Édition de Luxe

Memoirs of a Physician

IN THREE VOLUMES
VOL. I.

BY ALEXANDRE DUMAS

WITH ILLUSTRATIONS

BOSTON

ESTES AND LAURIAT

1895

MEMOIRS OF A PHYSICIAN.

VOLUME I.

CONTENTS.

vi CONTENTS.

LIST OF ILLUSTRATIONS.

VOL. I.

MEMOIRS OF A PHYSICIAN.

I. — MONT TONNERRE.

NEAR the source of the Seltz, on the left bank of the Rhine, some leagues from the imperial city of Worms, there begins a range of mountains, the scattered and rugged summits of which disappear northward like a herd of wild buffaloes vanishing in a mist.

These mountains, which from their lofty summits overlook an almost desert region, and seem but to form an attendant train to one which is their chief, have each a peculiar figure, and each bears a name indicating some tradition connected with it. One is the King's Chair, another the Wild-rose Stone; this the Falcon's Rock, that the Serpent's Crest.

The highest of all, which raises to the clouds its granite top, girt with a crown of ruins, is Mont Tonnerre.

When evening deepens the shadows of the lofty oaks, when the last rays of the sun die away on the peaks of this family of giants, we might imagine that silence descended from these sublime heights to the plain — that an invisible hand unfolded from their declivities the dark blue veil through which we see the stars, to wrap it over the world, wearied with the toil and the noise of day. Waking gives place to sleep, and all the tenants of earth and air repose.

Even then is not heard the stream of the Seltz, pursuing its mysterious course by the fir-trees on its banks,

stopping not by day or night, for it must hurry on to the
Rhine, which to it is eternity. The sands of its current
are so smooth, its reeds so flexible, its rocks so richly
clothed with moss, that not one of its waves murmurs,
from Morsheim, where it rises, to Freewenheim, where
it finishes its course.

A little above its source, between Albisheim and
Kircheim-Poland, a road, winding deep between two
rugged walls of rock, leads to Danenfels. Beyond Danenfels the road becomes a path; it narrows, is lost, and the
eye seeks in vain anything on which to rest, except the
slopes of Mont Tonnerre, whose lightning-blasted summit
is hidden by a belt of trees impenetrable to the eye.

In fact, once under those trees, leafy as the oaks of
Dodona of old, the traveller may in open day continue
his way unseen by any one on the plain below. Were
his horse hung with more bells than any mule in Spain,
not a sound would be heard; were his trappings of gold
and jewels like those of an emperor, not a ray from them
would pierce through the foliage, — so powerful is the
density of the forest in extinguishing sound, and its
darkness in dimming the brightest colours.

Even at the present day, when our highest mountains
have become mere observatories for every-day tourists, on
whose lips the most fearful of the legends of poetry call
up a smile of doubt, even now this solitude has its terrors.
A few miserable looking houses, outposts of neighbouring
villages, appear here and there, but at a distance from the
magic belt, to show that man is to be found in that region.
Their inhabitants are millers, who carry their flour to
Rockenhausen or Alzey, or shepherds who herd their flocks
around the mountain, they and their dogs trembling often
to hear some enormous fir-tree fall with age, crashing in
the unknown depths of the forest.

All the fireside tales of the country are gloomy, and
that path which is lost beyond Danenfels, among the
heath and furze of the mountains, has not always, they

say, led good Christians to a safe shelter. Perhaps there yet may live one of those country people who has heard his father or his grandfather tell what we are now about to relate.

On the 6th of May, 1770, at that hour when the waters of the great river are tinged with a pale rose colour, — that is to say, when the inhabitants of the Rhingau see the setting sun sink behind the spire of Strasburg Cathedral, which divides it into two hemispheres of fire, — a man who came from Mayence, having passed through Alzey and Kircheim-Poland, appeared beyond the village of Danenfels. He followed the path so long as the path was visible; then, when all trace of it vanished, dismounting from his horse, he fastened its bridle to the first fir-tree of the pathless forest.

The animal neighed uneasily, and the woods seemed to start at a sound so unusual.

"Gently, gently, Djerid! — twelve leagues are enough for you; here you must wait my return."

The traveller tried to peer into the recesses of the forest, but in vain; he could only see masses of dark shadows relieved upon shadows yet darker. Turning then to his horse, whose Arab name declared his race and swiftness, he took his head between his hands, approached his lips to the smoking nostrils of the animal, and said, "Farewell, my good horse! — farewell, if it be fated that we meet not again."

As he said these words he looked quickly around, as if he feared they might have been overheard, or as if he desired it. The horse shook his silky mane, pawed and neighed, as he would in the desert on the approach of the lion. The traveller nodded with a smile which seemed to say, "Thou art not wrong, Djerid, there is danger here."

Then, having decided beforehand, no doubt, not to oppose force against this danger, the unknown adventurer drew from his saddlebow two richly mounted pistols, took out their balls, and sprinkled the powder on the ground.

This done, he put them back in their place. Then he
unbuckled a sword with a steel handle, wrapped the belt
of it round it, and put all together under the saddle, so
that the pommel of the sword was towards the horse's
shoulder. After these formalities, the traveller shook off the
dust from his boots, took off his gloves, felt in his pockets,
and having found a pair of small scissors and a penknife
with a tortoise-shell handle, he threw first the one and
then the other over his shoulder, without looking where
they fell. That done, he again stroked Djerid, breathed
deeply, as if to expand his chest, feeling that his strength
was about to be taxed, and sought a pathway among the
trees. He found none, and at last entered the forest at
a venture.

It is time that we should give our readers some idea of
the traveller's appearance, as he is destined to play an
important part in our history.

He was a man apparently of thirty or two-and-thirty
years of age, of middle height, but admirably made, and his
every movement exhibited a fine combination of strength
and flexibility of limb. He was dressed in a travelling
coat of black velvet, with gold buttons, under which appeared an embroidered waistcoat; tight-fitting breeches
of leather, and polished boots on limbs which might have
served as a model for a sculptor, completed his costume.
As to his face, whose rapid changes of expression bespoke
him of a southern race, there were in it both tact and
power of character. His eye, which could express every
feeling, seemed to read the soul of any one on whom it
rested. His complexion, naturally dark, had been rendered
darker by exposure to a warmer sun than ours. His mouth,
large but well formed, showed a fine set of teeth, the
whiteness of which was heightened by contrast with the
darkness of his skin. His foot was long, but finely formed,
and his hand small, but sinewy.

Scarcely had he advanced ten steps among the dark fir-
trees, when he heard the quick tramp of hoofs in the direc-

tion where he had left his horse. His first movement was to turn back, but he stopped himself; however, he could not resist the wish to know the fate of Djerid — he raised himself on tiptoe and glanced through an opening. Djerid had disappeared, guided by an invisible hand which had untied his bridle. A slight frown contracted the brow of the unknown, yet something like a smile curled his chiselled lips.

Then he went on his way towards the centre of the forest.

For a few steps further the twilight aided him, then it left him, and in darkness so thick, that seeing no longer where to place his foot, he stopped.

"I got on very well to Danenfels, for from Mayence to Danenfels there is a road," said he aloud; "and from Danenfels to the Dark Heath, because there is a path; and from the Dark Heath hither, though there is neither road nor path, because I could see where I was going; but now I must stop — I see nothing."

Scarcely had he pronounced these words, in a dialect half French, half Sicilian, when a light appeared about fifty paces from the traveller.

"Thanks," said he; "now as the light moves I shall follow."

The light moved steadily on, with a gliding motion, as we sometimes see a light move over the stage of a theatre.

The traveller might have gone about a hundred steps farther when he thought he felt a breathing at his ear. He started.

"Turn not," said a voice on the right, "or thou art dead!"

"Good!" replied the immovable traveller.

"Speak not," said a voice on the left, "or thou art dead!"

The traveller bowed without speaking.

"But if thou art afraid," said a third voice, which, like that of Hamlet's father, seemed to come from the bowels of the earth, "turn back; that will declare that thou abandonest thy scheme, and thou shalt be permitted to go."

The traveller made a gesture of dissent with his hand, and went on.

The night was so dark and the forest so thick that he could not advance without occasionally stumbling, and his progress was slow. For nearly an hour the flame moved on, and he followed without a murmur, and without showing a symptom of fear.

All at once it disappeared.

The traveller was out of the forest. He raised his eyes, and in the dark blue sky saw some twinkling stars.

He continued to advance in the direction of the place where the light had disappeared, and soon saw arise before him a ruin, the spectre, as it were, of some ancient castle.

Next, his foot struck against some of its fragments. Then something cold passed his temples and sealed up his eyes, and he saw not even the shadows of outward objects.

A bandage of wet linen bound his head. This was only what he expected, no doubt, as he made no effort to remove it. He only silently stretched out his hand, like a blind man imploring a guide. His gesture was understood. A cold, dry, bony hand grasped the fingers of the traveller.

He knew that it was the hand of a skeleton, but if that hand had been endowed with sensation, it would have felt that his did not tremble.

Then the traveller felt himself rapidly drawn on for about a hundred paces. Suddenly the hand released its grasp, the bandage fell from his eyes, he stopped; he was on the summit of Mont Tonnerre.

II. — HE WHO IS.

In the midst of a glade formed by larches, bare with age, rose one of those feudal castles which the crusaders, on their return from the Holy Land, scattered over Europe. The gateways and arches had been finely sculptured, and in their niches were once statues; but these lay broken at the foot of the walls, and creeping plants and wild flowers now filled their places.

The traveller on opening his eyes found himself before the damp and mossy steps of the principal entrance; on the first of these steps stood the phantom by whose bony hand he had been led thither. A long shroud wrapped it from head to foot, and the eyeless sockets darted flames. Its fleshless hand pointed to the interior of the ruins as the termination of the traveller's journey. This interior was a hall, the lower part of which was but half seen, but from its vaults, heaped with ruins, flickered a dim and mysterious light.

The traveller bowed in assent. The phantom mounted slowly, step by step, to the hall and plunged into the ruins. The unknown followed calmly and slowly up the eleven steps which this spectre had trodden, and entered also. With the noise of a clashing wall of brass the great gate of the portal closed behind him.

At the entrance of a circular hall, lighted by three lamps, which cast a greenish light, the phantom stopped. The traveller, ten steps farther back, stopped in his turn.

"Open thine eyes!" said the phantom.

"I see!" replied the unknown.

The phantom then drew, with a proud gesture, a two-edged sword from beneath his shroud, and struck it against a column of bronze. A hollow metallic groan responded to its blow.

Then all around the hall arose stone seats, and numerous phantoms, like the first, appeared. Each was armed with a two-edged sword, and each took his place on a seat, and seen by the pale green light of the three lamps, they might have been taken, so cold and motionless were they, for statues on their pedestals. And these human statues came out in strange relief on the black tapestry of the walls.

Some seats were placed in advance of the others, on which sat six spectres who seemed like chiefs; one seat was vacant.

He who sat on the middle seat arose.

" Brethren, how many are present ? " he asked, turning to the assembly.

" Three hundred," replied the phantoms, with one voice. It thundered through the hall, and died away among the funereal hangings on the walls.

" Three hundred," replied the president, — "and each speaks for ten thousand companions ! Three hundred swords which are equal to three millions of poniards ! "

Then he turned to the traveller. " What dost thou wish ? " he asked.

" To see the light," replied the other.

" The paths which lead to the mountain of fire are rugged and difficult. Fearest thou not ? "

" I fear nothing."

" One step forward and you cannot return. Reflect ! "

" I stop not till I reach the goal."

" Wilt thou swear ? "

" Dictate the oath ! "

The president raised his hand, and with a slow and solemn voice, pronounced these words : " In the name of the crucified Son, swear to break all bonds of nature which unite thee to father, mother, brother, sister, wife, relation, friend, mistress, king, benefactor, and to any being whatever to whom thou hast promised faith, obedience, gratitude, or service ! "

The traveller, with a firm voice, repeated these words, and then the president dictated the second part of the oath.

" From this moment thou art free from the pretended oath thou hast taken to thy country and its laws; swear thou to reveal to the new head whom thou acknowledgest all that thou hast seen or done, read or guessed, and henceforward to search out and penetrate into that which may not openly present itself to thine eyes."

The president stopped; the unknown repeated the words.

"Honour and respect the *aqua tofana*, as a prompt, sure, and necessary means of ridding the world by the death or idiocy, of those who would degrade truth or tear it from us."

An echo could not have been more exact than the voice of the unknown in repeating the words of the president.

"Flee from Spain, flee from Naples, flee from every accursed land; flee from the temptation of revealing aught that thou shalt now see and hear! Lightning is not more quick to strike than will be the invisible and inevitable knife, wherever thou mayest be, shouldst thou fail in thy secrecy."

Spite of the threat conveyed in these last words, no trace of emotion was seen on the face of the unknown; he pronounced the end of the oath with a voice as calm as at the beginning.

"And now," continued the president, "put on his forehead the sacred band!"

Two phantoms approached the unknown; he bowed his head. One of them bound round it a crimson ribbon covered with silver characters, placed alternately with the figure of Our Lady of Loretto; the other tied it behind, just at the nape of the neck. Then they left his side.

"What wouldst thou ask?" inquired the president.

"Three things."

"Name them!"

"The hand of iron, the sword of fire, the scales of adamant."

"Why the hand of iron?"

"To stifle tyranny."

"Why the sword of fire?"

"To banish the impure from the earth."

"And why the scales of adamant?"

"To weigh the destinies of humanity."

"Canst thou withstand the necessary trials?"

"Courage is prepared for all trials."

"The trials! the trials!" cried many voices.

"Turn!" said the president.

The unknown obeyed, and found himself face to face with a man pale as death, bound and gagged.

"What seest thou?" asked the president.

"A malefactor or a victim."

"A traitor! One who took the oath as thou hast done, and then revealed the secrets of our order."

"A criminal, then."

"Yes."

"What penalty has he incurred?"

"Death."

The three hundred phantoms repeated, "Death!" and, in spite of all his efforts, the condemned was dragged into a darker part of the hall. The traveller saw him struggle with his executioners; he heard his choking voice. A dagger glimmered for an instant, a blow was struck, and a dead and heavy sound announced a body falling on the earthy floor.

"Justice is done!" said the unknown, turning to the ghastly assembly, who, from beneath their shrouds, had devoured the sight with greedy looks.

"Then," said the president, "thou dost approve what has been done?"

"Yes, if he who has fallen was really guilty."

"Thou wilt drink to the death of every man who, like him, would betray our secrets?"

"I will!"

"Whatever be the draught?"

"Whatever be the draught."

"Bring the cup," said the president.

One of the two executioners brought the unknown a red tepid liquor in a human skull. He took this frightful cup, and raised it above his head, saying, "I drink to the death of every man who shall betray the secrets of this holy society."

Then, bringing it to his lips, he drained it to the last drop, and returned it calmly to him who had presented it.

A murmur of surprise ran through the assembly, and the phantoms seemed to look at each other through their half-opened shrouds.

"Good," said the president. "The pistol!"

A phantom drew near the president, holding in one hand a pistol and in the other a ball and a charge of powder.

"Thou promisest passive obedience to our behests?"

"Yes."

"Even if this obedience be put to the proof against thyself?"

"He who enters here is no longer his own; he belongs to all."

"Then thou wilt obey whatever order be given thee?"

"I will obey."

"On the very instant?"

"On the very instant."

"Without hesitation?"

"Without hesitation."

"Take this pistol; load it!"

The unknown took the pistol and loaded it, all the dread assembly looking on the operation in a silence only broken by the sighs of the wind among the arches of the ruin.

"The pistol is loaded," said the unknown.

"Art thou sure?" asked the president.

A smile passed over the lips of the traveller as he tried the pistol, showing that it was loaded. The president bowed in token of being satisfied.

"Yes," said he, "it is loaded."

"What am I to do with it?"

"Cock it."

The unknown cocked the pistol, and its click was distinctly heard in the intervals of silence in the dialogue.

"Now put it to thy forehead," said the president.

He obeyed unhesitatingly. The silence seemed to deepen over the assembly, and the lamps to turn pale. These were real phantoms, for not a breath was then heard.

"Fire!" said the president.

The cock was heard to snap, the flint flashed, but the powder in the pan alone took fire, and no report accompanied its quick flame.

A shout of admiration burst from every breast, and the president involuntarily extended his hand to the unknown.

But two trials were not sufficient to satisfy all, and some voices shouted, "The dagger! the dagger!"

"You demand that, also?" said the president.

"Yes — the dagger! the dagger!" replied the voices.

"Bring the dagger," said the president.

"It is useless," said the unknown, making a disdainful movement with his head.

"Useless!" cried the assembly.

"Yes, useless!" he replied, with a voice which drowned every other; "useless! You lose time, and it is precious."

"What mean you?" asked the president.

"I tell you I know your secrets, — that these trials of yours are but child's play, unworthy of men. I tell you that I know the body which lies there is not dead; that I have not drunk blood; that, by a spring, the charge fell into the butt at the moment I cocked the pistol. Such things may frighten cowards. Rise, pretended corpse, thou hast no terrors for the brave."

A shout made the vaults ring.

"Thou knowest our mysteries, then?" said the president. "Thou art one of the illuminated, or a traitor!"

"Who art thou?" demanded the three hundred voices; and on the instant twenty swords, in the hands of the near-est phantoms, were pointed, with a motion as precise as if directed by a military signal, at the bosom of the unknown.

He smiled, shook the thick curls of his hair, which, unpowdered, were only retained by the ribbon which had been bound round his head, and said calmly, "*I am he who is.*"

Then he turned his eyes slowly around the living wall which hemmed him in, and gradually sword after sword sank before him.

"Thou hast spoken rashly," said the president. "Doubtless thou knowest not the import of thy words."

The stranger shook his head and smiled.

"I have spoken the truth."

"Whence comest thou?"

"I come whence comes the light."

"But we have learned that thou comest from Sweden."

"I might come from Sweden, and yet from the East."

"Then we know thee not. Who art thou?"

"Who am I? Ay, ye shall know more. Ye pretend not to understand me; but first I will tell you who you are!"

The phantoms started, and the clang of their swords was heard as they grasped them in their right hands and raised them to the level of the stranger's breast.

"First," said he, "thou who questionest me, who believest thyself a god, and who art but the forerunner of one, thou who representest Sweden, I shall name thee, that the rest may know I can also name them. Swedenborg, how comes it thy familiars told thee not that he whom thou waitedst for was on the road?"

"They did declare it to me," replied the president, putting aside a fold of his shroud in order to see him better who spoke; and in doing so, contrary to all the habits of the association, he showed a white beard and the venerable face of a man of eighty.

"Good!" replied the stranger. "On thy left is the representative of England or of Old Caledonia. I salute you, monseigneur. If the blood of your grandfather flows in your veins, England's extinguished light may be rekindled."

The swords sank — anger gave place to astonishment.

"Ah, captain," said the unknown, addressing one on the left of the president, "in what port waits thy good ship? A noble frigate the 'Providence.' Its name augurs well for America."

Then, turning towards him on the right —

"Look, Prophet of Zurich, thou hast carried physiognomy

almost to divination; read the lines on my face, and acknowledge my mission."

He to whom he spoke recoiled.

"Come," said he, turning to another, "descendant of Pelago, we must drive the Moors a second time from Spain, — an easy task if the Castilians yet retain the sword of the Cid !"

The fifth chief remained so still, so motionless, that the voice of the unknown seemed to have turned him to stone.

"And to me," said the sixth ; "hast thou naught to say to me ? "

"Ay," replied the traveller, turning on him a look which read his heart, "ay, what Jesus said to Judas ; but not yet."

The chief turned paler than his shroud, and a murmur running through the assembly seemed to demand the cause of this singular accusation.

"Thou forgettest the representative of France," said the president.

"He is not here," replied the stranger, haughtily ; "and that thou knowest well, since his seat is vacant. Learn, then, that snares make him smile who sees in darkness, who acts in spite of the elements, and who lives in spite of death."

"Thou art young," replied the president, "and thou speakest as if from divine authority. Reflect! boldness overcomes only the weak or the ignorant."

A disdainful smile played over the lips of the stranger.

"You are all weak since you have no power over me ! you are all ignorant, since ye know not who I am ! I on the other hand know you. Boldness, then, alone might overcome you ; but why should one all-powerful so overcome ? "

"Give us the proof of your boasted power ? " said the president.

"Who convoked you ? " asked the unknown, becoming the interrogator instead of the interrogated.

"The Grand Assembly."

"And not without a cause hast thou," pointing to the

president, " come from Sweden; thou," and he turned from
one to another of the five chiefs as he spoke, " thou from
London; thou from New York; thou from Zurich; thou
from Madrid; thou from Warsaw; and you all," looking
round the assembly, "from the four winds of heaven, to
meet in the sanctuary of the dreaded faith."

" No," replied the president, " not without cause, for we
came to meet him who has founded in the East a mysterious faith, joining two worlds in one belief, entwining
mankind with the bonds of brotherhood."

" Is there any sign by which you shall know him ? "

" Yes," said the president; "and an angel has revealed
it to me."

" You alone know it ? "

" I alone."

" You have revealed it to none ? "

" To none."

"Name it."

The president hesitated.

"Name it ! the hour is come."

" He will bear on his breast a diamond star, and on it
three letters, the signification of which is only known to
himself."

" Declare the letters."

" L. P. D."

The stranger rapidly threw open his coat and vest, and
on his fine Holland shirt shone like a flaming star the
diamond, and the three letters formed of rubies.

" It is HE ! " cried the president.

" He whom we await ? " asked the chiefs.

"The Great Copt ? " murmured the three hundred voices.

"Now," cried the stranger triumphantly, " do you believe
me when I say, I am he that is ? "

" Yes," said the phantoms, prostrating themselves before
him.

" Speak, master," said the president, "speak; we shall
obey ! "

III. — L. P. D.

There was silence for some moments, during which the unknown seemed to collect his thoughts. Then he began:

" Messieurs, ye but weary your arms with your swords; lay them aside, and lend an attentive ear, for you shall learn much from the few words which I am about to utter."

All were profoundly attentive.

" The sources of great rivers are sacred, therefore unknown. Like the Nile, the Ganges, the Amazon, I know to what I tend, not whence I come. All that I can reveal is that, when the eyes of my spirit first opened to comprehend external things, I was in Medina, the holy city, playing in the gardens of the Mufti Salaaym. He was a venerable man, kind as a father to me, yet not my father; for though he looked on me with love, he spoke to me with respect. Thrice a day he left me, and then came another old man, whose name I may pronounce with gratitude, yet with fear. He was called Althotas, and him the seven great spirits had taught all that the angels know in order to comprehend God. He was my tutor, my master, my friend, — a friend to be venerated indeed, for his age was double that of most among you."

His solemn tone, his majestic deportment, deeply impressed the assembly; they seemed trembling with anxiety to hear more.

He continued : —

" When I reached my fifteenth year I was initiated into the mysteries of nature. I knew botany, not as one of your learned men, who has acquired only the knowledge of the plants of his own corner of the world, — to me were known the sixty thousand families of plants of the whole earth. My master, pressing his hands on my forehead, made a ray of celestial light descend on my soul; then could I perceive beneath the seas the wondrous vegetations which are tossed by the waves, in the giant branches of which are cradled monsters unknown to the eye of man.

"All tongues, living and dead, I knew. I could speak every language spoken from the Dardanelles to the Straits of Magellan. I could read the dark hieroglyphics on those granite books, the pyramids. From Sanchoniathon to Socrates, from Moses to Jerome, from Zoroaster to Agrippa, all human knowledge was mine.

"Medicine I studied, not only in Hippocrates, in Galen, and in Averrhoes, but in that great teacher, Nature. I penetrated the secrets of the Copts and the Druses. I gathered up the seeds of destruction and of scarcity. When the simoom or the hurricane swept over my head, I threw to it one of those seeds, which its breath bore on, carrying death or life to whomsoever I had condemned or blessed.

"In the midst of these studies I reached my twentieth year. Then my master sought me one day in a grove, to which I had retired from the heat of the day. His face was at the same moment grave and smiling. He held a little vial in his hand. 'Acharat,' said he, 'I have told thee that nothing is born, nothing dies in the world, — that the cradle and the coffin are twins; that man wants only to see into past existences to be equal to the gods, and that when that power shall be acquired by him he will be as immortal as they. Behold! I have found the beverage which will dispel darkness, but I have not found that which destroys death. Acharat, I drank of it yesterday, — see, the vial is not full; drink thou the rest to-day.'

"I had entire confidence in my venerable master, yet my hand trembled as it touched the vial which he offered me, as Adam's might have done when Eve presented him with the apple.

"'Drink!' said he, smiling.

"I drank.

"Then he placed his hands on my head, as he always did when he would make light penetrate to my soul.

"'Sleep!' said he.

"Immediately I slept, and I dreamed that I was lying

on a pile of sandal-wood and aloes. An angel, passing by
on the behests of the Highest from the east to the west,
touched the pile with the tip of his wing, and it kindled
into flame. Yet I, far from being afraid, far from dreading the fire, lay voluptuously in the midst of it, like the
phœnix, drawing in new life from the source of all life.

"Then my material frame vanished away; my soul only
remained. It preserved the form of my body, but trans-
parent, impalpable; it was lighter than the atmosphere in
which we live, and it rose above it. Then, like Pythagoras,
who remembered that in a former state he had been at the
siege of Troy, I remembered the past. I had experienced
thirty-two existences, and I recalled them all. I saw ages
pass before me like a train of aged men in procession. I
beheld myself under the different names which I had borne
from the day of my first birth to that of my last death.
You know, brethren — and it is an essential article of our
faith — that souls, those countless emanations of the Deity,
fill the air, and are formed into numerous hierarchies,
descending from the sublime to the base; and the man
who, at the moment of his birth, inhales one of those pre-
existing souls, gives it up at his death, that it may enter on
a new course of transformations."

He said this in a tone so expressive of conviction, and
his look had something so sublime, that the assembly interrupted him by a murmur of admiration.

"When I awoke," continued the illuminated, "I felt
that I was more than man — that I was almost divine.
Then I resolved to dedicate not only my present existence,
but all my future ones, to the happiness of man.

"The next day, as if he had guessed my thoughts,
Althotas said to me, 'My son, twenty years ago thy mother
expired in giving birth to thee. Since that time, invincible
obstacles have prevented thy illustrious father revealing
himself to thee. We shall travel, we shall meet thy
father; he will embrace thee, but thou wilt not know
him.'

"Thus, in me, as in one of the elect, all was mysterious, — past, present, future.

"I bade adieu to the Mufti Salaaym, who blessed me and loaded me with presents, and we joined a caravan going to Suez.

"Pardon me, messieurs, if I give way for a moment to emotion, as I recall that one day a venerable man embraced me; a strange thrill ran through me as I felt his heart beat against mine.

"He was the Cheriffe of Mecca, a great and illustrious prince, who had seen a hundred battles; and at the raising of his hand three millions of men bent their heads before him. Althotas turned away to hide his feelings, perhaps not to betray a secret, and we continued our road.

"We went into the heart of Asia; we ascended the Tigris; we visited Palmyra, Damascus, Smyrna, Constantinople, Vienna, Berlin, Dresden, Moscow, Stockholm, Petersburg, New York, Buenos Ayres, the Cape of Good Hope, and Aden; then, being near the point at which we had set out, we proceeded into Abyssinia, descended the Nile, sailed to Rhodes, and, lastly, to Malta. Before landing, a vessel came out to meet us, bringing two knights of the order; they saluted me and embraced Althotas, and conducted us in a sort of triumph to the palace of the Grand Master, Pinto.

"Now, you will ask me, messieurs, how it came that the Mussulman Acharat was received with honour by those who have vowed the extermination of the infidels. Althotas, a Catholic, and himself a knight of Malta, had always spoken to me of one only God, omnipotent, universal, who, by the aid of angels, his ministers, made the world a harmonious whole, and to this whole he gave the great name of Cosmos. I was, then, not a Mussulman, but a theosophist.

"My journeyings ended; but in truth all that I had seen had awakened in me no astonishment, because for me there was nothing new under the sun, and in my preceding thirty-two existences I had visited the cities before through which I had lately passed. All that struck me was some change in their inhabitants. Now I would hover over events and watch the progress of man. I saw that all minds tend onward, and that this tendency leads to liberty. I saw that prophets had been raised up from time to time to aid the wavering advances of the human race; and that men, half blind from their cradle, make but one step towards the light in a century. Centuries are the days of nations.

"'Then,' said I to myself, 'so much has not been revealed to me that it should remain buried in my soul. In vain does the mountain hide veins of gold, in vain does the ocean hide its pearls; for the persevering miner penetrates to the bowels of the mountain, the diver descends to the depths of the ocean; but better than the mountain or the ocean, let me be like the sun, shedding blessings on the whole earth.'

"You understand, then, that it is not to go through some masonic ceremonies I have come from the East. I have come to say to you, Brethren, take the wings and the eyes of the eagle! rise above the world, and cast your eyes over its kingdoms!

"Nations form but one vast body. Men, though born at different periods, in different ranks, arrive all in turn at that goal to reach which they were created. They are continually advancing, though seemingly stationary, and if they appear to retreat a step from time to time, it is but to collect strength for a bound which shall carry them over some obstacle in their way.

"France is the advance-guard of nations. Put a torch in her hand, and though it kindle a wide-spreading flame, it will be salutary, for it will enlighten the world.

" The representative of France is not here; it may be that he has recoiled at the task imposed on him. Well, then! we must have a man who will not shrink from it, — I will go to France."

"You will go to France?" said the president.

"Yes, the most important post I take myself; the most perilous work shall be mine."

"You know what passes in France, then?" inquired the president.

The stranger smiled.

"I know, for I myself have prepared all. An old king, weak, vicious, yet not so old, not so weak, not so vicious as the monarchy which he represents, sits on the throne of France. He has but few years to live. Events must be prepared to succeed his death. France is the keystone of the arch; let but this stone be unfixed, and the monarchial edifice will fall! Ay, the day that Europe's most arrogant sovereigns shall hear that there is no longer a king in France, bewildered, they will of themselves rush into the abyss left by the destruction of the throne of Saint Louis!"

Here, he on the right of the president spoke, and his German accent announced that he was a Swiss. "Most venerated master, hast thou then calculated all?" he asked.

"All!" replied the Great Copt.

"Your pardon if I say more, but on our mountains, in our valleys, by our lakes, our words are free as the winds and the waters. Let me say, then, that a great event is on the eve of arriving, and that to it the French monarchy may owe its regeneration. I have seen, great master, a daughter of Maria Theresa travelling in state towards France to unite the blood of seventeen emperors with that of the successor of the sixty-one kings of France; and the people rejoiced blindly, as they do when their chains are slackened, or when they bow beneath a gilded yoke. I would infer, then, that the crisis is not yet come."

All turned to him who so calmly and boldly had spoken to their master.

"Speak on, brother," said the Great Copt; "if thy advice be good, it shall be followed. We are chosen of Heaven,

and we may not sacrifice the interests of a world to
wounded pride."

The deputy from Switzerland continued, amidst deep
silence: "My studies have convinced me of one truth,
that the physiognomy of men reveals, to the eye which
knows how to read it, their virtues and their vices. We
may see a composed look or a smile, for these, caused by
muscular movements, are in their power, but the great
type of character is still imprinted legibly on the countenance, declaring what passes in the heart. The tiger can
caress, can give a kindly look, but his low forehead, his
projecting face, his great occiput, declare him tiger still.
The dog growls, shows his teeth, but his honest eye, his
intelligent face, declare him still the friend of man. God
has imprinted on each creature's face its name and nature.
I have seen the young girl who is to reign in France; on
her forehead I read the pride, the courage, the tenderness,
of the German maiden. I have seen the young man who
is to be her husband; calmness, Christian meekness, and
a high regard for the rights of others characterise him.
Now, France, remembering no wrongs, and forgetting no
benefits, — since a Charlemagne, a Louis, and a Henry have
been sufficient to preserve on the throne twenty base and
cruel kings, — France, who hopes on, despairs never, will
she not adore a young, lovely, kindly queen, a patient,
gentle, economical king, after the disastrous reign of
Louis XV., after his orgies, his mean revenges, his
Pompadours and Dubarrys? Will not France bless her
youthful sovereigns, who will bring to her as their dowry
peace with Europe? Marie Antoinette now crosses the
frontier; the altar and the nuptial bed are prepared at
Versailles. Is this the time to begin in France your work
of regeneration? Pardon if I have dared to submit these
thoughts to you, whose wisdom is infallible!"

At these words, he whom the Great Copt had addressed
as the apostle of Zurich bowed as he received the applause
of the assembly, and awaited a reply.

He did not wait long.

"If you read physiognomy, illustrious brother, I read the future. Marie Antoinette is proud; she will interfere in the coming struggle, and will perish in it. Louis Auguste is mild; he will yield to it, and will perish with her, but each will fall through opposite defects of character. Now they esteem each other, but short will be their love; in a year they will feel mutual contempt. Why, then, deliberate, brethren, to discover whence comes the light? It is revealed to me. I come from the East, led, like the shepherds, by a star, which foretells a second regeneration of mankind. To-morrow I begin my work. Give me twenty years for it; that will be enough, if we are united and firm."

"Twenty years?" murmured several voices, "the time is long."

The Great Copt turned to those who thus betrayed impatience.

"Yes," said he, "it is long to those who think that a principle is destroyed, as a man is killed, with the dagger of Jacques Clément or the knife of Damiens. Fools! — the knife kills the man, but, like the pruning-hook, it lops a branch that the other branches may take its place. In the stead of the murdered king rises up a Louis XIII., a stupid tyrant; a Louis XIV., a cunning despot; a Louis XV., an idol whose path is wet with tears of blood, like the monstrous deities of India, crushing with chang-less smile women and children who cast garlands before their chariot wheels. And you think twenty years too long to efface the name of king from the hearts of thirty millions of men, who but lately offered to God their children's lives to purchase that of Louis XV.! And you think it an easy task to make France hate her lilies, which, bright as the stars of heaven, grateful as the odours of flowers, for centuries have borne light, charity, victory, to the ends of the world! Try! try, brethren! I give you, not twenty years, — I give you a century. You, scattered, trembling, unknown each to the others, known only to me, who only can sum up your divided worth, and tell its value, —to me, who alone can unite you in one fraternal chain, — I tell you, philosophers, political economists, theorists, that in twenty years those thoughts which you whisper in your families, which you write with uneasy eye in the solitude of your old sombre towers, which you tell one another with the dagger in your hands, that you may strike the traitor who would repeat them in tones louder than your own, — I tell you that these thoughts shall be proclaimed aloud in the streets, printed in the open face of day, spread through Europe by peaceful emissaries, or by the bayonets of five hundred thousand soldiers, battling for liberty with your principles inscribed on their standards. You who tremble at the name of the Tower of London, you who shrink at that of the prisons of the Inquisition, hear me, — me, who am about to dare the Bastille! I tell you that we shall see those dreaded prisons in ruins, and your wives and children shall dance on their ashes. But that cannot be until, not the monarch, but the monarchy, is dead, until religious domination is despised, until social inferiority is extinguished, until aristocratic castes and unjust division of lands are no more. I ask twenty years to destroy an old world, and make a new one, — twenty years, twenty seconds of eternity! — and you say it is too long!"

The silence of admiration and of assent followed the words of this dark prophet; he had obtained the sympathy of the representatives of the hopes of Europe who surrounded him.

The Great Copt enjoyed for some minutes his triumph; then, feeling that it was complete, he went on: "Now brethren, now that I am going to devote myself to our cause, to beard the lion in his den, to risk my life for the freedom of mankind, now, what will you do for that to which you say you are ready to give up life, liberty, and fortune? This is what I am here to demand."

A deeper silence fell on the assembly than when he last ceased to speak; it seemed as if the motionless phantoms around him were absorbed by a fateful thought, which, when expressed, should shake twenty thrones.

The six chiefs conversed for a moment apart, and then returned to the president. The president spoke:

"In the name of Sweden, I offer for the overthrow of the throne of Vasa the miners who established it, and one hundred thousand crowns."

The Great Copt made an entry in his tablets.

Another on the left spoke: —

"I, sent by Scotland and Ireland, can promise nothing from England, our firm opponent; but from poor Scotland, from poor Ireland, I shall bring three thousand men and three thousand crowns yearly."

He wrote again. "And you?" said he, turning to one whose vigorous frame and restless spirit seemed wearied by his phantom robe, and who replied: —

"I represent America, whose stones, whose trees, whose waters, whose every drop of blood are vowed to rebellion. Whilst we have gold we will give it, whilst we have blood we will shed it; let us but be free first. Though now divided, marked, and disunited, we are the links of a gigantic chain, and could some mighty hand join two of them, the rest will unite themselves. Begin, then, O great master, with us! If thou wouldst rid France of royalty, free us from a foreign yoke first."

"It shall be so," replied the master; "you shall first be free, and France shall help you. Wait! brother, but I promise thou shalt not wait long."

Then he turned to the Swiss deputy, who replied to his look: —

"I can promise nothing. Our republic has been long the ally of the French monarchy, to which it sold its blood at Marignan and Pavia. Its sons are faithful; they will give that for which they have been paid. For the first time, I am ashamed of their fidelity."

"So!—but we shall conquer without them, and in spite of them. And you, representative of Spain?"

"I am poor; I can offer only three thousand of my brothers, with a contribution of a thousand reals yearly. Our Spaniards are indolent, they sleep on a bed of pain; provided they sleep, they care not."

"Good! And you?" said he to another.

"I represent Russia and Poland. My people are either discontented nobles or wretched serfs. The serf, who owns not even his life, can offer nothing; but three thousand nobles have promised twenty louis d'or each annually."

Then all the representatives in turn declared what those from whom they came would give for the great cause. Some were deputies from small kingdoms, some from large principalities, some from impoverished States, but all declared that they would add something to what had been offered. Their promises were written on the tablets of the Great Copt, and they were bound by an oath to keep them.

"Now," said he, "you have seen and recognised the initials of our watchword. Let it be placed *on* your hearts, and *in* them; for we, the sovereign lord of the East and West, have decreed the downfall of the lily. Hear it, then, brethren: LILIA PEDIBUS DESTRUE."

Loud was their shout at this explanation of the mysterious letters,—so loud that the gorges of the mountain re-echoed to it.

"And now, retire," said the master, when silence had succeeded; "retire by those subterranean passages which lead to the quarries of Mont Tonnerre. Disperse before the rising of the sun. You shall see me once more, and it will be on the day of our triumph! Go!"

His words were followed by a masonic sign, understood only by the six heads of the assembly, so that they remained around him when the rest had disappeared.

"Swedenborg," said he, "thou art truly inspired. God thanks thee by me for thy efforts in his cause. I shall give thee an address in France to which thou shalt send the promised money."

The president bowed, and departed, full of astonishment at that intelligence which had discovered his name.

"I salute thee, Fairfax," continued the master, "thou art worthy of thy great ancestor. Remember me to Washington when next thou writest to him."

Fairfax bowed, and followed Swedenborg.

"Come, Paul Jones," said the Copt, "thou spokest bravely; thou shalt be a hero of America. Let her be ready at the first signal!"

The American thrilled in every nerve, as if the breath of some divine being had passed over him, and retired also.

"And now, as to thee, Lavater. Abjure thy theories; it is the time for action. Study no longer what man is, but what he may be. Go! Woe to thy countrymen if they rise against us; for our people will devour in its wrath, as the wrath of God devours."

The trembling Swiss bowed and departed.

"Hear, Ximenes," he went on, addressing the Spaniard, "thou art zealous, but distrustful. Thy country sleeps, but it is because none awakes her. Go! Castile is still the country of the Cid!"

The last of the six was advancing, but by a gesture the Copt forbade him.

"Scieffort of Russia, before a month thou wilt betray our cause, but in a month thou shalt be no more."

The Russian envoy fell on his knees, but a threatening movement of the master made him rise, and with tottering steps he also departed.

And now this singular man, whom we have introduced as the hero of our drama, left alone, looked around the empty, silent hall, buttoned up his black velvet coat, fixed his hat firmly on his head, touched the spring of the great bronze gate which had closed behind him, and sallied out into the defiles of the mountain. Though he had neither guide nor light, he went on rapidly, as if led by an invisible hand.

Having passed the thick belt of trees, he looked for his horse; but not seeing him, he listened, and soon thought he heard a distant neighing. He whistled with a peculiar modulation, and in a moment Djerid could be seen coming forward like a faithful and obedient dog. The traveller sprang to the saddle, and quickly disappeared in the darkness, which spread over the heath extending from Mont Tonnerre to Danenfels.

CHAPTER I.

THE STORM.

EIGHT days after the scene just related, about five in the evening, a carriage with four horses and two postilions left Pont-à-Mousson, a small town between Nancy and Metz. It had taken fresh horses at an inn, in spite of the recommendation of an attentive hostess who was on the lookout for belated travellers, and continued on its road to Paris. Its four horses had scarcely turned the corner of the street, when a score of children and half a score of gossips, who had watched the progress of their being put to, returned to their respective dwellings with gestures and exclamations expressive in some of great mirth, in others of great astonishment.

All this was because nothing like that carriage had for fifty years passed the bridge which good King Stanislaus threw across the Moselle to facilitate the intercourse of his little kingdom with France. We do not except even those curious vehicles of Alsace which bring from Phalsbourg to our fairs two-headed wonders, dancing bears, and the wandering tribes of harlequins and gipsies.

In fact, without being either a child or a curious old gossip, surprise might have arrested one's steps on seeing this primitive machine, on four massive wheels, roll by with such velocity that every one exclaimed, "What a strange way of travelling post!"

As our readers, fortunately for them, did not see it pass, we shall describe it.

First, then, the principal carriage — we say principal because in front it was a sort of cabriolet — the principal

carriage was painted light blue, and bore on its panels a
baronial scroll, surmounting a J and a B entwined.   Two
windows — large windows, with white muslin curtains —
gave it light; only, these windows, invisible to the profane
vulgar, looked frontwise into the cabriolet.   A grating
covered them, through which one might speak to the inhabitants of the carriage.

This carriage, which was eight feet long, had no light
but from the windows, and no air but from a ventilator on
the top; and then, to complete its oddity, a chimney rising
about a foot above the roof offered to the passers-by the
pleasant sight of a light cloud of smoke lengthening into a
bluish trail behind it.   At the present day we should only
have thought it a new invention, combining the power of
steam with that of horses.

This would have seemed so much the more probable,
that the carriage, preceded as we have said by four horses
and two postilions, was followed by one horse fastened to
it by his bridle.   His small head, slender legs, narrow
chest, and silky mane and tail bespoke him of Arab race.
He was ready saddled, which implied that one of the
travellers shut up in this Noah's ark sometimes enjoyed
the pleasure of riding beside the carriage.

At Pont-à-Mousson the postilion who left had received,
besides the pay for the horses, a double gratuity, presented
by a strong but white hand, slipped through the leather
curtains of the cabriolet, which shaded it as imperviously
as the muslin ones did the carriage.

"Many thanks, monseigneur," said the astonished postilion, quickly taking off his cap and bowing low.

A sonorous voice replied in German (for at Nancy
German is still understood, though no longer spoken),
"*Schnell! schneller!*" which means "Fast! faster!"

Postilions understand nearly all languages — above all,
when accompanied by the sound of certain metals, of which
it is said they are rather fond.   So the two new postilions
did their utmost to keep to a gallop; but after efforts which

did more honour to their arms than to the powers of their horses, wearied out, they fell into a trot, getting on at the rate of two and a half or three leagues an hour.

Towards seven, they changed at Saint Mihiel; the same hand passed through the curtains payment for the last stage, and the same voice uttered a similar injunction.

The strange vehicle excited there the same curiosity as at Pont-à-Mousson, for as night was fast approaching, its appearance was still more fantastic.

Beyond Saint Mihiel there is a steep hill, and travellers must be satisfied to let the horses walk. It took half an hour to proceed a quarter of a league.

On the top the postilions stopped a moment to breathe their horses, and the travellers in the carriage, by withdrawing the curtains, might have gazed on a wide prospect, had not the mists of evening begun to veil it slightly.

The weather had been clear and warm until three in the afternoon; towards evening, however, it became oppressive. A great white cloud from the south seemed as if intentionally to follow the carriage, threatening to overtake it before it reached Bar-le-Duc, where the postilions resolved at all risks to pass the night.

The road, shut in between the hill and a rugged declivity, descended to a valley, in which was seen the winding Meuse, and was so steep that it was dangerous to allow the horses to do anything but walk, which prudent plan the postilions adopted. The cloud advanced, and as it brooded over, and almost touched the ground, continually extended its limits by drawing the vapours arising from the soil; so was it observed in ill-boding whiteness to overwhelm the bluish clouds which seemed to take up their station to windward, like ships preparing for an engagement. Soon, with the rapidity of the flood-tide, it spread until it hid the last rays of the sun. A dim, grey light struggled through upon the scene, and although no breeze swept along, the leaves shivered, and put on the dark tinge which they assume in the deepening twilight succeeding sunset.

Suddenly a flash illuminated the cloud, the heavens burst into sheets of flame, and the startled eye might penetrate the immeasurable depths of the firmament. At the same moment the thunder rolled from tree to tree, shaking the earth, and hurrying on the vast cloud like a maddened steed. On went the carriage, sending forth its smoke, now changed in colour by the changes of the atmosphere.

In the mean time the heavens grew darker and darker, but a purple light appeared from the carriage, as if the person within, careless of the storm, had lighted a lamp, and went on with some work which he had to accomplish.

The vehicle was now on a level part of the mountain, and when about to begin the descent, a peal of thunder more violent than the first rent the clouds, and the rain fell, at first in large drops, then thick and smarting, like arrows darted from the heavens.

The postilions seemed to consult together, and then stopped.

"Well!" cried the voice which had before spoken, but now in excellent French; "what the devil are you doing?"

"We were consulting whether we should go on," replied the postilions.

"I think you ought to ask me, not one another. On with you!"

The postilions obeyed, for there was that in the voice which forbade all thought of disobedience, and the carriage began to descend.

"Good!" said the voice, and the leather curtains, which had been half opened, fell between the traveller and the postilions.

But the road had become so slippery from the torrents of rain that the horses stopped of themselves.

"Monsieur," said the leading postilion, "it is impossible to go any farther."

"Why?" asked the voice within.

"Because the horses only slip; they cannot get on; they will fall."

"How far are we from the next place where we change?"

"A long way, monsieur,— four leagues."

"Well, postilion, put silver shoes on your horses and they will get on;" and as he said this the stranger opened the curtain and held out four crowns.

"Many thanks!" said the postilion, receiving them in his broad hand, and slipping them into his great boot.

"The gentleman spoke, I think," said the other postilion, who had heard the sound of money, and did not wish to be excluded from so interesting a conversation.

"Yes, the gentleman says we must push on."

"Have you anything to say against that, my friend?" asked the traveller, in a kind voice, but with a firmness that showed he would brook no contradiction.

"Why, as to myself, I have nothing to say; but the horses won't stir."

"What is the use of your spurs, then?"

"I have buried them in the sides of the poor jades, and, if it has made them move a step, may Heaven —"

He had not time to finish his oath, for a frightful peal of thunder interrupted him.

"This is no weather for Christians to be out in," said the honest fellow. "See, monsieur, see! the carriage is going of itself; in five minutes it will go fast enough — *Jésus Dieu!* there we go!"

And, in fact, the heavy machine pressing on the horses, they lost their footing. It then made a progressive movement, and, according to the mathematical increase of forces, its velocity augmented till, with the rapidity of an arrow, it was visibly nearing the edge of a precipice.

It was not now only the voice of the traveller which was heard; his head was seen thrust out of the cabriolet.

"Stupid fellow!" cried he, "will you kill us? To the left! the leaders to the left!"

"Ah, monsieur, I wish from my heart I saw you on the left," replied the frightened postilion, vainly trying to recover the reins.

"Joseph!" cried a female voice, now first heard, "Joseph! help! help! Oh, holy Virgin!"

Indeed, danger so terrible and so imminent might well call forth that ejaculation. The carriage, impelled by its own weight, neared the precipice; already one of the leaders appeared suspended over it; three revolutions of the wheel, and horses, carriage, and postilions would all have been precipitated, crushed and mangled, to its base, when the traveller, springing from the cabriolet on the pole, seized the postilion by the collar, lifted him like a child, flung him two paces from him, leaped into the saddle, and gathering up the reins, called to the second postilion: —

"To the left, rascal, or I will blow out thy brains!"

The command acted like magic. By an extraordinary effort the postilion gave an impulse to the carriage, brought it to the middle of the road, on which it began to roll on rapidly, with a noise that contended with that of the thunder. "Gallop!" cried the traveller; "gallop! If you slacken your speed I will run you through the body, and your horses, too!"

The postilion felt that this was no vain menace; he redoubled his efforts, and the carriage descended with frightful speed. As it thus passed in the night, with its fearful noise, its flaming chimney, and its stifled cries from within, it might have been taken for some infernal chariot drawn by phantom horses, and pursued by a hurricane.

But if the travellers escaped from one danger, they met another. The cloud which had hung over the valley was as rapid as the horses. From time to time, as a flash rent the darkness, the traveller raised his head, and then, by its gleam, anxiety, perhaps fear, might have been seen on his face; for dissimulation was not wanted then, God only saw him. Just as the carriage had reached level ground, and was only carried on by its own impetus, the cloud burst with an awful explosion. A violet flame, changing to green and then to white, wrapped the horses; the hind ones reared, snuffing the sulphurous air; the leaders, as if the ground had given way beneath their feet, fell flat; but almost instantly the horse upon which the postilion was mounted regained his feet, and finding his traces snapped by the shock, he carried off his rider, who disappeared in the darkness, while the carriage, after proceeding ten feet farther, was stopped by encountering the dead body of the lightning-stricken horse.

All this was accompanied by piercing shrieks from the female in the vehicle.

There was a moment of strange confusion in which no one knew whether he was dead or living. The traveller felt himself all over to assure himself of his own identity. He was safe and sound, but the woman had fainted.

Although he suspected this from the silence which had succeeded to her shrieks, it was not to her that his first cares were directed. Scarcely had he lighted on the ground when he hastened to the back of the vehicle.

There was the beautiful Arabian horse of which we have spoken, terrified, rigid, with every hair rising as if life were in it. He tugged violently at his fastening, shaking the door to the handle of which he was secured. His eye was fixed, the foam was on his nostrils; but after vain efforts to break away, he had remained, horror-stricken by the tempest; and when his master whistled to him in his usual manner, and put out his hand to caress him, he bounded aside, neighing, as if he did not know him.

"Ay, always that devil of a horse," muttered a broken voice from the carriage; "curse him, he has broken my wall!"

Then, with double emphasis, this voice cried in Arabic, "Be still, demon!"

"Do not be angry with Djerid, master," said the traveller, loosing the horse, which he now tied to one of the
hind wheels; "he has been frightened, that is all; and
indeed one might well have been frightened at less."

Saying this, he opened the carriage door, let down the
step, entered, and closed the door after him.

CHAPTER II.

ALTHOTAS.

THE traveller found himself face to face with an old man with grey eyes, a hooked nose, and trembling but busy hands. He was half buried in a great chair, and turned with his right hand the leaves of a manuscript on parchment, called "La Chiave del Gabinetto;" in his left he held a silver skimming-dish.

His attitude, his occupation, his face, motionless and deeply wrinkled, alive only, as it were, in the eyes and mouth, may seem strange to the reader, but they were certainly very familiar to the traveller; for he scarcely cast a look on the old man, nor on all that surrounded him; and yet it was worth the trouble.

Three walls — so the old man called the sides of the carriage — were covered by shelves filled with books. These walls shut in his chair, his usual and principal seat, while above the books had been planned for his convenience several articles for holding vials, decanters, and boxes set in wooden cases, as earthen and glass ware are secured at sea. He could thus reach anything without assistance, for his chair was on wheels, and with the aid of a spring he could raise it and lower it to any height necessary to attain what he wanted.

The room, for so we must call it, was eight feet long, six wide, and six high. Opposite the door was a little furnace, with its shade, bellows, and tongs. At that moment there boiled in a crucible a mixture which sent out by the chimney the mysterious smoke of which we have spoken, and which excited so much surprise in old and young who saw the carriage pass.

Besides the vials, boxes, books, and papers strewed around, copper pincers were seen, and pieces of charcoal which had been dipped in various liquids; there was also a large vase half full of water, and from the roof, hung by threads, were bundles of herbs, some apparently gathered the night before, others a hundred years ago. A keen odour prevailed in this laboratory, which in one less strange would have been called a perfume.

As the traveller entered, the old man wheeled his chair with wonderful ease to the furnace, and was about to skim the mixture in the crucible attentively, — nay, almost respectfully, — but disturbed by the appearance of the other, he grumbled, drew over his ears his cap of velvet, once black, and from under which a few locks of silver hair peeped out. Then he sharply pulled from beneath one of the wheels of his chair the skirt of his long silk robe, — a robe now nothing but a shapeless, colourless, ragged covering. The old man appeared to be in a very bad humour, and grumbled as he went on with his operation.

"Afraid, — the accursed animal! Afraid of what? He has shaken the wall, moved the furnace, spilled a quart of my elixir in the fire. Acharat, in Heaven's name get rid of that brute in the first desert we come to!"

"In the first place," said the other, smiling, "we shall come to no deserts; we are in France. Secondly, I should not like to leave to his fate a horse worth a thousand louis d'or, or rather, a horse above all price, for he is of the race of Al Borach."

"A thousand louis d'or! I will give you them, or what is equal to them. That horse has cost me more than a million, to say nothing of the time, the life, he has robbed me of."

"What has he done — poor Djerid?"

"What has he done? The elixir was boiling, not a drop escaping, — true, neither Zoroaster nor Paracelsus says that none must escape, but Borri recommends it."

"Well! dear master, in a few moments more the elixir will boil again."

"Boil? See! there is curse on it; the fire is going out. Something, I know not what, is falling down the chimney."

"I know what is falling," said the disciple, laughing; "water!"

"Water? — water? Then the elixir is ruined; the operation must be begun again — as if I had time to lose! Heaven and earth!" cried the old man, raising his hands in despair, "water! What kind of water, Acharat?"

"Pure water, master, — rain from the sky. Have you not seen that it rained?"

"How should I see anything when I am at my work? Water! You see, Acharat, how this troubles my poor brain! For six months — nay, for a year — I have been asking you for a funnel for my chimney! You never think of anything; yet, what have you to do, you who are young? Thanks to your neglect, it is now the rain, now the wind, which ruins all my operations; and yet, by Jupiter! I have no time to lose! You know it. The day decreed is near; and if I am not ready for that day, if I have not found the elixir of life, farewell to the philosopher; farewell to the wise Althotas! My hundredth year begins on the 15th of July, at eleven at night, and from this time to that my elixir must attain perfection."

"But it is going on famously, dear master!"

"Yes, I have made some trials by absorption. My left arm, nearly paralysed, has regained its power; then, eating as I do, only once in two or three days, and taking a spoonful of my elixir, though yet imperfect, I have more time, and am assisted on by hope. Oh, when I think that I want but one plant, but one leaf of a plant, to perfect my elixir, and that we have perhaps passed by that plant a hundred, five hundred, a thousand times! perhaps our horses have trodden it, our wheels crushed it, Acharat, — that very plant of which Pliny speaks, and which no sage has yet found or discovered, for nothing is lost. But stay, Acharat, you must ask its name from Lorenza, in one of her trances."

"Fear not, master; I will ask her."

"Meantime," said the philosopher, with a deep sigh, "my elixir remains imperfect, and three times fifteen days will be necessary to reach the point at which I was to-day. Have a care, Acharat, your loss will be as great as mine, if I die, and my work incomplete. But what noise is that? Does the carriage move?"

"No, master; you hear thunder."

"Thunder?"

"Yes; we have all been nearly killed by a thunderbolt; but my silk coat protected me."

"Now, see to what your childish freaks expose me, Acharat. To die by a thunderbolt, to be stupidly killed by an electric fire that I would myself bring down from heaven, if I had time, to boil my pot — this is not only exposing me to accidents which the malice or awkwardness of men bring on us, but to those which come from heaven, and which may be easily prevented."

"Your pardon, master; I do not understand."

"What! did I not explain to you my system of points, — my paper-kite conductor? When I have found my elixir I shall tell it you again; but now, you see, I have not time."

"And you believe one may master the thunderbolt of heaven?"

"Certainly; not only master it, but conduct it where he chooses; and when I have passed my second half-century, when I shall have but calmly to await a third, I shall put a steel bridle on a thunderbolt, and guide it as easily as you do Djerid. Meantime, put a funnel on my chimney, I beg you!"

"I shall. Rest easy."

"I shall! — always the future, as if we could both look forward to the future. Oh, I shall never be understood!"

cried the philosopher, writhing in his chair, and tossing his arms in despair. "'Be calm!'—he tells me to be calm; and in three months, if I have not completed my elixir, all will be over. But so that I pass my second half-century, that I recover my powers of motion, I shall meet no one who says, 'I shall do;' I shall then myself exclaim, 'I have done!'"

"Do you hope to say that, with regard to our great work?"

"Yes; were I but as sure of—oh, heavens!—discovering the elixir as I am of making the diamond."

"Then you are sure of that?"

"It is certain, since I have already made some."

"Made some?"

"Yes, look!"

"Where?"

"On your right, in the little glass vase."

The traveller anxiously seized the little crystal cup, to the bottom and sides of which adhered an almost impalpable powder. "Diamond dust?" cried the young man.

"Yes, diamond dust; but look in the middle."

"Yes, yes; a brilliant of the size of a millet-seed."

"The size is nothing; we shall attain to the union of the dust, and make the grain of millet-seed a grain of hemp-seed, and of the grain of hemp-seed a pea. But first, my dear Acharat, put a funnel on my chimney, and a conductor on the carriage, that the rain may not descend through my chimney, and that the lightning may go and sport itself elsewhere."

"Yes, yes; doubt it not. Be calm!"

"Again, again, this eternal 'Be calm'! You make me swear. Youth!—mad youth!—presumptuous youth!" cried the old man, with a laugh which showed all his toothless gums, and made his eyes sink deeper in their hollow sockets.

"Master," said Acharat, "your fire is going out, your crucible cooling. But what is in the crucible?"

"Look into it."

The young man obeyed, uncovered the crucible, and found in it a heap of vitrified charcoal, about the size of a small seed.

"A diamond!" cried he. Then, after a slight examination of it, "Yes, but stained, incomplete, valueless."

"Because the fire was put out — because there is no funnel on the chimney."

"Let me look at it again, master," said the young man, turning in his hand the diamond, which sometimes shot forth brilliant rays, and sometimes was dull. "Good! — pardon me, and take some food."

"It is unnecessary; I took my spoonful of elixir two hours ago."

"You are mistaken, dear master; it was at six in the morning that you took it."

"Well, and what o'clock is it now?"

"Half-past eight in the evening."

"Heaven and earth! another day past! — gone forever! But the days are shorter than they were; there are not twenty-four hours in them now."

"If you will not eat, sleep at least for some minutes."

"Well, yes, I will sleep two hours — yes, just two hours. Look at your watch, and in two hours awake me."

"I promise to do so."

"Dost thou know, dear Acharat," said the old man, in a caressing tone, "when I sleep, I always fear it will be for eternity? So in two hours you will wake me, will you not? Promise it; swear it."

"I swear it, master."

"In two hours?"

"In two hours."

Just then something like the trampling of a horse was heard, and then a shout which indicated alarm and surprise.

"What does that mean?" cried the traveller; and hurriedly opening the carriage door, he leaped out.

CHAPTER III.

LORENZA FELICIANI.

WE shall now inform the reader what passed outside whilst the philosopher and the traveller were conversing inside the carriage.

At the noise of the thunderbolt, which struck down two of the horses, and caused the other two to rear so frightfully, the lady in the cabriolet, as we have said, had fainted. She remained for some minutes motionless; then, as fear alone had caused her to swoon, by slow degrees her consciousness returned.

"Ah, heaven!" she exclaimed, "abandoned here, helpless, with no human creature to take pity on me!"

"Madame," replied a timid voice, "I am here, if I can be of any service to you."

At the sound of this voice, which seemed close to her ear, the young lady rose, put her head out between the leather curtains, and found herself face to face with a young man who was standing on the step of the cabriolet.

"It was you who spoke, monsieur?" said she.

"Yes, madame," answered the young man.

"And you offered me your services?"

"Yes."

"But first tell me what has happened."

"The thunderbolt, which fell almost on your carriage, broke the traces of the front horses, and one of them ran off with the postilion."

The lady looked uneasily around.

"And he who rode the hinder horses?" she asked.

"He has just got into the carriage, madame."

"Has he not been injured?"

"Not in the least."

"Are you sure?"

"He leaped from his horse, at least, like a man all safe and sound."

"Heaven be praised!" and the young lady breathed more freely. "But who are you, monsieur, who are here so opportunely to offer me assistance?"

"Madame, overtaken by the storm, I was down in that hollow, which is merely the entrance to a quarry, when all at once I heard a carriage coming with alarming speed. I at first supposed the horses had run off, but soon saw that they were managed by a powerful hand. Then the thunderbolt fell with a tremendous explosion, and I thought for an instant that all was over with me. Indeed, on recovering, all that I have related seemed but a dream."

"Then you are not sure that the gentleman entered the carriage?"

"Oh, yes, madame; I had quite recovered, and distinctly saw him enter."

"Make yourself certain, I entreat you, that he is in the carriage."

"But how?"

"Listen; if he be there you will hear two voices."

The young man jumped down from the step and approached the door of the carriage.

"Yes, madame," said he, returning to her, "he is there."

The young lady, by a movement of her head, seemed to say, "It is well," but she remained for some time as if plunged in a deep reverie.

During this time the young man had leisure to examine her appearance. She was about twenty-three or twenty-four years of age,— a brunette in complexion, but of that rich brown which is more beautiful than the most delicate tint of the rose; her fine blue eyes, raised to heaven, from which she seemed to ask counsel, shone like two stars; and her black hair, which she wore without powder, notwithstanding the fashion of the day, fell in jetty curls on her neck. All at once she roused herself, as if she had decided on her part.

"Monsieur," said she, "where are we now?"

"On the road from Strasburg to Paris, madame."

"On what part of the road?"

"Two leagues from Pierrefitte."

"What is Pierrefitte?"

"A village."

"And, after Pierrefitte, what is the next stage?"

"Bar-le-Duc."

"Is it a town?"

"Yes, madame."

"A large one?"

"About four or five thousand inhabitants."

"Is there any cross-road by which one could get more directly to Bar-le-Duc?"

"No, madame — at least, I know of none."

"*Peccato!*" murmured she, falling back in the cabriolet.

The young man waited, expecting to be questioned further; but as she kept silence he moved a step or two away. This roused her, for, leaning out again, she called hurriedly, "Monsieur!"

The young man returned.

"I am here, madame," said he, approaching her.

"One question, if you please."

"Speak, madame."

"There was a horse behind the carriage?"

"Yes, madame."

"Is he there still?"

"No, madame; the person who got into the carriage untied him and fastened him to the wheel."

"Nothing, then, has injured the horse?"

"I think not."

"He is a valuable animal, and I should like to be sure that he is safe; but how can I reach him through this mud?"

"I can bring the horse here?" said the young man.

"Oh, yes, do so, I pray; I shall be forever grateful to you."

The young man approached the horse, who tossed his head and neighed.

"Do not be afraid," said the female; "he is as gentle as a lamb." Then, in a low voice, she murmured, "Djerid, Djerid!"

The animal evidently knew the voice to be that of his mistress, for he snorted, and stretched out his intelligent head towards the cabriolet. During this time the young man was untying him; but the horse no sooner felt his bridle in unpractised hands than at one bound he was free, and twenty paces from the carriage.

"Djerid!" repeated the young woman in her most caressing tones, "Djerid! here, here!"

The Arabian tossed his head, snuffed the air, and came towards the cabriolet, pawing as if in time to some musical air.

The lady leaned out. "Come, Djerid, come," said she.

And the obedient animal advanced towards the hand which she held out to caress him. Then with her slender hand she seized him by the mane, and sprang as lightly into the saddle as the goblin in the German ballads, who leaps behind unwary travellers and holds on by their belts.

The young man hurried towards her, but she waved him off imperiously. "Hearken!" said she; "though young, or rather, because you are young, you ought to be humane. Do not oppose my flight. I leave a man whom I love; but my religion is still dearer to me. That man will destroy my soul if I stay with him longer; he is an atheist and a necromancer. God has warned him by his thunders; may he profit by the warning. Tell him what I have said, and receive my blessing for what you have done for me. Farewell."

At that word, light as a vapour, she disappeared, borne away by the aërial Djerid. The young man, seeing her flee, could not prevent a cry of astonishment escaping his lips. It was this cry which startled the traveller in the carriage.

CHAPTER IV.

GILBERT.

THE cry had, as we have said, roused the traveller. He
leaped out, shut the door carefully after him, and looked
uneasily around.

The first object which he beheld was the young man
standing there in alarm. The lightning, which flashed
incessantly, enabled him to examine him from head to
foot, — a practice which seemed habitual with the traveller
when any unknown person or thing met his eye. He was
a youth of sixteen or seventeen years old, little, thin, and
muscular. His black eyes, which he fixed boldly on any
object which attracted his attention, wanted mildness, but
had a certain kind of beauty; his nose, small and turned
up, his thin lip and projecting cheek-bones, betokened
cunning and circumspection; and the strong curve of his
chin announced firmness.

"Did you shout just now?" asked the traveller.

"Yes, monsieur."

"And why?"

"Because—" He stopped short.

"Because?" repeated the traveller.

"Monsieur, there was a lady in the cabriolet."

"Yes."

And the eyes of Balsamo darted on the carriage as if
they could have penetrated its sides.

"There was a horse tied to the wheel."

"Yes; where the devil is he?"

"Monsieur, the lady has fled on the horse."

The traveller, without uttering a word, sprang to the cabriolet, undrew the curtains, and a flash of lightning showed him it was empty.

"*Sang du Christ!*" shouted he, loud almost as the thunder which pealed at that moment.

Then he looked round, as if for some means of recovering the fugitives, but soon felt that it was vain.

"To try to overtake Djerid," he muttered, "with a common horse, would be to hunt the gazelle with the tortoise; but I shall know where she is, unless —"

He felt hurriedly in the pocket of his vest and drew from it a little case, opened it, and took out of a folded paper a curl of black hair. At the sight of it the traveller's face lost its anxious expression, and his manner became calm, — at least, in appearance.

"Well," said he, wiping the perspiration from his forehead, "well, and did she say nothing on leaving?"

"Oh yes, monsieur."

"What did she say?"

"That she quitted you, not through hatred, but fear; that she is a good Christian, and that you —" He hesitated.

"And that I?"

"I know not how to tell it."

"*Pardieu!* tell it."

"That you are an atheist and an infidel; that God has given you a last warning by the storm; that she understood that warning, and conjures you not to be deaf to it."

A smile of contempt curled the lip of the traveller. "And this was all she said?"

"Yes, this was all."

"Well, let us speak of something else;" and all trace of disquietude passed away from the traveller's countenance.

The young man remarked all these emotions reflected on his face with a curiosity indicating no deficiency on his side of powers of observation.

"And now," said the traveller, "what is your name, my young friend?"

"Gilbert, monsieur."

"Gilbert! — that is merely a baptismal name."

"It is the name of our family."

"Well, my dear Gilbert, Providence has sent you to my aid."

"I shall be happy, if I can oblige you, monsieur."

"Thank you. At your age one is obliging for the mere pleasure of the thing; but what I am going to ask is only a trifle, — merely if you can direct me to a shelter for the night."

"Why, in the first place, there is that rock under which I was sheltering just now."

"Yes," said the traveller, "but I should like something more like a house, where I could have a good supper and a good bed."

"That would be very difficult to find."

"Are we then so far from the next village?"

"From Pierrefitte?"

"It is called Pierrefitte, then?"

"Yes, monsieur; it is about a league and a half off."

"A league and a half! Let us see, surely there is some habitation nearer?"

"There is the château of Taverney, about three hundred paces from this."

"Well, then — "

"What, monsieur!" and the young man opened his eyes in astonishment.

"Why did you not say so at once?"

"The château of Taverney is not a hotel."

"Is it inhabited?"

"Yes."

"By whom?"

"Why, by the Baron de Taverney, of course."

"What is this Baron de Taverney?"

"He is the father of Mademoiselle Andrée, monsieur."

"Very pleasing intelligence, indeed; but I mean what sort of a man is he?"

"An old nobleman, monsieur, sixty or sixty-five years of age; he once was rich, they say."

"Ay, and poor now; that is the history of all those old barons. Well, show me the way to this baron's abode."

"To the Baron de Taverney's?" he asked, in alarm.

"Then you refuse?"

"No, monsieur; but —"

"Well?"

"He will not receive you."

"He will not receive a gentleman in need of shelter? Is he a bear, your baron?"

"*Dame!*" said the young man, with an expression which said plainly, "Not much unlike one."

"Never mind, I'll run the risk."

"Remember, I do not advise it."

"Bah!" said the traveller, "bear as he is, he won't eat me."

"No; but he may shut the door in your face."

"Then I'll break it open; so, if you refuse to be my guide —"

"I don't refuse, monsieur."

"Show me the way, then."

"Willingly, monsieur."

The traveller leaped into the cabriolet and brought from it a little lantern. The young man hoped, as it was not lighted, that he should be obliged to open the carriage, and that then its interior would be disclosed. But the traveller did nothing of the kind; he put the lantern into Gilbert's hand.

"What shall I do with it, monsieur?"

"It will light you on the way whilst I lead the horses."

"But it is not lighted."

"I am going to light it."

"Oh, you have a fire in the carriage?"

"And in my pocket," replied the traveller.

"But in this rain the tinder won't kindle."

"Open the lantern," said the traveller, smiling.

Gilbert obeyed.

"Hold your hat over my hands."

Gilbert again obeyed, regarding with curiosity what followed, for he knew no other means of procuring a light than with a flint and tinder.

The traveller took from his pocket a very small silver case, drew from it a match, which he rubbed in some sort of inflammable paste, and it kindled instantly, with a slight crackling.

Gilbert started. The traveller smiled at his surprise, which was natural enough at that time, when phosphorus was only known to a few chemists, who kept the secret for their own advantage. The candle in the lantern being lighted by the match, he put up the little case. The young man followed his movements with greedy eyes; it was evident he would have given a great deal for such a treasure.

"Now that we have light, lead on."

"Follow now, then, monsieur;" and Gilbert advanced, whilst his companion, taking the horse by the bit, dragged him after.

The weather was now not so bad; the rain had ceased, and the thunder was only heard muttering at a distance. The traveller seemed to wish for more conversation.

"You know this baron, then, my good fellow?"

"Certainly, monsieur, since I have lived in his house from my infancy."

"A relation?"

"No, monsieur."

"Your guardian?"

"No."

"Your master?"

The young man started and coloured with anger at the word *master*. "I am not a servant, monsieur," said he.

"Well, but you are surely something or other?"

"I am the son of an old tenant of the baron's; my mother nursed Mademoiselle Andrée."

"I understand; being the young lady's foster-brother —
for I presume she is young — you live at free quarters in
the house."

"She is sixteen, monsieur."

Now in the traveller's last words there was something
like two questions, but Gilbert avoided any reply to that
which concerned himself. The traveller seemed to observe
this, and gave his interrogations another turn.

"How did you happen to be out during such weather?"

"I was under a rock near the road."

"What were you doing there?"

"I was reading."

"You were reading?"

"Yes."

"What were you reading?"

"'Le Contrat Social,' by Rousseau."

The traveller looked at the young man with surprise.

"Did you get that book in the baron's library?"

"No, monsieur; I bought it."

"Where? at Bar-le-Duc?"

"No, monsieur, from a pedler. They roam this way
now and then, and bring us some tolerably good books."

"Who told you 'Le Contrat Social' was a good book?"

"I soon found that out as I read it."

"Have you read bad books, then, that you know the
difference so well?"

"Yes."

"What do you call bad books?"

"Why, 'Le Sofa,' 'Tanzaï and Néadarme,' and books
of that description."

"But where the deuce did you get such books?"

"In the baron's library."

"And how does the baron get new novels in this den of
his?"

"They are sent him from Paris."

"So this poor baron spends his money on that sort of
trash?"

"No; they are given him."

"Given him? By whom?"

"By one of his friends, a great nobleman."

"A great nobleman! Do you know his name?"

"The Duc de Richelieu."

"What! the old marshal?"

"Yes, the marshal."

"I take it for granted he does not leave such books in Mademoiselle Andrée's way?"

"Indeed, monsieur, he leaves them in everybody's way."

"Is Mademoiselle Andrée of your opinion?" asked the traveller, with a sly smile, "that they are bad?"

"She does not read them, monsieur," replied Gilbert, dryly.

The traveller was silent for a minute; this character, a singular mixture of shame and boldness, of good and evil, interested him in spite of himself.

"And why did you read those books when you knew they were bad?"

"Because I did not know when I began them."

"But you soon found it out?"

"Yes."

"And nevertheless you went on?"

"Yes."

"But why?"

"They taught me things I did not know before."

"And 'Le Contrat Social'?"

"It teaches me things that I have guessed."

"How so?"

"Why, that men are brothers; that societies in which there are serfs or slaves are ill constituted; that one day we shall all be equal."

"Oh, ho!" said the traveller. There was a short silence.

"So, my good fellow," continued the traveller, in a low voice, "you wish to be instructed?"

"Yes, monsieur, that is my most ardent wish."

"And what do you wish to learn?"

"Everything."

"For what purpose?"

"To raise myself in the world."

"And how high would you rise?"

Gilbert hesitated. No doubt he had his mind made up on that point, but it was evidently a secret, and he would not reveal it.

"As high as man can rise," he replied.

"Well, have you studied anything?"

"Nothing. How can I study, not being rich, and living at Taverney?"

"Then you know nothing of mathematics?"

"No."

"Nor of natural philosophy?"

"No."

"Nor of chemistry?"

"No; I know only how to read and write; but I shall know all those things."

"When?"

"Some day or other."

"But how?"

"I don't know yet."

"Strange creature!" muttered the traveller.

"And then —" murmured Gilbert, speaking to himself.

"Well, then —?"

"Nothing."

They had now proceeded for about a quarter of an hour; the rain had ceased, and the earth sent up those odoriferous exhalations which in spring follow a great storm.

Gilbert seemed reflecting; all at once he said, "Monsieur, do you know the cause of storms?"

"Certainly."

"You really do?"

"Yes."

"You know the cause of the thunderbolt?"

The traveller smiled. "It is the meeting of two streams

of the electric fluid, — one from the clouds, the other from the earth."

Gilbert sighed. "I do not understand that," said he.

Perhaps the traveller would have explained the matter more clearly, but just then a light appeared through the trees.

"Ah! what is that?" asked the stranger.

"It is Taverney."

"We have reached it then?"

"Yes; this is the gate of the back entrance."

"Open it."

"And do you think the gate of Taverney, monsieur, can be opened with a push?"

"Is it a fortified place then? Knock."

Gilbert approached the gate, and timidly gave one knock.

"*Pardieu!* they will never hear that. Knock loudly!"

Nothing, indeed, indicated that Gilbert's knock had been heard; all was silent.

"You must take the responsibility upon yourself, monsieur, then," said Gilbert.

"Don't be troubled about that."

Gilbert hesitated no longer; left the knocker, and pulled a string which made a bell sound so loud one might have heard it a mile off.

"*Ma foi!* if your baron does not hear that," said the traveller, "he must be deaf."

"Hark! I hear Mahon barking."

"Mahon? That is no doubt a compliment from your baron to his friend, the Duc de Richelieu?"

"I don't know what you mean, monsieur."

"Mahon was the last place taken by the marshal."

"Oh, monsieur, I told you I know nothing," and Gilbert sighed again.

These sighs revealed to the stranger some hidden ambition, some secret cause of pain.

A step was heard. "Here is some one at last," said the stranger.

"It is Master La Brie," said Gilbert.

The gate opened, but La Brie, taken by surprise at seeing the stranger and the carriage when he expected no one but Gilbert, would have shut it again.

"Excuse me, my friend, but I have come here purposely, and you must not shut the door in my face."

"But, monsieur, I must tell the baron that an unexpected visitor — "

"Never mind; I shall run the risk of his looking a little cross at me; but he shall not turn me out, I can tell you, until I have got warmed, dried, and fed. They say you have good wine in this part of the country; do you happen to know?"

La Brie, instead of replying, was going to make farther resistance, but it was in vain; the traveller pushed in, and Gilbert closed the gate after him, the two horses and carriage being in the avenue. La Brie, seeing himself vanquished, proceeded as quickly as his old limbs would permit towards the house to announce his own defeat, shouting with all his strength, "Nicole Legay, Nicole Legay!"

"Who is this Nicole?" asked the stranger, calmly making his way to the house.

"Nicole Legay, monsieur?" replied Gilbert, with symptoms of some inward emotion.

"Yes; she whom Master La Brie is calling."

"Mademoiselle Andrée's waiting-maid, monsieur."

In the mean time, in answer to the calls of La Brie, a light appeared under the trees, borne by a beautiful young girl.

"What do you want, La Brie? What is all this fuss?" asked she.

"Quick, Nicole!" cried the quivering voice of the old man, "run and tell the baron a strange gentleman is come to ask shelter!"

Nicole did not wait to be told twice, but flew off towards the château so quickly that in a moment she was out of sight.

As to La Brie, having thus satisfied himself that the
baron should not be taken by surprise, he stopped and took
breath.

The message soon produced an effect. A sharp, commanding voice was heard from the house, repeating, with
an accent by no means indicating a wish to be hospitable:
"A strange gentleman? Who is he? Gentlemen don't
come in that way without sending up their names."

"Is it the baron himself?" asked he who was the cause
of all the disturbance.

"Oh, yes, monsieur," replied the poor frightened old
man; "you hear what he says?"

"He asks my name, I think?"

"Yes. I forgot to ask it, monsieur."

"Say the Baron Joseph Balsamo. Our titles being the
same, he will perhaps not be so angry."

La Brie, a little emboldened by the rank of the stranger,
announced him as he requested.

"Well," grumbled the voice from the house, "since he
is there, he must come in. Here, monsieur, this way, this
way."

The stranger advanced quickly; but just as he reached
the foot of the stone steps leading up to the door, he
turned to see whether Gilbert was there or not. Gilbert
had disappeared.

CHAPTER V.

THE BARON DE TAVERNEY.

ALTHOUGH in some degree forewarned by Gilbert of the poverty of the Baron de Taverney, the person who had caused himself to be announced as the Baron Joseph Balsamo could not help being surprised at the miserable appearance of the abode called by Gilbert, with emphasis, a château.

The house was built in the form of an oblong square of one story in height, with a square tower at each corner. Its irregular appearance had, however, something pleasing and picturesque, seen by the pale light of the moon, shining out from between the huge masses of the clouds left by the storm. There were six windows in the low building, and two in each tower, — that is, one window in each of its stories. A broad flight of steps led up to the hall-door, but they were so broken and rugged that they seemed rather a sort of precipice than a staircase.

Such was the dwelling on the threshold of which the stranger was received by the Baron de Taverney, in his dressing-gown, and holding a candlestick in his hand. The baron was a little old man from sixty to sixty-five years of age, with a keen eye and a high, retreating forehead. He wore an old wig, which, from frequent accidents with the candles on the mantelpiece, had lost all the curls which the rats, which frequented his wardrobe, had left it. He held in his hand a napkin of very dubious whiteness, which indicated that he had been disturbed when going to sit down to supper.

In his malicious countenance, which slightly resembled that of Voltaire, two expressions struggled for mastery, — politeness required a smile for his guest, but vexation turned it to a rather decided atrabilious sneer. And thus, lighted as he was by the candle in his hand, the flickering of which disturbed his features, the Baron de Taverney could not well be called anything but a very ugly nobleman.

"Monsieur," said he, "may I know to what fortunate circumstance I owe the pleasure of seeing you?"

"Simply, monsieur, to the storm, which frightened my horses and caused them very nearly to destroy my carriage ; one of my postilions was thrown from his horse, the other galloped off with his, and I know not what I should have done, had I not met a young man who conducted me to your château, assuring me that your hospitality was well known."

The baron raised his light to endeavour to discover the unlucky wight who had, by this piece of information, been the cause of the unwelcome visit. Balsamo also looked around for his guide, but he had retired.

"And do you know the name of the young man who pointed out my château?" asked the Baron de Taverney, as if he wanted to return him thanks.

"Gilbert, I think, is his name."

"Ha! Gilbert! I scarcely thought him fit even for that. An idle dog, — a philosopher, you must know, monsieur! "

The threatening tone in which these epithets were uttered showed that there was little sympathy between the lord and his vassal.

"However, monsieur," said the baron, after a moment's silence as expressive as his words, "will you be good enough to enter?"

"Allow me first, monsieur, to see after my carriage, which contains some very valuable articles."

"La Brie!" cried the baron, "La Brie! get some assistance, and put the gentleman's carriage under the shed in the yard; there are still some laths of a roof there. I can't answer for your horses, however, getting a good feed; but as they are not yours, but the postmaster's, you need not care very much."

"In truth, monsieur," said the traveller, beginning to get impatient, "I fear that I am giving you quite too much trouble."

"Not at all monsieur, not at all, — no trouble to me; but you will be rather poorly lodged, I warn you."

"Monsieur, I assure you I feel exceedingly grateful."

"Pray, do not deceive yourself as to what we can do for you," said the baron, raising his candle, so as to throw its rays in the direction where Balsamo was assisting La Brie to wheel his carriage under the shed, and elevating his voice in proportion as his guest retreated. "Pray do not deceive yourself; Taverney is a dull abode, a wretched place!"

The traveller was too busy to reply; he chose the best covered part of the shed to shelter the carriage, and having pointed it out to La Brie, slipped a louis-d'or into his hand, and returned to the baron.

La Brie put the louis in his pocket, supposing it only a crown, and thanking Heaven for his good fortune.

"Heaven forbid I should think so ill of your château as you speak of it!" said Balsamo, bowing to the baron, who, as the only proof of the truth of his assertion, shook his head, and led the guest through a wide, damp antechamber, grumbling as he proceeded: "Oh, all very good! but I know what I am saying; I know, unfortunately, my own means, and I assure you they are very limited. If you are a Frenchman, monsieur, — but your German accent shows you are not, and yet your name is Italian, but that is no matter, — if you are a Frenchman, I repeat, the name of Taverney may recall some recollections of splendour; it was once called Taverney the rich!"

Balsamo expected a sigh at this conclusion, but there was none. "Philosophy!" thought he.

"This way, this way!" cried the baron, opening the dining-room door. "Holà! Maître La Brie! wait at supper, now, as if you were yourself a hundred servants in one!"

La Brie bustled about in obedience to this command.

"I have no servant but this, monsieur," said Taverney; "he is a very bad one, but I have not the means of getting a better. The fool has been with me twenty years without getting a penny of wages. I feed him about as well as he waits on me. He is an ass, you see!"

Balsamo continued to study this character. "No heart," thought he; "yet perhaps all this is merely affectation."

The baron shut the door of the dining-room, and then, as he held his light high above his head, the traveller saw distinctly its size and its furniture.

It was a large, low hall, which had formerly been the principal apartment of a small farm-house, raised by its owner to the rank of a château. It was so scantily furnished that, at the first glance, it appeared empty. Straw chairs, with carved backs, some engravings from the battle-pieces of Lebrun, framed in black varnished wood, and a large oak cupboard, dark with age and smoke, were all its ornaments. In the middle stood a little round table on which was a dish of partridges and cabbage. The wine was in a stone jar, and the plate, unpolished, worn, and battered, consisted of three covers, one tankard and one salt-cellar; but this last article was very massive, exquisitely chased, and looked like a diamond among worthless pebbles.

"There, monsieur, there!" said the baron, offering a seat to his guest, whose scrutinising look on all around did not escape him. "Oh, you are looking at my salt-cellar. You admire it. Good taste, — and very polite, too, for you fix on the only thing here worth looking at. I assure you, monsieur, I am particularly obliged. But no, I forgot; I have one other valuable commodity, — my daughter!"

"Mademoiselle Andrée?" said Balsamo.

"Faith, yes! Mademoiselle Andrée! said the host, surprised that his guest was so well informed. "I shall present you to her. Andrée! Andrée! come hither, child; don't be afraid."

"I am not afraid, father," answered a sweet and clear voice; and a tall and beautiful girl entered the room, in a manner perfectly unembarrassed, and yet quite free from forwardness.

Joseph Balsamo, though, as we have seen, perfectly master of himself, could not prevent an involuntary bow at sight of all-powerful beauty like hers. Andrée de Taverney seemed indeed sent to adorn and brighten all around her. She had dark auburn hair, of a rather lighter shade at her temples and neck, black eyes, — clear, with dilated pupils, — and a steady and majestic look, like that of an eagle; yet the mildness of that look was inexpressible. Her small mouth, formed like Apollo's bow, was brilliant as coral; her tapering hands were antique in form, as were her arms, and dazzlingly fair. Her figure, flexible and firm, was like that of the statue of some pagan goddess to which a miracle had given life. Her foot might bear a comparison with that of the huntress Diana, and it seemed only by a miracle that it could support the weight of her body. Her dress was of the simplest fashion, yet suited her so well that it seemed as if one from the wardrobe of a queen would not have been so elegant or so rich.

All these details were perceived by Balsamo in the first glance, as the young lady passed from the door to the table. On his side, the baron had not lost a single impression produced on the mind of his guest by the rare union of perfections in his daughter.

"You were right," whispered Balsamo, turning to his host, "Mademoiselle Andrée is perfection."

"Do not not flatter poor Andrée, monsieur," said the baron, carelessly; "she has just returned home from her convent, and she will believe all you say. Not that I am afraid of her coquetry, — on the contrary, the dear child is not enough of a coquette; but, like a good father, I am cul-

tivating in her that first and most important quality for a
woman."

Andrée looked down and blushed; although she tried to
avoid listening, she could not but overhear her father's
words.

"Did they tell mademoiselle that at the convent?"
asked Joseph Balsamo, laughing; "and was that precept
part of the instructions of the nuns?"

"Monsieur," replied the baron, "I have my own way of
thinking on particular subjects, as you may see."

This was so self-evident that Balsamo merely bowed in
assent.

"No," continued he, "I do not imitate those fathers who
say to their daughters, 'Be prudes, be rigid, be blind;
think of nothing but honour, delicacy, devotion.' Fools!
It is as if the fathers of the knights of old had sent those
champions into the lists, after having taken off all their
armour, to fight an adversary armed cap-à-pie. *Pardieu!*
that is not the way I shall bring up my daughter Andrée,
though she be brought up in this miserable den."

Although Balsamo perfectly agreed with the baron as to
the propriety of this last epithet, yet he deemed it polite to
contradict it.

"Oh, all very well," resumed the old man, "but I know
the place, I tell you. Yet, though now so far from the sun
of Versailles, my daughter shall know the world which I
formerly knew so well myself; and if she enter it, it shall
be with an arsenal of weapons forged by my experience
and my recollections. But I must confess, monsieur, the
convent has ruined all my plans. As if that was what I
wanted, my daughter was the first boarder who really practised the precepts there taught, and followed the letter of
the Gospel. *Corbleu!* was not that being prettily served?"

"Mademoiselle is an angel," replied Balsamo, "and in
truth, monsieur, what you say does not surprise me."

Andrée bowed her thanks for this compliment, and sat
down in obedience to a look from her father.

"Be seated, baron," said the host, "and if you are hungry, eat. What a horrible ragout that fool La Brie has given us!"

"Partridges! Do you call that horrible?" said the guest, smiling. "You slander your supper. Partridges in May! Are they from your own estates?"

"My estates! it is long since I had one. My respectable father left me some land indeed, but it was eaten and digested long enough ago. Oh, Heaven be praised! I have not an inch of ground. That good-for-nothing Gilbert, who can only read and dream, must have stolen a gun, powder, and shot from some one or other, and he kills birds, poaching on the estates of my neighbours. He will be caught and sent to the galleys some day, and certainly I shall not interfere, — it will be a good riddance; but Andrée likes game, so I am obliged to overlook Monsieur Gilbert's freaks."

Balsamo watched Andrée's lovely face as this was said, but not a change, not the slightest blush, disturbed it.

He was seated at table between her and the baron, and she helped him, without appearing in the least annoyed at the scantiness of the repast, to a portion of the dish procured by Gilbert and cooked by La Brie, and so heartily abused by the baron. During this time poor La Brie, who heard all the eulogiums passed on himself and Gilbert, handed the plates with a deprecating air, which became quite triumphant at each word of praise the guest bestowed on his cookery.

"He has not even salted his abominable ragout!" cried the baron, after he had devoured two wings of a partridge, which his daughter had placed before him on a tempting layer of cabbage. "Andrée, pass the salt-cellar to the Baron Balsamo."

Andrée obeyed, extending her arm with exquisite grace.

"Ah, you are admiring the salt-cellar again!" said the host.

"No, monsieur, you are wrong this time," replied Balsamo; "I was admiring mademoiselle's hand."

"Ah! very good indeed, — a perfect Richelieu! But since you have the salt-cellar in your own hand, examine it; it was made for the regent by the goldsmith Lucas. It represents the loves of the satyrs and bacchantes, — a little free, but pretty."

Balsamo saw that the little figures so admirably executed were something worse than free, and he could not but admire the unconsciousness with which Andrée had offered him the salt-cellar.

But as if the baron had determined to put to the proof that innocence which carries with it such a charm, he began to point out in detail the beauties of his favourite piece of plate, in spite of all Balsamo's efforts to change the conversation.

"Come, eat, baron," said Taverney, "for I warn you there is no other dish. Perhaps you are expecting the roast, and other removes; if so, great will be your disappointment."

"Pardon me, monsieur," said Andrée, in her usual calm manner, "but if Nicole has rightly understood me, we shall have another dish. I have given her the receipt for one."

"The receipt! you have given a receipt to your maid! the *femme-de-chambre* turned cook! It only requires one step more — turn cook yourself, I beg you! Did the Duchesse de Châteauroux or the Marquise de Pompadour ever cook for the king? On the contrary, it was he who dressed omelets for them. *Jour de Dieu!* have I lived to see women cooking in my house? Baron, excuse my daughter, I beseech you."

"But, father, we must eat," said Andrée, quietly. "Well, Legay," added she in a louder tone, "is it done?"

"Yes, mademoiselle," replied the maid, bringing in a dish of a very tempting odour.

"I know one at least who will not eat of that dish!" said the baron, furious, and breaking his plate as he spoke.

"Perhaps you will eat some, monsieur?" said Andrée, coldly. Then, turning to her father, "You know, monsieur, we have now only seven plates of that set which my mother left me;" and, so saying, she proceeded to carve the smoking viands, which Mademoiselle Legay, the pretty waiting-maid, had just placed on the table.

CHAPTER VI.

ANDRÉE DE TAVERNEY.

THE searching intellect of Balsamo found ample food for study in each detail of the strange and isolated life led by this family in a corner of Lorraine.

The salt-cellar alone revealed to him one phase of the baron's character, or rather his character in all its bearings. He called up all his penetration, therefore, as he scrutinised the features of Andrée whilst she handed him that salt-cellar.

At length, whether moved by curiosity or some deeper feeling, Balsamo gazed on Andrée so fixedly that two or three times, in less than ten minutes, the eyes of the young girl met his. At first she bore his look without confusion, but its intensity became by degrees so great that a feverish impatience, which made the blood mount to her cheeks, took possession of her; then, feeling that this look had something supernatural in its power, she tried to brave it, and, in her turn, she gazed at the baron with her large, limpid, dilated eyes. But this time again she was obliged to yield, and, filled with the magnetic fluid which flowed in streams from his flaming orbs, her eyelids weighed down, sunk timidly, no longer to be raised but with hesitation.

Whilst this silent struggle went on between the young girl and the mysterious traveller, the baron grumbled, laughed, found fault, and swore like a true country gentleman, and pinched La Brie whenever he was within his reach, feeling that he must vent his spleen on some one. He was going to do the same to Nicole, when his eyes, for the first time no doubt, rested on the hands of the young waiting-maid. The baron was an adorer of fine hands; all his youthful follies might be attributed to the power of a fine hand over him.

"Only see!" cried he, "what pretty fingers this little rogue has! How the nail tapers! it would bend over the tip, — a great beauty if washing bottles and cutting wood did not wear down the horn; for it is horn you have at the ends of your fingers, Mademoiselle Nicole."

Not accustomed to compliments from her master, Nicole looked at him with a half-smile, in which there was more astonishment than gratification.

"Yes, yes," said the baron, who saw what passed in the mind of the young flirt, "turn away, — play the coquette, I beg of you; but I must inform you, my dear guest, that Mademoiselle Nicole Legay, this young lady here present, is not a prude like her mistress, and is not at all afraid of a compliment."

Balsamo turned quickly towards the baron's daughter, and saw an expression of supreme disdain on her handsome features. Then, thinking it right to adapt his expression to hers, he looked haughtily away; at which Andrée seemed pleased, and regarded him with less sternness, or rather with less uneasiness, than before.

"Would you think, monsieur," continued the baron, chucking Nicole under the chin, "would you think that this damsel had been in a convent with my daughter, and is really what one might call educated? Oh! Mademoiselle Nicole would not quit her mistress for a moment. There is a devotedness in her which would greatly delight the philosophers who maintain that these creatures have souls."

"Monsieur," said Andrée, displeased, "it is not devotedness which prevents Nicole from leaving me; it is because I order her to remain."

Balsamo raised his eyes to Nicole, to see the effect of these contemptuous words, and he observed, from her compressed lips, that she was not insensible to the humiliations to which her position in the family exposed her. But the

emotion was transitory; for, in turning away to hide it,
her eyes rested with interest on a window of the room
which looked into the courtyard. Everything roused the
curiosity of Balsamo, and, as he followed her eyes, he
thought he saw what interested her, — the face of a man
at the window. "In truth," thought he, "every one has
a mystery in this house, and I hope soon to know Mademoiselle Andrée's. I have found out the baron's, and I guess
what Nicole's is." Whilst he was thus communing with
himself, the baron observed his absence of mind.

"You are in a reverie, my dear guest," said he. "Well,
it is infectious here, — it attacks every one. Let me reckon :
first, Mademoiselle de Taverney falls into reveries; then
Mademoiselle Nicole does the same; then the good-for-
nothing fellow who shot the partridges is in a perpetual
reverie, and very likely the partridges were in a reverie
when he shot them."

"Gilbert ? " asked Balsamo.

"Yes. Oh, a philosopher like Monsieur La Brie here !
But as to the philosophers, — perhaps you are a friend of
theirs ? If so, I warn you you will be none of mine."

"No, monsieur, I am neither for them nor against them,"
replied Balsamo. "I know nothing of them."

"*Ventrebleu!* so much the better. They are wretches
as mischievous as they are ugly ; the monarchy will be
ruined by their opinions. No one laughs now ; every
one reads ! And what, I pray you ? Sentiments like this :
*Under a monarchical government it is difficult for a people
to be virtuous;* or this : *Monarchy is an institution invented
for the corruption of the morals of men, and the purpose of
enslaving them ;* or else this : *If the power of kings comes
from God, it comes as diseases and other scourges of the
human race come from him.* You call that improving, I
hope ! A virtuous people ! Now, I ask you, of what use
would they be ? Everything has gone wrong since the
king spoke to Voltaire and read Diderot ! "

At this moment Balsamo thought he saw the pale face

which he had seen before again appear at the window; but it vanished when he looked in that direction.

"Is mademoiselle a philosopher?" asked Balsamo, turning to Andrée, with a smile.

"I don't even know what philosophy is," replied Andrée. "I like what is serious."

"Ha! mademoiselle!" cried the baron, "then in my opinion, nothing is more serious than good living, — like that, I pray you."

"But mademoiselle does not hate life, I presume?" said Balsamo.

"That depends on circumstances," replied Andrée.

"What a stupid phrase," exclaimed the baron; "would you believe it, monsieur, my son once made me, word for word, a similar reply!"

"You have a son then, monsieur?"

"Oh, *mon Dieu!* monsieur, yes! I have that misfortune. The Chevalier de Taverney, lieutenant in the body-guard of the dauphin, — a most excellent young man!" And the baron uttered these four words as if he would have crushed each letter in them.

"I congratulate you, monsieur," said Balsamo, with a bow.

"Oh yes! another philosopher, monsieur! Upon the honour of a gentleman, it is sickening! Did he not speak to me the other day about giving the negroes their freedom? 'And what about sugar?' asked I, 'for I like my coffee very sweet, and so does Louis XV.' 'Monsieur,' replied he, 'is it not better to go without sugar than to make a whole race suffer?' 'A race of monkeys,' said I, and I think it was saying a great deal in their praise. Well, what do you think he said next? *Ma foi!* there must be something in the air to turn people's heads! He replied to me that all men were brothers! I the brother of a Hottentot!"

"Oh, that was going rather far!"

"Hey! what do you think of that? I am in great luck

with my two children, am I not ? No one will say that I
shall be truly represented in my descendants. The sister
is an angel, the brother an apostle ! Drink, monsieur,
drink ! The wine is detestable ! "

"I think it exquisite," said Balsamo, still looking at
Andrée.

"Then you *are* a philosopher! Take care, or I shall
order my daughter to preach you a sermon. But, no, philosophers have no religion. Still, religion was a very con-
venient thing; one believed in God and the king, and all
was settled. Now people believe in neither the one nor the
other; they must know so much, read so much. I prefer never doubting. In my time our only study was to
amuse ourselves, — to play at faro and dice, and to fence;
we ruined duchesses, and were ruined by opera-dancers.
That was my history to a tittle! The whole of Taverney
went to the opera. It is the only thing I regret, for a
ruined man is not worth the name of man. You think me
old, don't you ? Well, it is because I am ruined, and live
in this den; because my wig is shabby, and my coat a relic
of antiquity. But look at my friend, the marshal, with his
coats of the newest cut, and his well-curled wig, and his
ten thousand a year. He looks young, fresh, and gay, and
yet he is ten years older than I, monsieur ! — ten years,
I assure you ! "

"You speak of Monsieur de Richelieu ? "

"Yes, the same."

"The duke ? "

"Why, faith, not the cardinal, I think; I do not go
quite so far back. Besides, the cardinal never did what
his nephew did; he did not last so long."

"I am surprised that, with such powerful friends at
court, you should have left it."

"Oh, a temporary retreat! I shall return to it some
day or other," and the old baron cast a singular look on his
daughter. Balsamo did not allow it to pass unnoticed.

"But," said he, "the marshal might at least advance
your son ? "

"My son! He hates him."

"Hates the son of his friend?"

"He is quite right."

"And do *you* say so, monsieur?"

"*Pardieu!* I tell you he is a philosopher; he abhors him!"

"And Philip returns him the compliment," said Andrée, with perfect calmness. "Remove these things, Legay!"

The young girl, roused from her fixed contemplation of the window, hastened to obey.

"Ah," said the baron, sighing, "one used to sit after supper till two in the morning; we had what was fit to eat then, and when the eating was over, we drank. But how drink this stuff, when we are not occupied in eating? Legay, bring a flask of Maraschino, if there be one."

"Do so," said Andrée, for the maid seemed to wait for her orders before obeying those of the baron.

The baron threw himself back in his chair, shut his eyes, and sighed with a grotesque sort of melancholy.

"You were speaking of the Marshal de Richelieu," said Balsamo, who appeared not inclined to let the conversation drop.

"Yes," said Taverney, "I was speaking of him;" and he hummed an air as melancholy as his sighs.

"If he hate your son, and if he be right to hate him because he is a philosopher, he must retain all his friendship for you, since you are not one."

"Philosopher! no, Heaven be praised!"

"You must surely have claims on the administration? You have served the king?"

"Fifteen years. I was the marshal's aide-de-camp; we served together in the campaign of Mahon. Our friendship is of long standing. Let me see: it began at the siege of Philipsbourg; that was in the year 1742 or 1743."

"So," said Balsamo, "you were at the siege of Philipsbourg? I was there myself."

The old man sat upright in his chair and stared at the stranger.

"Excuse me; but what is your age, my respected guest?"

"Oh, I am not old," said Balsamo, holding out his glass to be filled with Maraschino by the fair hand of Andrée.

The baron interpreted the stranger's answer in his own way, and concluded that Balsamo had some reason for concealing his age.

"Monsieur," said he, "allow me to say that you do not appear to be old enough to have served at Philipsbourg; that siege took place twenty-eight years ago, and you seem to be about thirty."

"Oh, anybody might be taken for thirty."

"*Pardieu*, then, I wish *I* could; it is just thirty years since I was of that age."

Mademoiselle Andrée gazed with increasing and irresistible curiosity on the stranger, for every word revealed him in a new light.

"You astonish me, monsieur," said the baron, — "unless you are all this time mistaken in the name, and are thinking of some other town than Philipsbourg. I should say you were not more than thirty; would not you, Andrée, say the same?"

"Yes, indeed," replied she, trying to bear the powerful eye of their guest, but this time again in vain.

"No, no," said the latter, "I mean what I say; I mean the famous siege of Philipsbourg, at which the Duc de Richelieu killed his cousin, the Prince de Lixen, in a duel. The affair took place as they were returning from the trenches, on the high-road; he ran his sword right through his body! I passed just as he expired in the arms of the Prince de Deux-Ponts; he was seated against the side of a ditch, while Richelieu was coolly wiping his sword."

"On my honour, you amaze me, monsieur," said the baron; "it occurred precisely as you say!"

"You have heard the affair described?" asked Balsamo, coolly.

" I was there. I had the honour of being second to the marshal; he was not marshal then, but that is no matter."

" Let me think," said Balsamo, turning and gazing firmly on him. " Were you not then a captain ? "

" Precisely."

" You were in the queen's regiment of light horse, which was cut to pieces at Fontenoy ? "

" Perhaps you were at Fontenoy, too ? " asked the baron, endeavouring to jest.

"No," replied Balsamo; "I was dead at that time."

The baron stared, Andrée started, Nicole crossed herself.

"But to return to what we were saying. You wore the uniform of the light horse, I remember perfectly, at that time; I saw you as I passed; you were holding your own and the marshal's horse, whilst they fought. I went up to you and asked you about the duel; you gave me the details."

" I ? "

" Yes, you, *pardieu!* — I recognise you now; you bore the title of chevalier — they called you *the little chevalier.*"

" *Mordieu!* " cried the baron, all amazed.

"Excuse me that I did not sooner recognise you; but thirty years change a man. Let us drink the marshal's health, my dear baron."

He raised his glass, and drained it to the last drop.

" You saw me there ? " cried the baron; " impossible ! "

" I saw you," said Balsamo.

" On the high-road ? "

" On the high-road."

" Holding the horses ? "

" Holding the horses."

" Whilst the duel was going on ? "

" As the prince was expiring, I said."

"Then you are fifty."

"I am old enough to have seen what I tell you."

The baron threw himself back in his chair, but in so

ridiculous a pet that Nicole could not help laughing
Andrée, instead of laughing, seemed to be in a reverie, —
her eyes open, and fixed on those of Balsamo. He appeared now to have attained his object. Suddenly rising,
he sent from his flaming eyeball two or three lightning
flashes full on her. She started, as if from an electric
shock. Her arms stiffened, her neck bent, she smiled,
yet as if involuntarily, on the stranger, then closed her
eyes.

"Do you also, mademoiselle, believe I speak falsely when
I say that I was present at the siege of Philipsbourg ? "

"No, monsieur, I believe you," she articulated, making
a violent effort.

"Then it is I who am only a dotard," said the baron;
"the gentleman no doubt has come back from the other
world ! "

Nicole gazed on him with horror.

"Who knows ? " replied Balsamo, in so solemn a tone
that she was yet more horrified.

"Well, then, baron," resumed the old man, "to have
done with jesting, are you really more than thirty ?
You do not look more. "

"Monsieur," said Balsamo, "would you believe me if
I told you a very incredible thing ? "

"I do not promise that," said the baron, looking knowing, whilst Andrée listened with eager attention. "I
am very incredulous, I must candidly warn you."

"What use is there, then, in putting a question, when
you will not listen to my reply ? "

"Well, I will believe you. There ! — are you satisfied ? "

"Then, monsieur, I have only to repeat what I have told
you, and to add that I knew you personally at the siege
of Philipsbourg."

"Then you must have been a child ? "

"Undoubtedly."

"Four or five years old at most ? "

"No, I was forty-one."

The baron burst into a loud fit of laughter, which Nicole re-echoed.

"I told you you would not believe me," said Balsamo, gravely.

"But how is it possible to believe that? At least, give me some proofs."

"That is easy. I was forty-one then, but I do not say that I was the man I am."

"Oh," cried the baron, "this is going back to paganism. Was there not a philosopher, — for those wretches flourished in every century, — was there not a Greek philosopher who would not eat beans because he pretended they had had souls, as my son says negroes have? Who was he? — what the devil was his name?"

"Pythagoras," said Andrée.

"Yes, Pythagoras; the Jesuits taught me that. Father Porée made me compose Latin verses on it, with little Arouet. I remember they thought mine much the best. Pythagoras? — yes."

"Well, how do you know that I am not Pythagoras?" replied Balsamo, quietly.

"I do not deny that you may be Pythagoras, but Pythagoras was not at the siege of Philipsbourg; at least, I did not see him there."

"No; but you saw the Viscount Jean des Barreaux, who was in the Black Musketeers."

"Yes, I knew him well; but he was no philosopher, although he did hate beans, and never ate them when he could help it."

"Well, do you recollect, the day after the duel, Des Barreaux was in the trenches with you?"

"Yes, perfectly well."

"For you know the Black Musketeers, and the light horse always mounted guard together every seven days."

"True enough. What next?"

"That very evening the grape-shot fell like hail, and

Des Barreaux was dull; he asked you for a pinch of snuff, and you offered him your gold box."

"On which was the likeness of a female?"

"Exactly. I see her now. She was fair, was she not?"

"*Mordieu!*" cried the baron, terrified, "you are right. Well, then?"

"Well, then," continued Balsamo, "as he was taking that pinch of snuff, a ball carried off his head, just in the same way that Marshal Berwick's was carried away formerly."

"Alas! yes, I remember," said the baron. "Poor Des Barreaux!"

"And now, monsieur, you see I must have seen and known you at the siege of Philipsbourg, since I was that very Des Barreaux."

The baron fell back once more in his chair, almost stupefied at these words; but, recovering, he cried, "Why, this is sorcery — magic! A hundred years ago you would have been burnt, my dear guest. Upon my honour, I think I can smell a sort of corpse-like odour."

"Monsieur," said Balsamo, "no true sorcerer or magician has ever yet been burnt; it is fools who have anything to do with the fagot. But a truce to this conversation. Mademoiselle de Taverney is asleep; it seems that metaphysics and the occult sciences have few attractions for her."

In fact, Andrée, overcome by an unknown, irresistible power, felt her head sink on her breast, — like a flower whose cup bends under its weight of dew.

At the last words of Balsamo she made an effort to shake off the influence that like a subtle fluid stole upon her. She shook her head, arose, seemed about to fall, but, supported by Nicole, left the dining-room. At the same moment the face which had been looking in at the window, and which Balsamo had long ago recognised as Gilbert's, also disappeared. An instant after he heard Andrée begin to play with vigour on her harpsichord. He had followed her with his eye as she left the room, and could not help exclaiming triumphantly, as she disappeared, "I may say, like Archimedes, *Eureka!*"

"Archimedes! Who was he?" asked the baron.

"A good sort of a fellow,—a savant whom I knew two thousand one hundred and fifty years ago," said Balsamo.

CHAPTER VII.

EUREKA.

WHETHER this piece of extravagance was too much for the baron, whether he had not heard it, or whether, having heard it, he thought it best to get rid of his strange guest, we know not; but he made no reply to it. But when the sound of Andrée's harpsichord proved that she was engaged in the next apartment, he offered to procure Balsamo the means of proceeding to the nearest town.

"I have an old horse who, though on his last legs, will carry you so far; and you would at least procure good lodgings. There is, indeed, a room and a bed at Taverney; but my ideas of hospitality are rather peculiar. '*Good or none*' is my motto."

"Then you wish to send me away?" said Balsamo, hiding his vexation under a smile. "That is treating me like an intruder."

"No, indeed; it is treating you like a friend, my dear guest. Lodging you here would be really treating you as an enemy. I say this in all conscience, but with great regret, for I am delighted with your society."

"Then, pray do not force me to rise when I am tired, — to get on horseback when I would rather stretch my limbs in bed. Do not represent your hospitable resources as worse than they are, if you would not have me believe that I have been so unfortunate as to incur your dislike."

"Oh!" said the baron, "since you view the matter in that light, you shall stay."

Then looking round for La Brie, who was in a corner, he cried, "Come hither, you old rascal!" La Brie advanced

a few steps timidly. "*Ventrebleu!* come hither, I say!
Is the red room fit to accommodate a gentleman, think
you?"

"Oh, certainly, monsieur," replied the old servant;
"you know it is occupied by Monsieur Philip when he
comes to Taverney."

"It may do very well for a poor devil of a lieutenant
who comes to pass a month with a ruined father, and at
the same time be very unfit for a rich nobleman who travels
post with four horses."

"I assure you," said Balsamo, "I shall be perfectly content with it."

The baron grinned, as if he would have said, "I know
better;" then he added aloud, "La Brie, show the stranger
to the red room, since he is determined to be cured of all
wish to return to Taverney. Well, you have decided to
stay, I suppose?" said he, turning to Balsamo.

"Yes, if you permit it."

"Stay!" there are still other means."

"Means for what?"

"To avoid having to make the journey on horseback."

"What journey?"

"To Bar-le-Duc."

Balsamo waited quietly to hear this new plan developed.

"You were brought here by post-horses, were you not?"

"Yes; unless Satan brought me."

"I at first almost suspected he did, for you do not seem
to be on bad terms with him."

"You do me infinitely more honour than I deserve."

"Well, the horses that brought your carriage could now
take it away."

"No; there are only two horses left of the four, and the
carriage is heavy. Besides, post-horses must rest."

"Ha! another reason. You are determined, I see, to
remain."

"Because I wish to see you again to-morrow, and express
my gratitude to you for your hospitality."

"That you could easily repay."

"How?"

"Since you are on such good terms with his Satanic Majesty, beg him to permit me to discover the philosopher's stone."

"Why, Monsieur le Baron, if you really wish for it —"

"The philosopher's stone! *Parbleu!* if I really wish for it!"

"In that case you must apply to another individual than the devil."

"To whom, then?"

"To ME! as I heard Corneille say about a hundred years ago, when he was reciting to me a part of one of his comedies."

"Ha! La Brie, you old rascal!" cried the baron, who began to find the conversation rather dangerous at such an hour, and with such a man, "try and find a wax candle, and light the gentleman to his room."

La Brie hastened to obey, and during this search, almost as dubious in its result as that for the philosopher's stone, he desired Nicole to precede him upstairs and air the red room. Nicole being gone, Andrée was delighted to find herself alone; she felt as if she required to reflect. The baron bade Balsamo good-night, and retired to bed.

Balsamo looked at his watch, for he remembered the promise he had made to Althotas, — a promise now impossible to fulfil, the two hours having expired. He asked La Brie if the carriage was still in the place he had pointed out. La Brie replied that unless it would move away of itself, it must be there. He then asked what had become of Gilbert. La Brie assured him that the lazy fellow was no doubt in bed two hours ago. Then, after having studied the topography of the passage which led to the red room, Balsamo went out to waken Althotas.

The Baron de Taverney had not spoken falsely respecting the discomfort of this apartment; it was as poorly furnished as all the other rooms of the château.

An oaken bed with a faded green damask coverlet, and hangings of the same material looped up above it; an oaken table with twisted legs; a huge stone chimney-piece of the time of Louis XIII., to which in winter a fire might impart some appearance of comfort, but which now, wanting that, wanting all ornaments and utensils, wanting wood, and stuffed with old newspapers, only made the place look still more dreary, — such was the apartment of which Balsamo was for one night to be the fortunate possessor.

We must add that there were two chairs and a wardrobe painted of a grey colour.

Whilst La Brie was endeavouring to give a habitable appearance to the room, which Nicole had aired before retiring to her own apartment, Balsamo had wakened Althotas and returned to the house. When he reached Andrée's door, he stopped to listen. From the moment Andrée left the dining-room she felt that she had escaped from the mysterious influence which the stranger exercised over her, and to rouse herself completely from its power, she continued to play on her harpsichord. Its sound reached Balsamo through the closed door, and, as we have said, he stopped to listen.

After a minute or two he made several gestures with a sweeping circular motion, which might have been mistaken for a species of conjuration, since Andrée, struck again by the same sensation she had previously experienced, ceased to play, let her arms fall immovable by her side, and turned towards the door with a slow, stiff motion, as if she were obeying a command against her own free will. Balsamo smiled in the dark as if he saw through the door. No doubt this was all he wanted, for he stretched out his left hand, and, having found the balustrade of the staircase, which was steep and broad, he ascended to the red room. In proportion as he increased his distance, Andrée, with the same slow, rigid motion, returned to her harpsichord; and when Balsamo reached the highest stair, he heard her resume the first notes of the air which he had interrupted.

Having entered his chamber, he dismissed La Brie. La Brie was evidently a good servant, accustomed to obey on the instant; but now, after moving a few steps towards the door, he stopped.

"Well?" said Balsamo.

La Brie slipped his hand into his waistcoat pocket, and seemed feeling for something in its silent depths, but he did not reply.

"Have you anything to say to me, my friend?" inquired Balsamo, approaching him.

La Brie made a great effort over himself, and pulled his hand out of his pocket.

"I merely wished to say, monsieur, that you made a mistake this evening."

"Did I?" said Balsamo. "How so?"

"You meant to give me a livre, and you gave me a louis-d'or;" and he opened his hand and disclosed to view the new, shining piece.

Balsamo looked at the old servant with an expression of admiration which indicated he had not the highest opinion of men as far as probity was concerned.

"'*And honest?*'" said he, "as Hamlet says;" and, feeling in his own pocket, he drew out a second louis-d'or, which he laid beside the first in La Brie's hand.

La Brie's joy at this munificence could not be described. For twenty years he had not once seen gold, and in order to convince him that he was really the happy possessor of such a treasure, Balsamo had to put the money with his own hand into La Brie's pocket. He bowed to the ground, and was retiring without turning his back on the stranger, when the latter stopped him.

"At what hour does the family usually rise in the morning?" asked he.

"Monsieur de Taverney rises late, but Mademoiselle de Taverney is always up at a very early hour."

"At what hour?"

"About six o'clock."

"Who sleeps above this room?"

"I do, monsieur."

"And below?"

"No one; the vestibule is under this."

"Thank you, my friend; now you may go."

"Good-night, monsieur."

"Good-night; but, by the by, see that my carriage is safe."

"You may depend on me, monsieur."

"If you hear any noise, or see any light, do not be alarmed; I have an old lame servant in it who travels with me everywhere. Tell Monsieur Gilbert not to interfere with him; and tell him also, if you please, not to go out to-morrow morning until I have spoken to him. Can you remember all this?"

"Oh, certainly! But are you going to leave us so soon, monsieur?"

"I am not quite sure," said Balsamo, with a smile; "yet, strictly speaking, I ought to be at Bar-le-Duc to-morrow evening."

La Brie sighed resignedly, gave a last glance at the bed, and taking up the candle, went towards the fireplace to give a little warmth to the great damp room by setting fire to the papers, as he had no wood.

"No, never mind," said Balsamo, preventing him; "leave the old papers; if I do not sleep, I can amuse myself by reading them."

La Brie bowed and retired.

Balsamo listened until the steps of the old servant had died away on the stairs, and until he heard them overhead; then he went to the window. In the opposite tower there was a light in the window of a garret, the curtains of which were but half closed. It was Legay's room; she was thoughtfully unfastening her gown and handkerchief, and from time to time she opened her window and leaned out to see into the courtyard. Balsamo looked at her with more attention than he had chosen to bestow on her during supper. "What a singular resemblance!" he murmured to himself. At this moment the light in the garret was extinguished, although its occupant was not yet in bed.

Balsamo leaned against the wall, listening anxiously; the notes of the harpsichord still sounded in his ears. He assured himself that its harmony alone awoke the midnight silence around; then, opening the door which La Brie had shut, he cautiously descended the stairs, and gently pushed open the door of the salon.

Andrée heard nothing; her white hands continued to wander over the old yellow keys of the instrument. Opposite her was a mirror set in an old carved frame, the gilding of which had changed to a dull grey. The air she played was melancholy, or rather, she played merely harmonies instead of an air. No doubt it was all extempore; and she was thus reproducing in music her early recollections, or indulging in the dreams of her imagination. Perhaps her spirit, saddened by her residence at Taverney, had left the château to wander in the large, shady gardens of the convent of the Annonciades at Nancy, ringing with the merry voices of troops of happy boarders. Whether such were her dreams or not, her vague gaze seemed to lose itself in the sombre mirror before her, which reflected only indistinctly the different objects in the vast apartment, dimly lighted by the single candle placed on the harpsichord.

Sometimes she suddenly ceased. It was when she recalled the strange vision of the evening, and her unaccountable impressions; but before her thoughts had time to take any precise form, her heart beat, she felt a thrill run through her limbs, and she started as though a living being had come into contact with her. All at once, as she tried to account for these feelings, they returned; she felt a thrill as if from an electric shock; her eye became fixed, her floating thoughts become embodied as it were, and she perceived something move over the dim mirror.

The door of the salon had opened noiselessly, and in the doorway a shadow appeared. She shuddered, her fingers wandered involuntarily over the keys; yet nothing could be more easily accounted for than the appearance of the figure. Might it not be her father, or Nicole, or La Brie, who, before retiring, had returned to the apartment upon some household errand? La Brie's visits of that kind were frequent; and on these occasions the faithful creature never made a sound. But no; the eyes of her soul showed her that the being whom she did not see was none of those we have named.

The shadow drew nearer noiselessly, becoming more distinct in the mirror, and when within the circle of the light afforded by the candle, the stranger was seen, his dress of black velvet increasing the ghastly pallor of his face; he had, for some mysterious reason, laid aside the silk one which he wore at supper.[1]

She would have turned and screamed, but Balsamo extended his arms, and she remained motionless.

She made another effort. "Monsieur," said she, "in the name of Heaven, what do you want?"

He smiled; the glass reflected his smile, and she watched it with eager gaze; but he did not reply.

She tried once more to rise, but could not; an irresistible power, a paralysing feeling, which was not without a pleasurable sensation attending it, fixed her to her chair, whilst her eye never left the magic mirror. This new sensation alarmed her, for she felt that she was altogether in the power of the unknown. She made another almost supernatural effort to call for aid, but Balsamo extended both his hands above her head, and no sound escaped her lips. She continued dumb, her bosom loaded with a stupefying heat, which ascended slowly in invading billows to

---

[1] It is well known that silk is a bad conductor, and repels the electric fluid. It is almost impossible to magnetise a person who wears a dress of silk.

her brain. She had no longer strength or will; her head sank on her shoulder.

At this moment Balsamo thought he heard a slight noise. He turned; the face of the man he had seen before was at the window. He frowned, and, strange to say, the frown was reflected on the young girl's face.

Then, turning again to Andrée, he drew down his hands, which he had hitherto held above her head; then he raised them again gently, again drew them down, and continued thus to overwhelm her with column upon column of the electric fluid.

"Sleep!" said he.

She still struggled against his power.

"Sleep!" he repeated, in a voice of command; "sleep! it is my will!"

Then all her faculties yielded to that all-powerful will; she leaned her elbow on the harpsichord, drooped her head on her hand, and slept.

Balsamo now, without turning his face from her, left the room, closed the door, and went up to his own chamber. Scarcely had he retired when the face once more appeared at the window. It was Gilbert's.

CHAPTER VIII.

ATTRACTION.

GILBERT, whose menial position in the château of Taverney caused him to be excluded from the salon, watched all the evening those whose rank permitted them to enter. During supper he saw Balsamo's looks and gestures; he remarked Andrée's attention to him, the baron's unusual affability, and the respectful eagerness of La Brie.

When the party rose from table he hid in a clump of shrubs, lest Nicole, in closing the shutters, or in going to her own room, might see him, and put an end to his espionage. Nicole had, indeed, made her round to secure all for the night, but one of the shutters of the salon she was forced to leave open, the half-unfixed hinge of which would not permit it to close. Gilbert knew that such was the case, so he remained out, certain that he could continue his watchings when Legay was gone.

His watchings, have we said? What reason had Gilbert to watch? Having been brought up at Taverney, did he not know it perfectly, as well as the habits of the family? The reason was that on that evening he had other motives than those which usually actuated him; he not only watched, but waited.

When Nicole quitted the salon, leaving Andrée there, after having slowly closed the doors and shutters, she walked for a few minutes up and down in front of the house, as if she expected some one. Then she looked furtively on all sides, peeped into the salon, waited a little longer, and at length made up her mind to go to bed.

Gilbert, motionless, bending down close to the trunk of

a tree, and scarcely venturing to breathe, saw every movement and gesture of Nicole; and when she had disappeared,
and when he saw a light in the windows of her apartment,
he stole again on tip-toe to the window, leant forward,
and continued, although scarcely knowing why, with eager
eyes to devour Andrée, who was sitting at her harpsichord
in a listless attitude.

Just then Joseph Balsamo entered the salon. Gilbert
started, and every faculty was strained to enable him to
comprehend the scene which we have just described. He
thought that Balsamo complimented Andrée on her musical
talent, that she replied with her usual coldness; that, with
a smile, he repeated his praise, and that then she stopped
to reply, and to dismiss him for the night. He admired
the grace with which the stranger retired backwards; but
he had in reality understood nothing of the scene, as it
had all passed in silence. He had heard no words, he had
seen the lips and hands of the pair before him move, and
close observer as he was, he discovered no mystery in
what appeared to pass so naturally.

Balsamo gone, Gilbert remained no longer in an attitude
of observation, but apparently lost in observation of
Andrée, so beautiful in her careless attitude; but soon,
to his amazement, he discovered that she was asleep.
He remained for some moments longer in the same position, to be certain that such was the case; then, when he
was quite convinced, he clasped his forehead with both
hands, like one who feared for his senses in the flood of
thoughts and sensations which poured on his brain. "Oh!"
said he, "her hand! — that my lips might only touch her
hand! Gilbert, Gilbert, rouse thee! I WILL do it!"

As he spoke he rushed into the ante-room and reached
the door of the salon, which, as when Balsamo entered,
opened without noise. But scarcely was it open, scarcely
did he find the young girl before him without anything
separating them, when he felt all the importance of the
step he had taken. He, the son of a farmer, and a peasant

woman,— he, the timid young man, who in his lowness
dared hardly raise his eyes to his haughty mistress,— he
was going to press to his lips the hem of the robe or the
tip of the finger of this sleeping majesty, who, if she
awoke, would with a look crush him to the dust. At this
idea all that had intoxicated him and made him bold
vanished; he stopped and clung to the door-post, for he
trembled, and felt as if he should fall.

But Andrée's meditation or sleep (for Gilbert could not
yet decide whether she slept or was only buried in thought)
was so deep that he in no way disturbed her; yet one
might have heard the beating of his heart, which he tried
in vain to still. He remained a minute gazing on her.
She stirred not; she was so beautiful, with her head
gently bent forward on her hand, her long, unpowdered
hair falling on her shoulders, that the flame, which fear
for a moment had extinguished, rekindled. His madness
returned; he must at least touch something touched by
her. He made a step towards her; the floor creaked under
his unsteady footstep, a cold moisture stood on his forehead. But she seemed to have heard nothing.

"She sleeps!" he murmured; "oh, joy! she sleeps!"

But before he advanced three steps farther he stopped
again; it was the unusual brightness of the candle which
alarmed him now, for it had burnt down in the socket,
and gave, as is usual, a larger flame just before it expired.
But not a sound, not a breath in the house. La Brie had
retired to bed, and no doubt to sleep, and the light in
Nicole's chamber was extinguished.

"Courage!" said he, and he advanced anew. Strange,
the floor creaked again; but Andrée stirred not, and Gilbert
himself could scarcely avoid being frightened by this mysterious repose.

"She sleeps!" repeated he again, with that varying
resolution peculiar to the lover and the coward, — and he
who is not master of his heart is always a coward,—"she
sleeps! Oh, Heaven! oh, Heaven!"

In the midst of all these feverish alternations of fear and hope, he still advanced, and at last found himself within two paces of Andrée. Then he felt as if fascinated. He would have fled were flight possible; but once within the circle of attraction of which she was the centre, he felt himself rooted to the spot, and, conquered, subdued, he fell on both his knees.

Andrée remained motionless as a statue. Gilbert took the hem of her dress in both hands and kissed it; then he looked up slowly, breathlessly; his eyes met hers, which were wide open, yet she saw him not.

Gilbert no longer knew what to think; he was overwhelmed with astonishment. For a moment the horrible idea that she was dead flashed across his mind: he seized her hand,— it was warm, and the pulse beat softly; but this hand remained unresistingly in his. Then, bewildered by having touched it, he imagined that she saw, that she felt, that she had discovered his maddening passion, — poor blinded heart! — that she expected his visit, that her silence indicated consent, her immovability favour. He raised her hand to his lips, and imprinted on it a long and burning kiss. Immediately a shudder ran through her frame, and Gilbert felt that she repelled him.

"I am lost!" he murmured, relinquishing her hand, and throwing himself upon the floor.

Andrée rose as if moved by a spring, and not once casting her eyes to the floor, on which Gilbert lay overcome by shame and fear, without even strength to ask a pardon which he knew would not be granted, her head erect, her neck rigid, and with a painful and constrained step, she moved towards the door. She passed on like one drawn by a secret spell to an unseen goal, and in passing she touched Gilbert's shoulder. He raised himself on one hand, turned slowly, and followed her with eyes full of amazement. She opened the door, passed into the ante-room, and reached the foot of the stairs. Pale and trembling, Gilbert dragged himself after her on his knees.

"Oh," thought he, "she is so indignant that she would not herself deign to show her anger. She is going to the baron to relate my shameful infatuation, and I shall be turned out like a disgraced lackey."

The thought that he should be dismissed — that he should no longer see her who was his light, his life, his soul — gave him courage; he arose and hurried after her. "Oh, pardon, mademoiselle! in the name of Heaven, pardon!" murmured he.

Andrée appeared not to have heard him, passed on, but did not enter her father's apartment. Gilbert breathed more freely. She advanced towards the staircase, and began to ascend.

"Great Heaven!" murmured he, "where can she be going? That is the way to the red room, which the stranger occupies, and to La Brie's loft. It may be to call him — yet, she would ring; she must be going — oh, impossible, impossible!" and he wrung his hands with rage at the thought that she was going into Balsamo's apartment.

She stopped before the door. A cold perspiration trickled down Gilbert's forehead; he grasped the iron of the balustrade that he might not fall, — for he had continued to follow her, — and all that he saw and all that he fancied filled him with horror.

Balsamo's door was half open. Andrée did not knock, but pushed it wider, and entered the room. The light within fell on her noble features, and was reflected with a golden lustre from her large, open eyes. Gilbert could see the stranger standing in the middle of the chamber, with his eyes fixed, his brow contracted, and one hand extended with a commanding gesture.

This was all; the door was shut again.

Gilbert felt his strength abandon him; he put his hand to his head and fell heavily on the cold stone of the upper step of the stairs, but with his eyes turned on the accursed door, which entombed his past dreams, his present happiness, his future hopes.

CHAPTER IX.

CLAIRVOYANCE.

BALSAMO advanced to meet the young lady, who moved towards him in a direct line, rigid in her movement as the bronze statue in Don Juan. However strange her coming might seem to any other than Balsamo, he appeared in no degree surprised at it.

"I commanded you to sleep," said he; "do you sleep?"

She sighed, but did not answer. Balsamo drew nearer her, imparting to her still more of the electric fluid.

"It is my will that you speak," he said.

She started.

"Have you heard my command?"

Andrée assented by a gesture.

"Then why do you not speak?"

She put her hand to her throat, as if to indicate that she could not articulate.

"Well, sit down!" said Balsamo.

He took her by the hand which Gilbert had so lately kissed without her being conscious, and his touch gave her that shudder which she had then exhibited, but which had been caused by the electric fluid descending on her at that moment from the room above. Led by him, she made three steps backwards and sat down in an arm-chair.

"Do you see?" he asked.

Her eyes dilated as if she tried to take in all the rays of light in the apartment.

"I do not mean to ask if you see with your eyes. Do you see inwardly?" and drawing from under his embroidered coat a little rod of steel, he touched her heaving breast. She bounded as if a dart of flame had pierced her and entered her heart, and then her eyes closed.

"And now you begin to see?" he said.

She bowed in assent.

"And you will soon speak?"

"Yes," replied Andrée; but at the same moment she put her hand to her head in a manner expressive of great suffering.

"What is the matter?" asked Balsamo.

"I am in pain."

"Wherefore?"

"Because you force me to see and speak."

He made several movements over her head, as if to lessen the influence of the electricity.

"Do you suffer now?"

"Not so much."

"Well, then, see where you are."

Her eyes remained closed, but her face expressed great surprise.

"I am in the red chamber!" she murmured.

"With whom?"

"With you!" continued she, shuddering.

"What is the matter?"

"I am afraid; I am ashamed!"

"Of what?—are we not united by sympathy?"

"Yes, certainly!"

"And you know that I have caused you to come here with a pure intention?"

"True, true," said she.

"That I respect you as a sister?"

"I know it, indeed!" and her face grew calm, then again was troubled.

"You do not tell me all; you do not pardon me entirely."

"Because I see that though you would not wrong me, you would another, perhaps."

"Possibly," he muttered; "but look not at that!" he

added in an authoritative tone. Her face resumed its usual expression.

"Are all asleep in the house?"

"I do not know."

"Then look and see."

"Where shall I look?"

"Let me see — first, in your father's room; what is he doing?"

"He is in bed."

"Asleep?"

"No; he is reading."

"What is he reading?"

"One of those bad books which he wishes me to read."

"And you will not read them?"

"No!" said she, with an expression of the greatest scorn on her features.

"Well, we are safe, then; look in Nicole's room."

"There is no light in her room."

"But you do not want light to see."

"Not if you command me."

"See! it is my will."

"Ah, I see!"

"What?"

"She is half undressed; she is opening her door softly; she is going downstairs!"

"So! where is she going?"

"She stops at the courtyard gate; she waits behind it; she watches!"

Balsamo smiled. "Is she watching to see whether you are out?"

"No."

"Well, that is the principal matter; for when a young lady is free from her father's and her waiting-maid's eye, she has nothing to fear, unless —"

"No."

"You are replying to my thought."

"I see it."

"Then you have no lover?"

"I?" asked she, disdainfully.

"Yes; you might be in love,—young people do not leave their convents to be shut up. They give liberty to their hearts when their persons are set free."

Andrée shook her head. "My heart is free," she said, sadly; and such an expression of candour and virgin modesty lighted her features that Balsamo exclaimed with rapture, "A lily! a true pupil! a clairvoyante!" and he clasped his hands with joy and gratitude.

Then turning again to Andrée, "But if you do not love, you may be loved," said he.

"I do not know," replied she, softly.

"What? you do not know!" he cried, imperiously. "When I question I expect a proper answer!" and he touched her bosom again with the steel rod. She started, but without evincing so much pain as before.

"Yes, I see," said she; "but be gentle, or you will kill me."

"What do you see?"

"Oh — but no! It cannot be," said she.

"What, then, do you see?"

"A young man, who, ever since my leaving the convent, has followed me, watched me, brooded on me, yet always secretly."

"Who is the young man?"

"I do not see his face. I see his coat; it is like that of a workman."

"Where is he?"

"At the foot of the stairs. He seems in sorrow; he weeps."

"Why can you not see his face?"

"It is hidden in his hands."

"Look through his hands."

She made an effort; then exclaimed, "No! it is impossible! Gilbert?"

"Why impossible?"

"He? — he dares not love me!" cried she, with a lofty expression of disdain.

Balsamo smiled like one who knows mankind, and who is aware that there is no distance the heart will not overleap, were there an abyss between it and its object.

"And what is he doing at the foot of the staircase?"

"Stay! he removes his hands from his face; he seizes the balustrade; he rises; he ascends."

"Ascends where?"

"Up here; but no matter, he dares not come in."

"Why not?"

"Because he is afraid," said she, with a smile of contempt.

"But he will listen."

"Yes; for he is now putting his ear to the door."

"That annoys you?"

"Yes; he may hear what I say."

"And would he use it against her whom he loves?"

"Yes, in a moment of passion or jealousy; in such a moment he would be capable of anything."

"Then let us get rid of him," said Balsamo, and he walked noisily to the door.

Gilbert's hour to be courageous was not yet come, for, at the noise, fearing to be caught, he jumped astride on the balustrade, and slid down noiselessly to the bottom of the staircase.   Andrée uttered a stifled cry.

"Look no more in that direction," said Balsamo, returning towards her; "the loves of the vulgar are of no importance.   Speak to me of the Baron of Taverney, will you?"

"I will answer what you choose," said she, sighing.

"The baron is very poor, is he not?"

"Very poor."

"Too poor to allow you any amusement?"

"Oh, yes."

"You are heartily tired of Taverney?"

"Heartily!"

"You are ambitious, perhaps?"

"No."

"You love your father?"

"Yes," said the young girl, with hesitation.

"Yet I thought this evening your filial love was not very apparent," said Balsamo, smiling.

"I am vexed at him for having wasted my mother's fortune, so that poor Maison Rouge has to pass his time in garrison, and cannot worthily support the dignity of our family."

"Who is this Maison Rouge?"

"My brother Philip."

"Why do you call him Maison Rouge?"

"It is, or rather it was, the name of one of our castles, and the eldest of the family bears it until the death of the chief; then he is called Taverney."

"You love your brother, then?"

"Oh, dearly, dearly!"

"More than any one in the world?"

"More than any one in the world."

"Why do you love him so warmly, and your father so coldly?"

"Because he has a noble heart; he would die for me."

"And your father?"

She was silent. Doubtless Balsamo thought it better not to force her against her will on this point; and perhaps, also, he already knew as much of the baron as he wished.

"And where is the Chevalier Maison Rouge at this moment?"

"Where is Philip?"

"Yes."

"In the garrison at Strasburg."

"Do you see him there?"

"Where?"

"At Strasburg."

"I do not see him."

"Do you know that town?"

"No."

"I know it; let us visit it together, will you?"

"Yes; with pleasure."

"Now. Is he at the theatre?"

"No."

"Is he at the coffee-house in the square with the other officers?"

"No."

"Has he gone back to his apartment? I wish that you should look for him there."

"I see nothing. I think he is not in Strasburg."

"Do you know the road from thence?"

"No."

"I know it; follow me! Is he at Saverne?"

"No."

"Is he at Saarbrück?"

"No."

"Is he at Nancy?"

"Stay! stay!" The young girl seemed collecting all her powers; her heart beat, her bosom heaved. "I see him! I see him! Dear Philip, — what joy!"

"What is he doing?"

"Dear Philip!" continued Andrée, her eyes sparkling with joy.

"Where is he?"

"On horseback, riding through a town I know well."

"What town?"

"Nancy! Nancy! where I was at the convent."

"Are you sure that it is he?"

"Oh, yes; the torches around show his face."

"Torches?" said Balsamo, with surprise; "why, are there torches?"

"He is on horseback, at the door of a magnificent carriage, richly gilt."

"Ah!" cried Balsamo, who appeared to comprehend this, "who is in the carriage?"

"A young lady — oh, how majestic she is! how graceful! how beautiful! Strange, I almost fancy I have seen her before; no, it is Nicole's features which resemble hers."

"Nicole resembles the young lady who is so beautiful and so majestic?"

"Yes, yes; but as a jasmine may be said to resemble a lily."

"Let us see what is passing at Nancy at this moment."

"The young lady bends forward, and makes a sign to Philip to approach; he obeys, and takes off his hat respectfully."

"Can you hear what they say?"

"I am listening," said Andrée, impressing silence on Balsamo by a gesture. "I hear, I hear!" murmured she.

"What does the young lady say?"

"She orders him, with a sweet smile, to hasten the pace of the horses; she says she will require her escort to be ready at six in the morning, as she wishes to stop on the road."

"To stop? Where?"

"My brother is just asking her. Heavens! she wishes to stop at Taverney, to see my father! Such a great princess at our poor house! What shall we do, — without plate, almost without linen?"

"Do not be uneasy; that will be provided for."

"Oh, thanks, thanks!" And the young girl, who had half risen from her seat, sank back with a heavy sigh, completely exhausted.

Balsamo immediately approached her, and, by some magnetic passes in an opposite direction, changed the course of the electric fluid. A calm sleep then stole over her lovely frame, which had bent down exhausted, her head sinking on her palpitating bosom.

"Recover thy strength," said Balsamo, gazing at her with a stern delight; "I shall soon require thy light again. O Science!" continued he, with the rapture of exalted faith, "thou alone never deceivest us; to thee, then, man

ought to sacrifice every feeling.   This young girl is
beautiful, pure as an angel; and He who made beauty
and innocence knows how dear they ought to be to us.
But let the creature perish — how pure, how perfect, how
beautiful soever she be — if I can but make her speak the
words of truth!   Let all the delights of the world — love,
passion, rapture — exist no longer for me, if I can only
with a firm step advance on the path of light and science.
And now, young girl, now that my will has given thee
strength, awake! — or rather, sink again in the sleep
which reveals all things!   Speak again! but now it is for
me that thou must speak."

He spread his hands over her head, and forced her to
sit up by breathing upon her.   Seeing her ready and
submissive, he took from his pocket-book a curl of jet-
black hair, which he put into Andrée's hand.

"See!" he commanded.

"Again!" said she, with anguish.   "Oh, no, let me rest,
— it is too painful; and just now I felt so happy."

"See!" replied Balsamo, pitilessly, touching her again
with the steel rod.

She wrung her hands, struggling to evade the tyranny
of the experimenter.   The foam was on her lips, as formerly it gathered on those of the pythoness on her sacred
tripod.

"I see, I see!" cried she, with the despair of a subdued
will.

"What do you see?"

"A woman."

"Ah!" exclaimed Balsamo, with wild joy, "science is
not, then, a useless word, like virtue!   Mesmer is greater
than Brutus!   Describe the woman, that I may know you
really see her whom I would have you see."

"She is a brunette, tall, with blue eyes, jet-black hair,
and sinewy arms."

"What is she doing?"

"She gallops, she flies forward, carried by a splendid
horse, reeking with sweat and foam."

"In what direction?"

"There, there!" said the young girl, pointing to the west.

"On the highway?"

"Yes."

"Towards Châlons?"

"Yes."

"Good!" said Balsamo; "she takes the road which I shall take; she goes to Paris, as I do; I shall find her there. Now rest," said he; and he took from Andrée's hand the curl of hair.

Her arms fell powerless by her side.

"Now return to your harpsichord!"

Andrée arose and made a step towards the door, but, overcome by inexpressible fatigue, her limbs refused to support her. She staggered.

"Renew your strength and walk!" said Balsamo, enveloping her anew with magnetic passes; and she, like the generous steed that braces every nerve to fulfil his master's will, unjust though it be, walked erect. Balsamo opened the door, and, still sleeping, she descended the stairs.

CHAPTER X.

NICOLE LEGAY.

WHILST the scene of interrogation was passing in Balsamo's chamber, Gilbert remained under the railings at the foot of the staircase in a state of indescribable torture. Not daring to ascend again to listen at the door of the red chamber, he fell into despair, and this despair was increased tenfold by the feeling of his weakness and his inferiority.

Balsamo was only a man (for Gilbert, being a profound thinker, a philosopher in embryo, had small faith in sorcerers); but then this man was strong, and he was weak; this man was courageous, and Gilbert was not so yet. Twenty times he arose, determined to beard the stranger, and twenty times his trembling limbs bent under him, and he sank on his knees. Then the thought struck him that he would get a ladder used by La Brie (who was at the same time cook, butler, and gardener) for nailing the jessamine and honeysuckle against the walls, and, by propping it against the balcony of the apartment, be enabled to mount to the window, and witness what he so ardently desired to discover.

He passed stealthily into the courtyard, and ran to the spot where the ladder lay; but as he was stooping to take it up, he thought he heard a noise in the direction of the house, and he turned. He was almost certain that in the obscurity he saw a human form enter the dark frame of the open door, but moving so quickly and so noiselessly that it appeared rather a spectre than a living being. He let the ladder fall, and, his heart beating audibly, hastened back towards the château.

Some minds are constitutionally superstitious, and these are generally the most exalted and the richest in fancy. They admit the fabulous more readily than the rational, because what is natural is too common for them, impelled as they are towards the impossible, or at least the ideal. Such spirits delight in the darkness of the forest, the depths of which they people with phantoms or genii. The ancients, who were poets in all things, saw these fantastic beings in open day; but as their sun, warmer and brighter than ours, forbade the fancy to bring forth spectres and demons, they filled the forest with smiling dryads and wood-nymphs. Gilbert, born in a gloomier clime, imagined he saw a spirit. This time, in spite of his incredulity, he recalled the words of the woman who had fled from Balsamo, and the idea flashed across his mind that the sorcerer might have summoned up some evil spirit to do his bad behests. But Gilbert had always, after a first impression, a second, not more encouraging, for it was the result of reflection. He recalled all the arguments of powerful minds against the belief in the return of spirits to this world, and thinking of the article "Spectre" in the "Philosophical Dictionary" restored his courage; but it was only to give him another apprehension, better founded and more alarming.

If he had indeed seen any one, it must have been a real individual deeply interested in watching him. Fear suggested Monsieur de Taverney; his conscience whispered another name. He looked up to Nicole's apartment: her candle was out, not a ray of light was visible; not a whisper, not a movement, not a light in all the house, except in the stranger's room. He looked, he listened; then, seeing nothing, hearing nothing, he took up the ladder again, convinced that he had been deceived, and that this vision had been the result of a suspension of his observing faculties, rather than of their exercise.

Just as he was about to place his ladder, Balsamo's door opened and then shut. At this sound he hurried in, and saw Andrée glide out and descend the stairs without noise and without a light, as if guided and supported by a super-natural power. Having reached the landing-place, she passed by where he had now concealed himself in the shade, her dress touching him as she passed, and continued her way. The baron was asleep, La Brie in bed, Nicole in the other turret, Balsamo's door closed; he could not be surprised by any one. He made a violent effort and followed her, adapting his step to hers, and keeping at a distance from her. She passed through the ante-room into the salon; but, although she left the door open, he stopped just before he reached it. Should he enter? He hesitated, then resolved; but just as his foot was on the threshold, an arm was stretched out in the darkness, and he was firmly grasped. Gilbert turned, his heart panting as if it would burst his bosom.

"So I have caught you at last!" whispered an angry voice close at his ear. "Deny now, if you can, that you have meetings, — that you are in love with her!"

Gilbert had not strength to shake himself loose from the clutch which detained him, yet it was only that of a young girl; it was simply the hand of Nicole Legay that held him.

"What do you mean?" whispered he, impatiently.

"Oh, I am to speak it out, then?" and Nicole raised her voice nearly to the loudest pitch.

"No; for God's sake be quiet!" replied Gilbert, between his closed teeth, and dragging her away from the door.

"Well, come with me, then!"

This was what Gilbert wanted, for by going away with her he took her away from Andrée. He followed Nicole, who led the way into the courtyard, shutting the door behind her when he had passed.

"But," said Gilbert, "mademoiselle will be retiring to her apartment; she will call you to help her to undress, and you will not be in the house."

"Do you think I care for that now? Let her call or not, I must speak to you."

"You might put off until to-morrow what you have got to say, Nicole. You know Mademoiselle Andrée is strict."

"Yes, I would advise her to be strict,—particularly with me."

"To-morrow, Nicole, I promise."

"You promise! I know what your fine promises are. This very day you promised to meet me near Maison Rouge. Where were you? Why, in the very opposite direction, since you brought the traveller hither. Your promises, indeed! I believe them just as I did those of our confessor at the Annonciades, who swore to keep a secret what we confessed, and then told all our sins to the abbess."

"But, Nicole, you will be dismissed if you are seen."

"And you—will you not be dismissed for being in love with my young lady? Do you think the baron too generous for that?"

"He could surely have no motive for dismissing me," said Gilbert, endeavouring to defend himself.

"Oh, none in the world! The baron, perhaps, allows you to pay your addresses to his daughter. I really did not know he was quite so great a philosopher."

Gilbert might easily have proved to Nicole, by relating what he had just witnessed, that, if he was to blame, at least Andrée was not privy to his misconduct; and incredible as her visit to the stranger's apartment would have appeared, Nicole — thanks to the good opinion women have of one another — would have believed him. But deeper reflection arrested the words on his lips. Andrée's secret was one that might serve him, as it placed her completely in his power; and as he loved Andrée infinitely more than he feared Nicole, he was silent on the singular events he had just witnessed.

"Well," said he, "since you insist on having an explanation, let us understand each other."

"Oh, that is easily done. But you are right, — this is a bad place for it; let us go to my room."

"To your room?   Impossible!"

"Why so?"

"We might be surprised."

"Indeed! and who would surprise us?   Mademoiselle?
True she might be jealous about her sweet youth.   Unfortunately for her, since her secret is discovered, I am not
afraid of her.   Mademoiselle Andrée jealous of Nicole!
What an honour!"   And the forced laugh of the young
girl frightened Gilbert more than any invective or menace
could possibly have done.

"It is not mademoiselle of whom I am afraid," said he;
"I am only anxious on your own account, Nicole."

"Oh, most anxious, no doubt.   But you are going to my
room for no bad purpose; and you have often told me,
where there is no bad intention there should be no shame.
Philosophers are Jesuits sometimes; and our confessor at
the Annonciades told me all that before you.   Come, come,
no more false reasons!   Come to my room; I am resolved
you shall!"

"Nicole!" said he, grinding his teeth.

"Well! what more, pray?"

"Take care!" and he raised his hand.

"Oh, I am not afraid.   You struck me once; but you
were jealous then.   At that time you loved me, and I
allowed you to strike me; but I shall not now, — no, no,
no! for you no longer love me, and it is I who am jealous
now."

"But what will you do?" cried Gilbert, grasping her
wrist.

"I shall scream, and mademoiselle will hear me.   I
advise you to let go your hold of me."

Gilbert dropped her hand; then, seizing the ladder, and
dragging it cautiously after him, he placed it against the
wall of the turret, so that it reached to Nicole's window.

"See how things turn in this world," said she, maliciously: "the ladder which was to assist you to climb to
mademoiselle's apartment must merely serve you to de-

scend from my humble attic. Very flattering for me, is it not?"

Nicole, perceiving the advantage she had gained, declared her triumph with that precipitate eagerness which women, unless, indeed, of very superior minds, often exhibit, — a victory which is often too dearly purchased.

Gilbert, who felt himself in a false position, was silent, and followed the young girl, reserving all his powers for the approaching contest.

In the first place, however, like a prudent general, he satisfied himself on two points. The first was, in passing before the window, that Mademoiselle de Taverney was still in the salon; and the second, on reaching Nicole's chamber, that, in case of necessity, he could reach the ladder without much risk of breaking his neck, and thus allow himself to slide to the ground.

Nicole's room was as simple in its furniture as the rest of the house; it was a loft, the walls of which were covered with a drab and green paper. A wooden bed, and a large geranium placed near the window, were its whole furniture and decorations, except a large bonnet-box, given her by Andrée, which served both for table and wardrobe. Nicole sat down on the edge of the bed, Gilbert on a corner of the box. She had had time to calm down while ascending the stairs, and now, completely mistress of herself, she felt strong in having justice on her side. Gilbert, on the contrary, was agitated, and could not recover his coolness; his anger had increased as hers decreased.

"So," said she, "you are in love with mademoiselle, and you have attempted to deceive me?"

"Who told you I was in love with mademoiselle?"

"*Dame!* were you not going to a rendezvous with her?"

"How do you know that I had a rendezvous with her?"

"How do I know? Why, there was no one else to go to but the sorcerer."

"Well, I might have been going to him; I am ambitious."

"Say envious."

"It is the same word taken in a bad sense."

"Don't let us dispute about words. You love me no longer."

"Yes, I do; I love you still."

"Then why do you avoid me?"

"Because you quarrel with me whenever I meet you."

"That is because you always avoid me."

"You know I am shy, — that I love solitude."

"Yes; and you seek solitude ladder in hand."

Gilbert was beaten on his first move.

"Come, come! Be frank if you can, Gilbert, and confess that you no longer love me, or that you love two women at once."

"Well, and if I did, what would you say?"

"I should say it was monstrous."

"No, no! that there was an error somewhere."

"In your heart?"

"No, — in our social state. You know there are nations where every man is allowed seven or eight wives."

"They are not Christians," said Nicole, pettishly.

"They are philosophers," said Gilbert, with dignity.

"So, Master Philosopher, you would wish me to take a second lover, as you have done!"

"I would not be unjust and tyrannical; I should not wish to repress the impulses of your heart. Freedom, blessed freedom, respects free-will. If you change your love, Nicole, I shall not force you to a fidelity which, in my opinion, is unnatural."

"Ah, I see plainly you no longer love me!"

Gilbert was great in argument; not that he was skilful in logic, but he was an adept in paradox, and, however little he knew, he still knew more than Nicole. She had read only what amused her; he, what taught him a little also; and as they talked he regained his presence of mind, while Nicole began to lose hers.

"Has the great philosopher any memory?" asked Nicole, with an ironical smile.

"Sometimes," replied Gilbert.

"Then you have not forgotten, perhaps, what you said to me five months ago, when I came with mademoiselle from the Annonciades?"

"I have forgotten; tell it me."

"You said, 'I am poor;' it was the day we were reading among the old ruins."

"Well, go on."

"You trembled very much that day."

"Very likely,— I am naturally timid; but I do all I can to correct that fault, and some others also."

"So that when you have corrected all your faults," said Nicole, laughing, "you will be perfect."

"I shall be strong; wisdom gives strength."

"Where did you read that, pray?"

"Never mind; return to what you were saying."

Nicole felt that she was losing ground every minute.

"Well, you said to me, 'I am poor — no one loves me; yet there is something here,' and you pressed your hand on your heart."

"No, Nicole; if I pressed my hand anywhere when I said that, it must have been on my forehead. The heart is merely a forcing-pump, which drives the blood to the extremities of the body. Read the article 'Heart' in the 'Philosophical Dictionary;'" and Gilbert drew himself up proudly. Humble before Balsamo, he gave himself the airs of a prince before Nicole.

"You are right, Gilbert; it must have been your head which you struck. Well, striking your forehead, you said, 'I am treated here worse than a dog; indeed, Mahon is in a happier condition than I.' I replied that they were wrong not to love you; that if you had been my brother I should have loved you also. I think, however, I said that from my heart, not from my head; but perhaps I am wrong, for I never read the 'Philosophical Dictionary.'"

"You ought to read it, Nicole."

"Then you threw your arms round me. You said, 'You
are an orphan; I am one, too. Let us love one another as
if we were brother and sister, — no, better than if we were;
for if we were, we should be forbidden to love as I wish
we should;' then you kissed me."

"Very possibly!"

"Did you think then as you spoke?"

"Oh, yes; one generally thinks what one says at the
time one says it."

"So that now — ?"

"Now I am five months older than I was. 1 have learned
things of which I knew nothing then, and I look forward
to things which I do not yet know; I think differently
now."

"You are a deceiver, a hypocrite, a liar!" exclaimed she,
furiously.

"No more than a traveller, should he make two different
answers to the same question, — if you asked him in a
valley what he thought of the prospect, and again when
he had got to the top of a mountain which before had
closed his view."

"So, then, you will not marry me?"

"I never said I would marry you," said Gilbert, contemptuously.

"And yet," cried the exasperated girl, "I think Nicole
Legay fully the equal of Sebastian Gilbert."

"All human beings are equal; but nature or education
makes certain faculties greater in one man than another,
and according as these faculties are more or less developed,
men differ from one another."

"So that your faculties being more developed than mine,
you are raised above me?"

"Quite correct! — you do not reason yet, Nicole, but you
understand."

"Yes, yes! I understand!" cried Nicole, with redoubled
passion.

"What do you understand?"

"That you are a bad man."

"It is possible. Many are born with bad inclinations. Rousseau himself had such, but he corrected them; I shall do the same."

"Oh, heavens!" cried Nicole, "how could I ever love such a man?"

"You did not love me, Nicole," replied Gilbert, coldly; "I pleased you, that was all. You had just come from Nancy, where you had only seen students whom you laughed at, or soldiers who frightened you; so you took a fancy to me, and for a month or two we enjoyed our dream of love. But should we therefore be tied together to be eternally miserable? You see, Nicole, if we bound ourselves for our lives in a moment of happiness, we should give up our free-will, and that would be absurd!"

"Is that philosophy?" asked Nicole.

"I think so," replied Gilbert.

"Then there is nothing sacred in the eyes of philosophers?"

"Oh, yes! — reason is."

"Yet I think you once said something about being faithful to the choice of the heart. You recollect your theory on marriages?"

"On unions, Nicole, for I shall never marry."

"You will never marry?"

"No! I shall be a learned man, — a philosopher. Science requires perfect freedom of the mind, and philosophy that of the body."

"Monsieur Gilbert," said she, "you are a wretch; and whatever I am, I am at least better than you."

"Now," said Gilbert, rising, "we are only losing time — you in abusing me, I in listening to you; let us end! You loved me because you took pleasure in loving."

"Well?"

"Well! — there is no reason in the world that I should make myself unhappy, because you did a thing which gave you gratification."

"Fool!" she exclaimed, "you think you can confound my common-sense; and you pretend not to fear me."

"Fear you! Why, Nicole, jealousy is turning your brain!"

"Jealous!" she cried, stamping her foot, "and why should I be jealous! Is there a prettier girl in the province than I? — if I had but as white hands as mademoiselle; and I shall have some day, when I do no more hard work. You are my first lover, it is true, but you are not the first man who has paid court to me. Gilbert, Gilbert! do not force me to seek revenge on you; do not make me leave the narrow path in which a last remembrance of my mother and the regular repetition of my prayers have kept me. Gilbert, if you do, you may have to reproach yourself with bringing many evils on yourself and others."

"All in good time," said Gilbert. "So now that you have got to the summit of your dignity, Nicole, I am perfectly satisfied on one point."

"And what may that be?" inquired the girl.

"Simply that if I consented now to marry you —"

"What then?"

"Why, that you would refuse me."

Nicole paused, her clenched hands and gnashing teeth showing the workings of her mind.

"You are right," she exclaimed at length. "Yes, I also begin to ascend that mountain of which you spoke. I see a wider prospect before me. The wife of a learned man, a philosopher! No, I am destined for something greater than that! Mount your ladder! and don't break your neck; though I begin to think it would be a blessing for many persons if you would, — perhaps even a blessing for yourself."

She turned her back on him. Gilbert stood a moment wavering and irresolute; for Nicole, excited by anger and jealousy, was truly beautiful. But he had resolved to break with her; Nicole could blast at once his love and his ambition. His decision was made.

In a few seconds, Nicole, hearing no sound, looked behind her. She was alone in the apartment.

"Gone!" she murmured; "and mademoiselle — oh, I shall know to-morrow whether she loves him or not!"

She went to the window and looked out; all was dark, every light extinguished. She stole on tiptoe to her young lady's door and listened.

"She is in bed; she sleeps soundly," said she; "but to-morrow I shall know all!"

CHAPTER XI.

WAITING-MAID AND MISTRESS.

THE calmness with which Nicole returned to her room was not affected. Young, strong, full of an uncultivated self-confidence, she was blessed with that faculty so important for those who would govern where they love, — the faculty of forgetting; and she could sleep after she had arranged with the little malicious sprites that dwelt in her heart her plan of vengeance.

Mademoiselle de Taverney appeared to her even more guilty than Gilbert. This aristocratic girl, rigid in her prejudices, elevated in her pride, who at their convent would descend to familiarity with none below the daughters of marquises, — this statue, outwardly so cold, but yet with feeling in its marble bosom, — this statue, warming to life for a rural Pygmalion like Gilbert, became contemptible in her estimation. For Nicole felt that Gilbert was her inferior in everything but a little reading, and thought that she had condescended very much when she, the waiting-maid of the daughter of a ruined baron, put herself on a level with the son of a poor peasant.

What, then, could she think of her mistress, if she really returned Gilbert's love?

She calculated that, in relating what she had seen to the baron, she should fall into a great error: first, because he would only laugh at the affair, box Gilbert's ears, and turn him out of doors; next, because it would deprive her of her power over Gilbert and Andrée. What pleasure she should have — she, the waiting-maid — in seeing them turn pale or red as her eye fell on them! This idea flattered her pride and soothed her vindictive spirit; and at this idea her reflections ceased; she slept.

It was day when she awoke, fresh, light-hearted, and her mind prepared for everything. She took her usual time to dress, — that is, an hour. She looked at herself in the piece of broken glass which served as her mirror. Her eyes appeared to her more brilliant than ever; her lips had not lost their brightness nor their roundness; her teeth were perfect; her neck, which she took particular care to hide from the sun, was white as a lily. Seeing herself so handsome, she began to think she could easily make her young lady jealous. Thus armed personally and mentally, she opened Andrée's door, as she was authorised to do whenever, at seven o'clock, her mistress had not rung for her.

When Nicole entered the room she stopped in amazement.

Pale, her beautiful hair damp with perspiration, Andrée lay on her bed in a heavy sleep, in which she sometimes writhed as if in pain. She was still in the dress which she had worn the day before. Her breathing was hurried, and now and then a low groan escaped her lips. Nicole looked at her for a minute, then shook her head, for she acknowledged to herself that there could be no beauty which could contest the palm with Andrée's.

She went to the window and opened the shutters. A stream of light poured in, and made Mademoiselle de Taverney's violet-veined eyelids quiver. She awoke and tried to rise, but felt, at the same time, such great weakness and such excessive pain, that she fell back on her pillow with a cry of suffering.

"Oh! mademoiselle, what is the matter?" asked Nicole.

"Is it late?" said Andrée, rubbing her eyes.

"Very late, mademoiselle, — much later than your usual hour for rising."

"I do not know what is the matter with me, Nicole," said she, looking around her; "I feel so oppressed, so ill."

Nicole fixed her eyes on her mistress before replying:

"It is the commencement of a cold that you have caught,
mademoiselle, last night."

"Last night!" replied Andrée, surprised; then, looking
at her disordered dress, "Have I really lain down without
undressing? How could that be?"

"If mademoiselle would try to remember — "

"I don't recollect anything about it," replied Andrée,
leaning her head on her hand; "what has happened?
Am I going mad?" She sat up on the bed, and looked
round for the second time all bewildered. Then, after
reflecting: "Oh! yes, I remember I was very tired, very
much exhausted yesterday, — it was the storm, no doubt;
then I fell asleep on the music-stool at my harpsichord.
But after that I remember nothing; I must have come up
to my room half asleep, and thrown myself on my bed
without strength to undress."

"You should have called me, mademoiselle," said Nicole;
"mademoiselle knows that I am always ready to wait on
her."

"I either did not think of it, or had not strength to
do it."

"Hypocrite!" muttered Nicole to herself. Then she
added: "But mademoiselle must have stayed very late
at her harpsichord, then; for before she came up to her
room, hearing a noise, I went down — " She stopped,
hoping to discover in Andrée something like agitation, —
a blush, perhaps. No! Andrée was calm, and her countenance, that clear mirror of her soul, was undisturbed.
"I went down — " repeated Nicole.

"Well?"

"Well, mademoiselle, you were not at your harpsichord."

Andrée looked up, but there was only surprise to be
read in her lovely eyes. "Very strange!" said she.

"It is quite true, however."

"You say I was not in the salon? But I never left it
for a moment till I came to bed."

"Mademoiselle will pardon me for contradicting her."

"But where was I, then?"

"Mademoiselle must know that better than I," said Nicole, shrugging her shoulders.

"You must be wrong, Nicole," said Andrée, mildly; "I only remember feeling cold and stiff, and having great difficulty in walking."

"Oh, but when I saw mademoiselle, she walked very well," said Nicole, almost with a sneer.

"You saw me walk?"

"Yes, indeed, mademoiselle."

"But just now you said I was not in the salon?"

"It was not in the salon I saw mademoiselle."

"Where, then?"

"In the vestibule, near the staircase."

"I?"

"Yes; I think I ought to know mademoiselle when I see her," said Nicole with an affected laugh.

"I am certain, however," said Andrée, with great simplicity, after she had again tried to recall the events of the night, "that I did not stir out of the salon."

"I am, however, quite as certain that I saw mademoiselle in the vestibule. I thought, indeed, she had just come in from a walk in the garden. It was a beautiful night after the storm; and it is very pleasant to walk out when the air is so cool, and when the flowers smell so sweet, is it not, mademoiselle?"

"Oh, but you know I dare not walk out at night. I am too timid."

"Mademoiselle might have some one with her, and then she would not be afraid."

"And whom, pray, could I have with me?" asked Andrée, without the least suspicion that she was undergoing a cross-examination.

Nicole was afraid to proceed further in her investigation. Andrée's coolness she thought the height of dissimulation, but she judged it best to give the conversation another turn.

" Mademoiselle was saying that she felt in pain ? "

" Yes, indeed, I feel in great pain ; and so weak, so low.   I did nothing yesterday but what I do every day, yet I am so tired ! Perhaps I am going to be ill."

" It may be some sorrow which causes that feeling of weariness ; I have felt it myself."

" Oh, you have sorrows, have you, Nicole ? "

This was said with a disdainful carelessness which gave Nicole courage to speak more plainly.

" Oh, yes, mademoiselle," she replied ; " yes, I have."

Andrée got slowly out of bed, and, while proceeding to undress, that she might dress again, she said, " Well, let me hear them."

" Indeed I have just come to tell mademoiselle — " She stopped.

" To tell what ?   You look frightened, Nicole."

" I look frightened, and mademoiselle looks tired ; so, doubtless, we are both suffering."

This piece of familiarity displeased Andrée. She frowned slightly, exclaiming, " Oh ! "

The intonation of her voice might have made Nicole reflect, but she was not to be daunted.

" Since mademoiselle wishes me to speak, I shall do so."

" Well, go on."

" I wish to get married, mademoiselle."

" Oh ! Is that what you are thinking of ? Why, you are not seventeen yet."

" Mademoiselle is only sixteen, and yet does she not sometimes think of marrying ? "

" What reason have you to suppose so ? " asked Andrée, severely.

Nicole was just opening her mouth to say something impertinent, but she knew that that would cut short the conversation, which she had no desire should end yet.

" I beg mademoiselle's pardon ; I cannot certainly know her thoughts.   I am but a country girl ; I follow nature."

" That is a strange expression ! "

"Is it not natural for a woman to love, and to wish to be loved?"

"Perhaps so. Well?"

"Well; I am in love."

"And the person you love loves you?"

"I think so, mademoiselle." Then, reflecting that this reply was not decided enough under the circumstances, she added, "Indeed, I am sure of it."

"You are not wasting your time at Taverney, from your own account, Mademoiselle Nicole!"

"One must think of the future, mademoiselle; you are a lady, and doubtless some rich relation will leave you a fortune. I must do the best I can for myself."

All this appeared natural enough, and forgetting Nicole's little piece of impertinence, Andrée's goodness of heart began to resume the ascendency.

"Very true," said she; "but I should like to know who is your choice."

"Ah, you do know him, mademoiselle!" said Nicole, fixing her eyes on Andrée.

"I know him?"

"Yes, very well."

"Who is it, then? Do not keep me in suspense."

"I am afraid mademoiselle will be displeased."

"I displeased?"

"Yes, mademoiselle."

"Then it is some improper person you have chosen?"

"I do not say that, mademoiselle."

"Then tell it without fear. It is the duty of masters to take an interest in the welfare of their dependents who perform their duties satisfactorily; and you know I am satisfied with you."

"You are very kind, mademoiselle."

"Well, tell me quickly, and finish lacing me."

Nicole collected all her firmness and all her powers of penetration, as she said, "Well, mademoiselle, it is Gilbert whom I have chosen."

To her great surprise Andrée betrayed no emotion of any kind; she only said : —

"What, little Gilbert, — my nurse's son!"

"Yes, mademoiselle, the same."

"And he loves you ? "

Now was the decisive moment.

"He has told me so twenty times."

"Well, marry him," replied Andrée, calmly. "I see nothing to prevent it. You have no relations, he is an orphan; you are each of you free from control."

"Certainly," stammered Nicole, quite amazed at the matter ending so differently from what she had expected. "Mademoiselle gives her permission, then ? "

"My full permission; only, you are both very young yet."

"We shall live longer together."

"And neither of you has any money."

"We shall work."

"What can he work at ?   He is good for nothing."

This dissimulation was too much for Nicole. She could not contain herself.

"Mademoiselle must allow me to say that speaking so of poor Gilbert is treating him very ill ! "

"It is treating him as he deserves; he is a lazy fellow."

"Oh, mademoiselle, he reads a great deal; he wishes so to be well-informed."

"He will not work."

"For mademoiselle, he does all that he can."

"For me ? "

"Mademoiselle must know that, when she ordered him to procure game for her every day, and he does so."

"I ordered him ? "

"Yes; and he often goes twenty miles for it."

"Indeed ! I confess I never thought about it."

"About the game ? " asked Nicole, sarcastically.

"What does that witticism mean ? " asked Andrée, becoming a little impatient, for she felt irritable and unwell.

"I have no wit, mademoiselle ; wit is for great ladies. I
a poor girl, and tell things plainly as they are," replied
Nicole. " And mademoiselle is unjust to Gilbert, who is so
very attentive to all her wishes."

"He only does his duty as a servant, if he be so."

' "But Gilbert is not a servant, mademoiselle ; he receives
no wages."

"He is the son of an old tenant. He is kept, he is fed,
and he does nothing in return. But why defend so warmly
this lad, when he was not attacked ? "

" Oh, I knew very well that mademoiselle would not
attack him."

"More words that I do not understand ! "

"Mademoiselle will not understand."

"Enough ! Explain this moment what you mean."

"Mademoiselle must certainly have no difficulty to know
what I mean."

"I know nothing, — and I shall not take the trouble of
finding out. You ask my consent to your marriage ? "

"Yes, and I would beg of you, mademoiselle, not to be
angry with Gilbert for loving me."

" What can it matter to me whether he loves you or does
not love you ? You are really very tiresome."

"Perhaps mademoiselle has said the same to Gilbert ? "

"I ! — do I ever speak to your Gilbert ? You are crazy,
I think."

"If mademoiselle does not speak to him now, it is not
very long since she did speak."

Andrée turned on her a look of ineffable scorn. " You
have been trying for an hour to let me hear some specimen
of your impertinence ; say it at once, I command you."

"But —" began Nicole, a little alarmed.

"You say that I have spoken to Gilbert ? "

"Yes, mademoiselle, I say so ! "

A thought flashed across Andrée's mind, but it was so
absurd that she burst into a fit of laughter. "Heaven
forgive me ! " she exclaimed, "I do believe the poor girl is

jealous. Be not uneasy, Legay, I know so little of your
Gilbert, that I do not even know the colour of his eyes!"
And Andrée felt quite prepared to pardon what she now
thought not impertinence, but mere folly. But Nicole did
not want to be pardoned, because she looked on herself as
the injured person.

" It is not the way to know their colour to look at them
by night," said she.

" Did you speak?" asked Andrée, now beginning to
understand, but scarcely willing to allow herself to entertain
the thought.

" I said that if mademoiselle only speaks to Gilbert at
night, she will not see very well what his features are."

"Take care!" said Andrée, turning pale, " and explain
instantly what you mean."

" That is easily done. Last night I saw — "

" Be silent; some one calls me!"

In fact, a voice just then called, from the court in front
of the house, " Andrée! Andrée!"

" It is the baron, mademoiselle," said Nicole, " with the
strange gentleman."

" Go down, and say that I cannot appear, that I am indis-
posed; and then return and let me know the end of this
extraordinary history of yours."

" Andrée!" cried her father again, " it is merely the
Baron Balsamo, who wishes to bid you good-morning and
inquire after your health."

"Go, I tell you," said she to Nicole, and she pointed to
the door with the gesture of a queen.

But when Nicole was gone, Andrée felt a strange sensation; she had resolved not to appear, yet she was impelled
by an irresistible power to the window left open by her
waiting-maid. She saw Balsamo below; he bowed, at the
same time fixing his eyes steadily on her. She trembled,
and held by the window to prevent herself from falling.

" Good-morning, monsieur," said she, in reply to his salu-
tation; and just as she pronounced the words, Nicole, whom

she had sent to say she should not appear, advanced towards
the gentlemen, looking with open mouth at this instance of
caprice in her mistress.

Andrée had scarcely spoken, when she sank deprived of
strength on a chair; Balsamo still continued to gaze on
her.

CHAPTER XII.

THE traveller had risen early, in order to look after his carriage, and inquire how Althotas had got on. No one was up at that hour in the castle but Gilbert, who followed with his eyes every movement of the stranger. But he could discover little, as Balsamo closed the carriage door too carefully for his inquisitive looks to penetrate its mystery.

Seeing the baron's abode by the clear light of a sunny morning, Balsamo was struck by the different impression it made on him from what it had done the preceding night. In fact, the little white and red château — for it was built of stone and brick — made a pretty picture, surrounded as it was by a grove of sycamores and laburnums of a large size, the flowers of which hung on the roof of the low building, and girt the towers with a crown of gold. In front of the court there was a small piece of water, surrounded by a broad border of turf and a hedge of acacias, on which the eye rested with pleasure, confined as the view was on this side by the tall chestnut and ash trees of the avenue.

Balsamo turned along a broad walk on the left, and had scarcely advanced twenty paces when he found himself in the midst of a thick shrubbery of maples, palms, and lindens, amongst which the roses and syringas, steeped by the rain of the preceding night, sent forth a delicious perfume. Through the hedge of privet which bordered the walk peeped jasmine and honeysuckle, and in the distance could be seen a long alley, lined with pink hawthorn and wild roses, leading to a wood.

Balsamo at last arrived at the extremity of the demesne. Here, on a slight elevation, stood the massive ruins of an ancient castle, one of the towers of which was still standing almost uninjured, and clothed from its base to its summit with luxuriant shoots of the ivy and wild vine. Viewed from this point, the demesne of Taverney, though but seven or eight acres in extent, wanted neither dignity nor elegance.

After having spent about an hour in examining the ruins, Balsamo was returning towards the house, when he saw the baron leave it by a side-door, his slight frame buried in an Indian flowered dressing-gown, and proceed to prune and arrange his little parterre. He hastened to meet him, and now having still further sounded the poverty of his host, his politeness was more decided in its expression than it had been the night before.

" Allow me, monsieur," said he, " to offer you my excuses for the trouble I have given you, and, at the same time, my respectful thanks for your hospitality. I should not have ventured to come down before knowing that you were up, but the view of Taverney from my window was so charming that I could not resist my desire to revisit those imposing ruins, and to see your beautiful garden."

" The ruins," said the baron, after having politely wished the stranger good-morning, " the ruins, monsieur, are fine, — indeed, the only thing that is fine at Taverney."

" It was a large castle ! "

" Yes; it was mine, or rather my ancestors'. They called it Maison-Rouge, which name has long been joined to Taverney; indeed, our barony is Maison-Rouge. But, my dear guest, let us not talk of things no longer in being."

Balsamo bowed in submission.

" Allow me rather to make my excuses to you for your poor accommodation here. I told you beforehand what my house was."

" I have been delighted with it."

" A dog-kennel, a dog-kennel, monsieur ! — a very favourite place with the rats, since the foxes, lizards, and adders drove them from the other castle! Ah, *pardieu!* monsieur, you, who are a sorcerer or something very near it, you certainly ought to raise up with a stroke of your wand the old castle in its glory again, — above all, not forgetting the two thousand acres which formerly surrounded it. I'll wager, however, that instead of thinking of doing me such a service, you have been so polite as to go to sleep in an execrable bed!"

"Oh, monsieur—"

"No, no; don't attempt to say anything in its favour! it is an execrable bed, — it is my son's."

"You must permit me to say that, such as the bed is, it appeared to me excellent. I cannot but feel ashamed of having intruded on you, and I am deeply indebted for the kindness with which you have received me. It would give me sincere pleasure to make a return, if it were in my power."

"Well, there is an opportunity," replied the old man, with a mocking smile, and pointing to La Brie, who was coming with a glass of water on a splendid plate of Dresden china. "Just turn this into Burgundy, Chambertin, or any other good wine, and you will do me a most essential service."

Balsamo smiled; the old man took the smile for a refusal, and at one draught swallowed the water presented to him.

"An excellent specific," said Balsamo; "water is highest among the elements, for the Holy Spirit was borne on it before the creation of the world. Nothing can resist its action; it penetrates stone, and we may yet discover that the diamond can be dissolved by it."

"I shall be dissolved by it, I fear," replied the baron. "Will you pledge me? The water has some advantages over my wine; it is in capital order, and it is not yet exhausted. It is not like my Maraschino."

"If you had ordered a glass for me as well as for yourself, I might have been able to use it for your advantage."

"Good; explain that for me, — is there not still time?"

"Then tell your servant to bring me a glass of very pure water."

"La Brie, do you hear, you old rascal?"

La Brie hastened to obey.

"How!" said the baron, turning to his guest, "does the glass of water which I drink every morning contain any properties, any secrets which are unknown to me? Have I for ten years been making chemical experiments, as Monsieur Jourdain made prose, without being aware of it?"

"I do not know what you have been doing, but you shall see what I can do. Thank you, my good fellow," said Balsamo, taking the glass from La Brie, who had brought it with marvellous rapidity.

He held the glass on a level with his eyes, and seemed to interrogate the water which it contained; in the sunlight the little beads on its surface were bright as diamonds, and streaked with violet colour.

"Oh, the deuce!" cried the baron, laughing, "can anything beautiful be seen in a glass of water?"

"Yes, baron, to-day, at least, something very beautiful."

And Balsamo appeared doubly attentive in his occupation, the baron, in spite of himself, looking a little serious, and La Brie gazing with open mouth at what was going on.

"What do you see, pray? I am bursting with impatience to know. A good estate for me? A new Maison-Rouge to set me on foot again?"

"I see something which induces me to beg you to be on the alert."

"Ay! — am I going to be attacked?"

"No; but this morning you will receive a visit."

"Then, you have yourself ordered some one to meet you here. That was wrong, monsieur, very wrong. There may be no partridges this morning — remember that!"

"I speak seriously, my dear baron, and what I say is most important; some one is at this moment on the way to Taverney."

"Some one?   What sort of a visitor, tell me, pray? —
for I must confess (you must have perceived it from the
rather sour reception I gave you) that every one annoys me
who comes here.   So, what sort of visitor?   Be precise, my
dear sorcerer; if possible, be precise in your description."

"I can very easily tell all you wish," and Balsamo again
raised the glass to his searching eye.

"Well, do you see anything?"

"I see everything distinctly."

"Speak, oh speak, sister Anne!"

"I see a lady of great consequence coming."

"Bah! indeed! — coming without being invited?"

"She has invited herself; your son brings her."

"Philip brings her?"

"Yes, himself."

The baron laughed heartily.

"She is brought by my son?   The great lady brought
by my son?"

"Yes, baron."

"You know my son, then?"

"I never saw him in my life."

"And my son at this moment is — "

"Is about a mile off."

"My dear monsieur, he is in garrison at Strasburg, and
unless he has deserted, which he has not, I can swear, he is
bringing nobody hither."

"He is bringing a great lady hither, a very exalted
personage.   Ah, hold! there is one thing I ought to tell
you; you had better keep out of sight that little rogue
with the horn at her finger-ends."

"Nicole Legay?   Why, pray?"

"Because her features resemble those of the lady who is
coming."

"A great lady resemble Nicole!   That is absurd!"

"Why so?   I bought a slave once who resembled Cleo-
patra so much that there was some idea of sending her to
Rome to pass for that queen in Octavius's triumph."

"Ah! another attack of your old malady!"

"You must surely see, my dear baron, that this matter cannot concern me; I only speak for your own good."

"But why should Nicole's resemblance to the great lady offend her?"

"Suppose you were the King of France, which I am far from wishing, or the dauphin, which I wish still less; should you be flattered, on entering a house, to find among the servants one whose face was a counterpart of your august visage?"

"Oh, the devil! — that would be a sad dilemma! So, then, you think — "

"I think that the most high and mighty lady who is coming would not be pleased to see her living image in a short petticoat and cotton handkerchief."

"Oh, well," said the baron, still laughing, "we must see about it; but, after all, my dear baron, what delights me most in this affair is that my son is coming, — that dear Philip! — without giving us a note of warning;" and he laughed louder than before.

"So you are pleased with my prediction?" said Balsamo, gravely. "I am glad of it; but in your place I should set about giving some orders."

"Really?"

"Yes."

"I shall think of it, my dear guest, I shall think of it."

"You have very little time."

"And you are serious, then?"

"No one could be more serious. If you wish to receive properly the great personage who does you the honour of visiting you, you have not a minute to lose."

The baron shook his head.

"You still doubt?" asked Balsamo.

"I warn you, you have to do with a most confirmed sceptic." And just then he turned to call his daughter, in order to communicate his guest's prediction to her, as we have before related. We have seen how the young girl replied to her father's invitation, and how Balsamo's gaze had drawn her, as if by fascination, to the window.

Nicole stood looking with amazement at La Brie, who was making signs to her, and trying to understand what had been said.

"I am dreadfully hard of belief," repeated the baron, "and unless I saw — "

"Then, since you must see, look there," said Balsamo, pointing to the avenue, where a horseman appeared, galloping towards them.

"Ha!" cried the baron, "there indeed is — "

"Monsieur Philip!" said Nicole, standing on tiptoe.

"My young master!" exclaimed La Brie, joyfully.

"My brother, my brother!" cried Andrée, stretching out her arms at the window.

"Is it your son, my dear baron?" asked Balsamo, in a careless tone.

"Yes, *pardieu!* it is!" exclaimed he, stupefied with astonishment.

"This is but the beginning," said Balsamo.

"You are positively a sorcerer, then," said the baron, more submissively than before.

A triumphant smile hovered on the stranger's lips.

The horse came on at full speed, reeking with moisture, passed the last rows of trees, and, while still in motion, the rider leaped to the ground, and hastened to embrace his father, who only muttered, "What the devil! what the devil!"

"It is really I," said Philip, who saw his father's perplexity; "it is indeed."

"Doubtless — I see that plainly enough; but what brought you hither at this time?".

"Father, a great honour awaits our house!"

The old man looked up inquiringly.

Philip went on: "In an hour Marie Antoinette Josèphe, Archduchess of Austria and Dauphiness of France, will be here."

The baron looked as deeply humbled as he had before looked sarcastic, and, turning to Balsamo, said only, "Pardon me!"

"Monsieur," returned Balsamo, "I leave you with your son; it is long since you have met, and you must have much to say to each other."

Bowing to Andrée, who, full of joy at the arrival of her brother, had hastened down to meet him, he retired, making a sign to Nicole and La Brie, which they doubtless understood, for they disappeared with him among the trees of the avenue.

CHAPTER XIII.

PHILIP DE TAVERNEY.

PHILIP DE TAVERNEY, Chevalier de Maison-Rouge, did not in the least resemble his sister, yet was as fine a specimen of manly beauty as she was of feminine loveliness. His features were noble and regular, his figure and carriage graceful in the extreme, and the expression of his eyes was at the same time mild and haughty.

Like all distinguished minds, wearied by the narrow and chilling forms of life, he was disposed to melancholy, without being sad. To this, perhaps, he owed his mildness of temper, for he was naturally proud, imperious, and reserved. The necessity of associating with the poor, his real equals, as with the rich, his equals in rank, had softened a character inclined to be overbearing and scornful.

Philip had scarcely embraced his father when Andrée, roused from her magnetic torpor by his arrival, hastened down to throw herself on his bosom. The sobs which accompanied this action showed how dear he was to the heart of the tender girl.

Philip took her hand and his father's and drew them into the salon, where, being now alone, he sat down between them.

"You are incredulous, my dear father, — you are surprised, my dear sister," said he; "yet nothing is more true than that in a few minutes the dauphiness will be in our poor abode."

"*Ventrebleu!*" cried the baron; "she must be prevented, whatever it cost! The dauphiness here! — we should be dishonoured forever! This would be a specimen of the nobility of France to present her! No, no; it must not be. But tell me, what the deuce put my house into her head?"

"Oh, it is a complete romance."

"A romance!" said Andrée; "relate it, brother, — my dear, good brother."

"'My dear, good brother!'" repeated the baron; "she seems quite pleased."

"Yes; for is not Philip pleased, my dear father?"

"Because Master Philip is an enthusiast. But for me, who look at things in a more serious manner, I see nothing very agreeable in it."

"You will be of a different opinion when I relate what has occurred."

"Well, relate it quickly," grumbled the baron.

"Yes, yes, relate it!" exclaimed Andrée impatiently.

"Well, I was in garrison at Strasburg, as you know. Now, you are aware that it was by Strasburg that the dauphiness was to enter France."

"Know it! How should we know anything in this den?" asked the baron.

"Well, at Strasburg, brother?" said Andrée.

"Well, we were waiting on the glacis from six in the morning, for we did not know positively at what hour Madame la Dauphine would arrive. It rained in torrents, and our clothes were dripping. The major sent me forward to endeavour to discover the cortège. I had galloped about a league, when all at once, at a turn in the road, I found myself close to the advanced guard of the escort. I spoke a few words to them, and just then her royal highness put her head out of the carriage window, and asked who I was. It seems I had been called to to stop; but I had already set off at full gallop. All my fatigue was forgotten in an instant."

"And the dauphiness?" asked Andrée.

"She is not older than you, and beautiful as an angel."

"But, Philip," said the baron, rather hesitatingly.

" Well, father ? "

" Does she not resemble some one you have seen ? "

" Some one that I have seen ? "

" Yes ; endeavour to recollect."

" No, I know no one like Madame la Dauphine ! " he exclaimed enthusiastically.

" What ! not Nicole, for instance ? "

" Ha ! that is most strange ! Now you say so, I do think she is like her ; but oh, so much inferior in beauty and grace ! But how could you know that she was like her ? "

" Faith ! a sorcerer told me."

" A sorcerer ? "

" Yes ; and he predicted her coming and yours this morning."

" The stranger ? " asked Andrée, timidly.

" Is it he who was beside you, monsieur, when I arrived, and who retired so discreetly ? "

" Yes, the same ; but go on, Philip, go on."

" Perhaps it would be better to make some preparations," said Andrée.

" No, — the more you prepare, the more ridiculous we shall appear. Go on, Philip, I tell you ! "

" I returned to Strasburg, and told the governor, the Count de Stainville. We set out immediately to meet Madame la Dauphine, and we were at the Kehl gate when the procession came in sight. I was close to the governor."

" Stay ! " said the baron ; " I once knew a Count de Stainville."

" Brother-in-law to the prime minister, the Duke de Choiseul."

" It is the same. Go on, then, go on."

" The dauphiness, who is young, perhaps likes young faces, for she listened very inattentively to the governor, and all the time fixed her eyes on me, although I kept respectfully in the background. Then, pointing to me, she said, 'Is not that the gentleman who was the first to meet me ?' 'Yes, madame,' replied the governor. 'Approach, monsieur,' said she. I approached her. 'What is your name ?' asked the dauphiness, in the sweetest voice I ever heard. 'The Chevalier de Taverney Maison-Rouge,' I replied, stammering. 'Pray take a note of that name on your tablets, my dear friend,' said the dauphiness, turning to an old lady, who, I have since learned, is the Countess de Langershausen, her governess. My name was written. Then, turning again to me, she said, 'Ah, monsieur, you have suffered very much from your exposure to this frightful weather; I am extremely sorry for having been the cause of it.'"

"Oh, how good the dauphiness must be! What kindness and consideration!" said Andrée, with delight.

"Very well, very well indeed," muttered the baron, with a smile indicative of a father's partiality, and, at the same time, of his bad opinion of women, and even of queens. "But go on, Philip."

"What did you say ?" asked Andrée.

"I said not a word; I bowed to the very ground. She passed on."

"What! you said nothing ?" exclaimed the baron.

"I had no voice, I assure you, monsieur; my heart beat so rapidly, — I was so much agitated."

"What the devil! do you think I had nothing to say when, about your age, I was presented to the Princess Leczinska ?"

"But, monsieur, you had always a great deal of wit," Philip replied.

Andrée pressed his hand.

"I profited by her Royal Highness's departure," continued Philip, "to hasten to my apartment and change my clothes; for I was wet to the skin and covered with mud from head to foot."

"Poor, dear brother !" whispered Andrée.

"When the dauphiness," Philip continued, "reached

the town-hall, she had to receive the congratulations of the principal inhabitants; that being over, it was announced that dinner was served. A friend of mine, the major of my regiment, since told me that, whilst at table, she looked several times round on the officers who were present, and at last she said, 'I do not see the young officer who was sent to meet me this morning; has he not been told that I wished to thank him?' The major stepped forward. 'Madame,' said he, 'Lieutenant de Taverney was obliged to retire and change his dress, that he might present himself in a more suitable manner before you.' A moment after, I entered the room, and I had not been five minutes in it when the dauphiness perceived me. She made a sign to me to approach; I obeyed. 'Monsieur,' said she, 'should you object to follow me to Paris?' 'Oh, madame,' I cried, 'it would only make me too happy; but I am in garrison at Strasburg, and I am not my own master.' 'Well, I shall arrange that matter with the governor;' and she made a gesture for me to retire. In the evening she said to the governor, 'Monsieur, I have a vow to fulfil, and you must assist me in it.' 'I shall consider it a sacred duty, madame,' he replied. 'You must know,' she continued, 'that I made a vow to take into my own service the first Frenchman, whoever he should be, whom I should meet on touching the soil of France, and that I would make him and his family happy, if, indeed, princes can make any one happy.' 'Madame,' said the governor, 'princes are God's representatives on earth. But may I ask,' continued he, 'who was the person who had the good fortune to be first met by your Royal Highness?' 'The Chevalier de Taverney Maison-Rouge, a young lieutenant.' 'We shall all be jealous of the Chevalier de Taverney, madame,' replied the governor, 'but we shall not place any obstacle in the way of his high fortune; the ties which engage him here shall be broken, and he shall depart at the same time as you, madame.' So the day on which the dauphiness left Strasburg, I was

ordered to accompany her on horseback, and since then
have never left the door of her carriage."

"Oh!" said the baron, with his former singular smile,
"strange enough, but not impossible!"

"What, father?"

"Oh, never mind!"

"But, brother," said Andrée, "I don't see what all this
has to do with the dauphiness coming hither."

"Wait till you hear. Yesterday we arrived at Nancy
about eleven o'clock at night, and were passing through the
town by torch-light. The dauphiness called me to her. 'I
wish,' said she, 'to depart early to-morrow morning.'
'Madame is going to make a long march, then?' 'No,
but I wish to stop on the road; and can you guess where?'
she asked, smiling. 'No, madame.' 'I mean to stop at
Taverney, to see your father and sister.' 'My father and
my sister! What, madame knows —' 'I have made
inquiries, and know that they live only two hundred paces
from the road which we are travelling.' The perspiration
broke on my forehead, and trembling, as you may suppose,
I hastened to reply, 'My father's house, madame, is not
worthy to receive so great a princess; we are poor.' 'So
much the better,' replied she; 'I shall therefore, I am certain, be received more cordially and more simply. However
poor you may be, there will be always a cup of milk for a
friend who wishes to forget for a moment that she is Archduchess of Austria and Dauphiness of France.' 'Oh,
madame!' said I. This was all; respect forbade me to
go farther."

"Stupid fellow!" cried the baron.

"One might have thought that madame guessed what was
passing in my mind, for she added: 'Do not be afraid; I
shall not stay long; but since you think that I shall suffer
any inconvenience by this visit, it is only fair, for I caused
you to suffer on my arrival at Strasburg.' Who could
resist such charming words, father?"

"Oh, it would have been impossible!" cried Andrée;

"she is so sweet, so good, she will be satisfied with my flowers and a cup of my milk, as she says."

"Yes; but she will not be very well satisfied with my chairs, which will dislocate her bones, and my hangings, which will disgust her. Devil take all whims! So! France will be well governed with a woman who takes such caprices. Plague on it! A strange reign it will be, to judge from the commencement," said the baron, angrily.

"Oh, father, how can you say such things of a princess who is honouring us so highly?"

"Who is dishonouring us, rather!" cried the old man. "Taverney was forgotten, buried under the ruins of Maison-Rouge. I intended that if it came to light again it should be in a suitable manner; and now the whims of a girl are going to drag us into day, — dusty, shabby, wretched! And the gazettes, on the watch for everything absurd, will amuse their readers with the visit of a great princess to this den of Taverney. *Cordieu!* I have an idea —"

The young people started at the manner in which he pronounced these words.

"What do you mean, monsieur?" demanded Philip.

The baron muttered to himself: "If the Count of Medina burnt his palace that he might embrace a queen, I may well burn my kennel to get rid of the visit of a princess. Let her come! let her come!"

Philip and Andrée only heard the last words, and they looked at each other uneasily.

"It cannot be long before she will be here, monsieur," said Philip. "I took the way through the wood, in order to get some minutes in advance of the cortège; it will soon be here."

"Then I must not lose time," said the baron; and, with the agility of a youth of twenty, he left the salon. He hastened to the kitchen, snatched a flaming piece of wood from the hearth, and proceeded to his barns; but just as he raised his arm to throw it into a heap of straw, he was seized by Balsamo, who flung to a safe distance the burning brand.

"What are you about, monsieur?" cried he; "the Archduchess of Austria is not a Constable de Bourbon, whose presence contaminates, so that we should rather burn our house than permit her to enter it!"

The old man stopped, pale, trembling, and his habitual smile vanished from his lips; he had gathered all his strength to enable him to resolve on making his poverty yet greater by the destruction of his dwelling, rather than be disgraced, according to his ideas, by allowing its mediocrity to be seen.

"Come, monsieur, come," continued Balsamo; "you have only time to throw off your dressing-gown and put yourself in better trim. The Baron of Taverney whom I knew at the siege of Philipsbourg wore the grand cross of the order of St. Louis; any coat will be rich and elegant when decorated with that."

"But, monsieur, shall I show to our dauphiness that poverty which I wished to hide from you?"

"Be not uneasy; we shall manage to occupy her attention so that she shall not know whether your house be new or old, poor or rich. Be hospitable, monsieur; it is your duty as a gentleman! What will the enemies of the dauphiness — and she has many — what will they do, if her friends burn their castles rather than receive her under their roofs? Let us not thus anticipate that vengeance which is to come! Everything in its predestined time."

The baron again showed an involuntary submission to Balsamo, and hurried to his children, who, uneasy at his absence, were seeking him on every side.

As to Balsamo, he retired in silence, like a man intent on some work which he had undertaken, and which he must complete.

CHAPTER XIV.

MARIE ANTOINETTE JOSÈPHE, ARCHDUCHESS OF AUSTRIA.

As Balsamo had said, there was no time to be lost, for now
on the road, generally so peaceful, which led to the
Baron of Taverney's dwelling, a great sound of carriages,
horses, and voices was heard.

Three carriages, one of which was covered with gilding
and mythological bas-reliefs, and which, notwithstanding
its magnificence, was not less dusty and bespattered than
the others, stopped at the great gate of the avenue. Gilbert held it open, his eyes distended, his whole frame
trembling with feverish agitation at the sight of so much
magnificence. Twenty gentlemen on horseback, all young
and splendidly dressed, drew up near the principal carriage,
from which a young girl of sixteen, dressed with great simplicity, but with her hair elaborately piled on her forehead,
got out, assisted by a gentleman in black, who wore, saltier-
wise, under his mantle, the ribbon of St. Louis.

Marie Antoinette, for it was she, brought with her a
reputation for beauty, which the princesses destined to share
the thrones of the kings of France have not always possessed. It was difficult to say whether her eyes were beautiful or not, yet they were capable of every expression,
more particularly of the opposite expressions of mildness
and scorn. Her nose was finely formed, her upper lip
beautiful; but the lower lip, her aristocratic inheritance
from seventeen emperors, was too thick and prominent.
Her complexion was lovely ; her neck, shoulders, and bust
were of marble whiteness and beautifully formed; her
hands truly regal. At times, when roused to energy, her

carriage was majestic, firm, and decided; at other times, soft, undulating, — one might almost say caressing. No woman ever made a more graceful courtesy; no queen ever bowed with more tact and discrimination. This day the most expressive sweetness shone in her countenance. She had resolved to be only the woman, and to forget the dauphiness. She wore a dress of white silk, and her beautiful bare arms supported a mantle of rich lace.

Scarcely had she touched the ground when she turned to assist one of her ladies of honour whom age had weakened a little ; and, refusing the arm of the gentleman in black, she advanced, inhaling the fresh air, and looking around as if determined to enjoy to the utmost the few moments of freedom with which she was indulging herself.

" Oh, what a beautiful situation ! " she exclaimed ; " what magnificent trees ! and such a pretty little house ! How happy one might be in this healthful air, under those trees, which form so sweet a retirement ! "

At this moment Philip appeared, followed by Andrée, on whose arm the baron leaned. She was dressed in a simple gown of grey silk, and the baron in a coat of blue velvet, the remains of some of his old magnificence ; he had not forgotten Balsamo's recommendation, and wore his ribbon of St. Louis. On seeing the three approach, the dauphiness stopped. Her escort then grouped itself around her, — the officers holding their horses by the bridles, and the courtiers, hat in hand, whispering to one another. Philip drew near, pale with agitation, yet with a noble bearing.

" With madame's permission," said he, " I have the honour of presenting to madame the Baron de Taverney Maison-Rouge, my father, and Claire-Andrée de Taverney, my sister."

The baron bowed profoundly, like a man who knew how to bow to queens. Andrée showed, in her graceful timidity, the most flattering kind of politeness, — sincere respect. Marie Antoinette looked at the two young people, and recalling what Philip had said of their poverty, she guessed what they suffered at that moment.

"Madame," said the baron, with dignity, "does too much honour to the Château of Taverney; such an humble abode is not worthy to receive so much rank and beauty."

"I know that it is the abode of an old soldier of France," replied the dauphiness, "and my mother, the Empress Maria Theresa, who was a distinguished warrior, has told me that often in your country those richest in glory are the poorest in meaner treasures," and with ineffable grace she extended her lovely hand to Andrée, who, kneeling, kissed it.

The baron was, however, still haunted by the idea which had so much tormented him, — that the train of the dauphiness was about to crowd into his little house, in which there could not be found chairs for a fourth of their number. The dauphiness hastened to relieve him from all embarrassment.

"Gentlemen," said she, turning to those who formed her escort, "I must not impose on you the trouble of following me in all my caprices. You will wait here, if you please; in half an hour I shall return. Come with me, my good Langershausen," she added in German to the lady whom she had assisted out of the carriage, "and you, monsieur," said she to the gentleman in black, "have the goodness to follow us!"

This personage, though dressed thus simply, was remarkable for the elegance of his manners, and was about thirty years of age, and very handsome. He drew to one side to allow the princess to pass. Marie Antoinette took Andrée for her guide, and made a sign to Philip to come near his sister.

As to the baron, he was left to the personage, of high rank, doubtless, to whom the dauphiness had granted the honour of accompanying her.

"So you are a Taverney Maison-Rouge?" said he, playing with his splendid ruffles of the most expensive lace, and turning to the baron with truly aristocratic impertinence.

"Must I reply 'monsieur,' or 'monseigneur'?" asked the baron, with equal impertinence.

"You may say simply 'Prince,' or 'your Eminence,' which you choose," the other replied.

"Well, then, your Eminence, I am a Taverney-Maison-Rouge, — a real one!" said the baron, in that tone of raillery which he so seldom abandoned.

His Eminence, who had the usual tact of great nobles, felt that he had to do with no country clown, and continued, "This is your summer residence?"

"Summer and winter," answered the baron, who wished to put an end to disagreeable queries, but accompanying each reply with a low bow.

Philip could not help turning from time to time uneasily towards his father, for the house, as they drew nearer to it, wore an aspect threatening and ironical, as if pitilessly determined to show all their poverty. The baron had already resignedly extended his hand to point the way to the door of his house, when the dauphiness, turning to him, said, "Excuse me, monsieur, if I do not enter; these shades are so delightful that I could pass my life in them. I am tired of rooms. For fifteen days I have been received in rooms, — I, who love the open air, the shade of trees, and the perfume of flowers." Then, turning to Andrée, "You will bring me a cup of milk here, under these beautiful trees, will you not?"

"Madame," said the baron, turning pale, "how should we dare to offer you such poor refreshment?"

"I prefer it, sir, to anything else. New-laid eggs and milk formed my banquets at Schoenbrunn."

All at once La Brie, swelling with pride, in a splendid livery and with a napkin on his arm, appeared under an archway of jessamine, the shade of which had attracted the eye of the dauphiness. In a tone in which importance and respect were strangely mixed, he announced, "Madame is served!"

"Am I in the dwelling of an enchanter?" cried the princess, as she ran rather than walked to the perfumed alley.

The baron in his uneasiness, forgot all etiquette, left the gentleman in black, and hurried after the dauphiness. Andrée and Philip looked at one another with mingled astonishment and anxiety, and followed their father.

Under the clematis, jessamine, and woodbine was placed an oval table, covered with a damask cloth of dazzling whiteness, on which was arranged, in a brilliant service of plate, a collation the most elegant and rare. There were exotic fruits made into the most delicious confections: biscuits from Aleppo, oranges from Malta, and lemons of extraordinary size, all arranged in beautiful vases. Wines, the richest and most esteemed, sparkled like the ruby and the topaz in decanters ornamented and cut in Persia, and in the centre, in a silver vase, was placed the milk for which the dauphiness had asked.

Marie Antoinette looked around and saw surprise and alarm imprinted on the face of her host, and on the countenance of his son and daughter. The gentlemen of her escort were delighted with what they saw, without understanding it, and without endeavouring to understand it.

" You expected me, then, monsieur ? " said she to the baron.

" I, madame ! " stammered he.

" Yes ; you could not in ten minutes have all this prepared, and I have only been ten minutes here ; " and she looked at La Brie with an expression which said, " above all, when you have only one servant ! "

" Madame," answered the baron, " madame was expected, or rather your coming was foretold to me."

" Your son wrote to you ? "

" No, madame."

" No one knew that I was coming here, as I did not wish to give you the trouble which I see I have done. It was only late last night that I expressed my intention to your son, and he reached this but half an hour before me."

" Scarcely a quarter of an hour, madame."

" Then some fairy must have revealed to you what was to occur. Mademoiselle's godmother, perhaps ? "

" Madame," said the baron, offering a chair to the princess,
" it was not a fairy who announced my good fortune to
me."

" Who, then ? " asked she, observing that he hesitated.

" An enchanter, madame ! "

" An enchanter ! How can that be ? "

" I know nothing of the matter, for I do not meddle with
magic myself, yet to him, madame, I am indebted for being
able to entertain your highness in a tolerable fashion."

" In that case we must not touch anything, since the
collation is the work of sorcery. His Eminence," added she,
pointing to the gentleman in black, who had fixed his eye on
a Strasburg pie, " seems in a hurry to begin; but we shall
assuredly not eat of this enchanted collation. And you,
dear friend," turning to her governess, " distrust the Cyprus
wine, and do as I do ! " and she poured some water from
a globe-formed carafe with a narrow neck into a golden
goblet.

" In truth," said Andrée, with alarm, " Madame is
perhaps right ! "

Philip trembled with surprise, and ignorant of what had
passed the evening before, looked alternately at his father
and his sister for explanation.

" But I see," continued the dauphiness, " his Eminence
is determined to sin, in spite of all the canons of the
Church."

" Madame," replied the prelate, " we princes of the
Church are too worldly to be able to believe that Heaven's
wrath will fall on us about a little refreshment for the
body ; and, above all, too humane to feel the least inclination
to burn an honest sorcerer for providing us with good
things like these ! "

" Do not jest, I pray, monseigneur," said the baron. " I
swear to you that a sorcerer — a real sorcerer — foretold
to me about an hour ago the arrival of her Royal Highness
and my son ! "

" And has an hour been sufficient for you to prepare this

banquet ? " demanded the dauphiness. " In that case you
are a greater sorcerer than your sorcerer ! "

" No, madame, it was he who did all this, and brought
the table up through the ground, ready served as you see."

" On your word, monsieur ? "

" On the honour of a gentleman ! " replied the baron.

" Ha ! " said the cardinal, in a serious tone, putting back
the plate which he had taken, " I thought you were jesting.
Then you have in your house a real magician ? "

" A real magician !   And I should not wonder if he has
made all the gold on that table himself."

" Oh, he must have found out the philosopher's stone ! "
cried the cardinal, his eyes sparkling with covetousness.

" See how the eyes of his Eminence sparkle !   He who
has been seeking all his life for the philosopher's stone ! "
said the dauphiness.

" I confess to your Royal Highness," replied his very
worldly Eminence, " that nothing interests me more than
the supernatural ; nothing is so curious, in my estimation,
as the impossible."

" Ah ! I have touched the vulnerable part, it seems ! "
said the dauphiness. " Every great man has his mysteries,
particularly when he is a diplomatist ; and I — I warn
your Eminence, know a great deal of sorcery.   I sometimes
find out things, if not impossible, if not supernatural, at
least incredible ! " and the eye of the dauphiness, before so
mild, flashed as from an internal storm ; but no thunder
followed.   His Eminence alone doubtless understood what
this meant, for he looked evidently embarrassed.   The
dauphiness went on : —

" To make the thing complete, M. de Taverney, you must
show us your magician.   Where is he ?   In what box have
you hidden him ? "

" Madame," answered the baron, " he is much more able
to put me and my house in a box, than I to put him ! "

" In truth, you excite my curiosity," said Marie
Antoinette. " I must positively see him ! "

The tone in which this was uttered, although still retaining the charm which Marie Antoinette knew so well how to assume, forbade all idea of refusal to comply with her wish.

The baron understood this perfectly, and made a sign to La Brie, who was contemplating with eager eyes the illustrious guests, the sight of whom seemed to make up to him for his twenty years of unpaid wages.

"Tell Baron Joseph Balsamo," said his master, "that madame the dauphiness desires to see him." La Brie departed.

"Joseph Balsamo!" said the dauphiness. "What a singular name!"

"Joseph Balsamo!" repeated his Eminence, as if reflecting; "I think I know that name."

Five minutes passed in silence. Then Andrée felt a thrill run through her frame; she heard, before it was perceptible to other ears, a step advancing under the shade of the trees. The branches were put aside, and Joseph Balsamo stood face to face with Marie Antoinette.

CHAPTER XV.

MAGIC.

BALSAMO bowed humbly; but no sooner had he raised his head than he fixed his bright, expressive eyes firmly but respectfully on the face of the dauphiness, and waited calmly until she should interrogate him.

"If it is you of whom the Baron de Taverney has been speaking to us, draw near, monsieur, that we may better see what a magician is."

Balsamo advanced another step and bowed.

"Your profession is to foretell events, monsieur?" said the dauphiness, regarding him with more curiosity than she would herself have been willing to acknowledge, and sipping some milk which had been handed her.

"It is not my profession, but I do foretell events."

"We have been brought up in an enlightened creed," said the dauphiness, "and the only mysteries in which we believe are those of the Catholic faith."

"They are to be venerated," said Balsamo, reverently; "but here is Monseigneur the Cardinal de Rohan, who will tell your Royal Highness, though he be a prince of the Church, that they are not the only mysteries which deserve to be regarded with respect."

The cardinal started; he had not told his name, it had not been pronounced, yet this stranger knew it. Marie Antoinette did not appear to remark this circumstance, but continued: —

"You will confess, monsieur, that at least they are the only mysteries which cannot be controverted?"

"Madame," answered Balsamo, with the same respect, "as well as faith, there is certainty."

"You speak rather obscurely, monsieur. Although thoroughly French in heart, I am but indifferently acquainted with the niceties of the language, and must beg you to be less enigmatic if I am to comprehend you."

"And I, madame, would entreat that all may remain unexplained. I should deeply regret to unveil to so illustrious a princess a future which might not correspond to her hopes."

"This becomes serious," said Marie Antoinette; "the gentleman wishes to excite my curiosity, that I may command him to tell my fortune."

"God forbid that your Royal Highness should force me to do it!"

"Yes," replied the dauphiness; "for you would be rather puzzled to do it!" and she laughed.

But the dauphiness's laugh died away without meeting an echo from any of the attendants. Every one present seemed to submit tacitly to the influence of the singular man who was, for the moment, the centre of general attraction.

"Come, confess it frankly," said the dauphiness.

Balsamo bowed.

"Yet it was you who predicted my arrival to the Baron de Taverney," resumed Marie Antoinette, with a slight movement of impatience.

"Yes, madame, it was I."

"And how did he do it?" she added, turning to the baron, as if she felt the necessity of a third party taking share in this strange dialogue.

"Very simply, madame, — merely by looking in a glass of water."

"Was it so?" she asked of Balsamo.

"Yes, madame," answered he.

"Then, having read the future for the Baron de Taverney in a glass of water, surely you can read it for me in a decanter."

"Perfectly well, madame."

" And why do you refuse to do so ? "

" Because the future is uncertain ; and if I saw a cloud on it — " He stopped.

" Well ? "

" It would give me pain to sadden madame."

" Have you known me before, or do you now see me for the first time ? "

" I have had the honour of seeing madame when a child, in your native country, with your august mother."

" You have seen my mother, then ? "

" I have had that honour. She is a great and powerful queen."

" Empress, monsieur."

" I used the word ' queen ' in reference to the heart and mind; and yet — "

" Reservations concerning my mother ? " said the dauphiness, haughtily.

" The greatest hearts have weaknesses, madame, particularly where they think the happiness of their children is concerned."

" History, I trust, monsieur, will not discover one single weakness in Maria Theresa."

" Because history will not know what is known only to the Empress Maria Theresa, to your Royal Highness, and to myself."

" We have a secret, monsieur? — we three! " said the dauphiness, smiling disdainfully.

" We three, madame! " replied Balsamo, solemnly.

" Come, then, tell this secret, monsieur! "

" It will then be no longer one."

" No matter ; tell it! "

" Is it madame's will ? "

" It is."

Balsamo bowed. " There is in the Palace of Schoenbrunn," said he, " a cabinet, called the Dresden cabinet, on account of the splendid vases of porcelain, which it contains."

" Yes," said the dauphiness ; " go on."

" This cabinet forms a part of the private suite of rooms of the Empress Maria Theresa; in it she writes her letters."

" Yes."

" On a certain day, about seven in the morning, when the empress had not yet risen, madame entered this cabinet by a door through which you alone were permitted to pass; for madame is the favourite daughter of her Imperial Majesty."

" Well, monsieur ? "

" Madame approached a writing-desk, on which lay open a letter which her Imperial Majesty had written the night before. Madame read that letter ; and doubtless some expressions in it must have been displeasing to you, for you took a pen, and with your own hand erased three words."

The dauphiness blushed slightly. " What were the words erased ? " she asked anxiously.

" They were too condescending, doubtless, and showed too great affection for the person to whom they were addressed. This was a weakness, and to this it was I alluded in speaking of your august mother."

" Then you remember the words ? "

" Assuredly."

" Repeat them to me."

" They were : ' *My dear friend.*' "

Marie Antoinette bit her lip and turned pale.

" Shall I tell madame to whom the letter was addressed ? "

" No ; but you may write the name."

Balsamo drew out a pocket-book with gold clasps, and, having written some words on one of the leaves, he tore it out, and, bowing, presented it to the dauphiness. Marie Antoinette unfolded the leaf, read it, and looked with astonishment at the man who, though he bowed low before her, seemed to have it in his power to direct her fate.

The letter was addressed to the mistress of King Louis XV., — " *To the Marquise de Pompadour.*"

"All this is true, monsieur," said Marie Antoinette, after a pause; "and though I am ignorant by what means you have become acquainted with these circumstances, I cannot speak falsely, and I must declare that what you have said is true."

"Then," said Balsamo, "will madame permit me to retire, satisfied with this harmless proof of my art?"

"No, monsieur," replied the dauphiness; "the more I know of your powers, the more desirous I become to have my fate foretold. You have spoken only of the past; let me learn what the future will be."

The princess spoke these words with a feverish impatience, which she in vain endeavoured to conceal from her auditors.

"I am ready, if madame commands me, to declare it; yet let me supplicate you not to do so."

"I have never expressed a command twice; and you will recollect, monsieur, that I have already commanded once."

"Let me at least consult the oracle whether it may be revealed to madame or not," he said, entreatingly.

"Good or bad, monsieur," replied Marie Antoinette, "I will know it. If good, I shall take it for flattery; if bad, I shall hold it as a warning, and shall be obliged to you for it. Begin!"

Balsamo took the round carafe with the narrow neck, and placed it on a golden saucer; the rays of the sun, striking on this, shone dimly yellow in the water, and seemed to offer something worthy of deep consideration to the attentive soothsayer. Every one was silent. At length he placed the carafe again on the table, and shook his head.

"Well, monsieur?" said the dauphiness.

"I cannot speak it," replied Balsamo.

"You cannot, because you have nothing to tell me," replied Marie Antoinette, a little contemptuously.

"There are things which must never be said to princes, madame," replied Balsamo, in a tone which seemed to express his determination to oppose her wishes.

"Yes, when those things, I repeat, may be expressed by the word *nothing.*"

"It is not that which prevents me, madame; on the contrary, it is the very reverse."

The dauphiness smiled disdainfully, Balsamo appeared embarrassed, the cardinal began to laugh outright, and the baron drew near, grumbling: —

"So my magician has exhausted himself! His powers have not lasted very long! It only remains for us to see all these fine things turned into vine-leaves, as we have read in Eastern tales."

"I should rather have had the simple vine-leaves," said Marie Antoinette, "than these fine things displayed by the gentleman for the purpose of getting himself presented to me."

"Deign to remember, madame," replied Balsamo, who was deadly pale, "that I did not solicit this honour."

"It was not difficult for you to guess, monsieur, that I should ask to see you."

"Pardon him, madame," said Andrée, in a low voice; "he thought he was doing right."

"And I tell you he was doing wrong," replied the princess, so as only to be heard by Andrée and Balsamo. "No one can elevate himself by humiliating an old man; and when we can have the pewter goblet of a gentleman to drink in, we need not the golden one of a mountebank!"

Balsamo started as if a viper had bitten him. "Madame," said he, greatly agitated, "I am ready to let you know your destiny, since your blindness impels you to desire such knowledge."

He pronounced these words in a tone so firm and so threatening that all present felt the blood chilled in their veins.

"*Gib ihm kein Gehœr, meine Tochter,*"[1] said the old lady to Marie Antoinette.

---

[1] Do not listen to him, my daughter.

"*Lass sie hœren ; sie hat wissen wollen, und so soll sie wissen,*"[1] replied Balsamo.

These words, spoken in German, a language which was understood by only a few present, seemed to render more mysterious what was going on.

"No," said the dauphiness, resisting the entreaties of her venerable governess; "let him say what he desires to say; were I now to permit him to be silent, he would believe me afraid."

Balsamo heard these words, and a dark, furtive smile played for a second on his lips. "It is as I said," he muttered to himself, "the courage of bravado merely."

"Speak!" said the dauphiness; "speak, monsieur."

"Then madame is decided ? "

"I never go back from a decision once made."

"In that case, madame, I would entreat that we may be alone."

She made a sign which those around understood; all retired.

"This is not a bad plan for obtaining a private audience," said the dauphiness, turning to Balsamo; "is it monsieur ? "

"I would beg madame not to irritate me !" replied Balsamo. "I am but an instrument of Providence to enlighten you on those sorrows which await you. Insult fortune, if you will, — she can revenge herself; but for me, I am but the gloomy herald of the misfortunes she has in store for you."

"Then it appears that misfortunes await me ? " said the dauphiness, mildly, touched by Balsamo's respectful manner.

"Yes, — terrible misfortunes."

"First, will my family be happy ? "

"That which you have left, or that to which you are going ? "

"Oh, my own family, — my mother, my brother Joseph, my sister Caroline."

---

[1] Let her; she wishes to know, and she shall know.

" Your misfortunes will not reach them."

" They are mine alone, then ? "

" They are yours, and those of your new family."

" The royal family of France includes three princes:
the Duke de Berry, the Count de Provence, and the Count
d'Artois, what will be their fate ? "

" They will all reign."

" Then I shall have no children ? "

" You will have children."

" Not sons ? "

" Some of them sons."

" My sorrows then will be caused by their death ? "

" You will grieve that one is dead, but most will you
grieve that the other lives."

" Will my husband love me ? "

" Yes, too well."

" Shall I not, then, be able to bear my grief, supported
by my husband and my family ? "

" Neither will support you."

" The love of my people will still be mine."

" The people ! — the ocean in a calm ! Have you seen
the ocean in a storm, madame ? "

" By doing good I shall prevent the storm ; or, if it
rise, shall rise above it ! "

" The higher the wave the deeper the abyss."

" God will defend me."

" Alas ! these are heads which he himself foredooms ! "

" What mean you, monsieur ; shall I not, then, be queen ? "

" Yes, madame, but would to Heaven that you were not
to be ! "

She smiled disdainfully.

" Did you remark," he continued, " the tapestry of
the first room in which you slept after having entered
France ? "

" Yes, monsieur."

" What did it represent ? "

" The Slaughter of the Innocents."

"Have not the grim faces of the murderers haunted your memory ? "

"I confess that they have."

"Had you not a storm on the way hither ? "

"Yes; a thunderbolt fell, and nearly on my carriage."

"Were not those omens ? "

"Fatal omens ? "

"It would be difficult to interpret them as happy ones ! "

The dauphiness let her head fall on her bosom, and raising it after a minute's silence, "Speak!" said she; "in what manner shall I die ? "

He shook his head.

"Speak ! "

"I dare not."

"It is my will that you should," she said, imperiously.

"Have mercy, — have mercy on yourself ! "

"Speak, monsieur, or I shall say that all this is but an absurd fable. Take care ! the daughter of Maria Theresa is not to be jested with ! the woman who holds in her hand the destiny of thirty millions of men is not to be trifled with ! "

He continued silent.

"You know no more," she said contemptuously; "your imagination is exhausted."

"My knowledge of the future is not exhausted, madame; and if you will force me — "

"Yes, I will hear all."

He seized the carafe on the golden saucer, and placed it in a dark hollow, where some rocks formed a sort of grotto; then he took the hand of the archduchess, and drew her under the vault.

"Are you ready ? " he asked the princess, who was alarmed by his rapid movements.

"Yes."

"On your knees, then ! on your knees ! and pray to God to spare you the dreadful end of all your greatness, which you are now to witness ! "

She obeyed mechanically, and fell on both knees.

He pointed with a wand to the glass globe, in the centre of which must have appeared some dark and terrible form, for the dauphiness, in trying to rise, trembled and sank again to the ground with a shriek of horror; she had fainted.

The baron hastened to her assistance, and in a few minutes she came to herself. She put her hand to her forehead, as if to recall her thoughts, then suddenly exclaimed, "The carafe! the carafe!"

The baron presented it to her. The water was perfectly limpid; not a stain mingled with it. Balsamo was gone.

CHAPTER XVI.

THE baron was the first to perceive that the dauphiness
had fainted; he had kept on the watch, more uneasy than
any one else at what might take place between her and
the sorcerer. Hearing her cry of terror, and seeing Balsamo spring out of the grotto, he ran to the spot.

The dauphiness's first request was to see the carafe; her
second, that no injury should be done the magician; and
it was well she made this request, for no sooner had
Philip heard her cry than he bounded after him like an
angry lion.

When her lady of honour came near, and ventured to
question her in German, she only drew from her that
Balsamo had in no way been wanting in respect to her —
that she thought the storm of the preceding night, and her
long journey, had fatigued her and brought on a nervous
attack. Her replies were translated to the Cardinal de
Rohan, who stood by, but dared not himself ask for information. In courts, people are obliged to be satisfied with
half-answers; so what the dauphiness said satisfied nobody,
but every one appeared perfectly satisfied. Philip then
drew near and said : —

" I am obliged to obey madame's orders, yet it is with
regret that I do so; the half-hour during which you intended to stay is past, and the horses are ready."

" Thanks, monsieur," said she, with a smile full of fascinating languor, " but I must alter my determination ; I do

not feel able to set out just now. If I could sleep for a few hours I should be quite restored."

"Madame knows what a poor abode ours is," the baron stammered out.

"Oh, monsieur, any place will do; a little rest is all I want!" She said this as if again fainting, and her head sank again on her bosom.

Andrée disappeared to prepare her room for her, and having in a few minutes returned, she stood beside the dauphiness, not daring to speak until some indication was given that she might do so. At length Marie Antoinette raised her head, smiled to Andrée, and with her hand made a sign to her to draw nearer.

"The room is ready for madame; we entreat only — "

But she was not permitted to finish her apology; the dauphiness interrupted her.

"Thank you! thank you! May I ask you to summon the Countess de Langershausen, and to lead us to the apartment?"

Andrée obeyed; the old lady of honour advanced. "Give me your arm, my dear friend," said the dauphiness to her in German, "for indeed I have scarcely strength enough to walk without support." The baroness obeyed; Andrée approached to assist her. Turning soon after to Andrée, the dauphiness asked, —

"Do you understand German, then, mademoiselle?"

"Yes, madame; I even speak it a little," replied Andrée, in German.

"That is delightful!" exclaimed the dauphiness; "that makes my plan still more agreeable."

Andrée dared not ask her august guest what her plan was, although she longed to know it. The dauphiness leaned on the arm of the Countess de Langershausen, and advanced slowly, her limbs trembling under her. As she issued from the trees in front of the grotto, she heard the cardinal's voice.

"What!" said he, "Count de Stainville, do you mean to

insist on speaking to madame, notwithstanding her orders
to the contrary?"

"I must insist on doing so," replied the governor of
Strasburg, in a firm voice; "madame will pardon me, I
am certain."

"And I, monsieur, on the contrary, insist —"

"Let the governor come forward," said the dauphiness,
appearing at the opening of the trees, which formed a
verdant arch above her head. "Come forward, Count de
Stainville!"

Every one bowed at her command, and drew back to
allow free passage to the brother-in-law of the then all-
powerful minister who governed France. The count looked
around, as if to request a private audience. Marie Antoinette understood that he had something important to say
to her, but before she could express a wish to be left alone,
all had withdrawn.

"A despatch from Versailles, madame," said the count,
in a low voice, and presenting a letter which he had kept
concealed under his plumed hat.

The dauphiness took it, and read the address. "It is
for you, monsieur, not for me," she said. "Open it and
read it to me, if it contain anything that concerns me."

"The letter is addressed to me," he replied, "but in the
corner is a mark agreed on between my brother, Monsieur
de Choiseul, and myself, indicating that the letter is for
madame."

"Ah, that is true, — a cross; I did not observe it. Give
me the letter."

She opened the letter, and read the following lines: —

"The presentation of Madame Dubarry is decided on, if she
can only procure some noble lady to present her. We still hope
she may not find one; but the only sure means to prevent the
presentation will be for her Royal Highness the dauphiness to make
all speed. Madame once at Versailles, no one will dare to offer such
an insult to the court."

"Very well," said the dauphiness, folding up the letter, without the slightest symptom of emotion, or even of interest.

"Will madame now retire to repose a little?" asked Andrée, timidly.

"No, I thank you, mademoiselle; the air has revived me; I have quite recovered." And abandoning the arm of her lady of honour, she walked forward firmly and rapidly. "My horses immediately!" said she.

The cardinal looked with inquisitive surprise at the count.

"The dauphin is becoming impatient," whispered the latter, and this falsehood appearing a secret confided to him alone, his Eminence was satisfied. As to Andrée, her father had taught her to respect the whims of crowned heads, and she was not at all surprised at the change in Marie Antoinette's intentions. The latter, therefore, turning, and seeing no alteration in the sweet expression of her countenance, said: —

"Thanks, mademoiselle; your hospitable reception has made a deep impression on me."

Then turning to the baron, she continued: —

"Monsieur, you must know that on leaving Vienna I made a vow to advance the fortune of the first Frenchman whom I should meet on the frontiers of France. That Frenchman was your son. But I do not intend to stop there; your daughter shall not be forgotten either."

"Oh, madame!" murmured Andrée.

"Yes, I mean to make you one of my maids of honour. You are noble, are you not?" she added, again addressing the baron.

"Oh, madame!" cried the baron, with delight, for all his dreams seemed realised by what he heard; "although poor, our descent is unblemished. Yet so high an honour —"

"It is only due to you. Your son will defend the king, as you have done; your daughter will serve the dauphiness.

The one you will inspire with every loyal sentiment, the
other with every virtuous one.   Shall I not be faithfully
served, monsieur?" she said, turning to Philip, who knelt
in gratitude at her feet, without words to express his
emotion.

"But—" murmured the baron, for his feelings did not
prevent him from reflecting.

"Yes, I understand," said the dauphiness; "you have
preparations to make; yet they cannot take long."

A sad smile passed over the lips of Andrée and Philip,
a bitter one over those of the baron; and Marie Antoinette
stopped, for she felt that she might unintentionally have
wounded their pride.

"At least," she resumed, "if I may judge by your desire
to please me.   Besides, I shall leave you one of my carriages; it will bring you after us.   I must call the Count
de Stainville to my aid."

The count approached.

"I shall leave one of my carriages for the Baron de
Taverney, whom I wish to accompany me to Paris with
his daughter.   Appoint some one to accompany their
carriage, and to cause it to be recognised as belonging to
my suite."

"This very moment, madame," answered the count.
"Come forward, Monsieur de Beausire!"

A young man, about five-and-twenty years of age, with
an easy and graceful carriage, and a lively and intelligent eye, advanced, hat in hand, from the ranks of the
escort of the dauphiness.

"Let one of the carriages remain behind," said the count,
"for the Baron de Taverney; you will accompany the
carriage yourself."

"And, monsieur," said the dauphiness, "join us again
as soon as possible.   I authorise you to have double relays
of horses, if necessary."

The baron and his children were profuse in their
acknowledgments.

"This sudden departure will not put you to much inconvenience, I hope, monsieur," said the dauphiness.

"We are too happy to obey madame's orders," replied the baron.

"Adieu! adieu!" said she, with a smile. "Gentlemen, conduct me to my carriage! Chevalier de Taverney, to horse!"

Philip kissed his father's hand, embraced his sister, and leaped lightly into his saddle.

The glittering train swept on, and in a quarter of an hour had disappeared like an evening vapour; there remained no human being in the avenue of Taverney but a young man, who, sitting on one of the low pillars of the gate, pale and sorrowful, followed with a longing eye the last cloud of dust which was raised by the horses' feet, and which served to show the road they had taken. The young man was Gilbert.

Meantime, the salon of Taverney presented a singular scene. Andrée, with clasped hands, reflected on the unexpected and extraordinary event which had so suddenly interrupted the course of her calm life, and she believed herself in a dream. The baron was pulling some hairs, which were rather too long, out of his grey eyebrows, and settling the bosom of his shirt. Nicole, leaning against the door, looked at her master and mistress, and La Brie, with his arms hanging down and his mouth open, looked at Nicole.

The baron was the first to rouse himself from his reverie.

"Scoundrel!" cried he to La Brie, "are you standing there like a statue, and that gentleman, one of the king's body-guard, waiting without?"

La Brie made a bound towards the door, got one leg hooked in the other, staggered to his feet, and disappeared. In a short time he returned.

"What is the gentleman doing?" asked the baron.

"Making his horse eat the pimpernels."

"Leave him alone, then. And the carriage?"

"It is in the avenue."

"The horses harnessed?"

"Yes, monsieur; four horses, — such beautiful animals! They are eating the pomegranates."

"The king's horses have a right to eat whatever they like. By the by, the sorcerer?"

"He is gone, monsieur."

"And has left all the plate on the table! It is not possible. He will return, or will send some one for it."

"I don't think he will, monsieur. Gilbert saw him set out with his wagon."

"Gilbert saw him set out with his wagon!" the baron repeated, in a thoughtful tone.

"Yes, monsieur."

"That wretch, Gilbert, sees everything. Go and pack my trunk."

"It is packed, monsieur."

"What! — it is packed?"

"Yes; as soon as I heard what her Royal Highness the dauphiness said, I went into your room, and packed your clothes and linen."

"Who told you to do so, you officious rascal?"

"*Dame*, monsieur! I thought I was only anticipating your orders."

"Fool! Go, then, and help my daughter."

"Thank you, father; but I have Nicole."

The baron began to reflect again.

"But, zounds, scoundrel! it is impossible."

"What is impossible, monsieur?"

"What you have not thought of, for you think of nothing."

"But what is it, monsieur?"

"That madame would go without leaving something with Monsieur de Beausire, or the sorcerer without leaving a message with Gilbert."

At this moment a low whistle was heard from the courtyard.

"What is that?"

"It is a call for me, monsieur," replied La Brie.

"And who calls, pray?"

"The gentleman, monsieur."

"The gentleman left by the dauphiness?"

"Yes, monsieur. And here is Gilbert coming as if he had something to say to you."

"Go, then, stupid animal!"

La Brie obeyed with his usual alacrity.

"Father," said Andrée, approaching him, "I know what troubles you. Recollect, I have thirty louis-d'or, and that beautiful watch set with diamonds, which Queen Marie Leczinska gave my mother."

"Yes, my dear, yes!" replied the baron; "but keep them, keep them. You must have a handsome dress for your presentation. I may discover some means — Hush! here is La Brie."

"Monsieur," cried La Brie, as he came in, holding in one hand a letter, and in the other some money, "see what the dauphiness left for me, — ten louis-d'or, monsieur! ten louis-d'or!"

"And that letter, rascal?"

"Oh, the letter is for you, monsieur, from the sorcerer."

"From the sorcerer? Who gave it you?"

"Gilbert, monsieur."

"I told you so, stupid animal! Give it me! give it me!"

He snatched the letter, tore it open, and read these words: —

MONSIEUR, — Since a hand so august has touched the plate I left with you, it belongs to you; keep it as a relic, and remember sometimes your grateful guest,

JOSEPH BALSAMO.

"La Brie!" cried the baron, after a moment's reflection, "is there not a good goldsmith at Bar-le-Duc?"

"Oh, yes, monsieur,— the one who soldered Mademoiselle Andrée's silver brooch."

"Very well.   Andrée, lay aside the goblet out of which her Royal Highness drank, and let the rest of the service be put up in the carriage with us.   And you, beast that you are, help the gentleman outside to a glass of what remains of our good wine."

"One bottle, monsieur," said La Brie, with deep melancholy.

"That is enough."

"Now, Andrée," said the baron, taking both his daughter's hands, "courage, my child.   We are going to court; there are plenty of titles to be given away there,— rich abbeys, regiments without colonels, pensions going to waste.   It is a fine country, the court.   The sun shines brightly there; put yourself always in its rays, my child, for you are worthy to be seen.   Go, my love, go!"

Andrée went out, followed by Nicole.

"Hallo! La Brie, you monster," cried the baron, "attend to the gentleman, I tell you!"

"Yes, monsieur," answered La Brie from a distant part of the cellar.

"I," continued the baron, going towards his room, "must go and arrange my papers; we must be out of this hole in an hour.   Do you hear, Andrée?   And we are leaving it in good style, too.   What a capital fellow that sorcerer is!   I am becoming as superstitious as the devil.   But make haste, La Brie, you wretch!"

"I was obliged to go feeling about, monsieur, in the cellar; there is not a candle in the house."

"It was time to leave it, it appears," said the baron.

CHPATER XVII.

NICOLE'S TWENTY-FIVE LOUIS-D'OR.

In the mean time Andrée made active preparations for her departure, and Nicole assisted her with an ardour which quickly dissipated the little cloud that had arisen between them in the morning.

"She is a good girl," said Andrée to herself, "devoted and grateful; she has faults, but what human creature has not? Let me forget them."

Nicole was not a girl who was slow to observe the expression of her mistress's face. "Fool that I was!" said she to herself; "I was nearly quarrelling with my young lady, and all about that young good-for-nothing, Gilbert; and she going to Paris, and will take me with her. One is sure of making one's fortune in Paris."

Andrée was the first to speak.

"Put my lace in a bandbox," said she.

"What bandbox, mademoiselle?"

"Really, I don't know. Have we one at all?"

"Oh, yes, — the one you gave me; it is in my room."

And Nicole ran to bring it with an obliging air, which disposed Andrée still more in her favour.

"But this bandbox is your own," said Andrée, when she reappeared with the article in her hand, "and you may want it yourself, my poor Nicole."

"Oh, you have more need of it, mademoiselle; and besides, it ought to be yours, — you lent it me."

"When people get married and set up housekeeping, they require many little things; so just now you have most need of the box. Keep it to put your bridal finery in."

"Oh, mademoiselle," said Nicole, gaily, shaking her head, "my finery will not take up much room."

"But if you marry, Nicole, I should wish you to be happy, and rich."

"Rich?"

"Yes, rich according to your rank."

"Then you have found some fermier-general for me, mademoiselle?"

"No; but I have found a dowry."

"Indeed, mademoiselle?"

"You know what is in my purse?"

"Yes, madame; twenty-five shining louis-d'or."

"They are yours, Nicole."

"Twenty-five louis-d'or!" cried Nicole, with rapture; "it is indeed a fortune!"

"My poor girl! I am glad you think so."

"And you really give them to me, madame?"

"I wish I could give you more."

Nicole felt surprised — moved; the tears came to her eyes; she seized her young lady's hand and kissed it.

"Do you think your husband will be pleased?"

"Oh, well pleased!" said Nicole. "At least, I hope so."

She reflected that Gilbert had doubtless refused her hand through fear of poverty, and that now, when she was rich, matters would turn out differently. Then she determined immediately to offer him a share of her young lady's generous gift, and to attach him to her by gratitude. Such was Nicole's generous plan. Andrée looked at her as she reflected. "Poor girl!" sighed she; "may she be happy in her simple life!"

Nicole heard the words and started from her reverie; they opened to her fancy a whole Eldorado of silks, diamonds, lace, and love, — things of which Andrée had not thought. But Nicole turned away her eyes from the gold

and purple cloud brightening her horizon, and resisted the
temptation. "After all, madame," said she, " I shall be
happy here, in a humble way."

"Reflect seriously on what you are going to do."

"Yes, mademoiselle, I shall reflect on it."

"That is right.   Make yourself happy in the way you
propose, if you can; but do not be foolish."

" You are very kind, mademoiselle.   And let me say
now, that I was very foolish this morning; but I hope
mademoiselle will forgive me.   When one is in love — "

"Then you are really in love with Gilbert?"

"Yes, mademoiselle; I — I loved him," said Nicole.

"Is it possible?" said Andrée, smiling.   "What can you
see to admire in the young man?   The first time I meet
him I must take a look at this Monsieur Gilbert, who steals
young girls' hearts."

"Is he not going with us to Paris, mademoiselle?" inquired Nicole, who wished to be fully informed on every
point before taking the step she meditated.

"Of what use would he be there?   He is not a domestic,
and could not take charge of a house in Paris.   Idle people
at Taverney live like the birds; however poor the soil, it
feeds them.   But in Paris an idle person would cost too
much; we could not support him."

"But if I marry him?" stammered Nicole.

"Well, if you marry him, you shall live here with him
at Taverney; you shall take care of this house, which my
mother was so fond of."

Andrée pronounced these words in so firm a voice that
Nicole could no longer doubt.   Yet she hesitated before
speaking again.   Andrée, seeing her hesitation, thought
that her mind was wandering from the pleasures of a
Parisian life to those of the quiet country, and that she
knew not how to decide.   So she went on gently: " Nicole,
the decision which you are now to make will affect all your
future life; be not hasty.   I shall give you one hour; it
is little, but you are prompt, and I think it will be suffi-

cient to enable you to choose between continuing to serve
me or having a husband, — between me and Gilbert."

"An hour! Oh, yes, mademoiselle, I can decide in an
hour."

"Collect all my clothes, and my mother's. I would not
leave behind those relics so dear to me. Then go, and
return in an hour fully decided; but whatever your determination be, here are your twenty-five louis-d'or. If you
marry, they shall be your dowry; if you continue in my
service, your wages for two years."

Nicole took the purse from Andrée's hands and kissed
it. Then she completed her task, — not a great one, certainly, — hurried downstairs, and Andrée saw her cross
the courtyard and enter the avenue. Not finding Gilbert
there, she flew to a window on the ground-floor, which was
that of his room, and tapped at it. He was bustling about
with his back to the window; but hearing her drumming,
he turned, and like a thief caught in the fact, he quickly
abandoned his occupation.

"Oh, is it you, Nicole?" said he.

"Yes, it is!" she replied, smiling, but with something
very decided in her tone.

"You are welcome," said he, coming forward and opening the window.

Nicole felt that there was kindness in his reception of
her, and held out her hand. He took it and pressed it.
"This is a good beginning," thought she; "farewell my
journey to Paris!" and to Nicole's praise, it must be said,
she did not sigh at this thought.

"You know," said the young girl, leaning her elbows
on the window, "you know, Gilbert, that the family are
leaving Taverney and going to Paris?"

"Yes, I know."

"Well, I am to go to Paris too."

"I did not know that; but I congratulate you if you are
pleased at going."

"How you say that!"

"I say it plainly, I think,— if you are pleased at going."

"My being pleased depends —"

"Why do you stop? depends — ?"

"My being pleased or not depends on you."

"I don't understand you," said Gilbert, seating himself on the window so that his knees touched Nicole's arm, and they could thus converse unseen and unheard.

Nicole looked at him tenderly; he shook his head, insinuating that he understood her look no more than her words.

"Well," said she, "since all must be told, listen to what I am going to say."

"I hear you," replied Gilbert, coldly.

"In plain words, my young lady offers to take me to Paris with her —"

"Very well; go on!"

"Unless —"

"Unless what?"

"Unless I get married here."

"Then you still think of getting married?" he answered, quite unmoved.

"Yes; more particularly since I have become rich."

"Oh, you have become rich?" he asked, so phlegmatically that Nicole knew not what to think.

"Very rich, Gilbert."

"Indeed?"

"Yes, indeed!"

"And how did that miracle come about?"

"Mademoiselle has given me a marriage portion."

"You are very fortunate. I congratulate you, Nicole."

"Look!" said she, pouring out of the purse into her hand the twenty-five louis-d'or, and watching Gilbert's eyes to discover some ray of pleasure or covetousness in them.

Gilbert moved not a muscle. "On my word, it is a nice little sum!" said he.

"And that is not all," continued Nicole. "The baron

will be rich once more; the old castle will be rebuilt, and
the care of it given — ”

“To the fortunate husband of Nicole,” said Gilbert,
with an irony not so well concealed but that it grated on
Nicole’s fine ear; yet she restrained her anger.

“And Nicole’s husband — do you not know him?”

“I? No.”

“Have you, then, grown stupid, or do I no longer speak
French?” cried the young girl, who began to show symptoms of impatience.

“I understand you perfectly,” replied Gilbert; “you
offer to make me your husband, do you not, Mademoiselle
Legay?”

“Yes, Monsieur Gilbert.”

“And it is since you have become rich that you have
thought of this,” returned Gilbert, hastily. “I am truly
grateful to you indeed, — I am indeed!”

“Well,” said Nicole, frankly, and holding out her hand,
“take it!”

“I?”

“You accept it, do you not?”

“No; I refuse it!”

Nicole sprang up from her leaning position. “Gilbert,”
said she, “you have a bad heart; and, trust me, what you
now do will not bring you happiness. If I felt any warmer
sentiment in making the offer I have just done, than a
sense of duty and honour, trust me, I should now be miserable indeed; but, having become rich, I did not wish it to
be said that Nicole would look down on her old friend
Gilbert. However, all is now over between us.”

Gilbert made a gesture of indifference.

“What I think of your conduct in the matter, you must
be well aware. I, whose character you know to be as free
and independent as your own, had decided to bury myself
here, from an old prepossession for you, when I had it in
my power to go to Paris, which may be for me a scene of
triumph. I would have borne to see before me, every day

of the year, for a whole lifetime, that cold and impenetrable face, the mask of so many wicked thoughts. You have not realized that there was any sacrifice in this; so much the worse for you, Gilbert. I do not say that you will regret me; but remember, you may yet feel remorse for the contempt and scorn you have shown me. Guided by you, I should have been a virtuous, happy, and contented woman; now, I am abandoned on the ocean of life, without a keeping or a guiding hand. Gilbert, if I fall, God will not hold you innocent of my fall. Farewell!"

And the proud young girl turned away, without anger or impatience, but having shown, as all impassioned natures do in the time of trial, true generosity of soul.

Gilbert shut his window quietly and returned to the mysterious occupation in which she had interrupted him.

CHAPTER XVIII.

FAREWELL TO TAVERNEY.

NICOLE, before entering her mistress's apartment, stopped on the staircase to subdue some gathering emotions of resentment rising in her bosom. The baron encountered her as she stood motionless, thoughtful, her brows contracted and leaning on her hand, and, seeing her so pretty, he kissed her, as the Duke de Richelieu would have done at thirty years of age. Roused from her reverie by this piece of gallantry, Nicole hurried up to Andrée's room, and found her just closing her trunk.

"Well," said Mademoiselle de Taverney, "have you decided?"

"Yes, mademoiselle," replied Nicole, very decidedly.

"You will marry?"

"No, mademoiselle."

"What! after all your first love?"

"My love will never do for me what the kindness of mademoiselle has done for me. I belong to you, mademoiselle, and wish always to belong to you. I know the mistress I have; I do not know the master I might have."

Andrée was touched with this unlooked-for exhibition of affectionate feeling in the giddy Nicole, and was far from suspecting that this choice had been a forced one. She smiled, pleased to find one human being better than she had expected.

"You do well, Nicole," she replied, " to attach yourself to me. I shall not forget this trust to me; and if any good fortune befall me, you shall share it."

"Oh, mademoiselle, I have quite decided I will go with you!"

"Without regret?"

"Blindly."

"I do not like that answer, Nicole. I should not wish you at some future day to reproach yourself with having blindly trusted me and followed me."

"I shall never have to reproach any one but myself, mademoiselle."

"Then you have had an explanation with your lover? I saw you talking with him."

Nicole blushed, then bit her lip. She forgot that Andrée's window was opposite that at which she had spoken to Gilbert.

"It is true, mademoiselle," replied Nicole.

"And you told him all?"

Nicole thought Andrée had some particular reason for this question, and, all her former suspicions returning, she answered, "I told him I would have nothing more to do with him."

It was plain that the two women would never understand each other, — the one pure as the diamond, the other without any fixed principle of conduct, though having occasional impulses of goodness.

In the mean time, the baron had completed all his arrangements. An old sword, which he had worn at Fontenoy, some parchments establishing his right to travel in his Majesty's carriages, and a litter of old papers, formed the most bulky part of his baggage. La Brie followed, tottering under the weight of an almost empty trunk. In the avenue they found the gentleman of the king's body-guard, who, whilst waiting, had drained to the last drop his bottle of wine. The gallant had remarked the fine waist and pretty ankle of Nicole, who was going back and forward with messages, and he had kept peeping about in the hope of exchanging a word with her. He was roused, however, to more active occupation by the baron's request that he would order the carriage to the door; he started, bowed, and in a sonorous voice summoned the coachman.

The carriage drew up. La Brie put the trunk on behind with an indescribable mixture of joy and pride in his looks. "I am really," murmured he, carried away by his enthusiasm, and thinking he was alone, "going to get into the king's carriage!"

"Behind it, behind it, my worthy friend!" replied Beausire, with a patronising smile.

"What, monsieur, are you going to take La Brie with you?" said Andrée. "Who will take care of Taverney?"

"Why, *pardieu!* the good-for-nothing philosopher."

"Gilbert?"

"Yes; has he not a gun?"

"But how will he live?"

"By his gun, to be sure! Don't be uneasy; he will have excellent fare. Blackbirds and thrushes are not scarce at Taverney."

Andrée looked at Nicole; the latter began to laugh. "And is that all the compassion you show for him, ungrateful girl?"

"Oh, mademoiselle," replied Nicole, "he is very clever with his gun; he will not die of hunger!"

"But, monsieur," continued Andrée, "we must leave him two or three louis-d'or."

"To spoil him? Very fine indeed! He is vicious enough as he is!"

"He must have something to live on," persisted Andrée.

"The neighbours will help him, if he is in want."

"Don't be uneasy, mademoiselle," said Nicole; "he will have no cause to ask their assistance."

"At all events," replied Andrée, "leave him two or three crowns."

"He would not accept them."

"He would not accept them? Then he is proud, this Monsieur Gilbert of yours."

"Oh, mademoiselle, he is not mine, Heaven be praised!"

"Come, come!" said the baron, "let Gilbert go to the devil! The carriage is waiting; get in, my love."

Andrée did not reply. She cast a farewell look on the old château, and then got into the heavy and ponderous carriage. The baron seated himself beside her. La Brie, still wearing his splendid livery, and Nicole, who seemed never to have known such a person as Gilbert, mounted on the box. The coachman rode one of the horses as postilion.

"But where will the officer ride?" exclaimed the baron.

"On my horse, monsieur, on my horse," replied Beausire, still eying Nicole, who coloured with delight at having so soon replaced a rude peasant admirer by an elegant gentleman.

The carriage, drawn by four strong horses, started into rapid motion. The trees of the avenue glided away on each side, and disappeared one by one, sadly bending before the east wind, as if to bid farewell to their owners who abandoned them. The carriage reached the gate. Gilbert stood there, upright, immovable, his hat in his hand. He did not seem to see Andrée, yet he watched her least movement; her eyes were fixed on the dear home she was leaving, so as to keep it in view as long as possible.

"Stop an instant!" cried the baron to the postilion.

The carriage stopped.

"So, Monsieur Good-for-nothing, you are going to be happy, — quite alone, like a real philosopher! Nothing to do, nobody to scold you. Don't let the house take fire; and, hark ye, take care of Mahon!"

Gilbert bowed, but did not reply. He felt as if Nicole's looks were a weight too great to be borne; he feared to meet her triumphant ironical smile, as he would the touch of red-hot iron.

"Go on, postilion!" cried the baron.

Nicole did not smile; it even required more than her habitual power over herself to prevent her expressing aloud her pity for the poor young man thus heartlessly abandoned. She was obliged to keep her eye on Monsieur de Beausire, who looked so well on his prancing horse.

Now, as Nicole kept her eyes fixed on Monsieur de Beausire she did not see that Gilbert was gazing, his soul in his eyes, on Andrée. Andrée saw nothing but the house in which she was born, — in which her mother died. The carriage disappeared. Gilbert, a moment before of so little importance in the eyes of the travellers, was now nothing to them.

The baron, Andrée, Nicole, and La Brie having passed through the gates of the avenue, entered a new world. Each had a peculiar subject for reflection. The baron thought that at Bar-le-Duc he could easily raise five or six thousand crowns on Balsamo's plate. Andrée repeated a prayer her mother had taught her, to keep away the demon of pride and ambition. Nicole covered her neck more closely with her handkerchief, to the great chagrin of Monsieur de Beausire. La Brie, with his hand in his pocket, counted over the ten louis-d'or of the dauphiness, and the two of Balsamo. Monsieur de Beausire galloped at the side of the carriage.

Gilbert closed the gates of Taverney, whose hinges, as usual, creaked with a melancholy sound. Then he ran to his little room, pulled out his oaken chest of drawers, behind which he found a bundle ready tied up in a napkin, and slung it on his stick. After this, pushing his hands into his hay-stuffed mattress, he drew out something wrapped in a bit of paper; it was a shining crown-piece, — his savings for three or four years. He opened the paper, looked at his crown to assure himself that it had not been changed, and then put it in his pocket, still wrapped in its paper.

Mahon, on seeing Gilbert, began to howl loudly, making furious leaps the whole length of his chain. Seeing one by one his friends leave him, his fine instinct told him that Gilbert was also about to abandon him, and he howled louder and louder.

"Hush!" cried Gilbert, "hush, Mahon!"

Then smiling bitterly at the parallel which occurred

to his mind, he muttered, " Have they not abandoned me like a dog? Why should not I abandon thee like a man?" But, after a minute's reflection, he added, " They abandoned me free, at least, — free to seek for food. Well, then, Mahon, I will do for thee what they did for me, neither more nor less;" and going to the hook to which the dog's chain was fastened, he slipped it off. " You are free!" said he; "provide for yourself as you like!"

The dog bounded towards the house; but, finding the doors all closed, he sprang towards the ruins and disappeared.

" And now," said Gilbert, " we shall see which has most instinct, the dog or the man!"

So saying, he went out by the small gate, closed it, double-locked it, and threw the key over the wall.

But nature speaks with the same voice in almost all hearts. Gilbert felt something like what Andrée experienced in leaving Taverney; only, with her sentiments mingled regret for the quiet past; with his, hopes for a more stirring future.

"Farewell!" said he, turning to look for the last time at the château, whose pointed roof appeared peeping over the sycamores and laburnums. " Farewell, abode in which I have suffered so much, where every one hated me and threw me food grudgingly, as if I had been a hungry hound. Be cursed! My heart bounds with joy at my freedom, for thy walls enclose me no more! Farewell, prison! hell! den of tyrants! Farewell forever!"

And after this imprecation Gilbert sprang forward on the road which the carriage had taken, fancying that he yet heard the roll of its distant wheels.

CHAPTER XIX.

GILBERT'S CROWN-PIECE.

AFTER half an hour's headlong race, Gilbert uttered a wild shriek of joy; he saw the carriage about a quarter of a league before him, slowly ascending a hill. He felt his heart dilate with pride as he thought that he, with only youth, strength, spirit, was about to do all that wealth, power, and rank could accomplish. Then, indeed, might the baron have called Gilbert a philosopher, had he seen him, his stick on his shoulder, his small bundle slung on it, walking on with rapid strides, leaping down every slope which could shorten his path, and stopping at every ascent, chafing with impatience, as if saying to the horses, "You do not go fast enough for me; see, I am obliged to wait for you."

Philosopher? Yes! and he deserved the name, if it be philosophy to despise all that contributes to ease and to enjoyment. It was an interesting spectacle, one worthy of the Creator of energetic and intelligent creatures, to see the young man bounding forward on his way, all dusty and panting, for an hour or more, until he had almost overtaken the carriage, and then resting with delight when the horses were compelled to pause for breath. Gilbert that day must have inspired every one with admiration who could have followed him in spirit as we do; and who knows but that even the proud Andrée might have been moved could she have seen him, and that her contempt for his indolence would have changed to admiration of his energy?

The day passed on in this manner. The baron stopped
an hour at Bar-le-Duc, which gave Gilbert time to get
in advance of him. He had heard the order to stop at
the goldsmith's; so, having passed the town, by a detour,
without entering it, he hid in a thicket until he saw
the carriage coming, and when it had passed, followed
it as before. Towards evening it came up with the train
of the dauphiness, at the little village of Brillon, the
inhabitants of which were crowded on a neighbouring hill,
and made the air resound with their shouts of welcome.
Gilbert had not eaten a morsel during the entire day,
except a morsel of bread which he had brought with him
from Taverney; but, in return, he had drunk plentifully
from a rivulet which crossed the road, and the water
of which was so fresh and limpid that Andrée had requested that the carriage might stop, and alighted herself
to fill the chased cup, the only article of Balsamo's service which the baron could be persuaded to retain. Gilbert
saw all this, hidden by some trees on the road-side. Then,
when the carriage had passed on, he emerged from his
hiding-place, and advancing to the stream, at the same
spot where Mademoiselle Taverney had stood he lifted
the water in his hand, and drank from the same source.

Evening came on, shrouding the landscape in her dusty
mantle, until at last he saw nothing but the light from
the large lanterns which were fastened on each side of
the carriage; this pale gleam, ever hurrying onward in the
distance, looked like a phantom impelled forward by some
strange destiny. Then night came on. They had travelled
twelve leagues; they were at Combles. The equipages
stopped; Gilbert was sure that it was for the night, that
he should have time to stop for a couple of hours in a barn;
and how vigorously should he afterwards pursue his way!
He approached to listen for Andrée's voice; the carriage
still continued stationary. He glided into a deep doorway;
he saw Andrée by the glare of the torch-light, and heard
her asking what hour it was. A voice replied, "Eleven

o'clock." At that moment Gilbert no longer felt fatigue, and would have rejected with scorn an offer of a seat in a vehicle. Versailles already appeared in view, — Versailles, all gilded, shining, the city of nobles and kings! And beyond appeared Paris, grim, immense, — the city of the people!

Two things roused him from his ecstasy, — the noise of the carriages setting out again, and the complaints of his stomach, which cried, "Hunger!" very distinctly. On went the carriages, Gilbert following, his hunger unappeased. At midnight they stopped at Saint Dizier. For the night? No! only to change horses; whilst, in the mean time, the illustrious travellers took a little refreshment by torch-light.

Gilbert had need of all his courage, and he sprang to his feet from the bank where he had seated himself, as he heard them depart, with an energy of determination which made him forget that, ten minutes before, his wearied legs had bent under him in spite of all his efforts.

"Well," cried he, "go, go! I shall stop also for re-freshment at Saint Dizier; I shall buy some bread and a slice of bacon; I shall drink a glass of wine, and for five sous I shall be refreshed as well as *the masters.*"

Gilbert entered the town. The train having passed, the good folks were closing their doors and shutters; but our philosopher saw a good-looking inn not yet shut up, where the large dishes of fowls and other things showed that the attendants of the dauphiness had only had time to levy a very slight contribution. He entered the kitchen resolutely; the hostess was there, counting what her gains had been.

"Excuse me, madame; but can I have some bread and ham?" said Gilbert.

"We have no ham, but you can have fowl."

"No, thank you; I ask for ham because I wish for ham, — I don't like fowl."

"That is a pity, my little fellow, for we have only fowl; but it shall not be dearer," she added, smiling, "than ham.

Take half a one, or, indeed, take a whole one for tenpence, and that will be provision for you for to-morrow. We thought Madame la Dauphine would have stayed all night, and that we should have sold all these things to the attendants ; but, as she only just passed through, they will be wasted."

One would have thought that, the offer being so good, and the hostess so kind, Gilbert would have gladly embraced it; but that would be to have misunderstood his character entirely.

"No, thank you," replied he, "I shall satisfy myself in a more humble manner ; I am neither a prince nor a footman."

"Well, then," said the good woman, "I will give you the fowl, my little Artaban."

"I am not a beggar either," replied he, in a mortified tone, "I buy what I wish, and pay for it."

And he majestically plunged his hand into his breeches-pocket; it went down to the elbow. In vain he fumbled in his vast pocket, turning paler and paler. The paper in which the crown had been, he found; but the crown was gone! Tossed about by his rapid movements, it had worn the paper, then the thin lining of his pocket, and had slipped out at his knee; for he had unfastened his garters to give freer play to his limbs.

His paleness and trembling touched the good woman. Many in her place would have rejoiced at his pride being brought down; but she felt for him, seeing suffering so powerfully expressed in the changes of his countenance.

"Come, my poor boy!" said she, "you shall sup and sleep here; then, to-morrow, if you must go on, you shall do so."

"Oh, yes, yes!" exclaimed Gilbert, "I must go on, — not to-morrow, but now, now!"

And snatching up his bundle without waiting to hear more, he darted out of the house, to hide his shame and grief in the darkness. He rushed on, alone, truly alone in

the world; for no man is more alone than he who has just
parted with his last crown, — more particularly if it be the
only one he ever possessed.

To turn back to look for his crown would have been to
begin a hopeless task; besides, it would make it impossible for him ever to come up with the carriages. He resolved to continue his way. After he had gone about a
league, hunger, which his mental suffering had made him
forget for a time, awoke more keen than ever. Weariness
also seized on every limb, on every sinew; yet, by incredible efforts, he had once more come in sight of the
carriages. But fate, it would seem had decided against
him. They stopped only to change horses, and so quickly
that he had not five minutes to rest himself.

Again he set out. The day began to dawn; the sun
appeared above a broad circle of dark clouds, foretelling one
of those burning days of May which sometimes precede
the heats of summer. How could Gilbert bear the noon of
that day? In his pride he thought that horses, men,
the destinies, had united against him, him alone! Like
Ajax, he shook his clenched fist at the heavens; and if he
did not say, like him, "I shall escape in spite of the gods!"
it was because he knew by heart "The Social Contract,"
better than the Odyssey. At last, however, as Gilbert had
dreaded, the moment arrived when he found the utter
impossibility of proceeding much farther. By a last and
almost despairing effort, he summoned up all his remaining
force, and once more overtook the carriages, of which he had
previously lost sight, and which, under the influence of his
heated and feverish imagination, he fancied were surrounded
with a strange, fantastic halo. The noise of the wheels
sounded like thunder in his ears, and almost maddened his
brain; he staggered on, his blackened lips wide apart,
his eyes fixed and staring, his long hair clinging to his
forehead bathed in perspiration; and his movements
seeming rather the effect of some clever piece of mechanism
than those of a thinking being. Since the evening before

he had travelled upwards of twenty leagues, and his weary and fainting limbs now refused to carry him farther. A mist overspread his eyes, strange noises sounded in his ears, the earth seemed to reel under him ; he endeavoured to utter a cry, and staggered forward, beating the air wildly with his arms. At last his voice returned to utter hoarse cries of rage against his conquerors. Then, tearing his hair with both hands, he reeled forward, and fell heavily to the ground, — with the consolation of having, like a hero of antiquity, fought the battle to the last !

"Hallo, there! Hallo, madman!" cried a hoarse voice, just as he fell, accompanying his shouts with the loud cracking of a whip.

Gilbert heard him not; he had fainted.

"Hallo! I say. Hallo! *Morbleu!* the fellow will be smashed!" And this time his words were accompanied by a vigorous lash, which reached Gilbert's waist, and cut into the flesh.

But Gilbert felt nothing; he remained immovable under the feet of the horses of a carriage, which was issuing into the highroad from a by-way between Thiéblemont and Vauclère.

A shrill cry was heard from the carriage, which the horses carried along like a whirlwind. The postilion made an almost superhuman effort, but could not prevent one of the horses, which was placed as a leader, from leaping over Gilbert; the other two, however, he succeeded in pulling up. A lady stretched her body half out of the carriage. "Heavens!" cried she, "you have killed the poor boy!"

"Why, faith, madame," replied the postilion, endeavouring to discover the body amidst the cloud of dust which the horses' feet had raised, "I am almost afraid we have."

"Poor creature! poor boy! Do not move a step farther!" And opening the door of the carriage herself, she sprang out.

The postilion had already alighted, and dragging Gil-

bert's body from between the wheels, he expected to find
it bruised and bloody; the lady assisted him with all her
force.

"What an escape!" he cried; "not a scratch,—not a
kick!"

"But he has fainted," said the lady.

"Only from fear. Let us place him against the bank;
and, since madame is in haste, let us go on."

"Impossible. I would not leave any creature in such a
state."

"Pooh! it's nothing, madame; he will soon recover."

"No, no! Poor fellow! he is some runaway lad from
college, and has undertaken a journey beyond his strength.
See how pale he is; he might die. No, I will not leave
him. Lift him into the carriage, on the front seat."

The postilion obeyed; the lady got in; Gilbert was laid
lengthwise on a good cushion, his head supported by the
well-stuffed side of the carriage.

"And now," cried the lady, "we have lost ten minutes;
a crown if you make up for them."

The postilion cracked his whip above his head; the
horses knew what this threatened, and set off at a gallop.

CHAPTER XX.

GILBERT RECOVERS THE LOSS OF HIS CROWN.

WHEN Gilbert returned to consciousness, he was in no small degree surprised to find himself placed as he was, with a young lady watching him anxiously.

This young lady was about five-and-twenty, with large grey eyes, a nose slightly *retroussé*, cheeks embrowned by a Southern sun, and a delicately formed little mouth, which added to the naturally cheerful and laughing expression of her face something of circumspection and *finesse*. Her neck and arms, which were beautifully formed, were displayed to advantage by a closely-fitting bodice of violet-coloured velvet with golden buttons, while the skirt of her dress of grey silk was so enormously wide as to fill almost the entire carriage.

Gilbert continued for some time to gaze on this face, which looked on his smilingly and with much interest, and he could scarcely persuade himself that he was not in a dream.

"Well, my poor fellow," said the lady, "are you not better now?"

"Where am I?" asked he, languidly.

"You are in safety now, my little fellow," replied the lady, who spoke with a strong Southern accent; "but just now you were in great danger of being crushed under the wheels of my carriage. What could have happened to you, to make you fall in that manner just in the middle of the highway?"

"I was overcome by weakness, madame, from having walked too much."

"Then you have been some time on the road?"

"Since yesterday, at four in the afternoon."

"And how far have you travelled?"

"I think about eighteen leagues."

"What! in fourteen hours?"

"Oh, I ran all the way!"

"Where are you going, then?"

"To Versailles."

"And you came from —"

"From Taverney."

"Taverney! Where is that?"

"It is a château, situated between Pierrefitte and Bar-le-Duc."

"But you have scarcely had time to eat on the way."

"I not only had not time, but I had not the means."

"How so?"

"I lost my money on the way."

"So that since yesterday you have eaten nothing?"

"Only a few bits of bread, which I brought with me."

"Poor fellow! but why did you not beg something?"

"Because I am proud, madame," said he, smiling scornfully.

"Proud! It is all very fine to be proud; but when one is dying of hunger —"

"Better death than dishonour."

The lady looked at the sententious speaker with something like admiration.

"But who are you, my friend," said she, "who speak in this style?"

"I am an orphan."

"What is your name?"

"Gilbert."

"Gilbert what?"

"Gilbert nothing."

"Ah!" said the lady, still more surprised.

Gilbert felt that he had produced an effect, and felt as if he were another Rousseau.

"You are very young to wander about in this way," continued the lady.

"I was left, deserted and alone, in an old château, which the family had abandoned. I did as they had done, — I abandoned it in my turn."

"Without any object in view?"

"The world is wide; there is room for all."

"And you lost your purse? Was it well filled?"

"There was only one crown in it," said he, divided between the shame of confessing his poverty and the fear of naming a large sum, which might have excited the suspicion that it had not been fairly obtained.

"One crown for such a journey! Why, it would scarcely have been sufficient to purchase bread for two days; and the distance! good heavens! from Bar-le-Duc to Paris is nearly sixty-five leagues!"

"I never counted the leagues, madame; I only said, 'I must get to Paris.'"

"And, thereupon, you set out, my poor simpleton?"

"Oh, I have good legs."

"Good as they are, they failed, you see."

"Oh! it was not my legs, it was hope which failed me."

"Why, indeed, you looked before you fell as if in great despair."

Gilbert smiled bitterly.

"What was passing in your mind? You struck your forehead with your clenched hand, and tore out your hair by handfuls."

"Indeed, madame?" asked Gilbert, rather embarrassed.

"Oh! I am certain of it; and it was that, I think, which prevented your hearing or seeing the carriage."

Gilbert's instinct told him that he might increase his consequence, and still more awaken the interest of the lady, by telling the whole truth.

"I was, indeed, in despair," said he.

"And about what?" said the lady.

"Because I could not keep up with a carriage which I was following."

"Indeed," said the young lady, smiling, "this is quite a romance. Is there love in the case?"

All Gilbert's resolution could not keep him from blushing.

"And what carriage was it, my little Roman?"

"A carriage in the train of the dauphiness."

"What do you tell me! Is the dauphiness before us?"

"She is, indeed."

"I thought her scarcely yet at Nancy. Are no honours paid her on the way, that she advances so rapidly?"

"Oh, yes, madame; but her Royal Highness seems to have some reason for being in haste."

"In haste? Who told you so?"

"I guessed it."

"On what grounds?"

"Why, she said at first she would stay two or three hours at Taverney, and she only stayed three-quarters of an hour."

"Do you know if she received any letters from Paris?"

"I saw a gentleman in a dress covered with embroidery, who had one in his hand as he entered."

"Did you hear his name mentioned?"

"No, madame, I merely know that he is the governor of Strasburg."

"What! the Count de Stainville, brother-in-law to the Duke de Choiseul? Horrible! Faster, postilion, faster!"

A vigorous lash was the reply, and Gilbert felt the speed of the carriage increase.

"But she must stop to breakfast," said the lady, as if speaking to herself, "and then we shall pass her. Postilion, what is the next town?"

"Vitry, madame."

"How far are we from it?"

"Three leagues."

"Where shall we change horses?"

"At Vauclère."

"Well, drive on, and if you see a train of carriages on the road before us, let me know."

Whilst the lady was exchanging these words with the postilion, Gilbert had again nearly fainted. When she once more turned towards him he was pale, and his eyes were closed.

"Poor child!" said she, "he is fainting again. It is my fault; I made him talk when he was dying of hunger, instead of giving him something to eat."

She took from the pocket of the carriage a richly carved flask, with a little silver goblet hanging round its neck by a chain, and poured out some of the contents for Gilbert. On this occasion he did not require to be asked twice.

"Now," said the lady, "eat a biscuit; in an hour or so you shall breakfast more solidly."

"Thank you, madame," said Gilbert, gladly taking the biscuit, as he had done the wine.

"As you have now recovered a little strength," said she, "tell me, if you are disposed to make a confidant of me, what induced you to follow a carriage in the train of the dauphiness?"

"Well, madame, you shall hear the truth. I was living with the Baron de Taverney when Madame la Dauphine came. She commanded him to follow her to Paris; he obeyed. I was an orphan, and consequently nobody thought of me; they left me there, without food and without money. So I resolved, since everybody was going to Versailles, with the assistance of good horses and fine coaches, I, with the assistance of only my legs, would go to Versailles, and as soon as the horses. But fate was against me. If I had not lost my money, I should have had something to eat last night; and if I had eaten last night, I should have overtaken them this morning."

"Very well. You showed courage, and I like that; but you forgot that at Versailles people cannot live on courage alone."

"I shall go to Paris."

"But in that respect Paris resembles Versailles exceedingly."

"If courage will not support me, labour will!"

"A good answer, my little fellow. But what sort of labour? Your hands do not seem those of a workman or porter."

"I shall study."

"I think you seem to know a great deal already."

"Yes, for I know that I know nothing!" replied Gilbert, remembering the aphorism of Socrates.

"And may I ask, my young friend, what branch of study you would choose?"

"I think, madame, that the best is that which teaches man to be most useful to his fellows; besides, man is so frail a being that he should learn the cause of his weakness, in order that he may know his strength. I should like to know, some day, why my stomach prevented my legs from carrying me any farther this morning; and if it was not that weakness of my stomach which summoned up the phantoms which distressed my brain."

"Really, you would make an excellent physician; and you speak already most learnedly on the science of medicine. In ten years you shall have me for a patient."

"I shall try to deserve that honour, madame."

They had now reached the place where they were to change horses. The young lady asked for information respecting the dauphiness, and found that she had passed through that place a quarter of an hour before; she intended to stop at Vitry, to change horses and to breakfast.

A fresh postilion took the place of the former one. The lady allowed him to leave the village at the usual speed; but when they had got a little beyond the last house, —

"Postilion," said she, "will you undertake to come up with the carriages of the dauphiness?"

"Certainly, madame."

"Before they reach Vitry?"

"*Diable!* they are going full trot."

"Yes; but if you were to go at a gallop?"

The postilion looked at her.

"Treble pay," said she.

"If you had said so at first," replied he, "we should have been a quarter of a league farther by this time."

"Well, here is a crown on account; make up for lost time."

The postilion's arm was stretched back, the lady's forward, and their hands met. The horses received a sharp lash, and the carriage started off like the wind.

During the change of horses Gilbert had alighted and washed his face and hands at a fountain, had smoothed down his hair, which was very thick, and had altogether improved his appearance very much.

"In truth," said the lady to herself, "he is handsome enough for a physician;" and she smiled.

Having finished her dialogue with the postilion, she turned once more to Gilbert, whose paradoxes and sententious humour amused her exceedingly. From time to time she interrupted herself in a burst of laughter which his philosophising caused her, to lean out of the carriage and look anxiously before her. They had gone about a league in this way, when she uttered a cry of joy, — she had caught a sight of the last wagons of the dauphiness's train as they were slowly ascending a steep hill, and now there appeared in advance of them about twenty carriages, from which many of the travellers had got out, and were walking beside them. Gilbert slipped out his head also, desirous to catch a glimpse of Mademoiselle de Taverney in the midst of the crowd of pygmies, and thought he discovered Nicole by her high cap.

"And now, madame," said the postilion, "what must we do?"

"We must get before them."

"Get before them! But you know we cannot pass the carriage of the dauphiness."

" Why not? "

"Because it is expressly forbidden. *Peste!* pass the king's horses ! I should be sent to the galleys."

"Now listen, my good fellow; manage it as you please, but I must positively get before those carriages."

"I thought you belonged to the train of Madame la Dauphine?" said Gilbert, inquiringly.

"It is very proper to wish for information," replied she, "but we should not ask indiscreet questions."

"I beg your pardon, madame," said he, reddening.

"Well, postilion, what are we to do?"

"Why, faith! this: keep behind till we reach Vitry, and then, if her Highness stops, obtain her permission to go on before her."

"Ay; but then it would be asked who I am; I should have to tell. No, no, that will not do; we must find out some other way."

"Madame," said Gilbert, " if I might give an opinion — "

"Yes, yes, my young friend; if you have any good advice, give it."

"Could we not take some by-road which would bring us round to Vitry, and so get before the dauphiness without having been wanting in respect to her?"

"Excellent! The boy is right!" cried the young lady. "Postilion, is there a by-road?"

"To go where?"

"Where you like, provided you leave the dauphiness behind."

"There is, in fact, a by-road leading round Vitry, and joining the high-road again at Lachaussée."

"That is it! that is the very thing!" cried the lady.

"But, madame, if I take that road, you must double the pay."

"Two louis-d'or for you if we get to Lachaussée before the dauphiness."

"Madame is not afraid, then, of her carriage being broken?"

"I care for nothing.   If it breaks, I shall proceed on horseback."

And turning to the right, they entered a cross-road full of deep ruts, bordered by a little river, which falls into the Marne between Lachaussée and Martigny.

The postilion kept his word: he did all that human power could do to break the carriage, but, at the same time, to arrive before the dauphiness.   A dozen times Gilbert was thrown into the lady's arms, and a dozen times she into his.   Intimacy springs up quickly from jolting on in the loneliness of a carriage; and after two hours' travelling on this by-road, it seemed to Gilbert as if he had known his companion ten years, and she, on her part, would have sworn she had known him since his birth.   About eleven o'clock they came again on the high-road between Vitry and Châlons.   A courier whom they met told them that the dauphiness was not only staying to breakfast at Vitry, but that she meant to take two hours' repose.   He added that he had been sent forward to desire those who attended to the horses to have them in readiness between three and four o'clock.   This news filled the lady with joy; she gave the postilion the two louis-d'or which she promised him, and, turning to Gilbert, "So now," said she, "we shall be able to dine at the next stopping-place."

But fate had decided that Gilbert should not dine there.

CHAPTER XXI.

IN WHICH A NEW PERSONAGE MAKES HIS APPEARANCE.

FROM the top of the hill which the lady's carriage was ascending, the village of Lachaussée might be seen; it was there she was to change horses and stop to dine. It was a lovely little village, with its thatched cottages scattered here and there at the caprice of the owners; some in the very middle of the road, some half hidden under the shade of a little grove which bordered the highway, and some following the course of the little river which we have mentioned, over which the inhabitants had placed temporary and rustic bridges to reach their dwellings.

At that moment, however, the most remarkable feature in the village was a man, who, looking down the brook, was standing right in the middle of the road, as if he had been ordered to keep watch there. Sometimes he looked up, sometimes down the road; then he turned a longing eye towards a beautiful grey horse with long mane and tail, which was fastened to the window-shutter of a cabin, which he shook in his impatient tossing of his head, — an impatience which was the more excusable as, from the fact of his being saddled, it might be presumed he was waiting for his master, who was inside.

From time to time the stranger ventured to approach the horse to pat his side, or pass his hand down his slender legs; and then, when he luckily escaped the kick which was always vouchsafed him at each attempt, he returned to his occupation of watching the road. Wearied at last by this fruitless watching, he knocked on the window-shutter.

"Hallo in there!" he shouted.

"Who is there?" replied a man's voice, and the shutter was opened.

"Monsieur," said the stranger, "if your horse is to be sold, the buyer is here at hand."

"You can see he has no wisp at his tail," answered the other, who appeared to be a countryman; and he shut the window.

This answer did not appear to satisfy the stranger, so he knocked again. He was a tall, stout man, with a ruddy complexion, a black beard, and large, sinewy hands peeping out from fine lace ruffles. He wore a hat edged with gold lace, and set on crosswise, like those officers of the provinces who try to look fierce in the eyes of the poor Parisians. He knocked a third time; but no answer. He got impatient.

"Do you know, my honest fellow," cried he, "you are not very polite; and if you don't open your shutter, I'll break it in!"

At this threat the shutter opened, and the same face as before appeared.

"But when you were told the horse is not for sale," replied the peasant, for the second time, "what the devil — is not that enough?"

"But when I tell you that I want a fast animal!"

"Well, if you want one, can you not go to the post-house?" there are sixty of the king's there; you surely can choose from among them. But leave a man who has only one, that one!"

"I tell you this is the very one I want!"

"A nice proposal, indeed! An Arabian —"

"That is the reason I want it."

"Very possibly; but it is not for sale."

"Whose is it?"

"You are very curious."

"And you mighty discreet."

"Well, it belongs to a person asleep in the house."

"A man, or a woman?"

"A woman."

"Tell the woman, then, that I will give her five hundred pistoles for her horse."

"Oh! ho!" said the peasant, staring; "five hundred pistoles! That is a sum!"

"Tell her it is the king who wants her horse."

"The king?"

"Yes, in person."

"Oh, come! you are not the king, are you?"

"No, but I represent him."

"You represent him?" said the peasant, taking off his hat.

"Come, come! make haste! The king is in a hurry!" and the burly stranger cast another impatient glance towards the highway.

"Well, when the lady awakes I will tell her."

"Yes; but I can't wait till she wakes."

"What is to be done, then?"

"*Parbleu!* awaken her!"

"Awaken her? certainly not."

"Well, I shall do it myself!"

But just as the stranger, who pretended to be the representative of his Majesty, advanced to knock at the window of the upper story with the handle of his long whip, he caught a glimpse of a carriage coming along at the utmost speed of the worn-out horses. His quick eye recognised it instantly, and he sprang forward to meet it; it was that in which were Gilbert and his guardian angel. On seeing this man, who made signs to him to stop, the postilion gladly obeyed, for he scarcely knew whether the horses could take him to the post-house.

"Chon! my dear Chon! is it you at last?"

"It is, Jean," replied the lady addressed by this singular name. "And what are you doing here?"

"*Pardieu*, a pretty question! I am waiting for you."

And he leaped on the step of the carriage, and putting in his long arms, seized her and covered her with kisses.

"Ha!" said he, all at once observing Gilbert, who looked on with surprise at these strange proceedings. "What the deuce have you here?"

"Oh, a little philosopher, and very amusing," replied Mademoiselle Chon, little caring whether she hurt or flattered the pride of her new acquaintance.

"And where did you pick him up?"

"On the road; but that is not the question."

"True," said the person who was called Jean. "What about our old Comtesse de Béarn?"

"All settled."

"What! settled?"

"Yes; she will come."

"But what did you say to her?"

"That I was her lawyer's daughter, that I was passing through Verdun, and that my father desired me to tell her her lawsuit was coming on. I merely added that her presence in Paris is now indispensable for its success."

"What did she say to that?"

"She opened her little grey eyes, took a long pinch of snuff, said that Monsieur Flageot was the cleverest man in the world, and gave orders for her departure."

"Admirable, Chon! I shall make you my ambassador extraordinary. And now, shall we breakfast?"

"With all my heart; for this poor child is dying of hunger. But we must be quick, for she will soon overtake us."

"Who,— the old countess? Nonsense."

"No; the dauphiness."

"Bah! The dauphiness is scarcely at Nancy yet."

"She is at Vitry; three leagues off."

"*Peste!* That alters the case. Drive on, drive on, postilion!"

"Where, sir?"

"To the post-house."

The carriage drove off, with the stranger still standing on the step, and soon drew up before the inn door.

"Quick! quick!" said Chon. "Let us have some cutlets, a fowl, some eggs, and a bottle of Burgundy! We must set out again instantly."

"Excuse me, madame," said the innkeeper, stepping forward, "but in that case it must be with your own horses."

"How!" said Jean, leaping heavily down from the step of the carriage. "With our own horses?"

"Certainly; or at least with those that brought you."

"Impossible!" said the postilion; "they have already done a double stage. See what a state they are in!"

"In good earnest," said Chon, "it would be utterly impossible to proceed farther with them."

"But what prevents your giving us fresh horses?" asked Jean.

"Merely that I have none."

"What the devil! you know the regulations; it is your duty to have horses."

"By the regulations, monsieur, I ought to have fifteen horses; now, I have eighteen."

"Why, all we want is three."

"Yes, but they are all out."

"What! all the eighteen?"

"Yes, monsieur."

"Damnation!" thundered the traveller.

"Oh, viscount! viscount!" cried Chon.

"Yes, yes, Chon; don't be afraid, I will keep calm. And when will your miserable hacks be in?" continued the viscount, turning to the host.

"Faith, sir, I don't know; it all depends on the postilions. Perhaps in an hour; perhaps in two hours."

"Now, my good fellow," said Viscount Jean, placing his hat on one side, and setting out his right leg, "I wish you just to understand this: I never jest."

"I am sorry for it, monsieur. I should like you much better if you did."

"Now, take my advice! Let the horses be harnessed before I get angry!"

"Go into the stable yourself, monsieur; and if you find a horse there, you shall have it for nothing."

"Indeed! and what if I should find sixty?"

"It would be just the same as if there were none; for these sixty horses are the king's."

"Well, what then?"

"What then!—they are not to be hired out."

"What the devil are they here for, then?"

"For the use of madame, the dauphiness."

"*Mon Dieu!* sixty horses, and we cannot get one!"

"But you know, monsieur—"

"I know one thing, and that is, that I am in a hurry."

"It is a pity."

"And," continued the viscount, without heeding the post-master's interruption, "as the dauphiness will not be here before the evening—"

"What do you say?" exclaimed the host, all alarmed.

"I say that the horses will be back before she arrives!"

"Can it be possible you would propose—"

"*Parbleu!*" said the viscount, going into the stable, "I will have three horses; I don't want eight, like royal personages, although I have a right to them,—by alliance at least."

"But I say you shall not have one!" said the host, throwing himself, in desperation, between the stranger and his horses.

"Scoundrel!" cried the viscount, turning pale with anger; "do you know who I am?"

"Viscount, viscount, in Heaven's name, no broils!" cried Chon.

"You are right, my good little Chon." Then, after a moment's thought, he turned with his most charming smile to the host. "My good fellow, no more words, now for deeds. I shall take the responsibility off your shoulders."

"How so?" asked the host, by no means satisfied even with the stranger's now gracious visage.

"I shall help myself; these three horses suit me exactly."

"And you call that freeing me from all responsibility?"

"Certainly; you have not given them to me; it was I who took them."

"I tell you the thing is impossible!"

"We shall see that. Where is the harness?"

"Let no one stir, at his peril!" cried the host to two or three grooms loitering about.

"Scoundrels!" cried the viscount.

"Jean, my dear Jean!" exclaimed Chon, "you will only bring us into some disagreeable situation. When on a mission like this we must endure —"

"Everything except delay," said Jean, with the utmost coolness; "and, since these rogues won't help me, I shall do the business myself." And Jean coolly took from the wall three sets of harness, and fitted them on three of the horses.

"Jean, Jean, I entreat you, do not be rash!" cried Chon, clasping her hands.

"Do you wish to arrive in Paris or not?" said the viscount, grinding his teeth.

"Of course I wish to arrive. All is lost if we do not hasten on!"

"Well, then, leave me alone." And separating three horses — not the worst — from the others, he led them to the carriage.

"Take care, monsieur, take care!" cried the host; "it is high treason to steal those horses!"

"I am not going to steal them, you fool; I'm only going to borrow them. Come on, my little pets!"

The host sprang forward to catch the reins; but before he could touch them he was rudely repulsed by the stranger.

"Brother, brother!" cried Mademoiselle Chon.

"Ah, he is her brother!" muttered Gilbert to himself, breathing more freely.

At this moment a window was opened on the opposite side of the way, and a lovely female face was seen. She appeared quite alarmed at the noise.

"Oh, it is you, madame?" cried Jean, who immediately perceived her.

"How, monsieur? I!" she replied, in bad French.

"Yes, you are awake now. Will you sell your horse?"

"My horse?"

"Yes, the grey Arabian, tied to the window-shutter there. You know I offered you five hundred crowns."

"My horse is not for sale, monsieur," said she, shutting the window.

"Well, I am not in luck to-day, — people will neither sell nor hire; but, *corbleu!* I'll take the Arabian if she won't sell it; and I'll drive these hacks to the devil, if they won't hire them. Come, Patrice!"

The footman on his sister's carriage jumped down.

"Harness them!" said Jean.

"Help! help!" shouted the host.

Two grooms ran forward.

"Jean! viscount!" cried poor Chon, writhing in the carriage, and endeavouring in vain to open the door. "You are mad; we shall all be slaughtered!"

"Slaughtered! It is we who shall slaughter them, I hope. We are three against three! Come out, my young philosopher!" thundered Jean, addressing Gilbert, who never stirred, so great was his astonishment; "come out, and do something, — sticks, stones, or fists; anything will do! *Morbleu!* you look like a saint carved on stone!"

Gilbert gave an inquiring and supplicating glance at his protectress, but she held him by the arm. The host, in the mean time, bawled incessantly, dragging the horses to one side, whilst Jean pulled them to the other. But the struggle could not last forever. Jean, wearied and heated, dealt the defender of the horses such a blow with his clenched fist that the latter fell back into the horse-pond, among his frightened ducks and geese, shouting, as he plunged in, "Help! murder! murder!"

The viscount, thus rid of his adversary, lost no time in harnessing the horses.

"Help, in the name of the king! Help!" cried the host, rising, and endeavouring to rally his frightened grooms.

"Who calls for help in the name of the king?" cried a cavalier, riding at full speed into the yard of the post-house, and reining up his horse, bathed in sweat and foam, in the very midst of the actors in this tumultuous scene.

"The Chevalier Philip de Taverney!" muttered Gilbert to himself, sinking down in the carriage to escape observation.

Chon, who lost no opportunity of acquiring information, heard the young man's name.

CHAPTER XXII.

VISCOUNT JEAN.

THE young lieutenant of the body-guard of the dauphin — for it was he — leaped from his horse at the aspect of this strange scene, which began to collect about the post-house all the women and children of the village. On seeing Philip, the post-master was ready to throw himself on his knees before his protector, whom Providence had sent him so opportunely.

"Monsieur, monsieur!" cried he, "do you know that this person is about to take by force some of the horses of madame the dauphiness?"

Philip drew back, as if he heard what was absolutely incredible. "And who has made this attempt?" he inquired.

"I, monsieur! — *mordieu!* — I myself!" said Jean.

"It cannot be, monsieur; otherwise you are either mad or not a gentleman!"

"Excuse me, monsieur. I am in my perfect senses, and have the *entrée* at court."

"How! — you are in your perfect senses, and are received at court, and yet you dare to take the horses of the dauphiness?"

"In the first place, there are sixty horses; madame can only employ eight, and it would be strange, indeed, if I should unluckily pitch upon the very ones she wanted."

"True, monsieur, there are sixty horses," replied the young man, "and madame will only employ eight; but that does not hinder every horse, from the first to the six-

tieth, being for her service; and between these horses no
distinction can be made."

"You are mistaken, monsieur,—it is made!" said the
viscount, contemptuously, "since I have taken these three
for myself. Shall I go on foot, when rascally lackeys are
drawn by four horses? *Mordieu!* let them be satisfied, as
I am, with three, and there will be enough for us all."

"If the lackeys have four horses, monsieur, it is by the
king's order; and now have the goodness to order your
footman to take those horses back to the stable." These
words Philip pronounced firmly, but with so much politeness that none but a ruffian would have answered otherwise
than respectfully.

"You may be right, my dear lieutenant," answered Jean,
"to speak in this manner, if it be a part of your duty to
attend to the cattle; but I did not know that the gentlemen of the dauphin's body-guard had been raised to the
rank of grooms. Therefore take my advice: shut your
eyes, tell your people to do the same, and a good-day to
you."

"Monsieur, whether I have been raised or lowered to
the rank of groom is not the question; what I do is my
duty, and I am commanded by the dauphiness herself to
attend to the relays."

"Oh, that alters the case; but allow me to tell you that
you are filling a sorry office, Monsieur Lieutenant. And if
this is the way the young lady begins to treat the army —"

"Of whom do you speak, monsieur?" interrupted Philip.

"Why, *parbleu!* of the Austrian."

The chevalier turned as pale as death. "Do you dare,"
he exclaimed, "to speak —"

"I not only dare to speak," interrupted Jean, "but I
dare to act! Come, Patrice, hasten, we are pressed for
time."

Philip seized the first horse by the bridle. "Monsieur,"
said he, in a perfectly calm voice, "do me the favour to
give your name."

"Do you wish particularly to know it?"

"Yes."

"Well, then, I am the Viscount Jean Dubarry."

"What! you are the brother of her —"

"Who will send you to rot in the Bastille, if you say one word more!" and Jean jumped into the carriage.

Philip approached the door. "Viscount Jean Dubarry," said he, "you will do me the honour to come out."

"Yes, *ma foi !* I have a great deal of time for that!" said the viscount, endeavouring to shut the door.

"If you hesitate one instant, monsieur," replied Philip, preventing him with his left hand from closing the carriage door, "I give you my word of honour, I will run you through the body!" and as he spoke, he drew his sword.

"Oh!" cried Chon, "we shall be murdered. Give up the horses, Jean, give them up!"

"What! you threaten me," shouted Jean, grinding his teeth and snatching up his sword, which he had laid on the seat of the carriage before him.

"And the threat shall be followed up — do you hear? — in a moment!" and the young man's sword glanced before Jean's eyes.

"We shall never get away," whispered Chon, "if you do not manage this officer by gentle means."

"Neither gentleness nor violence shall stop me in the discharge of my duty," said Philip, who had overheard the advice, bowing. "I recommend you, madame, to advise Monsieur le Viscount to submit in time, or in the name of the king, whom I represent, I shall be forced to kill him if he resists, or to arrest him if he does not."

"And I tell you I shall have the horses in spite of you!" shouted Jean, leaping out of the carriage and drawing his sword.

"That remains to be proved, monsieur," said Philip, putting himself on his guard. "Are you ready?"

"Lieutenant," said the brigadier commanding under Philip, "there are six of our men near; shall I —"

"Do not stir! Do not stir! This is a personal quarrel. Now, monsieur, I am at your service."

Mademoiselle Chon shrieked, and Gilbert wished the carriage had been as deep as a well, to hide him.

Jean began the attack; he was a good swordsman, but anger prevented him from turning his skill to advantage. Philip, on the contrary, was as cool as if he had been playing with a foil in the fencing-school. The viscount advanced, retired, leaped to the right, to the left, shouting in making his passes like the fencing-master of a regiment; while the chevalier, with closed teeth and steady eye, immovable as a statue, watched all his adversary's movements, and divined his intentions. Every one in the yard was silent, attentively looking on; even Chon ceased to scream. For some minutes the combat continued without Jean's feints, shouts, and movements producing any effect, but also without his having permitted Philip, who was studying his opponent's play, to touch him once. All at once, however, the viscount sprang back, uttering a cry of pain; and at the same moment his ruffles were stained with blood, which ran down his fingers in large drops. He was wounded in the arm.

"You are wounded, monsieur," said Philip.

"Sacrebleu! I feel it well enough," said he, turning pale and letting his sword fall.

The chevalier took it up and restored it to him. "Take it, monsieur," said he, "and never again be guilty of a similar folly."

"Plague take it! — if I have my follies, I pay for them," growled the viscount. "Come and dress this scrape, dear Chon," added he to his sister, who sprang from the carriage and hastened to his assistance.

"You will do me the justice, madame," said Philip, "to acknowledge that all this has not been caused by my fault. I deeply regret having been driven to such extremities before a lady," and bowing, he retired. "Let those horses be unharnessed and taken back to the stable," said he to the post-master.

Jean shook his fist at him.

"Oh!" cried the host, "this is just in the nick of time: three horses coming in that have been out! Courtin, Courtin, quick! put them to the gentleman's carriage."

"But, master—" said the postilion.

"Come, come! no reply; the gentleman is in a hurry. Don't be uneasy, monsieur, you shall have the horses."

"All very fine; but your horses should have been here half an hour ago," growled Dubarry, stamping with his foot as he looked at his arm, pierced through and through, which Chon was binding up with her handkerchief.

Meantime Philip had mounted his horse again, and was giving his orders as if nothing had occurred.

"Now, brother, now! let us go," said Chon, leading him towards the carriage.

"And my Arabian?" said he. "Ah, *ma foi!* let him go to the devil, for I am in for a day of ill-luck;" and he got into the carriage.

"Oh," said he, perceiving Gilbert, "I cannot stretch my legs with this fellow."

"Let me out, pray," said Gilbert, "and I will walk."

"In the devil's name, go, then!" replied Jean.

"No, no," said Chon, "I must keep my little philosopher. Sit opposite me, and you will not annoy him;" and she held Gilbert by the arm. Then, bending forward, she whispered to her brother, "He knows the man who wounded you."

A gleam of joy flashed from the viscount's eyes: "Oh, very well, let him stay. What is the fellow called?"

"The Chevalier Philip de Taverney."

Just then the young officer passed the carriage.

"Oh, you are there, my little gendarme," shouted the viscount. "You look wonderfully fierce just now, but my turn will come some day."

"I shall be at your service, monsieur, whenever you please," answered Philip, calmly.

"Yes, yes, we shall see that, Monsieur Philip de Taverney," said the viscount, leaning forward to see what effect the mention of his name would have on the young man, when he must be so far from expecting to hear it.

Philip looked up with surprise, and indeed with a slight feeling of uneasiness; but immediately recovering his self-possession, and taking off his hat with the utmost grace, "A pleasant journey, Viscount Jean Dubarry," said he.

The carriage rolled on rapidly. "Thousand devils!" said the viscount, making a horrible grimace; "do you know, my little Chon, I am suffering dreadful pain."

"The first place where we change I shall send for a doctor for you, while this poor fellow breakfasts," replied Chon.

"Ah! true, true, we have not breakfasted; but the pain I suffer — and I am in agony with thirst — takes away all appetite."

"Will you drink a glass of wine from my flask?"

"Certainly! give it me."

"Monsieur," said Gilbert, "will you allow me to remark that wine is very bad for you in your present condition?"

"Really, you are quite a physician, my little philosopher!"

"No, monsieur, but I hope to be so one day. I have read, however, in a treatise written for people in the army, that the first things forbidden the wounded are spirits, wine, and coffee."

"Ah, you read that? Well, I shall not drink the wine."

"But if Monsieur le Viscount would permit me to take his handkerchief and dip it in that brook, and then wrap it round his arm, I am sure it would ease his pain."

"Do, do!" said Chon. "Stop, postilion!"

Gilbert got out to follow up his proposition. "This boy will be a horrid plague to us," said the viscount; "I have a great mind to tell the postilion to drive on and leave him there, handkerchief and all."

"You would be wrong; that boy can be very useful to us."

"How so?"

"He has already given me some important information about the dauphiness; and did he not just now tell you the name of your adversary ? "

"True! Well, let him stay."

Gilbert returned, and the application of the wet bandage to the viscount's arm, as he had foretold, relieved him greatly.

"Faith, he was right, — I feel much better," said he; "let us have a little chat." Gilbert opened his ears to their utmost extent. The conversation which ensued, and which was conducted in the lively and brilliant patois of Provence, would have sadly puzzled a Parisian ear, and Gilbert, master of himself as he was, could not avoid a slight movement of impatience, which Mademoiselle Chon having perceived, quieted with a gentle smile. This smile reminded the poor boy of the kindness with which he was treated. Circumstances had brought him in contact with a nobleman honoured with the royal favour. "Ah," thought he, "if Andrée saw me in this magnificent carriage!" — and his heart swelled with pride. New ideas and hopes took possession of him, and Nicole no longer cost him a thought.

In the mean time, the brother and sister resumed their conversation, still however in the Provençal dialect.

Suddenly the viscount leaned forward. "See, there he is! " cried he.

"What ? "

"The Arabian which I wished to buy."

"Oh! " exclaimed Chon, "what a splendid woman the rider is ! "

"Call her, Chon; she will not perhaps be so much afraid of you. I would give a thousand crowns for the horse."

"And how much for the woman ? " said Chon, laughing.

"I would give all I have for her, — but call her."

"Madame ! " cried Chon, "madame ! "

But the stranger appeared not to hear, or not to understand. Wrapped in a long white mantle, and her face shaded by a large beaver hat with drooping feathers, she flew past them like an arrow, crying, *"Avanti, Djerid! avanti!"*

"She is an Italian," said the viscount. *"Mordieu,* what a splendid woman! If it were not for the pain in my arm, I would jump out and run after her."

"I know her," said Gilbert.

"Why, the little fellow is a directory for the whole province; he knows every one."

"Who is she?" asked Chon.

"Her name is Lorenza, and she is the sorcerer's wife."

"What sorcerer?"

"The Baron Joseph Balsamo."

The brother and sister looked at each other with an expression which said, "We did well to keep him!"

CHAPTER XXIII.

THE COUNTESS DUBARRY'S MORNING LEVEE.

WHILST Mademoiselle Chon and Viscount Jean are travelling post on the Châlons road, let us introduce the reader to another member of the same family.

In the suite of rooms at Versailles which Madame Adelaide, daughter of Louis XV., had once occupied, his Majesty had installed his mistress, the Countess Dubarry, not without keenly studying beforehand the effect which this piece of policy would produce on his court. The favourite, with her merry whims and her careless, joyous humour, had transformed that wing of the palace, formerly so quiet, into a scene of perpetual merriment and tumult; and every hour she issued thence her commands for a banquet or a party of pleasure.

But what appeared still more unusual on these magnificent staircases was the never-ceasing stream of visitors ascending them, and crowding an antechamber filled with curiosities from all parts of the globe, — certainly containing nothing so curious as the idol worshipped by this crowd.

On the day following, at her accustomed hour, nine in the morning, Jeanne de Vaubernier, dressed in a muslin embroidered robe which disclosed through its gauzy texture her rounded limbs and alabaster arms, — Jeanne de Vaubernier, afterwards Mademoiselle Lange and then Countess Dubarry by the grace of Jean Dubarry, her former protector, rose from her bed, we will not say like to Venus but surely more beautiful than Venus to the eyes of a man who prefers the real to the ideal.

Her blond hair, artistically dressed, a skin of white satin with blue veins, eyes in turn languishing and spiritual, a small mouth pencilled with purest carmine, and which when opened disclosed to view a double row of pearls, dimpled cheeks, chin and fingers and a throat like that of the Venus de Milo, the suppleness of an adder, and perfectly developed breasts, — thus behold Madame Dubarry about to disclose these charms to the chosen ones at her little levee.

Thus behold what his Majesty Louis XV., the chosen one for the night, did not neglect in the morning, like the others who profit by the old proverb which advises old people not to lose the crumbs which fall from the table of life. For some time the favourite had been awake. At eight o'clock she had allowed the sunlight, her first courtier, to enter the chamber little by little.

There was no sign of drowsiness in the eyes, bright as carbuncles, which laughingly questioned a small hand-glass with a gold rim studded with pearls.

The supple body which we have tried to describe glided from the bed where it had reposed, lulled by sweet dreams, to the ermine rug, where feet of which Cinderella would not have been ashamed touched hands holding two slippers, one of which would have made a woodman in Jeanne's native forest rich for life.

As the seductive form arose, becoming more and more alive, an attendant threw over it a superb wrap of Malines lace, while upon the rounded feet, taken from the slippers for a moment, were placed silk stockings of a texture so fine that it would have been hard to distinguish it from the skin they covered.

"No news of Chon?" she asked one of her tiring-women.

"No, madame."

"Nor of the viscount?"

"No, madame."

"Do you know, has Bischi received any?"

"A message was sent to your sister's, madame, this morning, but there were no letters."

"It is very tiresome waiting in this way," said the countess, pouting her lovely mouth. "I am in a wretched humour; I pity all who may come near me to-day. Will some means never be invented of conversing at a hundred leagues' distance? Is my antechamber passably filled?"

"Can madame think it necessary to ask?"

"*Dame!* but listen, Dorée; the dauphiness is coming! I shall be abandoned for that sun, — I, who am only a little twinkling star. But tell me, who is there?"

"The Duke d'Aiguillon, madame, the Prince de Soubise, Monsieur de Sartines, the President Maupeou, — "

"And the Duke de Richelieu?"

"Not yet, madame."

"How? — neither to-day nor yesterday?   He is afraid of compromising himself. Send one of my servants to the Hôtel du Hanovre to inquire if the duke be ill."

"Yes, madame. Will you receive all who are waiting at once, or do you wish to give any one a private audience?"

"Monsieur de Sartines first; I must speak to him alone."

The order was transmitted by the countess's woman to a tall footman who waited in the corridor leading from her bed-chamber to the ante-rooms, and the lieutenant of police immediately appeared, dressed in black, and endeavouring by an insinuating smile to moderate the severe expression of his grey eyes and thin lips.

"Good morning, my dear enemy!" said the countess, without looking round, but seeing him in her mirror.

"Your enemy, madame!"

"Yes; my world is divided into only two classes, — friends and enemies. I admit no neutrals, or class them as enemies."

"And you are right madame; but tell me how I, not-

VOL. I. — 15

withstanding my well-known devotion to your interests, deserve to be included in either of these classes ? "

" By allowing to be printed, distributed, sold, and sent to the king, a whole ocean of pamphlets, libels, verses, — all against me.   It is ill-natured, stupid, odious! "

" But, madame, I am not responsible."

" Yes, monsieur, you are; for you know the wretch who wrote them."

" Madame, if they were all written by one author, we should not have the trouble of sending him to the Bastille; Hercules himself would sink under such a labour ! "

" Upon my word, you are highly complimentary to me."

" If I were your enemy, madame, I should not speak the truth thus."

" Well, I believe you!   We understand each other now. But one thing still gives me some uneasiness."

" What is that, madame ? "

" You are on good terms with the Choiseuls."

" Madame, Monsieur de Choiseul is prime minister; he issues his orders and I must obey them."

" So if Monsieur de Choiseul orders that I am to be vexed, tortured, worried to death, you will allow me to be vexed, tortured, worried !   Thank you ! "

" Let us discuss matters a little," said Sartines, sitting down without being asked to do so, but without any displeasure being exhibited on the part of the favourite; for much must be pardoned in the man who knew better than any other all that was doing in France.   " Let us discuss this a little; and first, what have I done for you these three days past ? "

" You informed me that a courier had been sent from Chanteloup to hasten the arrival of the dauphiness."

" Was that done like an enemy ? "

" But about the presentation, on which you know my heart is set, — what have you been doing for me ? "

" Doing all I possibly could."

"Monsieur de Sartines, you are not candid!"

"Ah, madame! I assure you, you are unjust. Did I not find and bring you Viscount Jean from the back room of a tavern, in less than two hours, when you wanted to send him I don't know where, or rather I do know where?"

"I had much rather you had allowed my brother-in-law to stay there," said Madame Dubarry, laughing, — "a man allied to the royal family of France!"

"Well, but was that not a service to be added to my many other services?"

"Oh, very well! — but just tell me what you did for me yesterday."

"Yesterday, madame!"

"Oh, you may well endeavour to recollect; that was your day for obliging others."

"I don't understand you, madame."

"Well, I understand myself. Answer, monsieur, what were you doing yesterday?"

"Yesterday morning I was occupied as usual, writing with my secretary."

"Till what hour?"

"Till ten."

"What did you do then?"

"I sent to invite a friend of mine from Lyons, who had made a wager he would come to Paris without my knowing, and my footman met him just at the barrier."

"Well, after dinner?"

"I sent to the Austrian lieutenant of police information of the haunt of a famous robber whom he couldn't find."

"And where is he?"

"At Vienna."

"So you are not only the minister of police at Paris, but perform the same duties for foreign courts?"

"Yes, madame, in my leisure moments."

"Well, I shall take a note of that. Then, after having despatched the courier to Vienna?"

"I went to the opera."

" To see the little Guimard ? Poor Soubise! "

" No, to arrest a famous pickpocket, whom I did not disturb so long as he kept to the farmers-general, but who had the audacity to rob two or three noblemen."

" You should say 'the indiscretion.' Well, after the opera ? "

" After the opera ? "

" Yes. That is rather a puzzling question, is it not ? "

" No. After the opera ? let me think — "

" So! How much your memory has failed of late ! "

" Oh! after the opera — yes, I remember."

" Well ? "

" I went to the house of a certain lady who keeps a gaming-table, and I myself conducted her to Fort-l'Evêque."

" In her carriage ? "

" No, in a fiacre."

" Well ? "

" Well, that is all."

" No, it is not ! "

" I got into my fiacre again."

" And whom did you find in it ? "

He reddened.

" Oh ! " cried the countess, clapping her little hands, " I have really had the honour of making a minister of police blush! "

" Madame — " stammered Sartines.

" No, I shall tell you who was in the fiacre; it was the Duchesse de Grammont ! "

" The Duchesse de Grammont ? "

" Yes, the Duchesse de Grammont, — who came to ask you to contrive to get her admitted to the king's private apartments."

" *Ma foi*, madame! " said the minister, shifting uneasily in his chair, " I may give up my portfolio to you. It is you who manage the police of Paris, not I."

" To tell the truth, sir, I have a police of my own. So beware ! Oh, the Duchesse de Grammont in a fiacre with

the minister of police at midnight! It was capital! Do
you know what I did?"

"No, but I am afraid it was something dreadful. Fortunately it was very late."

"But night is the time for vengeance!".

"And what, then, did you do?"

"As I keep a police of my own, I keep a body of writers
also, — shocking, ragged, hungry scribblers!"

"Hungry? you must feed them badly."

"I don't feed them at all. If they became fat they
would be as stupid as the Prince de Soubise. Fat, we are
told, absorbs the gall."

"Go on; I shudder at the thought of them."

"I recollected all the disagreeable things you have
allowed the Choiseuls to do against me, and determined
to be revenged. I gave my legion of famishing Apollos
the following programme: First, Monsieur de Sartines,
disguised as a lawyer, visiting an innocent young girl who
lives in a garret, and giving her, on the thirtieth of every
month, a wretched pittance of a hundred crowns."

"Madame, that is a benevolent action which you are
endeavouring to misconstrue."

"It is only such actions which can be misconstrued. My
second scene was Monsieur de Sartines, disguised like a
reverend missionary, introducing himself into the convent
of the Carmelites of the Rue Saint-Antoine."

"I was taking those good nuns some news from the
Indies."

"East or West Indies, — which? My third scene is
Monsieur de Sartines, disguised as lieutenant of the police,
driving through the streets at midnight in a fiacre with
the Duchesse de Grammont."

"No, madame," exclaimed he. "No, you would not bring
ridicule on my administration in that manner!"

"Why, do you not bring ridicule on mine?" said the
countess, laughing. "But wait! I set my rogues to work,
and they began like boys at college, with exordium, narra-

230 MEMOIRS OF A PHYSICIAN.

tion, and amplification; and I have received this morning
an epigram, a song, and a ballad."

"Ah! *mon Dieu!*"

"All of them frightful. I amused the king with them
this morning; also with the new *Pater Noster*, ridiculing
him, which you have allowed to circulate. You know it,
of course : —

"'Our father who art in Versailles, unhallowed be thy
name as it ought to be. Thy kingdom is in chaos, thy will
is not done on earth, nor is it done in heaven. Give us
each day our daily bread which thy favourites have stolen
from us, and forgive thy parliaments which sustain thy
interests as we forgive thy ministers who have betrayed
them. Succumb not to the temptations of the Dubarry,
but deliver us from thy devil of a minister. Amen.'"

"Where did you find that," said Monsieur de Sartines,
clasping his hands.

"Oh, my God, there was no need to find it. Some one has
the courtesy to send me daily the best things of this kind
as they appear. I even gave you the credit for those daily
missives."

"Oh, madame!"

"And so, by way of return, to-morrow you will receive
the epigram, the song, and the ballad in question."

"Why not to-day?"

"I must have some time first to distribute them. Is not
that the way? Besides, the police ought always to hear last
about any new affair. I assure you, you will be very much
amused! I laughed three-quarters of an hour at them
this morning, and the king was nearly dead with laughing;
it was that which made him so late."

"I am ruined!" cried Sartines, clasping his hands.

"Ruined? Nonsense! You are only celebrated in song.
Am I ruined by all the verses made on me? No, I only
get in a passion at them, and then for revenge I determine
to put somebody else in a passion too. Ah, what delightful verses! I have ordered some wine to my literary

scorpions, and I expect by this time their senses are wrapped up in happy oblivion."

"Ah, countess, countess!"

"But, *pardieu*, you must hear the epigram:—

> " ' Oh, France, how wretched is thy fate,
>   When women hold the helm of state.'

No, no — I am wrong; that is the scandal perpetrated against myself. But there are so many, I confound them. Listen, listen! here it is:—

> " ' A perfumer once sought of a painter a sign,
>   His skill than his genius was duller;
>   For in a huge bottle, with knavish design,
>   He makes Boynes, Maupeou, and Terray to shine,
>   Displayed in their own proper colour.
>   But for Sartines still room in the vessel he leaves,
>   And he labels the mixture " The Essence of Thieves." ' "

"Cruel woman, you will send me mad!" cried Sartines.

"Now we must look at the poem. You must know it is Madame de Grammont who speaks:—

> " ' Dear minister, you know my skin
>   Is to the purest snow akin;
>   Then grant to me this single thing —
>   Oh, say so, say so, to the king.' "

"Madame, madame!" cried Sartines, more furious than ever.

"Nonsense!" said the countess. "You need not be so uneasy about these little poems; I have only had ten thousand copies of them struck off."

"You have a press, then?"

"Certainly. Has not the Duke de Choiseul one?"

"Let your printer take care!"

"Oh, it is kept in my own name; I am the printer."

"Shocking, shocking! And the king laughs at these calumnies ? "

"Laughs ? He sometimes gives me rhymes himself, when my own inspiration fails."

"You know how I serve you, and you treat me thus ? "

"I know that you are betraying me; the Duchesse de Grammont wishes to ruin me."

"Madame, I declare to you she took me quite unawares ! "

"You confess, then, that I was informed correctly ? "

"I am forced to confess it."

"Why did you not tell me ? "

"I came now for that purpose."

"I don't believe you."

"Upon my honour ! "

"I bet two to one against that pledge."

"Behold me at your feet ! " and he fell on his knees. "I beg forgiveness."

"You are in the position in which you ought to be."

"Let us make peace, countess, in Heaven's name."

"So you are afraid of a few bad verses, — you a man, a minister ! Yet you never reflect how many wretched hours such things make me spend, — me, a poor weak woman ! "

"You are a queen."

"A queen, not presented at court ! "

"I swear to you I have never done anything hurtful to your interests ! "

"No, but you have allowed others to do so. The matter, however, is now, not the doing nothing against them, but the doing all in your power to forward them. Are you on my side, — yes or no ? "

"Certainly, on your side."

"Will you assist me ? Will you allow nothing to interpose to hinder my presentation ? "

"For myself, I promise everything."

"No," said the countess, stamping with her foot, "Punic faith! I will not accept that; there is a loophole in it to creep out at ! You will be supposed to do nothing against me yourself, but the Duke de Choiseul will do all. Give me up the Choiseul party, bound hand and foot, or I will annihilate you, — destroy you! Take care! verses are not my only weapons!"

"Do not threaten me, madame," said Sartines, thoughtfully; "there are difficulties about this presentation which you cannot understand."

"Obstacles have purposely been thrown in the way of it. You can remove them."

"It would require a hundred persons to do so."

"You shall have a million!"

"The king will not give his consent."

"He shall give it!"

"And, when you have got it, how get a lady to present you?"

"I am seeking for one now."

"It is quite useless; there is a league against you."

"At Versailles?"

"Yes. All the ladies have refused, in order to pay their court to the Duke de Choiseul, the Duchesse de Grammont, the dauphiness, and the whole prudish party."

"Do not fear; I have nearly obtained what I want."

"Ha! it was for that you sent your sister to Verdun!"

"So you know that, do you?" said she, angrily.

"Oh, I have also my police, you know!" said Sartines, laughing.

"And your spies?"

"And my spies."

"In my apartments?"

"In your apartments."

"In my stable, or in my kitchen?"

"In your antechamber, in your salon, in your bedroom, under your pillow."

"Now, as the first pledge of our peace," said the countess, "give me the names of those spies."

"No, countess; I should not wish to embroil you with your friends."

" But name only the last who told you a secret."

" What would you do ? "

" I would turn him out."

" If you begin in that way, you will soon have to live in an empty house."

" This is frightful ! "

" Yet perfectly true. Oh, you know we could not govern without spies ! So excellent a politician as you must have discovered that long ago."

Madame Dubarry leaned her elbow on a table, and seemed to reflect for some minutes; then she said, " You are right. Let us say more on the subject. What are to be the conditions of our treaty ? "

" Make them yourself. You are the conqueror."

" I am as magnanimous as Semiramis. Let me hear what you wish."

" Well, then, you are never to speak to the king about petitions on the subject of wheat; for, traitress ! you have promised your support to those petitions."

" Very well. Take away all the petitions with you; they are in a box there."

" As a reward, here is a document drawn up by the peers of the kingdom respecting presentations, and the right of sitting in the royal presence."

" A document which you were charged to give his majesty ? "

" Yes."

" But what will you say to them ? "

" That I have given it. You will thus gain time; and you are too clever in your tactics not to take advantage of it."

At this moment the folding-doors were thrown open, and an attendant announced, " The king ! "

The two allies hastened to hide their mutual pledges of peace and good understanding, and turned to salute his Majesty, Louis, the fifteenth of that name.

CHAPTER XXIV.

KING LOUIS THE FIFTEENTH.

THE king entered with head erect, with a firm step, his eye full of life, and a smile on his lips. As the doors were opened, a double file of bowing heads was seen belonging to the courtiers, who had been long waiting in the ante-chamber, and who were now more desirous of admittance than ever, since they could thus pay their court to two powers at once; but the doors closed on them, for the king made a sign that no one should follow him. He found himself alone, therefore, with the countess and the minister of police (for we need not reckon the waiting-maid or the little negro boy).

"Good-morning, countess!" said the king, kissing Madame Dubarry's hand. "Ha! fresh as any rose, I see! Good-morning, Sartines! Is this your cabinet, where you write your despatches? Heavens! what heaps of papers! Hide them, hide them! Ha! what a beautiful fountain, countess!"

And, with the versatile curiosity of one always in search of something to amuse him, he fixed his eyes on a large china ornament, which had been brought in since the evening before and placed in a corner of the countess's bedroom.

"Sire," replied the countess, "it is a Chinese fountain; by turning this cock, the water comes out and makes these birds sing and these fishes swim; then the doors of the pagoda open, and there comes out a procession of mandarins."

"Very pretty, very pretty indeed!"

At this moment the little negro walked across the room, dressed in the fantastic fashion in which, at this period, they dressed their Osmans and Othellos; he wore a little turban, ornamented with a lofty plume of feathers, on one side of his head; a vest embroidered with gold, which permitted his ebony arms to be seen; and slashed breeches of white brocaded satin; round his waist was a scarf of various bright colours, which connected the breeches with a richly embroidered jacket; and in the scarf a dagger, ornamented with precious stones.

"*Peste!*" cried the king, "how splendid Zamore is to-day!"

The negro stopped to admire himself before a mirror.

"Sire, he has a favour to ask of your Majesty."

"Madame," replied the king, with a courtly smile, "I am afraid Zamore is very ambitious."

"How so, sire?"

"Because he has already been granted the greatest favour he can desire."

"What is that?"

"The same that has been granted me."

"I do not understand you, sire."

"You have made him your slave."

"Oh, how charming, sire!" cried the countess.

The countess, drawing near to the king, said in a low voice, "France, I adore thee!"

The minister of police bowed in assent, and bit his lip to prevent himself from smiling.

"But," asked the king, "what can Zamore desire?"

"The reward of his long and numerous services."

"Yes; he is twelve years old!"

"His long and numerous future services."

"Oh, very well!"

"Yes, indeed, sire. Past services have been rewarded long enough; it is now time to begin and reward future ones. There would not then be so much ingratitude."

"Ha! not a bad idea," said the king. "What do you think of it, Sartines?"

" That it would benefit all devoted servants of your
Majesty, sire; therefore I support it."

" Well, countess, what does Zamore want? "

" Sire, you know my little country seat of Luciennes? "

" I have merely heard it spoken of."

" It is your own fault; I have invited you to it a hundred
times."

" You know the etiquette, dear countess : unless on a
journey, the king can only sleep in a royal château."

" And for that very reason I wish you to make Luciennes
a royal château, and Zamore its governor."

" But, countess, that would be a burlesque."

" I love burlesques, sire."

" The governors of the other castles would all exclaim,
and this time with reason."

" Let them exclaim; they have often done so without
reason.   Kneel down, Zamore."

The little fellow knelt.

" For what is he kneeling? " asked the king.

" For the reward you are going to give him for bearing
my train, and putting all the prudes of the court in a
rage."

" He is really a hideous creature," said the king, bursting
into a fit of laughter.

" Rise, Zamore," said the countess; " you are appointed
governor of Luciennes."

" But indeed, madame — "

" I shall send Zamore all the writings necessary for his
governorship.   And now, sire, you may come to Luciennes ;
you have one more royal château from this day."

" Is there any way of refusing her anything, Sartines ? "

" There may be a way, sire," replied Sartines, " but it
has not yet been discovered."

" And if it should be found, sire, there is one thing certain, — it is Monsieur de Sartines who will find it."

" How can you think so, madame," asked Sartines,
trembling.

" Sire, only imagine that I have requested a favour of
Monsieur de Sartines for three months past, and it is not
yet granted."

"And what is it ? " asked the king.

" Oh, he knows very well ! "

" I — I swear to you, madame — "

" Does it fall under the duties of his office ? "

" Yes, — either in his or those of his successor."

" Madame," cried Sartines, " you really make me
uneasy."

" What is the request ? " again inquired the king.

" To find me a sorcerer."

Sartines breathed more freely.

" To burn him ? " said the king. " It is rather too hot,
countess ; wait till the winter."

" No, sire ; I wish to present him with a golden wand."

" Then the sorcerer foretold you some misfortune which
has not befallen you ? "

" On the contrary, sire, he predicted a piece of good
fortune which has come to pass."

" Let us hear it then, countess," said the king, throwing
himself back in an arm-chair, like one who was not quite
sure whether the tale would tire him or amuse him, but
who must run the chance.

" With all my heart ; but if I tell the tale, you must con-
tribute the half of the sorcerer's reward."

" The whole, if you like ! "

" Royally said ! Now listen."

" I am all attention."

" There was once — "

" It begins like a fairy tale."

" It *is* one, sire."

" Delightful ; I love enchanters ! "

" There was once a poor young girl, who, at the time my
story commences, had neither page, nor carriage, nor negro,
nor parrot, nor monkey — "

" Nor king," added Louis.

"Oh, sire!"

"And what did the poor young girl do?"

"She trotted about through the streets of Paris like any other common mortal, only she always went very quick; for it is said she was very pretty, and she was afraid of meeting some rude man."

"The young girl was a Lucretia, eh?"

"Oh, your Majesty knows there have been no Lucretias since the year — I don't know what — of the foundation of Rome."

"Oh, heavens! countess, are you going to become learned?"

"No; if I were learned I should have given you a wrong date; now I gave you none."

"True," said the king; "go on."

"The young girl one day was trotting along, as usual, when all at once, whilst crossing the Tuileries, she discovered that a man was following her."

"Oh, the deuce! Then she stopped, I presume."

"Ah, sire, what a bad opinion you have of women! It is easily seen you have only associated with marchionesses and duchesses."

"And princesses, eh?"

"I am too polite to contradict your Majesty. But what frightened the young girl was that a fog came on, which became every moment denser."

"Sartines, do you know what causes fogs?"

The minister, thus taken unawares, started.

"*Ma foi*, no, sire!"

"Nor I. Well, go on, dear countess."

"She ran as fast as she could, passed through the gate, and found herself in the square which bears your Majesty's name, when she found the unknown, from whom she thought she had escaped, face to face with her. She uttered a cry —"

"Was he so very ugly, then?"

"No, sire, he was a handsome young man, of six or eight

and twenty, of a dark complexion, with large, speaking eyes, and a pleasing voice."

"And the heroine was afraid? *Peste!* how easily she was frightened!"

"She was not quite so much so when she looked at him; still, it was not a pleasant situation in that dense fog. So, clasping her hands, she said, 'I implore you, monsieur, not to do me any harm.' The unknown shook his head, smiled, and replied, 'Heaven is my witness, I have no evil intentions towards you.' 'What then, do you want?' I asked. 'To obtain a promise from you.' 'What can I promise you, monsieur?' 'Promise to grant me the first favour I shall ask when —' 'When?' repeated the young girl likewise. 'When you are queen.'"

"And what did the young girl do?" said the king.

"Sire, she thought it would be engaging herself to nothing, so she promised."

"And what became of the sorcerer?"

"He disappeared."

"And Sartines refuses to find him? He is wrong."

"Sire, I do not refuse; but I cannot find him."

"Oh, monsieur," said the countess, "that word *cannot* should never be in the dictionary of the police."

"Madame, we are on his track."

"Yes, — what you always say when you are baffled."

"It is the truth; but consider what trivial directions you have given."

"How! trivial! 'Young, handsome, dark complexion, black hair, splendid eyes, a pleasing voice.'"

"Oh, the devil! how you speak of him, countess! Sartines, I forbid you to find that young man," said the king.

"You are wrong, sire: for I only wish to ask one simple question."

"Is it about yourself?"

"Yes."

"Well, what is it? His prediction is accomplished."

"Do you think so?"

"Yes, you are queen."

"Very nearly."

"What has the sorcerer, then, to tell you more?"

"He has to tell me when the queen will be presented. It does not suffice to reign at night only; one must reign also a little by day."

"That is no concern of his;" and the king made a grimace which showed that he thought they were getting on dangerous ground.

"And whose concern is it?"

"Your own."

"Mine?"

"Yes; you must find a lady to present you."

"Oh! very likely, among the prudes of the court! Your Majesty knows they are all sold to Choiseul and Praslin."

"What! was there not an agreement made between us that the ministers should never be named here?"

"I did not promise, sire."

"Well, I request you to leave them in their places, and keep your own place. Believe me, the best is yours."

"Alas, then, for foreign affairs and the navy!"

"Countess," interrupted the king, "in Heaven's name, no politics!"

At this moment Dorée entered, and whispered a word or two in her mistress's ear.

"Oh, certainly, certainly!" cried she.

"What is it?" asked the king.

"Chon, sire, who has just returned from a journey, and wishes to pay her respects to your Majesty."

"Let her come in! let her come in! Indeed, for some days past I felt that I wanted something, without knowing exactly what it was."

"Thanks, sire!" said Chon as she entered. Then, going up to her sister, she whispered, "It is all settled!"

The countess uttered an exclamation of joy.

"Well, what now?" asked the king.

"Nothing, sire. •I am only glad to see her again."

" I am glad, too.   How do you do, little Chon ? "

" May I say a word or two, sire, to my sister ? "

" Yes, yes, child; and while you are talking together, I shall ask Sartines where you have been."

" Sire," said the minister, wishing to avoid being questioned on that point, " may I beg your Majesty to allow me a few moments on business of the utmost importance ? "

" Oh, I have very little time now, Monsieur de Sartines," said the king, beginning to yawn.

" Only two words, your Majesty."

" About what ? "

" About these people with the second sight, — these illuminati, these workers of miracles."

" Pooh ! jugglers ! Give them permission to exercise their trade, and there will be nothing to fear from them."

" The matter is more serious than your Majesty supposes. Every day we have new masonic lodges formed.   They are now a powerful sect, attracting to them all the enemies of monarchy, — the philosophers, the encyclopedists.   Voltaire is to be received by them in great state."

" He ? he is dying."

" He, sire ! Oh ! no, sire, he is not such a fool."

" He has confessed."

" Merely a trick."

" In the habit of a Capuchin."

"That was an impiety, sire.   But, with regard to these freemasons, they are always active ; they write, they talk, they form associations, correspond with foreign countries. They intrigue, they threaten ; even now they are full of expectation of a great chief, or head, of the whole body, as I have learned from some words which escaped from one of their number."

" Well, Sartines, when this chief comes, catch him and put him in the Bastille, and the whole affair is settled."

" Sire, these persons have great resources."

"Have they greater than you, monsieur, who have the whole police of a large kingdom ? "

"Your Majesty was induced to expel the Jesuits; it was the philosophers whom you should have expelled."

"Come, come! — no more about those poor quill-drivers!"

"Sire, those quills are dangerous which are cut by the pen-knife of Damiens."

Louis XV. turned pale.

"These philosophers, sire, whom you despise — "

"Well, monsieur ? "

"Will destroy the monarchy, sire."

"How long will they take to do that ? "

Sartines stared at this coolness.

"How can I tell, sire ? Perhaps fifteen, twenty, or thirty years."

"Well, my dear friend, in fifteen or twenty years I shall be no more; so talk of all these things to my successor."

And the king turned to Madame Dubarry, who seeming to have waited for this movement, said, with a heavy sigh, "Oh, heavens! what is it you tell me, Chon ? "

"Yes, what is it ? " asked the king; "for you both look very wretched."

"Oh, sire, there is good cause for it!"

"Speak; let me hear what has happened."

"My poor brother!"

"Poor Jean!"

"Do you think it must be cut off ? "

"They hope not."

"Cut off! — what ? " asked the king.

"His arm, sire!"

"Cut off the viscount's arm! — why, pray ?

"Because he has been seriously wounded."

"Wounded in the arm ? "

"Oh, yes, sire."

"Ay, in some drunken squabble in a filthy tavern."

"No, sire; on the highway."

"But how did that happen ? "

"It happened because an enemy wished to assassinate him, sire."

"Ah, the poor viscount!" exclaimed the king, who had very little feeling for the sufferings of others, although he could look wonderfully compassionate. "But to assassinate him! This is a serious matter, is it not, Sartines?"

The minister looked much less moved than the king, but was, in reality, a great deal more uneasy on the subject. He drew near the sisters.

"Can it be possible," asked he, anxiously, "that such a misfortune has occurred?"

"Oh, yes, monsieur, it is but too possible," said Chon, very mournfully.

"Assassinated! — but how?"

"He was waylaid."

"Waylaid? Ha! Sartines, this is an affair for you," said the king.

"Relate all the circumstances, madame," said the minister, "and do not, I entreat you, allow your just resentment to exaggerate them. We shall, by being strictly just, be most severe; and where things are looked at closely and coolly they are often not so very serious as we at first apprehended."

"Oh," cried Chon, "this is not an affair which has been related to me! I saw the whole!"

"Well, but what did you see, Chon?" inquired the king.

"I saw a man fall on my brother, and, having forced him to draw in self-defence, wound him shockingly."

"Was the man alone?" asked Sartines.

"No, indeed; he had six others with him."

"The poor viscount!" said the king, looking at the countess, that he might know exactly what degree of grief to exhibit, — "forced to fight! Poor fellow!" But seeing that she did not relish this pleasantry, — "And he was wounded?" he added, in a compassionate voice.

"But how did the quarrel come about?" asked the minister of police, trying if it were possible to betray her into telling the truth.

"Oh, in the most trifling way in the world! All about post-horses which I wanted in order to hasten back to my sister, as I had promised to be with her this morning."

"Ha! Sartines, this merits punishment, does it not?" said the king.

"It does, sire, and I shall take all the necessary information on the subject. What was the name of the aggressor, madame, his condition, his rank?"

"His rank? He is a military man, — an officer in the bodyguard of the dauphin, I think. As to his name, he is called Baverney, Faverney, Taverney, — yes, Taverney, that is it."

"Madame, to-morrow he shall sleep in the Bastille."

"Oh, no!" said the countess, who until now had very diplomatically kept silence. "Oh, no!"

"Why 'Oh, no'?" asked the king. "Why should not the fellow be imprisoned? You know I detest the military."

"And I repeat, sire," said the countess, doggedly, "that I am quite sure nothing will be done to the man who assassinated the viscount."

"Ha! countess, this is very curious. Explain it, if you please."

"That is easily done; he will be protected."

"And who will protect him?"

"The person at whose instigation he acted."

"And that person will protect him against us? Oh, that is rather too much, countess!"

"Madame —" stammered the Count de Sartines; for he felt that a blow was coming, and he was not prepared to ward it off.

"Yes!" exclaimed the countess; "he will be protected against you, and there will be nothing said. Do you suppose you are the master, sire?"

The king felt the blow which the minister had foreseen, and he determined to bear it.

"I see that you are going to plunge into politics," said he, "and find out some reasons of state for a paltry duel!"

"There, now! you abandon me already; the assassination has become nothing but a duel, now that you suspect the quarter whence it comes!"

"So! I am in for it!" said the king, going to the great Chinese fountain, turning the cock, and making the birds sing, the fishes swim, and the mandarins come out.

"And you don't know who aimed this blow?" asked the countess, pulling the ears of Zamore, who was lying at her feet.

"No, on my word!" said the king.

"Or suspect?"

"I swear I don't. Do you, countess?"

"No, I don't suspect; I know positively. I am going to tell you, and it will be no news to you, I am certain!"

"Countess, countess, do you know that in what you said you gave the lie to your king?" and Louis tried to look dignified.

"Sire, I know I am a little warm, but if you think I shall quietly allow my brother to be killed by the Duke de Choiseul —"

"Yes, there it is, — Choiseul again!" exclaimed the king in a loud voice, as if he had not expected this name, which for the last ten minutes he had been dreading.

"Well, it is because your Majesty is determined not to see that he is my worst enemy; but I see it plainly, for he does not even take the trouble to hide his hatred from me."

"He is far from hating any one to that degree that he would cause him to be assassinated."

"There, you see! — when Choiseul is mentioned you are on his side immediately!"

"Now, my dear countess, politics again!"

"Oh, Monsieur de Sartines!" cried she, "is it not dreadful to be treated thus?"

"No, no; if it be as you think —"

"I know what I think," she interrupted passionately, "and what I am sure of, — the affair will be given up!"

"Now, do not get angry, countess," said the king; "it

shall not be given up. You shall be defended, and so well — "

"So well what?"

"So well that he who attacked poor Jean shall pay dearly for it."

"Yes, the instrument will be broken, but the hand that directed it will be taken and kindly pressed!"

"Well, but is it not right to punish this Monsieur Taverney, who actually committed the assault?"

"Oh, certainly, but it is nót right that what you do for me is no more than would be done to a soldier who should give a blow to a shopkeeper at the theatre. I will not be treated like every common person. If you do not do more for those whom you love than for those who are indifferent to you, I had rather remain alone in obscurity like these latter; their relations, at least, are not assassinated!"

"Oh, countess!" said the king, imploringly, "I got up for once in such good spirits, disposed to be gay, happy, and pleased with every one, and now you are spoiling my morning completely."

"Very fine, indeed! It is a delightful morning for me, of course, when my relations are being massacred!"

The king, in spite of his internal fears of the terrible storm that was gathering, could not help smiling at the word "massacred." The countess started up in a towering passion.

"Ah! is that the way you pity me?" said she.

"Now, now, do not get angry."

"Yes, I will get angry!"

"You are very wrong; you look lovely when you smile, but really ugly in a passion."

"What matters it to me how I look, when my beauty does not prevent me from being sacrificed to state intrigues."

"Now, my dear countess — "

"No, no. Choose between me and Choiseul!"

"Dear creature, it is impossible to choose; you are both necessary to me."

"Well, then, I shall retire and leave the field to my
enemies; I shall die of grief, but the Duke de Choiseul
will be satisfied, and that will console you."

"I swear to you, countess, that he has not any dislike to
you; on the contrary, he admires you. He is an excellent
man, after all," added the king, in a louder tone, that the
minister of police might hear him.

"An excellent man! Sire, you wish to drive me to desperation. An excellent man who causes people to be assassinated?"

"Mere suspicion," said the king.

"And, besides," Sartines ventured to say, "a quarrel, a
duel between military men is so common, so natural!"

Ha! Monsieur de Sartines, and are you also against
me?" cried the countess.

The minister of police understood this *tu quoque*, and
retreated before her anger. There was a moment of deep
and ominous silence.

"Ah, Chon!" said the king, in the midst of the general
consternation, "you see your handiwork!"

"Your Majesty will pardon me," said she, "if the grief
of the sister has made me forget for a moment my duty as
a subject."

"Kind creature!" murmured the king. "Come, countess, forget and forgive!"

"Yes, sire, I shall forgive; only, I shall set out for
Luciennes, and thence for Boulogne."

"Boulogne-sur-mer?" asked the king.

"Yes, sire; I shall quit a kingdom where the king is
afraid of his minister."

"Madame!" exclaimed Louis, with an offended air.

"Sire, that I may not any longer be wanting in respect
to you, permit me to retire;" and the countess rose, observing with the corner of her eye what effect her movement
had produced.

The king gave his usual heavy sigh of weariness, which
said plainly, "I am getting rather tired of this." Chon

understood what the sigh meant, and saw that it would be dangerous to push matters to extremity. She caught her sister by the gown, and approaching the king, —

"Sire," said she, "my sister's affection for the poor viscount has carried her too far. It is I who have committed the fault; it is I who must repair it. As the humblest of your Majesty's subjects, I beg from your Majesty justice for my brother. I accuse nobody; your wisdom will discover the guilty."

"Why, that is precisely what I wish myself," said the king, — "that justice should be done. If a man have not committed a certain crime, let him not be reproached with it; but if he have, let him be punished." And Louis looked towards the countess as he spoke, with the hope of once more catching the hopes he had entertained of an amusing morning, — a morning which seemed turning out so dismally. The good-natured countess could not help pitying the king, whose want of occupation and emptiness of mind made him feel tired and dispirited except when with her. She turned half round, for she had already made a step towards the door, and said, with the sweetest submission, "Do I wish for anything but justice? only, let not my well-grounded suspicions be cruelly repulsed."

"Your suspicions are sacred to me, countess," cried the king; "and if they be changed into certainty, you shall see. But now I think of it — how easy to know the truth! Let the Duke de Choiseul be sent for."

"Oh, your Majesty knows that he never comes into these apartments; he would scorn to do so. His sister, however, is not of his mind; she wishes for nothing better than to be here."

The king laughed. The countess, encouraged by this, went on: "The Duke de Choiseul apes the dauphin; he will not compromise his dignity."

"The dauphin is religious, countess."

"And the duke a hypocrite, sire."

"I promise you, my dear countess, you shall see him

here, for I shall summon him. He must come, as it is on state business, and we shall have all explained in Chon's presence, who saw all; we shall confront them, as the lawyers say. Eh, Sartines? Let some one go for the Duke de Choiseul."

"And let some one bring me my monkey. Dorée, my monkey!" cried the countess.

These words, which were addressed to the waiting-maid, who was arranging a dressing-box, could be heard in the ante-room when the door was opened to despatch the usher for the prime minister, and they were responded to by a broken, lisping voice,—

"The countess's monkey!—that must mean me; I hasten to present myself."

And with these words entered a little hunchback, dressed with the utmost splendour.

"The Duke de Tresmes!" said the countess, annoyed by his appearance; "I did not summon you, duke."

"You asked for your monkey, madame," said the duke, bowing to the king, the countess, and the minister, "and seeing among the courtiers no ape half so ugly as myself, I hastened to obey your call;" and the duke laughed, showing his great teeth so oddly that the countess could not help laughing also.

"Shall I stay?" asked the duke, as if his whole life could not repay the favour.

"Ask his Majesty, duke; he is master here."

The duke turned to the king, with the air of a suppliant.

"Yes, stay, duke, stay!" said the king, glad to find any additional means of amusement. At this moment the usher threw open the doors.

"Oh!" said the king, with a slight expression of dissatisfaction on his face, "is it the Duke de Choiseul already!"

"No, sire," replied the usher, "it is monseigneur the dauphin, who desires to speak to you."

The countess almost started from her chair with joy, for she imagined the dauphin was going to become her friend; but Chon, who was more clear-sighted, frowned.

"Well, where is the dauphin?" asked the king, impatiently.

"In your Majesty's apartments; his Royal Highness awaits your return."

"It is fated I shall never have a minute's repose," grumbled the king. Then, all at once remembering that the audience demanded by the dauphin might spare him the scene with Monsieur de Choiseul, he thought better of it. "I am coming," said he, "I am coming. Good-by, countess. See how I am dragged in all directions!"

"But will your Majesty go just when the Duke de Choiseul is coming?"

"What can I do? the first slave is the king. Oh, if those rogues of philosophers knew what it is to be a king! —but above all a king of France."

"But, sire, you can stay."

"Oh, I must not keep the dauphin waiting. People say already that I have no affection except for my daughters."

"But what shall I say to the duke?"

"Oh, tell him to come to my apartments, countess."

And, to put an end to any farther remonstrance, he kissed her hand, and disappeared, running, as was his habit whenever he feared to lose a victory gained by his temporising policy and his petty cunning. The countess trembled with passion, and clasping her hands she exclaimed, "So he has escaped once more!"

But the king did not hear those words; the door was already closed behind him, and he passed through the ante-rooms, saying to the courtiers, "Go in, gentlemen, go in,— the countess will see you; but you will find her very dull, on account of the accident which has befallen poor Viscount Jean."

The courtiers looked at one another in amazement, for they had not heard of the accident. Many hoped that the viscount was dead, but all put on countenances suitable to the occasion. Those who were best pleased looked the most sympathetic, and they entered.

CHAPTER XXV.

THE SALON OF CLOCKS.

In that large hall of the palace of Versailles which was called the Salon of Clocks, a young man walked slowly up and down, with his arms hanging and his head bent forward. He appeared to be about seventeen years of age, was of a fair complexion, and his eyes were mild in their expression; but it must be acknowledged that there was a slight degree of vulgarity in his demeanour. On his breast sparkled a diamond star, rendered more brilliant by the dark violet-coloured velvet of his coat; and his white satin waistcoat, embroidered with silver, was crossed by the blue ribbon supporting the cross of St. Louis.

None could mistake in this young man the profile, so expressive of dignity and kindliness, which formed the characteristic type of the elder branch of the house of Bourbon, of which he was at once the most striking and most exaggerated image. In fact, Louis Auguste, Duke de Berry, Dauphin of France (afterwards Louis XVI.), had the Bourbon nose even longer and more aquiline than in his predecessors. His forehead was lower and more retreating than Louis XV.'s, and the double chin of his grandfather was so remarkable in him that, although he was at the time we speak of young and thin, his chin formed nearly one-third of the length of his face.

Although well made, there was something embarrassed in the movement of his legs and shoulders, and his walk was slow and rather awkward. Suppleness, activity, and strength seemed centred only in his arms, and more par-

ticularly in his fingers, which displayed, as it were, that
character which in other persons is expressed on the forehead, in the mouth, and in the eyes. The dauphin continued to pace in silence the Salon of Clocks, — the
same in which, eight years before, Louis XV. had given
to Madame de Pompadour the decree of the parliament
exiling the Jesuits from the kingdom, — and as he walked
he seemed plunged in reverie.

At last, however, he seemed to become impatient of
waiting there alone, and to amuse himself he began to
look at the timepieces, remarking, as Charles V. had done,
the differences which are found in the most regular clocks.
These differences are a singular but decided manifestation
of the inequality existing in all material things, whether
regulated or not regulated by the hand of man. He
stopped before the large clock at the lower end of the
room, — the same place it occupies at present, — which, by
a clever arrangement of machinery, marks the days, the
months, the years, the phases of the moon, the course of
the planets, — in short, exhibiting to the still more curious
machine called man, all that is most interesting in his
progressive movement through life to death.

The prince examined this clock with the eye of an
amateur, and leaned now to the right, now to the left, to
examine the movement of such or such a wheel. Then he
returned to his place in front, watching how the second-
hand glided rapidly on, — like those flies which, with their
long, slender legs, skim over the surface of a pond without
disturbing the liquid crystal of its waters. This contemplation naturally led him to think that a very great number
of seconds had passed since he had been waiting there. It
is true, also, that many had passed before he had ventured
to send to inform the king that he was waiting for him.

All at once the hand on which the young prince's eyes
were fixed stopped as if by enchantment, the wheels
ceased their measured rotation, the springs became still,
and deep silence took possession of the machine, but a

moment before so full of noise and motion. No more ticking, no more oscillations, no more movement of the wheels or of the hands. The timepiece had died.

Had some grain of sand, some atom, penetrated into one of the wheels, and stopped its movements? Or was the genius of the machine resting, wearied with its eternal agitation? Surprised by this sudden death, this stroke of apoplexy occurring before his eyes, the dauphin forgot why he had come thither, and how long he had waited. Above all, he forgot that hours are not counted in eternity by the beating of metal upon metal, nor arrested even for a moment in their course by the hindrance of any wheel, but that they are recorded on the dial of eternity, established even before the birth of worlds by the unchangeable hand of the Almighty.

He therefore opened the glass door of the crystal pagoda the genius of which had ceased to act, and put his head inside to examine the timepiece more closely. But the large pendulum was in his way; he slipped in his supple fingers, and took it off. This was not enough; the dauphin still found the cause of the lethargy of the machine hidden from him. He then supposed that the person who had the care of the clocks of the palace had forgotten to wind up this timepiece, and he took down the key from a hook and began to wind it up like a man quite accustomed to the business. But he could only turn it three times, — a proof that something was astray in the mechanism. He drew from his pocket a little file, and with the end of it pushed one of the wheels; they all creaked for half a second, then stopped again.

The malady of the clock was becoming serious; the dauphin, therefore, began carefully to unscrew several parts of it, laying them all in order on a console beside him. Then, drawn on by his ardour, he began to take to pieces still more and more of the complicated machine, and to search minutely into its most hidden and mysterious recesses. Suddenly he uttered a cry of joy; he discovered that a screw which acted on one of the springs had become loose, and had thus impeded the movement of the motive wheel.

He immediately began to screw it; and then, with a wheel in his left hand, and his little file in his right, he plunged his head again into the interior of the clock.

He was busy at his work, absorbed in contemplation of the mechanism of the timepiece, when a door opened, and a voice announced, "The king!"

But the dauphin heard nothing but the melodious sound of that ticking which his hand had again awakened, as if it were the beating of a heart which a clever physician had restored to life.

The king looked around on all sides, and it was some minutes before he discovered the dauphin, whose head was hidden in the opening, and whose legs alone were visible. He approached, smiling, and tapped his grandson on the shoulder.

"What the devil are you doing there?" said he. The dauphin drew out his head quickly, but, at the same time, with all the care necessary to avoid doing any harm to the beautiful object which he had undertaken to mend.

"Sire, your Majesty sees," replied the young man, blushing at being surprised in the midst of his occupations; "I was amusing myself until you came."

"Yes, in destroying my clock, — a very pretty amusement!"

"Oh no, sire; I was mending it. The principal wheel would not move; it was prevented by this screw. I have tightened the screw, and now it goes."

"But you will blind yourself with looking into that thing. I would not put my head into such a trap for all the gold in the world."

"Oh, it will do me no harm, sire; I understand all about it. I always take to pieces, clean, and put together again, that beautiful watch which your Majesty gave me on my fourteenth birthday."

"Very well; but stop now, if you please, and leave your mechanics. You wish to speak to me?"

"I, sire?" said the young man, colouring again.

"Of course, since you sent to say you were waiting for me."

"It is true, sire," replied the dauphin, looking down.

"Well what is it? Answer me. If it is of no importance I must go, for I am just setting off for Marly." Louis XV., as was his custom, already sought to escape.

The dauphin placed his wheel and his file on a chair, which indicated that he had really something important to say, since he interrupted his important work for it.

"Do you want money?" asked the king, sharply. "If so, I shall send you some;" and he made a step towards the door.

"Oh, no, sire; I have still a thousand crowns remaining of the sum I received last month."

"What economy!" said the king; "and how well Monsieur de la Vauguyon has educated him! I think he has precisely all the virtues I have not."

The young prince made a violent effort over himself. "Sire," said he, "is the dauphiness yet very far distant?"

"Do you not know as well as I how far off she is?" replied the king.

"I?" stammered out the dauphin.

"Of course; you heard the account of her journey read yesterday. Last Monday she was at Nancy, and she ought to be now about forty-five leagues from Paris."

"Sire, does not your Majesty think her Royal Highness travels very slowly?"

"By no means," replied the king; "I think she travels very fast for a woman. And then, you know, there are the receptions and the rejoicings on the road. She travels at least ten leagues every two days, one with another."

"I think it very little, sire," said the dauphin, timidly.

Louis XV. was more and more astonished at the appearance of impatience, which he had been far from suspecting.

"Come, come," said he, smiling slyly, "don't be impatient; your dauphiness will arrive soon."

"Sire, might not these ceremonies on the road be shortened?" continued the dauphin.

"Impossible; she has already passed through two or three towns, where she should have made a stay, without stopping."

"But these delays will be eternal; and then, sire, I think, besides — " said the dauphin, still more timidly.

"Well, what do you think? Let me hear it; speak!"

"I think that the service is badly performed."

"How? what service?"

"The service for the journey."

"Nonsense! I sent thirty thousand horses to be ready on the road, thirty carriages, sixty wagons, I don't know how many carts. If carts, carriages, and horses were put in file, they would reach from this to Strasburg. How can you say, then, there is bad attendance on the road?"

"Well, sire, in spite of all your Majesty's goodness, I am almost certain that what I say is true; but perhaps I have used an improper term, and instead of badly performed I should have said badly arranged."

The king raised his head and fixed his eyes on the dauphin; he began to comprehend that more was meant than met the ear in the few words which his Royal Highness had ventured to utter.

"Thirty thousand horses," he repeated, "thirty carriages, sixty wagons, two regiments. I ask you, Monsieur Philosopher, have you ever heard of a dauphiness entering France with such an attendance as that before?"

"I confess, sire, that things have been royally done, and as your Majesty alone knows how to do them. But has your Majesty specially recommended that these horses and carriages should be employed solely for her Royal Highness and her train?"

The king looked at his grandson for the third time. A vague suspicion began to sting him, a slight remembrance to illuminate his mind; and a sort of confused analogy between what the dauphin was saying and a disagreeable circumstance of late occurrence began to suggest itself to him.

"A fine question!" said he. "Certainly, everything has been ordered for her royal highness, and for her alone; and therefore, I repeat, she cannot fail to arrive very soon. But why do you look at me in that way?" added he, in a decided tone, which to the dauphin seemed even threatening. "Are you amusing yourself in studying my features as you study the springs of your mechanical works?"

The dauphin had opened his mouth to speak, but became silent at this address.

"Very well," said the king, sharply; "it appears you have no more to say, hey? Are you satisfied now? Your dauphiness will arrive soon; all is arranged delightfully for her on the road; you are as rich as Crœsus with your own private purse. And now, since your mind is at ease, be good enough to put my clock in order again."

The dauphin did not stir.

"Do you know," said the king, laughing, "I have a great mind to make you the principal watchmaker for the palace, with a good salary."

The dauphin looked down, and, intimidated by the king's look, took up the wheel and the file which he had laid on the chair. The king, in the mean time, had quietly gained the door. "What the devil," said he, looking at him, "did he mean with his badly arranged service? Well, well! I have escaped another scene, for he is certainly dissatisfied about something."

In fact, the dauphin, generally so patient, had stamped with his foot as the king turned away from him.

"He is commencing again," murmured the king, laughing; "decidedly, I have nothing for it but to fly." But just as he opened the door, he saw on the threshold the Duke de Choiseul, who bowed profoundly.

CHAPTER XXVI.

THE COURT OF KING PÉTAUD.

THE king made a step backwards at the sight of this new actor in the scene, come, no doubt, to prevent him from escaping as he had hoped.   "Ha !" thought he, "I had forgotten him; but he is welcome, and I will make him pay for what the others have made me suffer."

"Ha! you are there!" cried he.   "I sent for you; did you know that?"

"Yes, sire," replied the minister, coldly; "I was dressing to wait on your Majesty when your orders reached me."

"I wished to speak to you on serious matters," said the king, frowning in order, if possible, to intimidate his minister. Unfortunately for the king, Monsieur de Choiseul was one of the men least likely to be daunted in his dominions.

"And I also, if it please your Majesty," said he, bowing, "have serious matters to speak of."   At the same time he exchanged a look with the dauphin, who was still half hidden by the clock.

The king stopped short. "Ha!" thought he, "now I am caught between two fires; there is no escape."

"You know, I presume," said the king, hastily, in order to have the first word, "that poor Viscount Jean has had a narrow escape from assassination, — that is to say, that he has received a wound in his arm."

"I came to speak of that affair to your Majesty."

"I understand; you wished to prevent unpleasant reports?"

"I wished, sire, to anticipate all remarks."

"Then you know the whole particulars, monsieur?" inquired the king, in a significant manner.

"Perfectly."

"Ha!" said the king, "I was told so in a place likely to be well informed."

The Duke of Choiseul seemed quite unmoved. The dauphin continued turning the screw in the clock, his head bent down, but he lost not a syllable of the conversation.

"I shall now tell you how the affair happened," said the king.

"Does your Majesty think that you have been well informed?" asked Monsieur de Choiseul.

"Oh, as to that —"

"We are all attention, sire."

"We!" repeated the king.

"Yes; monseigneur the dauphin and I."

"Monseigneur the dauphin?" repeated the king, turning his eyes from the respectful Choiseul to the attentive Louis Auguste, "and pray in what does this squabble concern monseigneur?"

"It concerns monseigneur," said the duke, bowing to the young prince, "because madame the dauphiness was the cause of it."

"The dauphiness the cause?" said the king, starting.

"Certainly; if you are ignorant of that, sire, your Majesty has been very badly informed."

"The dauphiness and Jean Dubarry!" said the king; "this is likely to be a curious tale. Come, explain this, Monsieur de Choiseul; conceal nothing, even though it were the dauphiness herself who pierced Dubarry's arm!"

"Sire, it was not the dauphiness," replied Choiseul, still calm and unmoved; "it was one of the gentlemen of her escort."

"Oh," said the king, again becoming grave, "an officer whom you know."

"No, sire; but an officer whom your Majesty ought to

know, if you remember all who have served you well, — an officer whose father's name was honoured at Philipsbourg, at Fontenoy, at Mahon, — a Taverney-Maison-Rouge."

The dauphin seemed to draw a deeper breath, as if to inhale this name, and thus preserve it in his memory.

"A Maison-Rouge," said the king; "certainly I know the name. And why did he attack Jean, whom I like so much? Perhaps because I like him! Such absurd jealousies, such discontents, are almost seditious."

"Sire, will your Majesty deign to listen to me?" said Monsieur de Choiseul.

The king saw there was no other way for him to escape from this troublesome business but by getting in a passion, and he exclaimed, "I tell you, monsieur, that I see the beginning of a conspiracy against my peace, an organised persecution of my family!"

"Ah, sire," said Monsieur de Choiseul, "is it for defending the dauphiness, your Majesty's daughter-in-law, that these reproaches are cast on a brave young man?"

The dauphin raised his head and folded his arms. "For my part," said he, "I cannot but feel grateful to the man who exposed his life for a princess who in a fortnight will be my wife."

"Exposed his life! exposed his life!" stammered the king; "what about? Let me know that; what about?"

"About the horses of madame the dauphiness," replied the duke. "Viscount Jean Dubarry, who was already travelling very fast, took upon him to insist on having some of those horses which were appropriated to the use of madame, — no doubt that he might get on still faster."

The king bit his lip and changed colour; the threatening phantom from which he had so lately hoped to escape now reappeared in all its horrors. "It is not possible," murmured he, to gain time. "I know the whole affair; you have been misinformed, duke."

"No, sire, I have not been misinformed; what I have the honour to tell your Majesty is the simple truth.

Viscount Jean Dubarry offered an insult to the dauphiness by insisting on taking for his use horses appointed for her service. After having ill-treated the master of the post-house, he was going to take them by force when the Chevalier Philip de Taverney arrived, sent forward by her Royal Highness to have horses in readiness for her, and after he had several times summoned him in a friendly and conciliating manner — "

"Oh, oh!" grumbled the king.

"I repeat, sire, after he had several times, in a friendly and conciliating manner, summoned the viscount to desist, he was at length obliged to draw his sword."

"Yes," said the dauphin, "I pledge myself for the truth of what the duke asserts."

"Then you also know of this affair?" said the king, exceedingly surprised.

"I know all the circumstances perfectly, sire," replied the dauphin.

The minister bowed, delighted at having such a supporter. "Will your Royal Highness deign to proceed?" said he. "His Majesty will doubtless have more confidence in the assertions of his august son than in mine."

"Yes, sire," continued the dauphin, without testifying for the Duke de Choiseul's zeal in his cause all that gratitude which might have been expected; "yes, sire, I know the circumstances, and I had come to tell your Majesty that Viscount Dubarry has not only insulted the dauphiness in interfering with the arrangements made for her journey, but he has also insulted me, in opposing a gentleman of my regiment who was doing his duty."

The king shook his head. "We must inquire," said he; "we must inquire."

"I have already inquired, sire," said the dauphin, gently, "and have no doubt in the matter; the viscount drew his sword on my officer."

"Did he draw first?" asked the king, happy to seize any chance of putting his adversary in fault.

The dauphin coloured, and looked to the minister for assistance. "Sire," said the latter, "swords were crossed by two men, one of whom was insulting, the other defending, the dauphiness; that is all."

"Yes, but which was the aggressor?" asked the king; "I know poor Jean; he is as gentle as a lamb."

"The aggressor, in my opinion, sire," said the dauphin, with his usual mildness, "is he who is in the wrong."

"It is a delicate matter to decide," replied the king; "the aggressor he who is in the wrong? — in the wrong? — but if the officer was insolent?"

"Insolent!" cried the Duke de Choiseul; "insolent towards a man who wanted to take by force horses sent there for the use of the dauphiness? Is it possible you can think so, sire?"

The dauphin turned pale, but said nothing. The king saw that he was between two fires.

"I should say warm, perhaps, not insolent," said he.

"But your Majesty knows," said the minister, taking advantage of the king's having yielded a step, to make a step forward; "your Majesty knows that a zealous servant can never be in the wrong."

"Oh, perhaps. But how did you become acquainted with this event, monsieur?" said he, turning sharply to the dauphin, without ceasing, however, to observe the duke, who endeavoured vainly to hide the embarrassment which this sudden question caused him.

"By a letter, sire," replied the dauphin.

"A letter from whom?"

"A letter from a person concerned for madame, the dauphiness, and who thinks it singular that any one should dare to affront her."

"Ha!" cried the king, "more mysteries, secret correspondences, plots! Every one is beginning again to plan annoyances for me, as in the time of the Marquise de Pompadour!"

"No, sire," said the minister; "this affair is no plot, and

can be settled very simply. It is the crime of treason in the second degree; let the guilty person be punished, and all will be settled."

At this word, "punished," Louis XV. saw in fancy the countess furious, and Chon in a rage; he saw peace flying from his dwelling (peace, which he had been seeking all his life, but had never been able to find), and intestine war, with crooked nails and eyes red with tears, entering in her stead.

"Punished!" cried he, "without the accused having been heard; without knowing which side is in the right? You make a very extraordinary proposal to me, duke; you wish to draw odium on me!"

"But, sire, who will henceforward respect madame the dauphiness, if a severe example is not made of the person who first insulted her?"

"Certainly, sire," added the dauphin; "it would be a scandal."

"An example? a scandal?" cried the king. "*Mordieu!* if I make an example of all the scandalous things that go on around me, I may pass my life in signing arrests for the Bastille! I have signed enough of them as it is, Heaven knows!"

"In this case it is necessary, sire," said the duke.

"Sire, I entreat your Majesty," said the dauphin.

"What! do you not think him punished already, by the wound he has received?"

"No, sire; for he might have wounded the Chevalier de Taverney."

"And in such a case, what would you have done?"

"I should have demanded his head."

"But that was only what was done in the case of Monsieur de Montgomery, for killing King Henry II.," said the king.

"He killed the king by accident, sire; Viscount Dubarry insulted the dauphiness intentionally."

"And you, monsieur," said the king, turning to the dauphin, "do you wish to have Jean's head?"

"No, sire; I am not in favour of the punishment of death, as your Majesty knows; I shall merely demand from you the viscount's banishment."

The king started up.

"Banishment for a tavern quarrel? Louis, you are severe, notwithstanding your philanthropical notions; it is true that before becoming philanthropist you were a mathematician, and—"

"Will your Majesty deign to proceed?"

"A mathematician would sacrifice the universe to his problem."

"Sire," said the dauphin, "I have no ill-will towards the Viscount Dubarry, personally."

"With whom, then, are you angry?"

"With the insulter of madame the dauphiness."

"What a model for husbands!" cried the king, ironically; "but I am not so easy of belief. I see very well who is attacked under all this; I see to what people would lead me with their exaggerations!"

"Sire," said Monsieur de Choiseul, "do not be misled,— nothing has been exaggerated; the public are indignant at the insolence which has been shown in this affair."

"The public?—there is another monster with which you frighten yourself, or rather with which you would frighten me. Shall I listen to this public, which by the thousand mouths of libellists, and pamphleteers, and ballad-mongers, tells me that I am robbed, tossed in a blanket, betrayed on all hands? No, no; I let the public talk, and I laugh. Do as I do. *Pardieu!* close your ears; and when your great public is tired of bawling it will stop. There you are again, making your discontented bow; and Louis is putting on a sulky face. Heavens! is it not singular that what is done for the lowest individual cannot be done for me? I cannot be allowed to live quietly in my own fashion! Everybody hates what I love, and eternally loves what I hate! Am I in my senses, or am I a fool? Am I the master, or am I not?"

The dauphin took up his file, and returned to his work in the clock. The Duke de Choiseul bowed exactly as before.

"There now, no answer! Answer something, will you? *Mordieu!* you will kill me with vexation,—first at your talk, then at your silence; with your petty hatreds and your petty fears!"

"I do not hate the Viscount Dubarry," said the dauphin, smiling.

"And I do not fear him, sire," said the minister, haughtily.

"You are both very ill-natured," cried the king, pretending to be in a great passion, when he was in reality only out of temper. "You wish to make me the laughing-stock of all Europe, — to give my cousin of Prussia something to make jests on; to make me realise the court of King Pétaud, which that rascal Voltaire has described; but I will not be what you wish!—no! you shall not have that satisfaction. I know what concerns my own honour, and I shall attend to it in my own way, and only as I choose myself!"

"Sire," said the dauphin, with that immovable mildness which characterised him, but at the same time with that constant perseverance of his, "this is not a matter which concerns your honour, it is the dignity of the dauphiness which has been attacked."

"Monseigneur is right, sire," said the duke; "let but your Majesty speak the word, and no one will again dare to insult her."

"And who would insult her? No one intended to insult her. Jean is a stupid fellow, but he is not malignant."

"Well, then, sire," continued the minister, "let it be placed to the account of stupidity, and let him ask pardon of the Chevalier de Taverney for his mistake."

"I said before," cried the king, "that I have nothing to do in the affair. Let Jean ask pardon, he is at liberty to do so; or let him decline, he is at liberty also."

"The affair given up in that way, sire, I must take the liberty to inform your Majesty, will be talked about."

"So much the better!" exclaimed the king, "let it be talked about until I am deafened with it, provided I don't hear all this nonsense of yours!"

"Then," replied the minister, with his imperturbable coolness, "I am authorised by your Majesty to say that Viscount Dubarry did right?"

"Authorised by me? authorised by me? and in an affair of which I understand nothing! You mean, I see, to drive me to extremities; but take care, duke! take care! And, Louis, I advise you to be more cautious how you conduct yourself towards me! I shall leave you to think of what I have said, for I am tired out; I cannot bear this any longer. Good-by, gentlemen! I am going to see my daughters, and then I shall take refuge at Marly, where I may hope for some tranquillity, if you do not follow me."

At this moment, and as the king was going towards the door, it was opened, and an usher appeared.

"Sire," said he, "Madame Louise is awaiting your Majesty in the gallery, to bid you farewell."

"To bid me farewell?" exclaimed the king, in alarm, "where is she going?"

"Madame says that she has had your Majesty's permission to leave the palace."

"Ha! another scene! This is my bigot daughter going to show off some of her follies. In truth, I am the most wretched of men."

And he left the apartment, running.

"His Majesty has given us no answer," said the Duke de Choiseul; "what has your Royal Highness decided on?"

"Ah, there it strikes!" said the young prince, listening with either a real or a pretended joy to the clock, which he had made to go once more.

The minister frowned and retired backward from the Salon of Clocks, leaving the dauphin alone.

CHAPTER XXVII.

MADAME LOUISE OF FRANCE.

THE king's eldest daughter awaited him in the great gallery of Lebrun, the same in which Louis XIV., in 1683, had received the Doge Imperiali and the four Genoese senators sent to implore pardon for the republic.

At the farther end of the gallery, opposite the door by which the king must enter, were three or four ladies of honour, who seemed in the utmost consternation. Louis arrived just at the moment when groups began to form in the vestibule; for the resolution which the princess had taken only that morning was now spreading on all sides through the palace.

Madame Louise possessed a majestic figure and a truly regal style of beauty; yet a secret sadness had left its lines on her fair forehead. Her austere practice of every virtue, and her respect for the great powers of the state — powers which for the last fifty years had only obtained a semblance of respect from interest or from fear — had caused her to be regarded with veneration by the court. We must add that she was loved even by the people, although a feeling of disaffection towards their *masters* was now general. The word "tyrants" had not yet been heard.

She was loved because her virtue was not stern. She was not loudly talked of, but all knew that she had a heart; she manifested this every day by works of charity, while others only showed it by shameless self-indulgence. Louis XV. feared this daughter, for the simple reason that he esteemed her. There were even times when he went

so far as to be proud of her; and she was the only one of
his children whom he spared in his sharp raillery or his
silly familiarities. He called her madame, whilst the
Princesses Adelaide, Victoire, and Sophie, he named Loque,
Chiffe, and Graille.[1] Since the period when Marshal Saxe
carried with him to the tomb the soul of the Turennes and
the Condés, and with the Queen Maria Leczinska passed
away the governing mind of a Maria Theresa, all became
mean and worthless around the throne of France. Madame
Louise, whose character was truly regal, and, compared
with those around her, seemed even heroic, alone remained
to adorn the crown, — like a pearl of price amidst false
stones and tinsel.   We should be wrong in concluding
from this that Louis XV. loved his daughter; Louis, it
is well known, loved no one but himself: we only affirm
that he preferred her to all his other children.

When he entered, he found the princess in the centre of
the gallery, leaning on a table inlaid with crimson jasper
and lapis lazuli. She was dressed entirely in black, and
her beautiful hair, which was without powder, was covered
by a double roll of lace. A deeper shade of sadness than
usual rested on her brow. She looked at no one in the
apartment, but from time to time her melancholy gaze
wandered over the portraits of the kings of Europe which
ornamented the gallery, at the head of whom were those
of her ancestors, the kings of France.

The black dress which she wore was the usual travelling
costume of princesses; it concealed large pockets, still
worn as in the times of the good housewife-like queens,
and the Princess Louise, imitating them in that also, had
the numerous keys of her chests and wardrobes suspended
at her waist by a gold chain.

The king's face assumed a very serious expression when
he saw how silent all in the gallery were, and how attentively they awaited the result of the interview between

---

[1] Tag, Rag, and Scrap.

him and his daughter. But the gallery was so long that
the spectators at either end might see, but they could not
hear what passed. They had a right to see; it was their
duty not to hear.

Madame advanced a few steps to meet the king, and
taking his hand, she kissed it respectfully.

"They tell me you are setting out on a journey, madame,"
said he; "are you going into Picardy?"

"No, sire," she replied.

"Then, I presume," said he, in a louder voice, "that
you are about to make a pilgrimage to Noirmontiers?"

"No, sire; I am going to retire to the convent of the
Carmelites at St. Denis, of which you know I have the
right to be abbess."

The king started, but he preserved his countenance unmoved, although in reality his heart was troubled.

"Oh, no, no! my daughter!" he said, "you will not
leave me! It is impossible you can leave me!"

"My dear father, it is long since I decided on abandoning the world, — your Majesty permitted me to make that
decision. Do not now, I entreat you, my dear father,
oppose my wishes."

"Yes, certainly, you wrung from me the permission of
which you speak. I gave it, but still hoped that when
the moment of departure came your heart would fail you.
You ought not to bury yourself in a cloister; by acting
so, you forget what is due to your rank; it is grief or want
of fortune which makes the convent be sought as a refuge.
The daughter of the King of France is certainly not poor;
and if she be unhappy, the world ought not to know it."

The king's thoughts and even his language seemed to
become more elevated as he entered more and more into
the part he was called on to play, — that of a king and a
father. This is, indeed, a part never played ill, when
pride and regret inspire the actor.

"Sire," replied the princess, perceiving her father's
emotion, and fearful that it might affect her more deeply

than she desired at that moment, "Sire, do not by your tenderness for me weaken my resolution. My grief is no vulgar grief; therefore, my resolution to retire from the world is not in accordance with the usual customs of our day."

"Your grief?" exclaimed the king, as if from a real impulse of feeling. "Have you, then, sorrows, my poor child?"

"Heavy, heavy sorrows, sire!"

"Why did you not confide them to me, my dearest daughter?"

"Because they are sorrows not to be assuaged by any mortal hand."

"Not by that of a king?"

"Ah, no, sire."

"Not by a father's hand?"

"No, sire, no."

"But you are religious, Louise; does not religion give you strength?"

"Not sufficient strength yet, sire; therefore I retire to a cloister in order to obtain more. In silence God speaks to the heart of man; in solitude man communes with God."

"But in acting thus you are making a sacrifice for which nothing can compensate. The throne of France casts a majestic shadow over the children of its kings; ought not this reflected greatness to be sufficient for you?"

"The shadow of the cell is better, sire, — it refreshes the weary spirit; it soothes the strong as well as the weak, the humble as well as the proud, the high as well as the low."

"Do you fear any danger by remaining? In that case, Louise, cannot the king defend you?"

"Sire, may God, in the first place, defend the king!"

"I repeat, Louise, that mistaken zeal leads you astray. It is good to pray, but not to pray always; and you — so good, so pious! — can you require such constant prayer?"

"Oh, my father! never can I offer up prayers enough to avert the woes which threaten you. If God has given me a portion of goodness, if for twenty years my only effort has been to purify my soul, I fear, alas! that I am yet far from having attained the goodness and the purity necessary for an expiatory sacrifice."

The king started back and gazed at the princess with surprise. "Never have I heard you speak thus before, my dear child," said he; "your ascetic life is making your reason wander."

"Oh, sire, do not speak thus of a devotion the truest that ever subject offered to a king, or daughter to a father, in a time of need. Sire, that throne, of which you but now so proudly spoke as lending a protecting shade to your children, — that throne totters. You feel not the blows which are dealt at its foundations, but I have seen them. Silently a deep abyss is preparing, which will engulf the monarchy. Sire, has any one ever told you the truth?"

The princess looked around to discover whether the attendants were far enough to be out of hearing of her words, then she resumed: —

"Well, sire, I know the truth. Too often have I heard the groans which the wretched send forth, when, as a Sister of Mercy, I visited the dark, narrow streets, the filthy lanes, the dismal garrets of the poor. In those streets, those lanes, those garrets, I have seen human beings dying of cold and hunger in winter, of heat and thirst in summer. You see not, sire, what the country is, — you, who go merely from Versailles to Marly, and from Marly to Versailles. But in the country there is not grain, I do not say to feed the people, but even to sow for a new harvest; for the land, cursed by some adverse power, has received, but has given nothing back. The people, wanting bread, are filled with discontent. The air is filled in the twilight and at night with voices telling them of weapons, of chains, of prisons, of tyranny; and at these voices they awake, cease to complain, and commence to threaten. The parliaments demand the right of remonstrance, — that is, the right to say to you openly what they whisper in private, 'King, you are ruining the kingdom; save it, or we shall save it ourselves.' The soldiers, with their idle swords, furrow the land in which the philosophers have scattered the seeds of liberty. Men now see things which they formerly saw not, for our writers have laid all open to them; they know all that we do, and frown whenever their *masters* pass by. Your Majesty's successor is soon to be married. When Anne of Austria's son was married, the city of Paris made presents to the new queen; now, it is not only silent, and offers nothing, but you have been obliged to use force to collect the taxes to pay the expense of bringing the daughter of Cæsar to the palace of the son of St. Louis. The clergy had long ceased to pray to God; but, seeing the lands given away, privileges exhausted, coffers empty, they have begun again to pray for what they call the happiness of the people. And then, sire, must I tell you what you know so well, — what you have seen with so much bitterness, although you have spoken of it to none? The kings, your brothers, who formerly envied us, now turn away from us. Your four daughters, sire, princesses of France, have not found husbands; and there are twenty princes in Germany, three in England, sixteen in the States of the North, without naming our relations, the Bourbons of Spain and Naples, who forget us, or turn away from us like the others. Perhaps the Turk would have taken us, had we not been daughters of his most Christian Majesty. Not for myself, my father, do I care for this, or complain of it. Mine is a happy state, since it leaves me free; since I am not necessary to any one of my family, and may retire from the world, — in meditation and in poverty may pray to God to avert from your head, and from my nephew's, the awful storm I see gathering on the horizon of the future."

"My child! my daughter! it is your fears which make the future appear so dreadful."

"Sire, sire, remember that princess of antiquity, that royal prophetess! She foretold to her father and to her brothers war, destruction, conflagration, and her predictions were laughed at, — they called her mad. Do not treat me as she was treated. Take care, oh, my father! reflect, my king!"

Louis XV. folded his arms, and his head sank on his bosom. "My daughter," said he, "you speak very severely. Are those woes which you denounce caused by me?"

"God forbid that I should think so! They are the fruit of the times in which we live. You are whirled on in the career of events as we are all. Only listen, sire, to the applause in the theatre which follows any allusion against royalty! See, in the evenings, what joyous crowds descend the narrow stairs of the galleries, while the grand marble staircase is deserted! Sire, both the people and the courtiers have made for themselves pleasures quite apart from our pleasures; they amuse themselves without us; or rather, when we appear in the midst of their pleasures, they become dull. Alas!" continued the princess, her eyes swimming with tears, "alas! poor young men, affectionate young women! — love, sing, forget, be happy! Here, when I went amongst you, I only disturbed your happiness; yonder, in my cloister, I shall serve you! Here, you hid your glad smiles in my presence, for fear of displeasing me; there, I shall pray — oh, God! with all my soul — for my king, for my sisters, for my nephews, for the people of France, for all whom I love with the energy of a heart which no earthly passion has exhausted."

"My daughter," said the king, after a melancholy silence, "I entreat you not to leave me, — not at this moment, at least; you will break my heart!"

Madame Louise seized his hand, and, fixing her eyes full of love on his noble features, "No!" said she, "no, my father; not another hour in this palace! No, it is time for me to pray: I feel in myself strength to redeem,

by my tears, those pleasures for which you sigh,—you,
who are yet young. You are the kindest of fathers, you
are ever ready to pardon!"

"Stay with us, Louise! stay with us!" said the king,
pressing her to his heart.

Madame Louise shook her head. "My kingdom is not
of this world," said she, disengaging herself from her
father's embrace. "Farewell, my father! I have told
you to-day what, for ten years, has lain heavy on my
heart. The burden became too great. Farewell! I am
satisfied; see, I can smile. I am now, at length, happy;
I regret nothing."

"Not even me, my daughter?"

"Ah, I should regret you, were I never to see you again;
but you will sometimes come to St. Denis? You will not
quite forget your child?"

"Oh, never, never!"

"Do not, my dear father, allow yourself to be affected.
Let it not appear that this separation is to be a lasting
one. My sisters, I believe, know nothing of it yet; my
women alone have been my confidants. For eight days I
have been making all my preparations; and I wish that
the report of my departure should only be spread when the
great doors of St. Denis shall have closed on me; their
heavy sound will prevent me from hearing any other."

The king read in his daughter's eyes that her resolution
was irrevocable; he wished, therefore, that she should go
without disturbance. If she feared that sobs might shake
her resolution, he feared them still more for his nerves.
Besides, he wished to go to Marly that day, and too much
grief at Versailles might have obliged him to put off his
journey. He reflected, also, that when issuing from some
orgies unfit both for a king and a father, he should never
more meet that grave, sad face, which seemed always to
reproach him for the careless, worthless existence which
he led; and this thought was not disagreeable to him.

"Be it, then, as you wish, my child," said he; "but, at

least, receive, before you go, the blessing of a father whom
you have always made perfectly happy."

"Give me your hand only, sire, and let me kiss it.
Bestow your precious blessing on me in thought."

To those who knew the decision of the princess, it was
a solemn spectacle to see her, at every step she made,
advancing, yet in life, to the tombs of her ancestors, —
those ancestors who, from their golden frames, seemed to
thank her that she hastened to rejoin them.

At the door of the gallery the king bowed, and returned
without uttering a word. The court, according to etiquette,
followed him.

CHAPTER XXVIII.

LOQUE, CHIFFE, AND GRAILLE.

THE king passed on to what was called the Cabinet of the Equipages. It was there that he was accustomed, before going to hunt or to drive out, to pass a few minutes in giving particular orders concerning the vehicles and attendants he should require during the rest of the day.

At the door of the gallery he bowed to the courtiers, and, by a wave of his hand, indicated that he wished to be alone. When they had left him, he passed through the cabinet to a corridor which led to the apartments of the princesses. Having reached the door, before which hung a curtain, he stopped for a moment, shook his head, and muttered between his teeth: —

"There was but one of them good, and she is gone!"

This very flattering speech for those who remained was answered by a shrill chorus of voices; the curtain was raised, and the furious trio saluted their father with cries of "Thank you, father, thank you!"

"Ha, Loque!" said he, addressing the eldest of them, Madame Adelaide, "you heard what I said, — so much the worse for you. Be angry or not, just as you like; I only spoke the truth."

"Yes," said Madame Victoire, "you tell us nothing new, sire. We always knew that you preferred Louise to us."

"In faith, quite true, Chiffe."

"And why do you prefer Louise?" asked Madame Sophie, in a sharp voice.

"Because Louise never gave me any trouble," replied the king, showing that good-humoured frankness of which, when he was perfectly pleased, Louis XV. was so complete a type.

"Oh, but she will give you trouble yet, rest assured!" replied Madame Sophie, with such a peculiar emphasis that it drew the attention of the king more particularly to her. "I should be rather surprised if she did not, for she is not very fond of you."

"And pray, what do you know about her, Graille?" said he. "Did Louise, before going away, make you her confidante?"

"I can say most truly," answered the princess, "that I return her affection with interest."

"Oh, very well. Hate one another, detest one another as much as you choose; I am perfectly content: only, do not summon me to restore order in the kingdom of the Amazons. However, I should like to know how poor Louise is to give me trouble."

"Poor Louise!" repeated Madame Victoire and Madame Adelaide, making different grimaces at the words. "You wish to know how she will give you trouble? Well, I shall tell you," said Madame Sophie.

The king stretched himself in a large easy-chair, placed near the door, so that he could at any moment make his escape.

"Louise is retiring to a convent because she wishes to carry on some experiments which she cannot make so well in the palace."

"Come, come," said the king, "no insinuations against the virtue of your sister! No one beyond these walls has ever dared to sully that, though many things are said of you for which it were well there were no grounds. Do not *you* begin this subject!"

"I?"

"Yes, *you!*"

"Oh, I was not going to attack Louise's virtue," said Madame Sophie, very much hurt by the peculiar accent her father had given to the *you*, and by the marked

repetition of it; "I only said she was going to make
experiments."

"Well, and if she does make experiments in chemistry,
if she does make fire-arms, and wheels for chairs, if she
does play on the flute, the drum, or the harpsichord, or
even the violin,— what harm would there be in it?"

"The experiments to which I alluded were experiments
in politics."

The king started; the princess went on.

"She is going to study philosophy and theology; she
will continue the commentaries on the bull 'Unigenitus.'
Indeed, we must seem very useless beings when compared
with her,— a lady who writes theories concerning govern-
ments, systems of metaphysics, and theology!"

"And if these pursuits lead your sister to heaven, what
harm can you see in them?" said the king, struck, however, with the connection there was between what Madame
Sophie was saying and the manner of Madame Louise's
departure, accompanied as it had been by a political ex-
hortation.   "If you envy her happiness you are very bad
Christians."

"No, on my honour!" said Madame Victoire; "she has
my full permission to go, but I shall take care not to follow
her."

"Nor I!" responded Madame Adelaide.

"Nor I!" said Madame Sophie.

"Besides, she always detested us," said the first.

"You all?" the king asked.

"Yes, detested us all," they replied.

"Oh, then, I see," he said; "poor Louise has chosen to
go to heaven, that she may not meet any of her family
again."

This sarcasm made the three sisters laugh, but rather
constrainedly, and Adelaide, the eldest, brought all her
wit into play in order to deal her father a more weighty
blow than he had given them.

"Ladies," said she, with the sneering tone which was

peculiar to her when roused from that habitual indolence
which had procured for her the name of Loque, "you have
either not found out, or you do not dare to tell the king,
the real cause of Louise's departure!"

"Come, Loque, come! you have got some wicked tale to
tell, I see. Let us hear it!"

"Sire, I fear it might vex you a little."

"No, no; say you hope it will vex me, that would be
nearer the truth."

Madame Adelaide bit her lips. "Then I shall tell you
the truth, sire."

"Very fine! If you ever do tell the truth, cure yourself
of the habit. The habit? Do I ever tell it? and yet you
see I am not the worse for it, heaven be praised!" and he
shrugged his shoulders.

"Speak, sister, speak!" said the other two sisters, impatient to hear anything that might wound their father.

"Sweet little creatures!" growled the king; "see how
they love their father!"

But he consoled himself by thinking that he returned
their love in kind.

"Well," continued Madame Adelaide, "what Louise
dreaded most — for she was very precise on the score of
etiquette — was — "

"Was what?" exclaimed the king; "come, finish, since
you have gone so far!"

"It was, sire, then, the intrusion of new faces at court."

"Do you say intrusion?" asked he, by no means pleased
with this beginning, for he saw to what it tended. "Intrusion? Are there intruders, then, in my palace? Am I
forced to receive persons against my will?"

By this adroit turn he hoped to change the course of the
conversation. But Madame Adelaide felt herself on the
right scent, and she was too cunning and too malicious to
lose it, when she had so good an end in view as the annoy-
ance of her father.

"Perhaps I was not quite correct, — perhaps I used the

wrong word; instead of 'intrusion' I should have said
'introduction.' "

"Oh, ah!" said the king, "that is an improvement; the
other word was a disagreeable one, I confess. I like 'introduction better.' "

"And yet," continued Madame Adelaide, "that is not
the right word either."

"What is it, then?"

"It is 'presentation.' "

"Yes," cried the other sisters, "yes, you have found the
right word now."

The king bit his lip. "Oh, do you think so?" said he.

"Yes," replied Madame Adelaide, "my sister was very
much afraid of new presentations."

"Well?" said the king, feeling what must come, and
thinking it best to have done with it as speedily as possible, "well? go on!"

"Well, sire, she was consequently afraid of seeing the
Countess Dubarry presented at court."

"Ha!" cried the king, with a burst of passion which
he could not repress; "so you have been all this time
getting this out! *Mordieu!* Madame Tell-truth, how you
beat about the bush!"

"Sire," replied the princess, "if I have so long delayed
in telling your majesty this, it is because respect closed
my lips, and I should not have opened them but by your
own command."

"Yes, yes; you would never have opened them, I suppose, to yawn, or to speak, or to bite."

"I am quite certain, however, sire, that I have discovered the real motive which has made my sister retire
into a convent."

"Well, you are wrong!"

"Oh, sire!" they all three repeated, shaking their heads,
"oh, sire! we are quite certain of what we say!"

"Pshaw! You are all of a tale, I see. There is a conspiracy in my family. This is the reason the presentation

cannot take place; this is the reason the princesses can never be seen when persons wish to visit them, — that they give no answers to petitions, or requests for an audience."

"What petitions? What requests for an audience?" asked Madame Adelaide.

"Oh, you know," replied Madame Sophie, "the petitions of Mademoiselle Jeanne Vaubernier." (This was the Countess Dubarry's name in the days of her poverty.)

"Yes," added Madame Victoire, "the requests for an audience of Mademoiselle Lange." (Another name which she had borne.)

The king started up, furious with passion; his eye, generally calm and mild, now flashed in a manner rather alarming for the three sisters, and as none of this royal trio of heroines seemed courageous enough to bear the paternal wrath, they bent their heads before the storm.

"And now," cried he, "was I wrong when I said the best had left me?"

"Sire," said Madame Adelaide, "you treat us very ill,— worse than you treat your dogs!"

"And justly, too. My dogs, when I go near them, receive me kindly, caress me; they are real friends. So, adieu, ladies! I shall go to Charlotte, Bellefille, and Gredinet. Poor animals! Yes, I love them! And I love them more particularly because they do not bark out the truth."

The king left the apartment in a rage; but had not taken three steps in the ante-room, when he heard his daughters singing in chorus the first verse of a ballad ridiculing the Countess Dubarry, which was then sung through the streets of Paris.

He was about to return,— and perhaps the princesses would not have fared well had he done so,— but he restrained himself, and went on, calling loudly, that he might not hear them, "Holà! the captain of the greyhounds! the captain of the greyhounds!"

The officer who bore this singular title hurried forward.

"Let the dogs be loosed!"

"Oh, sire," cried the officer, placing himself in the king's way, "do not advance another step!"

"What now? what now?" said the king, stopping before a door, from under which was heard the snuffing of dogs, aware that their master was near.

"Sire," said the officer, "pardon me, but I cannot permit your Majesty to enter here."

"Oh, I understand, the kennel is out of order. Well, then, let Gredinet be brought out."

"Sire," continued the officer, with alarm depicted on his face, "Gredinet has neither eaten nor drunk for two days, and it is feared he is mad."

"Oh," cried the king, "I am really the most wretched of men! Gredinet mad! This alone was wanting to complete my vexation!"

The officer of the greyhounds thought it his duty to shed a tear to make the scene more perfect. The king turned on his heel, and retired to his private cabinet, where his valet was waiting. He, seeing the king's face so disturbed, hid himself in the recess of a window; and the king, looking upon him rather as a piece of furniture than a man, strode up and down his room talking to himself.

"Yes, I see it, I see it plainly," said he. "The Duke de Choiseul laughs at me, the dauphin looks upon himself as already half master, and thinks he will be wholly so when he has his little Austrian beside him on the throne. Louise loves me, — but so sternly, that she preaches me a sermon and leaves me. My three other daughters sing songs, in which I am ridiculed under the name of Blaise. My grandson, the Count de Provence, translates Lucretius; and his brother, the Count d'Artois, is a dissipated scapegrace. My dogs go mad, and would bite me. Decidedly, there is only the poor countess who loves me. To the devil, then, with those who would annoy her!"

Then with a sort of settled despair, he seated himself at that table on which Louis XIV. wrote his proudest letters and signed his latest treatise.

" I know now," continued he, " why every one wishes to hasten the arrival of the dauphiness. They think when she shows herself I shall become her slave, and be governed by her family. I' faith, I shall see her soon enough, that dear daughter-in-law of mine, particularly if her arrival is to be the signal for new troubles. Let me be quiet as long as I can, and for that purpose the longer she is delayed on the road the better. She was to have passed through Rheims and Noyon without stopping, and to come immediately to Compiègne. I shall insist on the first arrangement. Three days at Rheims, and one — no, faith, two! — bah! *three* days at Noyon! That would be six days I should gain, — yes, six good days!"

He took a pen, and wrote in person an order to the Count de Stainville to stop three days at Rheims and three days at Noyon.

Then, sending for a courier, "Don't draw bridle," said he, "until you have delivered this according to its address."

Then with the same pen he wrote: —

DEAR COUNTESS, — To-day we instal Zamore in his government. I am just setting out for Marly. This evening, at Luciennes, I shall tell you all I now think.

FRANCE.

" Here, Lebel," said he to the valet, " take this letter to the countess, and keep on good terms with her, I advise you."

The valet bowed and left the room.

CHAPTER XXIX.

THE COUNTESS DE BÉARN.

THE principal object of all the fury of the court, and their stumbling-block on this dreaded occasion — the Countess de Béarn — was, as Chon said, travelling rapidly to Paris. Her journey thither was the result of one of those bright ideas which sometimes came to Viscount Jean's assistance in his times of trouble.

Not being able to find among the ladies of the court one who would present the Countess Dubarry, and since she could not be presented without a lady to introduce her, he cast his eye on the provinces. He examined country-seats, searched carefully in the towns, and at last found what he wanted on the banks of the Meuse, in an old Gothic-looking country-seat, but one kept in good order.

Now, what he wanted was an old lady fond of law, and having a lawsuit on hand. The old lady with the lawsuit was the Countess de Béarn.

The lawsuit was an affair on which all her fortune depended, and which was to be heard before Monsieur de Maupeou, who had lately taken up the cause of the Countess Dubarry, — having discovered, what had remained hidden until then, that he was related to her, — and now called her cousin. Looking forward to the appointment of lord chancellor through her interest, he showed the king's favourite all the warmth of a friendship naturally arising from such a substantial basis. This friendship and this interest had procured for him from the king the office of vice-chancellor, and from the world in general the pithy denomination of *the Vice*.

The Countess de Béarn was a thin, angular, agile little woman, always on the alert, always rolling her eyes like those of a frightened cat, from under her grey eyebrows. She still wore the dress which had been fashionable in her youth, and as the capricious goddess of fashion has sensible fits now and then, it so happened that the costume of the young girl of 1740 should be precisely that of the old woman of 1770.

Broad guipure, pointed mantelet, an enormous coif, an immense bag, and a neck-handkerchief of flowered silk — such was the costume in which Chon, the well-beloved sister and confidante of the Countess Dubarry, found the Countess de Béarn arrayed when she presented herself before her as Mademoiselle Flageot, the daughter of the lawyer in Paris who had the management of her suit. The old countess wore the costume of her early days as much from taste as from economy. She was not one of those persons who blush for their poverty, because her poverty had not been caused by her own fault. She regretted, indeed, not being rich for her son's sake, to whom she would have wished to leave a fortune worthy of his name. The young man was thoroughly country-bred, timid to a fault, caring much more for what belonged to the substantial things of life than to the honours of renown.

The countess's sole consolation was in calling the lands which were contested with the Saluce family " my estate ; " but as she was a woman of sense, she felt that if she wanted to borrow money on that estate, not a usurer in France — and there were some bold enough in running risks at that period — would lend it to her ; not an attorney — and there were some not very scrupulous then, as there have been at all times — would procure her the smallest sum on such a guarantee.

Forced, then, to live on the annual rents of those lands that were not disputed, the Countess de Béarn, having only one thousand crowns a year, kept very far from court; for there she must have spent nearly twelve livres a day in the hire of a carriage to take her to her lawyer's and to the judge's. She was still more determined in keeping aloof, since she had despaired of her cause being heard for four or five years at least. Law-suits, even in the present day, are, in truth, tedious affairs; but still, without living to the age of the patriarchs, a person who commences one has some hope of seeing it to an end; but formerly a suit extended through two or three generations, and was like those fabulous plants of the Arabian tales, which blossomed only at the end of two or three centuries.

The Countess de Béarn, therefore, did not wish to lose the remains of her patrimony in recovering the ten-twelfths of it which were disputed. She was what is always called "a woman of the old school," sagacious, prudent, firm, avaricious. She could certainly have managed her suit much better herself than any advocate, lawyer, or attorney; but she was called Béarn, and that name prevented her from doing many things which economy might have prompted. Like the divine Achilles in his tent, suffering a thousand deaths when he heard the trumpet, although feigning to be deaf to it, she in her retirement was devoured by regret and anguish. She passed her days in deciphering old parchments, her spectacles on her nose; and at night, on her pillow, she pleaded with such eloquence the cause of the estate claimed by the Saluces that she was always successful, — a termination of the affair which she could but wish her advocate to arrive at.

It may readily be imagined that, in such a temper of mind, the arrival of Chon and the news she brought were very agreeable to Madame de Béarn.

The young count was with his regiment.

We always believe what we wish to believe; so Madame de Béarn was very easily caught by the young lady's tale.

There was, however, a shadow of suspicion in the countess's mind. She had known Master Flageot twenty years, and had visited him two hundred times in his narrow, dark street; but she had never seen a child playing

on the square bit of carpet which looked so little on the
floor of his large office; and had there been children there,
they would surely have found their way into it to get a
toy or a cake from the clients.

But what was the use of thinking about the lawyer and
his office, and his carpet? What was the use of trying to
remember anything about it? Flageot's daughter was
Flageot's daughter, and — there she was! Moreover, she
was married, and — what banished the last shadow of
suspicion — she had not come on purpose to Verdun; she
was going to join her husband at Strasburg.

Perhaps the countess ought to have asked Mademoiselle
Flageot for a letter from her father, to assure herself of
her identity; but if a father could not send his own child
without a letter, to whom could he entrust a confidential
mission? Then why such fears? What could cause
such suspicions? Why should any one travel sixty leagues
to tell her a tale without any foundation on fact?

If she had been rich, a banker's or a financier's wife,
taking with her carriages, plate, and diamonds, she might
have thought it was a plot got up by robbers. But she
laughed to herself when she thought what a disappointment any robbers would experience who should be so ill-
advised as to attack her.

So, Chon having disappeared with her plain dark dress,
and her shabby little one-horse chaise which she had taken
at the last post, leaving her carriage behind her, the
countess, convinced that the time was come for her to
make a sacrifice, got into her old coach, and urged on the
postilions so well that she passed through Lachaussée an
hour before the dauphiness, and reached the gate of Saint-
Denis five or six hours after Chon herself.

As she had little luggage, and as the most important
thing for her was to receive information from her lawyer,
she ordered her coach to drive to the Rue du Petit-Lion,
and stop before Master Flageot's door. The vehicle, we
may be assured, did not stop there without attracting a

great number of curious spectators, — and the Parisians are all curious, — who stared at the venerable machine which seemed to have issued from the coach-house of Henry IV., — so antique was it in its solidity, its monumental form, and its scalloped leather curtains, which ran with a disagreeable creaking on a copper rod, covered with verdigris.

The Rue du Petit-Lion was not wide, and the countess's equipage filled it up very majestically. Having alighted and paid the postilions, she ordered them to take it to the inn where she usually stopped, — Le Coq Chantant, in the Rue Saint-Germain-des-Prés.

She ascended Monsieur Flageot's dark stairs, holding by the greasy cord which served instead of a hand-rail. The staircase was cool, and it refreshed the old lady, who was tired by her long and rapid journey. When Margaret, his servant, announced the Countess de Béarn, Master Flageot pulled up his stockings, which he had allowed to fall nearly to his ankles on account of the heat, with one hand, fixed on his wig with the other, then hastily threw on a dimity dressing-gown, and, so adorned, advanced smiling to the door. In this smile, however, there was such an expression of surprise, that the countess could not help saying, "Well, well! my dear sir, it is I."

"Yes, indeed," replied he, "I see plainly enough, madame, that it is you!"

Then, modestly wrapping his dressing-gown round him, he led the countess to a large leathern arm-chair, in the lightest corner of the apartment, carefully putting aside the papers which covered his desk, for he knew the old lady to be curious in the extreme.

"And now, madame," said Master Flageot, gallantly, "permit me to express my pleasure at this agreeable surprise."

The countess had leaned back in her chair, and raised her feet from the floor to allow Margaret to slip between it and her brocaded satin shoes a leather cushion; but at this phrase she started up hastily. "How?" exclaimed she, drawing her spectacles from their case, and putting

them on, so that she might see his face the better, —
"surprise?"

"Most assuredly; I thought you at your estates,
madame," replied the lawyer, adroitly flattering the old
lady by bestowing this title on the countess's three acres of
kitchen-garden.

"Well, I was there; but, on the first intimation from
you, I left them."

"Intimation from me?" said the astonished advocate.

"Yes, at your first word, or counsel, or advice, or whatever you please to call it."

Flageot's eyes looked as large as the countess's glasses.

"I have been very expeditious," continued she, "and
I hope you are satisfied."

"I am delighted to see you, madame, as I always am;
but allow me to say that I do not see how I have been
the cause of your visit."

"Not the cause? Most certainly you have been the
entire cause of it!"

"I?"

"Yes, you, undoubtedly. Well, have you no news to
tell me?"

"Oh, yes, madame; it is said the king is meditating
some great stroke of policy with regard to the parliament.
But may I offer you some refreshment?"

"But what does it matter to me about the king and
his strokes of policy?"

"About what, then, did you inquire, madame?"

"About my suit, of course. Is there anything new
about it?"

"Oh, as to that," said Flageot, shaking his head sorrowfully, "nothing, absolutely nothing!"

"That is to say, nothing —"

"No — nothing, madame."

"You mean nothing since your daughter spoke to me
about it; but as that was only the day before yesterday,
I can readily understand that there may not be much new
since then."

"My daughter, madame ? "

"Yes."

" Did you say my daughter ? "

" Yes, your daughter, whom you sent to me."

" Pardon me, madame; but it is quite impossible that I could send my daughter to you."

" Impossible ? "

" Yes, for a very simple reason, — I have no daughter."

" Are you sure ? " asked the countess.

"Madame," replied Flageot, " I have the honour to be a bachelor."

"Come, come ! " said the countess, as if she supposed him jesting.

Master Flageot became uneasy; he called Margaret to bring in some refreshment, but, more particularly, that she might watch the countess. "Poor woman ! " said he to himself, " her head is turned."

"What," said she, returning to the charge, "you have not a daughter ? "

"No, madame."

" Not one married at Strasburg ? "

" No, madame, by no means."

" And you did not send that daughter," pursued the countess, " on her way thither, to tell me that my suit was called on ? "

" Nothing of the kind, madame."

The countess started from her chair, and clasped her hands.

"Drink a little of something, madame; it will do you good," said Master Flageot; and at the same time he made a sign to Margaret to bring a tray, on which were two glasses of beer. But the old lady was not thinking of her thirst, and she pushed away the tray so rudely that Dame Margaret, who appeared to be a privileged sort of person, was affronted.

" But let us understand each other," said the countess, eyeing Master Flageot over her spectacles; "explain all this, if you please."

"Certainly, madame. Margaret, you need not go; the countess will perhaps drink something presently. Let us explain."

"Yes, let us explain; for, upon my honour, my dear monsieur, you are quite incomprehensible to-day. I begin to think the hot weather has turned your brain."

"Do not be angry, dear madame," said Flageot, manœuvring with the hind-feet of his chair, so that he got by degrees farther from the countess, "Do not get angry and let us talk over the matter quietly."

"Yes, yes, certainly. You say you have not a daughter?"

"No, madame, I have not one, and I regret it deeply, since it appears you would be pleased that I had, although —"

"Although what?" repeated the countess.

"Although, for my own part, I should prefer a son. Boys succeed better in the world, or rather, don't turn out so ill as girls in the present day."

The countess looked more and more alarmed.

"What!" said she, "have you not sent for me to Paris by a sister, a niece, a cousin, — by some person, in short?"

"I never thought of such a thing, madame, knowing how expensive it is staying in Paris."

"But my suit?"

"I should always have taken care to let you know in time, before the pleading came on."

"Before it came on?"

"Yes."

"Has it not come on, then?"

"Not that I know of, madame."

"It has not been called?"

"No."

"And it is not likely to come on soon?"

"Oh, no, madame, certainly not."

"Then," cried the old lady, rising, "I have been tricked! I have been most basely deceived!"

Flageot pushed back his wig, muttering, "I fear it, indeed, madame."

"Master Flageot!" cried the countess.

The lawyer started on his seat, and made a sign to Margaret to keep near, in order to defend him.

"Master Flageot," continued the countess, "I will not submit to such an indignity as this; I will address the minister of police, to discover the impudent creature who insulted me thus!"

"Oh," said Flageot, "it is a very doubtful affair."

"And when she is found," continued the countess, almost speechless with anger, "I shall bring an action against her."

"Another lawsuit!" said the lawyer sorrowfully.

These words made the poor lady fall from the height of her passion, and a heavy fall it was.

"Alas," said she, "I came here so happy!"

"But what did that woman say to you, madame?"

"First, that she was sent by you."

"Shocking intriguer!"

"That you desired her to say that the trial was coming on, was very near, — that I could scarcely be in time with all the speed I could make."

"Alas! madame," repeated Flageot, in his turn, "the trial is very far from coming on."

"Yes, so far from it, I suppose, that it is quite forgotten."

"Forgotten! — sunk, buried, madame; and unless a miracle were to happen — and you know miracles are very rare nowadays —"

"Oh, yes!" murmured the countess, with a sigh.

Master Flageot replied by another sigh, a faithful echo of the countess's.

"Well, monsieur, one thing is certain," added she.

"What is it, madame?"

"I shall not survive this."

"Oh, don't say so! you would be quite wrong."

"Oh, Heaven! oh, Heaven!" exclaimed the poor countess; "my strength is completely exhausted."

"Courage, madame, courage!" said Flageot.

"But have you no advice to give me, — none?"

"Oh, yes! my advice is to return to your estates, and after this never believe anybody who does not bring you a letter from me, in my own hand."

"I must return, indeed."

"It will be the wisest plan."

"Well, monsieur," said the countess with a groan, "believe me, we shall never meet again, — at least, not in this world."

"What an infamous affair!"

"I must have some very cruel enemies."

"It has been a trick of the opposite party, I would swear!"

"It is a very mean trick, I must say."

"A mean, sorry trick, indeed!"

"Justice! justice!" cried the countess, "my dear monsieur, she is the cave of Cacus!"

"And why is it?" he replied. "Because justice is not what it was; because the parliament is opposed; because Monsieur de Maupeou must be chancellor, forsooth, instead of remaining what he ought to be, president."

"Master Flageot, I think I could drink something now."

"Margaret!" cried the lawyer; for Margaret had left the room, seeing the peaceable turn affairs were taking. She now entered with the tray and the two glasses which she had carried away. The countess drank her glass of beer very slowly, after having touched the lawyer's glass with hers; then she gained the ante-room, after a sad and solemn curtsey and a still more sorrowful leave-taking.

The lawyer followed her, his wig in his hand. She was in the lobby, and was reaching out her hand for the cord to aid her in her descent, when a hand was laid on hers and a head gave her a thump on the chest. The head and the hand were those of a clerk, who was mounting the stairs four steps at a time.

The old lady muttering and grumbling, arranged her

petticoats aud continued on her way, whilst the clerk, having reached the lobby, pushed open the lawyer's door, and with the open and joyous voice for which the clerks of the parliament were noted, cried out, "Here, Master Flageot! here! it is about the Béarn business;" and he held out a paper.

To rush up the stairs at that name, push by the clerk, to throw herself on Flageot, to snatch the paper from him, to shut herself up with him in his office, all this was effected by the countess before the clerk had recovered from two boxes on the ear which Margaret bestowed or seemed to bestow on him, in return for two kisses.

"Well!" cried the old lady, "what is it? Master Flageot, what is it?"

"Faith, I can't tell, madame; but if you will give me back the paper, I shall let you know."

"True, true, my good Master Flageot! Read it, read it!"

He looked at the signature.

"It is from Guildou, our attorney," said he.

"Good heavens!"

"He desires me," continued Flageot, with surprise amounting almost to bewilderment, — "he desires me to be ready to plead on Tuesday, for your affair is to come on!"

"To come on?" cried the countess; "take care, Master Flageot, take care! No more tricks; I should never recover from another."

"Madame," replied Flageot, still bewildered at the intelligence, "if there be any trick, any jest in this, Guildou is the author of it; and it is certainly the first time in his life that he has jested."

"But are you certain the letter is from him?"

"It is signed Guildou — see!"

"I see it is. To be called this morning and pleaded on Tuesday. Well, then, you see, dear monsieur, the lady who came to me was not a cheat."

"It appears not."

"Then, since she was not sent by you — but are you sure she was not?"

"*Pardieu!* — am I sure of it?"

"By whom was she sent, then?"

"Yes, by whom?"

"For she must have been sent by some one."

"It is a complete riddle to me."

"And to me also. Let me read the paper again. Yes, my dear Master Flageot, the pleading is to come on; it is written so — and before the president, Maupeou."

"The devil! is that there?"

"Yes, certainly."

"That is vexatious."

"How so?"

"Because Monsieur Maupeou is a great friend of your opponents."

"You know that?"

"He is always with them."

"Ha! I am truly unfortunate! Now we are more embarrassed than ever!"

"But, for all that," said the lawyer, "you must wait on him."

"He will receive me very badly!"

"That is probable."

"Oh, Master Flageot, what do you tell me?"

"The truth, madame."

"What! you not only lose courage yourself, but you try to deprive me of mine?"

"With the Chancellor Maupeou you must not hope for anything favourable."

"You, so timid! you, a Cicero!"

"Cicero would have lost the cause of Ligarius had he pleaded before Verres instead of Cæsar," replied Master Flageot, finding nothing more humble to say in return for the high compliment of his client.

"Then you advise me not to wait on him?"

"Heaven forbid, madame, I should advise anything so

irregular; but I pity you sincerely for having to undergo
such an interview."

"You really speak like a soldier who meant to desert his
post. One would think you feared to undertake the
business."

"Madame," replied the lawyer, "I have lost causes
which seemed much more likely to be gained by me than
this of yours does."

The countess sighed, but summoning all her energy, she
said, with a kind of dignity which made a complete contrast to all that had been comic in the scene, "I shall carry
the matter through; it shall not be said that having right
on my side I gave way before a cabal. I shall lose my
cause, but I shall, at least, act as a woman of rank and
character, — such as there are few at court in the present
day. You will accompany me, will you not, Master Flageot, my visit to the vice-chancellor?"

"Madame," replied the lawyer, also calling up all his
dignity to his aid, "we opposition members of the parliament of Paris have sworn to have no intercourse beyond
necessary audiences with those who betrayed the parliament in the affair of Monsieur d'Aiguillon. 'Union is
strength,' and as the vice-chancellor tacked about perpetu-
ally in that business, we have determined to keep aloof
until he shows his real colours."

"My suit is doomed, I see," sighed the countess; "the
lawyers quarrel with the judges, the judges with the
clients. No matter! I shall persevere to the end!"

"May Heaven assist you, madame!" said Flageot, flinging his dressing-gown over his left arm as a Roman senator
might have done his toga.

"This is but a poor sort of an advocate," murmured she
to herself. "I am afraid I shall have less chance with
him before the parliament than I had at home on my pillow." Then aloud, with a smile, under which she strove to
hide her uneasiness, "Adieu, Master Flageot, adieu. Study
the case thoroughly, I entreat you; we know not how
things may turn out."

"Oh, madame," said Master Flageot, "do not fear as to the pleading. I shall do you justice; I shall make some terrible allusions."

"Allusions to what, monsieur?"

"To the corruption of Jerusalem, madame, which I shall compare to the accursed cities on which the fire of heaven descended. You understand? — no one can mistake; by Jerusalem I mean Versailles."

"Master Flageot," exclaimed the old lady, "do not compromise yourself; or rather, do not compromise my cause."

"Oh, madame, with Monsieur de Maupeou for judge, your cause is lost. But then, let the world hear of us; since we cannot obtain justice, let us at least strike terror to the wicked."

"Monsieur, monsieur!"

"Let us be philosophic; let us thunder — "

"Deuce take you with your thunder!" muttered the countess. "Fool of a lawyer, you are thinking only of making a figure with your fag-ends of philosophy. Come, I will go to the vice-chancellor; he at least is no philosopher. I may do better with him than with you, after all."

And the old countess left M. Flageot, having, poor old lady, in two days, mounted all the degrees of the scale of hope, and descended all those in that of disappointment.

CHAPTER XXX.

THE VICE.

THE old countess trembled in every limb as she proceeded towards Monsieur de Maupeou's residence. However, one thought had quieted her a little on the road, — it was so late that in all probability she would not be admitted, and she should merely have to tell the porter when she should come again.

In fact, it was about seven in the evening, and although it was still light, the habit of dining at four, which the nobility had adopted, had caused all business to be suspended from dinner until the next day. Although Madame de Béarn anxiously longed to see the chancellor, she was, nevertheless, consoled by the thought that she should not see him. This is one of the frequent contradictions of the human mind which we can always understand, but never explain.

The countess presented herself, therefore, quite certain that the porter would refuse her admittance; and had even prepared a crown to offer the Cerberus to induce him to put her name on the list of those who requested an audience. On reaching the house, she found an usher talking to the porter, as if giving him an order. She waited discreetly, that she might not interrupt these two personages; but on perceiving her in her hackney-coach, the usher withdrew. The porter approached and demanded her name.

"Oh, I know," said she, "that it is not probable I shall have the honour of seeing his Excellency."

"No matter, madame," replied the porter; "have the goodness to tell me your name."

"The Countess de Béarn," she replied.

"Monseigneur is at home," answered he.

"What did you say?" asked the countess, almost dumb with astonishment.

"I say that monseigneur is at home," repeated he.

"But of course he will not receive visitors?"

"He will receive you, madame."

Madame de Béarn got out of the coach, hardly knowing whether she was asleep or awake.

The porter pulled a cord; a bell rang twice. The usher appeared at the top of the steps, and the porter made a sign to the countess to enter.

"You wish to speak to monseigneur?" asked the usher.

"I wish for that honour, but I scarcely hoped to obtain it."

"Have the goodness to follow me, madame."

"And yet people speak so ill of this chancellor," said the countess to herself, as she went along, following the usher; "yet he has certainly one good quality,— he admits persons on business at all hours. A chancellor? it is strange!"

Yet still she shuddered at the idea that she should find him so much the more stern, so much the more ungracious, because he was assiduous at his duties. Monsieur de Maupeou, buried under a great wig, and dressed in a suit of black velvet, was waiting in his cabinet, with the doors open. The countess, on entering, cast a rapid glance around. She saw with surprise that he was alone; that the mirrors reflected no other face than her own, and that of the meagre, yellow, busy chancellor.

The usher announced, "Madame the Countess de Béarn." The chancellor rose up stiffly, as if he had no joints, and by the same movement leaned his back against the chimneypiece.

The countess made the necessary three curtseys.

Her short complimentary speech which followed the curtseys was rather embarrassed,—she did not expect the honour; she did not think that a minister who had so much to do would deprive himself of the hours necessary for recreation, etc., etc.

The chancellor replied that time was, no doubt, as precious to his Majesty's subjects as to his Majesty's ministers; that, nevertheless, he admitted there were distinctions to be made as to the importance of the affairs brought before him; consequently, he always gave the greater part of his time to those whose business was most urgent.

Fresh curtseys on the part of the countess, then an embarrassed silence; for compliments were ended, and her request must now be made.

The chancellor waited, stroking his chin.

"Monseigneur," said she, "I have presented myself before you to explain to you an affair on which my whole fortune depends."

The chancellor bowed, as if to intimate that she should go on.

"Monseigneur," she continued, "you must know that all my property, or rather my son's, is at stake in a suit now pending between us and the family of the Saluces."

The vice-chancellor continued to stroke his chin.

"But your equity is so well known to me, monseigneur, that although I am aware of your interest in — indeed, I may say your friendship for — the adverse party, I have not hesitated an instant in coming to entreat you to hear me."

The chancellor could not help smiling on hearing himself praised for his equity, — a quality for which he was about as famous as Dubois was for the apostolical virtues on which he had been complimented fifty years before.

"You are right, madame," said he, "in saying that I am a friend of your opponents, but you are also right in thinking that, when I accepted the seals, I laid aside all friendship. I shall reply to you, then, without any bias, as becomes the supreme head of justice."

"Heaven bless you, monseigneur!" cried the old countess.

"I shall examine your affair as a simple jurisconsult," continued the chancellor.

"I thank your Excellency; your skill in these matters is well known."

"Your cause comes on soon, I think."

"Next week, monseigneur."

"In the mean time, what are your wishes respecting it?"

"That your Excellency would look into the documents."

"I have already done so."

"Well," asked the old countess, trembling, "and what do you think of it, monseigneur?"

"I think that there is not a doubt on the subject."

"Not a doubt of my gaining?"

"No; of your losing."

"Then you think, monseigneur, I shall lose?"

"Undoubtedly; I shall, therefore, give you one piece of advice."

"What is it?" asked the countess, with a last ray of hope.

"It is, — if you have any payments to make, the cause being tried and sentence pronounced, — to have your funds ready."

"Oh, monseigneur, we shall be ruined, then?"

"Surely you know, madame, that justice never takes into account anything respecting the consequences of her decrees."

"But monseigneur, there should be mercy as well as justice."

"And for fear of justice being influenced by mercy, she is made blind, madame."

"But your Excellency will not refuse me your advice?"

"Certainly not; ask it, madame. I am ready."

"Is there no means of entering into an arrangement by which the sentence might not be so harsh?"

"Do you know any of your judges?"

"Not one of them, monseigneur."

"That is unfortunate. Messieurs de Saluces, your opponents, are connected with three-fourths of the parliament."

The countess shuddered.

"But observe," continued the chancellor, "that that does not alter the main grounds of the question; for a judge does not permit himself to be influenced by private feelings."

This was about as true as that he possessed the virtue of equity, or Dubois the apostolic virtues; but it made the poor countess nearly faint.

"But, after all," continued the chancellor, "the judge having done all that integrity demands, of course leans more to a friend than to a person about whom he is indifferent. That is only just, when it is just; and as it will be just that you should lose your cause, they may, in their sentence, make the consequences of that loss very unpleasant to you."

"But all that your Excellency says is very alarming."

" As far as I am concerned, I shall refrain from saying anything that might have an influence on the minds of others; but, as I am not a judge myself, I may speak to you of the state of affairs."

" Alas, monseigneur, I suspected one thing!"

The vice-chancellor fixed on her his little grey eyes.

"I suspected that, the adverse party living in Paris, they might become connected with the judges, and thus be all-powerful."

"Because, in the first place, they have justice on their side."

"How painful, it is, monseigneur, to hear such words from the lips of a man infallible as you are!"

"I merely say all this to you because it is the truth; and yet," continued Monsieur de Maupeou, with an affected frankness, "I should like, upon my word, to serve you."

The countess started; she thought that she saw some hidden meaning, if not in the chancellor's words, at least in his thoughts, which concealed behind it something favourable to her.

"Besides," he proceeded, "the name you bear is one of the noblest in France, and that is in itself a powerful recommendation to me."

"Ah, monseigneur, it will not prevent me from losing my suit."

"As to that, I have no power either one way or the other."

"Oh, monseigneur, monseigneur!" cried the countess, shaking her head, "how things go in this world now!"

"You seem to imply, madame, that in the good old times they went better."

"Alas, monseigneur, I cannot but think so. I recall with pleasure the time when you were merely a king's advocate in the parliament, and when you made those beautiful speeches which I, then a young woman, went to listen to, and which I applauded with such enthusiasm. What fire! what eloquence! what virtue! Ah, monseigneur, in those times there were no plots, no cabals, no favouritism! I should have gained my suit then."

"Yet we had Madame de Phalaris then, who tried to reign occasionally when the regent shut his eyes; and we had, too, La Souris, who went about picking up what crumbs she could manage to gather."

"Oh, monseigneur, but Madame de Phalaris was really a lady of rank, and La Souris was such a good-natured girl."

"Yes; so nothing was refused them."

"Or, rather, they could refuse no one."

"Come, madame," said the chancellor, laughing in a manner that astonished the old lady more and more, it was so open and natural, "come, do not make me speak ill of my own administration, through affection for my youthful days."

"But, monseigneur, when I think of those days I must lament my lost fortune, my ruined family."

"You see, countess, what it is not to go with the times, not to sacrifice to the idols of the day."

"Alas, monseigneur, those idols care not for worshippers who come with empty hands!"

"What can you know about them?"

"I?"

"Yes; you have never tried them, I think."

"Monseigneur, you speak to me really like a friend."

"Well, are we not about the same age, countess?"

"Oh! why am I not twenty, — and you, monseigneur, a simple advocate again? You would plead for me, and I should gain my suit."

"Unhappily, we are not twenty, countess," said the vice-chancellor, with a gallant sigh; "we must only, therefore, beg those who are twenty to assist us, since you confess that that is the age to have influence. What! you do know no one at court?"

"Some old noblemen who have left it now, I once knew, but they would blush for their old friend in her poverty. Stay, monseigneur, I have still the privilege of being received at court! I might go to Versailles; yet of what use would it be? Oh, had I again only my two hundred thousand livres of income, people would come to visit me! Perform that miracle for me, monseigneur!"

The chancellor pretended not to hear this last phrase. "In your place," said he, "I should forget the old, as they have forgotten you; I should apply to the young, and beat up for recruits among them. Do you happen to know the princesses at all?"

"They must have forgotten me."

"And besides, they have no influence. Do you know the dauphin?"

"No."

"And, after all, he is so busy about his archduchess, who is about to arrive, that he can think of nothing else. Let me see; among the favourites is there any one —"

"I don't even know their names."

"Monsieur d'Aiguillon?"

"A coxcomb, of whom such shameful things are said,—
that he hid in a mill whilst others were fighting! Fie!
fie!"

"Pooh! we must not believe the half of what we hear.
But stay! let me think—"

"Do, do, monseigneur; think of some one!"

"Yes; why not? Yes! ha! yes!"

"Who, monseigneur, who?"

"Why not apply to the countess herself?"

"To the Countess Dubarry?" said the old lady, spreading out her fan.

"Yes; she is really a kind creature."

"Indeed!"

"And anxious to be useful."

"I am of too ancient a family to please her, monseigneur."

"You are mistaken, countess; she tries to attach high
families to her."

"Do you think so?" asked the old countess, already
beginning to waver in her opposition.

"Do you know her?" said the chancellor.

"Oh, good heavens! no!"

"Ah, there is the mischief! She is the person who has
real influence."

"Yes, yes, she has influence; but I never saw her."

"Nor her sister Chon?"

"No."

"Nor her sister Bischi?"

"No."

"Nor her brother Jean?"

"No."

"Nor her negro, Zamore?"

"What! her negro, monseigneur?"

"Yes, her negro is one of the governing powers."

"What! that little fright, whose picture is sold in the
streets, which looks like that of a dressed-up pug dog?"

"Yes, the same."

"*I* know that African!" cried the countess, with offended dignity. "How should I know him, monseigneur?"

"Well, well! I see you do not wish to keep your estates, countess."

"How is that?"

"Because you speak contemptuously of Zamore."

"But what has Zamore to do in the matter?"

"He might gain your suit for you, that is all."

"He? That Moor! that Hottentot! How could he gain it for me?"

"By saying to his mistress that you wished to gain it. You know what influence is; he makes his mistress do what he chooses, and she makes the king do what she chooses."

"Then Zamore governs France, monseigneur?"

"Hum!" replied the chancellor, nodding his head, "he has a great deal of influence; and I had rather quarrel with — with the dauphiness, for instance, than with Zamore."

"Great Heaven!" exclaimed the countess; "if it were not a grave person like your Excellency who told me such things, I could not believe them."

"Oh, I am not the only one who will tell them you; everybody can tell them. Ask any of the dukes and peers if they ever forget, when going to Marly or Luciennes, to take comfits for Zamore to put in his mouth, or pearls for him to hang in his ears. I, who speak to you, am I not the chancellor of France, or something very near it? Well, what was I doing when you came in? I was drawing up a governor's commission for Zamore."

. "A governor's commission?"

"Yes; Monsieur Zamore is appointed governor of the castle of Luciennes."

"The very same title with which they rewarded the Count de Béarn after twenty years' service."

"Yes; he was made governor of the castle of Blois. I remember that."

"But what a degradation! Good heavens! the monarchy
is dead!"

"It is very ill, at least; and you know, countess, when
an invalid draws near his end, people try to get all they
can from him."

"No doubt, no doubt; but the question is how to get
near this invalid."

"Do you know what you must do to be well received by
the Countess Dubarry?"

"What?"

"You must get admitted by being the bearer of this
commission for her negro."

"I?"

"It will be an excellent beginning."

"Do you think so, monseigneur?" said the poor countess, all alarmed.

"I am sure of it; but—"

"But what?"

"Do you know any one acquainted with her?"

"No one but yourself, monseigneur."

"Oh, as for me, it would be difficult for me to introduce
you."

"Assuredly," said the poor old lady, tossed to and fro
by alternate hopes and fears, "assuredly, fortune is hostile
to me! Monseigneur has received me in a manner quite
unexpected,— for indeed I did not expect to be admitted to
an audience; then, you have inclined me to pay my court
to Madame Dubarry,— me, a Béarn!—and I am ready to
undertake the hateful task of delivering the commission
for her wretch of a negro; and now I cannot even get an
introduction to her!"

The chancellor began again to stroke his chin, and
appeared very thoughtful, when suddenly the usher announced, "Monsieur le Viscount Jean Dubarry!"

At this name the chancellor made a gesture of amazement, and the countess sank back breathless in her chair.

"Now say that fortune has abandoned you! Ah! countess, countess, Heaven is working in your favour."

Then, turning to the usher, without giving the old lady time to recover, he desired that the viscount should be admitted instantly. The usher withdrew, and in a moment after our old acquaintance, Jean Dubarry, entered with his arm in a sling.

After the usual number of bows were made on both sides, and as the countess, trembling and undecided, was trying to rise in order to take leave, — for the chancellor, by a slight movement of the head, had indicated to her that her audience was ended, — "Pardon me, monseigneur," said the viscount ; "pardon me, madame. I interrupt you, I fear, — but I beg of you not to go away; I have only two words to say to his lordship."

The countess sat down again without requiring to be pressed, her heart full of joy and expectation.

"But perhaps, monsieur, I shall be in your way?" she stammered.

"Oh, madame, not at all, not at all. I merely wish to lodge a short complaint with monseigneur."

"A complaint! Against whom?" exclaimed the chancellor.

"An attack upon me, monseigneur! an assassination! One cannot pass over such things as that. Let them abuse us, make ballads about us, blacken us, — we can survive all that ; but when it comes to cutting our throats, *mordieu!* we die!"

"Explain the affair, I beg," said the chancellor, pretending to be very much horrified.

"It is easily done; but I fear I am interrupting this lady's audience."

"The Countess de Béarn," said the chancellor, introducing the old lady to the Viscount Jean Dubarry.

Dubarry retreated gracefully to make his bow, the countess to make her curtsey; and both saluted as ceremoniously as if they had been at court.

"After you, monsieur," said she.

"Madame, I would not be guilty of such treason against gallantry for the world."

"Oh, monsieur, my business only concerns money, in yours honour is concerned; yours is therefore more urgent."

"Then, madame," said the viscount, "since it is your wish, I shall take advantage of your obliging permission." And he related his tale to the chancellor, who listened very gravely.

"You will require witnesses," said Monsieur de Maupeou, after a moment's reflection.

"Ah," cried Dubarry, "how easily one discovers, even in those words, the upright judge who can only be influenced by irrefutable truth! Well, I can procure witnesses."

"Monseigneur," said the countess, "the viscount has found one already."

"What witness?" they both asked.

"I, myself," the countess replied.

"You?" exclaimed the chancellor.

"Monsieur," said she, addressing the viscount, "did not this affair happen at the village of Lachaussée?"

"Yes, madame."

"At the post-house?"

"Yes."

"Well, I shall be your witness. I passed through the place where the attack was made on you two hours after it happened."

"Really, madame?" said the chancellor.

"Yes," continued the countess, "and everybody was talking of what had just taken place."

"Take care!" said the viscount, "take care, madame! If you consent to aid me in this matter, very likely the Choiseuls will find some means of making you repent of it."

"Ah!" said the chancellor, "and the more easily that the Countess de Béarn is engaged in a lawsuit, her chance of gaining which is very doubtful, I am afraid."

"Oh, monseigneur," cried the old lady, putting her hand to her head, "I sink from one difficulty to another!

"Lean upon the viscount," said the chancellor, in a half whisper; "he has a powerful arm to assist you."

"Only one at present," said Dubarry, with a simper. "But I know a certain person who has two good arms; they can reach far, and I offer you their aid."

"Oh, Monsieur le Viscount, are you serious in making me such an offer?"

"It is only service for service, madame. I accept your aid, you accept mine. Is it agreed?"

"Do I accept yours? Oh, monsieur, you do me too much honour!"

"Then, madame, will you take a seat in my carriage? I am just going to pay a visit to my sister."

"Without any reason; without any preparations? Oh, monsieur, I dare not."

"You have a reason; madame," said the chancellor, slipping into her hand Zamore's commission.

"Monseigneur, you are my tutelary genius!" cried the old lady, taking the document. "Monsieur le Viscount, you are the flower of the French nobility."

"At your service," said the viscount, pointing the way to the countess, who was as quick as a bird to take it.

"Thanks for my sister," whispered Jean in the chancellor's ear; "thank you, cousin. But did I play my part well, eh?"

"Admirably," said Maupeou; "but pray make the countess laugh by telling her how I played mine. But, take care! the old lady is as sharp as a needle."

At that moment the countess turned; the two gentlemen bowed formally to one another, as if taking a ceremonious adieu.

A splendid carriage, with attendants in the royal livery, waited at the door; the old lady took her place in it quite elated; Jean seated himself beside her, and they departed.

After the king left Madame Dubarry, as we have formerly related, after a very cold and constrained reception, the countess was left alone with Chon and her brother, who had not appeared at first, for fear of his wound being examined, it being, in reality, very trifling. The result of this family council was that the countess, instead of going to Luciennes as she had told the king, set off for Paris. She had there, in the Rue de Valois, a snug little house which served as a place of rendezvous for all her family, every member of which was constantly running backwards and forwards, hither and thither, as business or pleasure led them.

The countess being installed in this domicile of hers, took a book and waited. Meantime the viscount prepared his battery.

It might be about half-past seven by the large dial of the church of St. Eustache when the Countess de Béarn and Viscount Dubarry passed by on their way to his sister's.

The conversation on her side expressed great reluctance to avail herself of the good fortune which had fallen in her way. On his, there was the assumption of a sort of dignity in being her patron, with repeated exclamations at the happy chance which enabled him to introduce her to the Countess Dubarry. In return, the old lady never ceased praising the politeness and affability of the chancellor. All these fibs on both sides, however, did not prevent the horses from going as fast as they could, and they reached their place of destination a little before eight.

"Permit me, madame," said the viscount, leaving the old lady in an ante-room, "to inform the Countess Dubarry of the honour you have done her."

"Oh, monsieur," said the countess, "do not, I entreat you, allow my unseasonable visit to disturb her!"

Jean approached Zamore, who was watching for his return out of one of the windows, and whispered something in his ear.

"What a dear little negro!" cried the countess; "is he your sister's, monsieur?"

"Yes; he is one of her favourites, madame."

"I congratulate her on having such a one."

At this moment a footman opened the folding-doors of the salon where Madame Dubarry usually granted audiences, and requested the countess to walk in there. Whilst the old lady was sighing over the luxurious furniture of the apartment, Jean was with his sister announcing his prize.

"Is it really she?" asked Madame Dubarry.

"Flesh and blood."

"Does she suspect anything?"

"Nothing in the world."

"And how did the Vice behave?"

"Admirably!—everything conspired to favour us."

"Do not let us leave her too long alone, lest she should suspect something."

"You are right; for I assure you, she seems to me cunning enough."

"Where is Chon?"

"At Versailles, you know."

"Well, she must not by any means let herself be seen."

"Oh, I warned her."

"Now, princess, enter."

Madame Dubarry gently pushed open the door of her boudoir and entered the salon.

All the ceremonial necessary to the etiquette of those days was scrupulously gone through by the two actresses, mutually desirous of pleasing. Madame Dubarry was the first to speak.

"I have already thanked my brother, madame, for having procured me the honour of this visit; allow me now to thank you also for having consented to his wish."

"I know not, madame," replied the old lady, "in what terms to thank you for this gracious reception of me."

"Madame," said the countess, in her turn, with a curtsey of profound respect, "it is only due to a lady of your rank to place myself at your disposal, if I can be of service to you in any way."

And three more curtseys having been made on each side, the countess invited Madame de Béarn to be seated.

CHAPTER XXXI.

ZAMORE'S COMMISSION.

"MADAME," said the favourite, "pray let me hear your wishes; I am all attention."

"Permit me, sister," said Jean, who continued standing, "to disabuse your mind of the idea that the Countess de Béarn comes with a petition. Not at all; the chancellor has simply asked her to perform a little office for him."

The old lady turned a grateful look on the viscount, and held out to the countess the patent signed by the vice-chancellor, declaring Luciennes a royal castle, and Zamore its governor.

"Then it is I who am the person obliged," said the countess, glancing at the document; "if I could only be so fortunate, madame, as to be of any service to you in return."

"Oh, that you can readily be!" exclaimed the old lady, with a frankness which enchanted the brother and sister.

"Pray let me know how, madame."

"You were kind enough to say that my name is not quite unknown to you, madame."

"Unknown? — a Béarn!"

"Then you have perhaps heard of a lawsuit which threatens my whole property."

"Oh, yes, — a suit between you and the family of the Saluces?"

"Alas, madame, yes."

"I know all about it, madame; I heard his Majesty the other evening speak of it to my cousin, the chancellor."

"His Majesty, speak of my lawsuit?"

"Yes, madame."

"And in what terms, pray?"

"Alas! my dear madame!" and Madame Dubarry shook her head.

"As lost, as lost, was it not?" exclaimed the old lady, with anguish.

"If I must speak the truth, madame, it was."

"His Majesty said so?"

"His Majesty had too much prudence and delicacy to pronounce sentence decidedly, but he seemed to look upon the adverse party as already in possession of the estate."

"Oh, heavens! madame, if his Majesty were but rightly informed on the subject; if he knew that all this was about a bond really discharged! Yes, madame, the two hundred thousand francs have been paid. I have not a receipt for the money, certainly; but I have a moral certainty that it was paid. I could, if I was allowed to plead in person before the parliament, demonstrate it by inference."

"By inference?" exclaimed Madame Dubarry, who did not understand one word of what she said, but who appeared to pay the most serious attention.

"Yes, madame, by inference."

"The proof by inference is admissible," said Jean.

"Do you think so, monsieur?" asked the old lady.

"Yes, I think it is," replied the viscount, with profound gravity.

"Well, then, by inference I could prove that the bond for two hundred thousand francs with the interest accumulated, amounting to a total of about one million, — I could prove that this bond, bearing date 1406, was discharged by Guy Gaston, the fourth Count of Béarn, on his deathbed in 1417; for there it is written by his own hand in his will, "Being on my deathbed, and *owing nothing to any man*, and ready to appear before God — '"

"Well?" said Madame Dubarry.

"Well, madame, if he owed nothing to any man, he

owed nothing to the family of the Saluces; otherwise he would have said 'owing two hundred thousand francs,' instead of saying 'owing nothing to any man.' "

"Most undoubtedly he would have said so," exclaimed Jean.

"But have you no other proof?" asked the favourite.

"Than his word? None, madame; but he was called ' Gaston the Irreproachable.' "

"And your opponents have the bond?"

" Yes, they have; and that is just what makes the affair more intricate."

She should have said, "That is just what clears up the matter;" but she looked at things from her own point of view.

"So your conviction is, madame, that the bond was discharged?" said Jean.

"Yes, monsieur, that is my decided conviction," exclaimed Madame de Béarn, warmly.

"Do you know," said the countess, turning to her brother, as if deeply penetrated by that conviction, "the proof by inference, as the Countess de Béarn calls it, changes the face of things wonderfully."

"Oh, wonderfully!" returned Jean.

" And very unpleasantly for my opponents," continued the countess. "The terms of Gaston IV.'s will are most positive, — 'owing nothing to any man.' "

"It is not only clear, it is logical," said Jean. "He owed nothing to any man; therefore, of course, he had paid what he owed."

"Therefore he had paid what he owed," repeated the Countess Dubarry.

"Oh, madame, why are you not my judge?" ejaculated the old lady.

"Formerly," said the viscount, "we should not have had recourse to the tribunals to settle an affair of that kind; the judgment of Heaven would have been enough. For my part, I am so convinced of the goodness of your cause that,

did the old custom still exist, I should willingly offer myself for your champion."

"Oh, monsieur!"

"Yes, I should act as did my grandfather, Dubarry-
Moore, who had the honour of being connected with the
royal family of the Stuarts, when he fought in the lists
for the beautiful Edith of Scarborough, and made his
adversary confess that he lied in his throat. But unhappily," continued the viscount, with a sigh of disdain for
the degeneracy of the age, "we live not in those glorious
times; and gentlemen, when they claim their rights, must
submit their causes to the judgment of a set of pettifoggers,
who have not the sense to understand a phrase so clear as
'owing nothing to any man.'"

"But, brother," said the countess, "it is three hundred
years since those words were written; so you must allow
that the gentlemen of the long robe may well pause a little
before deciding on them."

"Oh, no matter, no matter; I am certain that if his
Majesty heard the Countess de Béarn state her case herself,
as she has done to us —"

"I should convince his Majesty; should I not, monsieur?"

"I am certain of it."

"Yes, but how am I to obtain an audience of his
Majesty?"

"You must come and visit me at Luciennes; and as his
Majesty does me the honour of coming sometimes to see
me there —"

"My dear," interrupted the viscount, "that is all very
well, but it depends on chance."

"Viscount," replied the favourite, with a sweet smile,
"you know that I depend a good deal on chance, and I
have no reason to complain."

"Yes, but the Countess de Béarn might go to Luciennes
for a week or a fortnight, and yet not meet his Majesty."

"That is true."

"In the mean time her cause is to come on on Monday
or Tuesday."

"On Tuesday, monsieur."

"And this is Friday evening."

"Ah, then," said Madame Dubarry, with a countenance all disappointment, "we must not reckon upon that."

"What shall we do?" said the viscount, as if in deep thought. "What a devil of a business!"

"I might have an audience at Versailles," suggested the old lady, timidly.

"Oh, you will not obtain it."

"But through your influence, madame?"

"Oh, my influence would be of no avail. His Majesty detests business matters; and, besides, his mind is now full of one thing only."

"The parliaments?" asked Madame de Béarn.

"No, my presentation."

"Ah!" said the old lady.

"For you know, madame, in spite of the opposition of Monsieur de Choiseul and Madame de Grammont, the king has decided that I shall be presented."

"I was not aware, madame."

"It is a settled affair," said Jean.

"And when will the presentation take place, madame?"

"Oh! very soon."

"You see the king wishes it to be before the arrival of the dauphiness, that he may invite my sister to share the festivities at Compiègne."

"Ah! I understand. Then you have all the arrangements made for your presentation," said the old countess, sighing.

"Oh, yes," replied the viscount; "the Baronne d'Alogny —do you know the Baronne d'Alogny?"

"No, monsieur. Alas! I scarcely know any one now. It is twenty years since I was at court."

"Well, it is the Baronne d'Alogny who is to present my sister. The king loads her with favours: her husband is chamberlain; he is to be raised from a baron to a count; the son is to go into the guards; her orders on the king's privy purse are to be made payable by the city of Paris, and the day of the presentation she is to receive twenty thousand crowns paid down; so she is eager for it, you may be sure."

"Yes, I can readily understand that," said the old lady, smiling.

"Oh, but now I think of it —" cried Jean.

"Of what?" asked the Countess Dubarry.

"What a misfortune! what a misfortune!" continued he, "that I did not meet madame a week sooner at our cousin the vice-chancellor's."

"Why, pray?"

"Why, we had no positive engagement then with the Baronne d'Alogny."

"Dear brother, you speak like a sphinx; I do not understand you."

"You do not understand?"

"No."

"I will wager something the Countess de Béarn understands!"

"No, monsieur, I do not, indeed."

"Last week you had not decided who should present you?"

"Undoubtedly."

"Well, the Countess de Béarn — But perhaps, madame, I am taking too great a liberty."

"No, monsieur, no."

"Then madame could have presented you, and the king would have done for her what he is going to do for the Baronne d'Alogny."

"Alas!" said the old lady, opening her eyes to their utmost extent.

"Oh, if you knew," continued Jean, "all the favours his Majesty heaped on the family of the baroness as soon as he knew she had offered to introduce Jeanne! There was only one thing in the affair that vexed him."

"Ah, one thing vexed him?"

"Yes, one single thing. 'One thing vexes me,' said he. 'The lady who presents the Countess Dubarry I should have wished to bear an historical name,' and as he said that, he looked at the picture of Charles I., by Vandyck."

"Yes, I understand," said the old lady; "his Majesty turned to that picture on account of the alliance between the Dubarry-Moores and the Stuarts, of which you spoke just now."

"Precisely."

"The fact is," said the old lady, with a slight air of hauteur, "I never heard of the family of D'Alogny."

"A good family, however," said the countess; "they have brought forward all the necessary proofs, or nearly all."

"*Pardieu!*" cried Jean, suddenly starting in his chair.

"Well, what is the matter?" said Madame Dubarry, scarcely able to refrain from laughing outright at the contortions of her brother-in-law.

"Monsieur has hurt himself, perhaps?" asked the old lady, anxiously.

"No," said Jean, sinking slowly back again into his chair, "it was an idea which just then occurred to me."

"What idea?" said the countess, laughing; "it almost overturned you."

"It must certainly have been a good one," said Madame de Béarn.

"Excellent!"

"Well? we are all anxiety to hear it."

"It has only one fault."

"Well?"

"It is impossible."

"No matter; let us hear it."

"Suppose you were to tell the Baronne d'Alogny the king's remark when he looked at Charles I.'s portrait?"

"Oh, brother, that would not be polite; we cannot think of it."

The old lady sighed.

"It is vexatious, too," continued the viscount, as if speaking to himself; "the affair could have been so easily arranged. The Countess de Béarn, who not only bears such an ancient name, but is besides a woman of distinguished talent, would offer herself in the place of the Baronne d'Alogny; she would have gained her lawsuit; her son would have got a commission as lieutenant in the guards, and as madame must, of course, have been put to considerable expense in her frequent visits to Paris, there would have been adequate compensation allowed. Such an opportunity does not occur twice in a lifetime."

"Alas, no!" exclaimed the old lady, quite overcome by this unforeseen blow.

The fact is that any one in the position of the old litigant would have felt inclined to echo her exclamation, and like her would have sunk back, overwhelmed, in the easy chair.

"Now, brother," said the countess, in a tone of great compassion, "you see you are giving pain to Madame de Béarn. Was it not enough that I was forced to tell her I could do nothing for her with the king before my presentation?"

"Oh, if I could delay my suit," sighed the countess.

"For only eight days," said Dubarry.

"Yes, in eight days," resumed Madame de Béarn, "in eight days madame will be presented."

"Yes; but the king will be at Compiègne in eight days; he will be in the midst of festivities; the dauphiness will have arrived."

"Stop! I have another idea. No — yes — no — yes, yes! I have hit it!"

",What is it, monsieur?" said Madame de Béarn, whose whole soul seemed to hang upon the viscount's lips, and who repeated mechanically the monosyllables he uttered.

"Your presentation is still a secret; no one knows that you have got a lady to present you?"

"No, for the king wishes it to fall like a thunderbolt on the court."

"Well, the Countess de Béarn will demand an audience of the king, as she is not supposed to know any more about your presentation than others, for the purpose of offering to present you. The king, at such an offer from a lady of her rank, will be delighted; he will receive her, thank her, will ask her what he can do for her. She will introduce the subject of her lawsuit, and explain her views respecting it; his Majesty will give them a favourable consideration, and the suit which she thought lost is gained!"

The favourite fixed her eager gaze on the old lady, who probably began to suspect that there was some snare laid for her. "I am a poor, unknown creature," said she; "his Majesty would not, perhaps—"

"Enough. I merely wished to give you a friendly advice on the matter," said Jean.

"Oh, monsieur, I am only too sensible—" said the countess, hesitating.

"It is not a bad idea," replied Madame Dubarry, smiling; "but perhaps madame would not like to descend to anything like a trick, even to gain her lawsuit."

"Quite true, madame," said the old lady, hoping to get off by this means; "I had much rather do you some real service to obtain your friendship."

"Indeed, nothing could be more condescending," said the favourite, with a slight shade of irony which did not escape the penetration of Madame de Béarn.

"Well, I have still another means," said Jean. The old lady listened anxiously.

"Really, brother, your imagination is as fertile in resources as that of Monsieur de Beaumarchais. Let us hear this last idea."

"It is that the Countess de Béarn shall render you the real service which she wishes to do. Can you not persuade the Baronne d'Alogny to yield her rights to the countess? You need not tell her plumply the king's observation, but you could, with your tact, make her understand that he preferred the countess's ancient name."

This time the attack was direct; he thought there could be no evasive answer, but the countess found one.

"I should not like to interfere with that lady's arrangements," said she; "among persons of quality a certain attention to these engagements must be observed."

Madame Dubarry made a gesture of anger and disappointment, but the viscount, by a look, restrained her.

"Observe, madame," said he, "I insist on nothing. Like many in the world, you have a lawsuit, which very naturally you wish to gain. It appears, however, that on the contrary, you are likely to lose it; you are in despair; just at that moment I arrive; I feel for you; I take an interest in an affair which does not in the remotest degree concern me; I endeavour to make it turn out favourably for you. I am wrong; let us say no more about it;" and Jean rose from his seat.

"Oh, monsieur," exclaimed the old lady, in despair, for she now saw that the Dubarrys, who had been till then indifferent, were going to use their influence against her; "oh, monsieur, believe me, I am truly grateful to you! I feel how benevolent have been your intentions."

"As for myself," replied Jean, playing to the life the part of a person perfectly unconcerned, "it matters not whether my sister be presented by the Baronne d'Alogny, the Countess de Polastron, or the Countess de Béarn."

"Oh, certainly, monsieur."

"Only I confess I felt annoyed that the royal favour should be bestowed on some mean spirit, actuated by sordid interest, — a spirit yielding to our power, because it is impossible to undermine it."

"Oh, that is what will most probably happen," said the favourite.

"Whilst," continued Jean, "the Countess de Béarn, almost an entire stranger to us, and coming forward without any solicitation on our part, and prompted solely by her kindness and good nature to offer her services, appears to me worthy of all the advantages which would thereby accrue to her."

The old lady was probably about to disclaim that good-will which the viscount did her the honour to attribute to her, but Madame Dubarry did not give her time.

"The fact is," said she, "the king would not refuse anything to a lady who would act as you describe."

"What! the king would not refuse anything, do you say?"

"Even more; he would say with his own lips to the vice-chancellor, 'Monsieur de Maupeou, I wish that everything should be settled about the lawsuit as the Countess de Béarn wishes.' But it seems, however, as if you saw some difficulty in the matter. Very good. But you will at least do me the justice, I hope, to believe that I was actuated by a sincere wish to serve you, madame;" and the viscount bowed.

"Indeed, monsieur, my heart is filled with gratitude to you!"

"Pray do not speak of it," said the gallant viscount.

"But the Baronne d'Alogny would not yield up her right," resumed the old lady, after a short pause.

"Still, his Majesty would not be the less grateful to you for your offer."

"But supposing," persisted the old lady, who was determined to view the matter in the worst light, in order to see to the bottom of the affair, — "supposing the baroness would yield her privilege to me, she would not so readily give up the accompanying advantages."

"The king's kindness is inexhaustible, madame," said the favourite.

"If I offered my services, madame," replied the old lady, drawn on more and more both by her interest and by the clever manner in which they played their parts, "I should leave out of view the gaining of my cause, — for, to say the truth, a suit which every one thinks lost to-day, will not be easily gained to-morrow."

"Oh, but if the king were favourable!" exclaimed Jean, eager to combat her new doubts.

"Well," said the favourite, "I confess I am of the countess's opinion, viscount."

"You are?" said he, staring at her with open eyes.

"Yes, I think it would be more honourable for a lady of her ancient name to allow her suit to go as it may. Then there would be nothing binding on the king, — nothing to impede his munificence to her; and if he did not wish, in the present state of the parliaments, to interfere with the course of justice, he might offer her compensation for the loss of the suit."

"Ah!" sighed the old lady, "how could he offer anything to compensate for the loss of two hundred thousand francs?"

"Why, in the first place," replied Madame Dubarry, "there might, for instance, be a royal gift of one hundred thousand francs."

The partners in this scheme looked at their victim with eager eyes.

"I have a son," said she.

"So much the better. One more loyal servant of the state."

"But do you think, madame, there would be anything done for my son?"

"I can answer for it," said Jean, "that the least he might expect would be a lieutenancy in the guards."

"Have you any other relations?" inquired the Countess Dubarry.

"I have a nephew."

"Well, we should find out something for your nephew," said the viscount.

"I think we may leave that in your hands, viscount," said the favourite, laughing, "as you have just given us proofs of so brilliant an imagination."

"Well," continued the viscount, apparently determined to bring matters to an issue, "if his Majesty did all these things for you, would you think it tolerably well?"

"I should think him extremely generous, and should offer you, madame, all my thanks, — convinced that it was to you alone I should be indebted for his generosity."

"Then," asked the favourite, "you really take our proposal seriously into consideration?"

"Yes, madame, most seriously," replied the old lady, turning pale at the very thought of the obligation to which she pledged herself.

"And you permit me to mention you to his Majesty?"

"Pray do me that honour," replied she, with a deep sigh.

"Madame, I shall do so with the least possible delay, — indeed, this very evening," said the favourite, rising to terminate the interview. "And in the mean time, I trust that I have secured your friendship."

"I feel so highly honoured by yours, madame," said the old lady, beginning her curtseys again, "that I almost feel as if all this were a dream."

"Let us see, once more," said Jean, wishing to fix the matter so firmly in the old countess's mind that it might be secure from all change. "One hundred thousand francs first, to make up for the loss of the suit; a lieutenancy for the young count; and something for a nephew."

"Something?"

"I shall find out something good; that is my affair."

"And when shall I have the honour of seeing you again, madame?" asked the old lady.

"To-morrow morning my carriage shall be at your door to take you to Luciennes; the king will be there. To-morrow, at ten o'clock, I shall have fulfilled my promise. His Majesty will be informed, and will expect you."

"Allow me to accompany you, madame," said Jean, offering his arm.

"By no means, monsieur!"

"Well, then, to the top of the stairs?"

"Since you insist on it;" and she took the viscount's arm.

"Zamore!" cried the countess.

Zamore appeared.

"Light this lady downstairs, and order my brother's carriage forward to the door."

The two ladies exchanged a last curtsey. At the top of the staircase Jean bade the old countess adieu, and returned to his sister, while Madame de Béarn majestically descended the grand staircase. Zamore marched first; then came two footmen with lights; and then the old lady, her train (rather a short one) borne by a third footman.

The brother and sister watched at the window, following with their eyes to the very carriage the precious chaperon, sought with so much care, and found with so much difficulty. Just as she reached the door a chaise entered the courtyard, and a young lady sprang out.

"Ah, Mistress Chon!" cried Zamore, opening his enormous mouth to its widest extent with delight. "How do you do this evening, Mistress Chon?"

The Countess de Béarn stood petrified. In the new arrival she recognised her visitor, the false daughter of Master Flageot. Dubarry hurriedly opened a window, and made frantic signs to his sister; but she did not see them.

"Has that little fool, Gilbert, been here?" inquired Chon of a lackey, without perceiving the countess.

"No, madame," replied one of the footmen; "we have not seen him."

It was just then that, looking up, she saw her brother, and following the direction of his hand, discovered Madame de Béarn. Chon recognised her, hastily pulled down her hood, and rushed into the vestibule.

The old lady, without appearing to have remarked anything, got into the carriage and gave her address to the coachman.

CHAPTER XXXII.

THE KING GETS TIRED.

THE king, who had gone to Marly, as he had said he would, ordered his carriage at three o'clock in the afternoon, and drove from there to Luciennes. He supposed that Madame Dubarry, on receiving his note, would immediately leave Versailles, and hasten there to wait for him.

He was rather surprised, therefore, on entering the château, to find Zamore, looking very little like a governor, occupied in plucking out the feathers of a parrot, which, in return, was endeavouring to bite him.

The two favourites were rivals, like the Duke de Choiseul and the Countess Dubarry.

The king installed himself in the small salon, and dismissed his attendants. Although the most inquisitive gentleman in his kingdom, he was not in the habit of questioning servants or lackeys; but Zamore was neither a servant nor a lackey; he occupied a middle place between the monkey and the parrot. The king therefore questioned Zamore.

"Is the countess in the garden?"

"No, master." This word the favourite, in one of her whims, had ordered to take the place of Majesty, at Luciennes.

"Is she at the lake, feeding the carp?"

This lake had been dug at a vast expense out of the side of the hill; it was fed with water from the aqueduct, and filled with great numbers of the finest carp, brought from Versailles.

"No, master," again answered Zamore.

"Where is she, then?"

"In Paris, master."

"What! Did the countess not come to Luciennes?"

"No, master; but she sent Zamore."

"What to do?"

"To wait for the king."

"Ah, ha! so you are delegated to receive me? Very agreeable, indeed. Thank you, countess. Thank you. I am to have the society of Zamore!" And he rose from his chair rather piqued.

"Oh, no, the king is not to have the society of Zamore," said the negro.

"Why not?"

"Because Zamore is going away."

"Where are you going?"

"To Paris."

"Then I am to be left alone? Better and better. But why go to Paris?"

"To find Mistress Barry and tell her the king is at Luciennes."

"Oh, the countess desired you to tell me that then?"

"Yes, master."

"And did she tell you what I was to do till she came?"

"She said you were to sleep."

"Ah!" said the king to himself, "she will not be long, and she has some surprise for me." Then he added aloud, "Go, then, and bring back the countess. But how will you travel?"

"On the great white horse with the scarlet housings."

"And how long does it take for the great white horse to go to Paris?"

"I do not know," said the negro boy; "but he goes fast, fast, fast! Zamore likes to go fast."

"Indeed! I am extremely fortunate to find that Zamore likes to go fast."

And he stationed himself at the window to see Zamore depart.

A tall footman lifted him on the horse, and with the happy ignorance of childhood, the little negro set off at a gallop on his gigantic steed.

The king, being left alone, asked a footman at last if there were anything new at Luciennes. The servant replied that there was only Monsieur Boucher, who was painting the countess's boudoir.

" Oh, Boucher, poor Boucher, is he here ? " said the king, with a slight appearance of satisfaction; "and where is he ? "

" In the summer-house; shall I show your Majesty the way to it ? "

" No, no; I should rather go and see the carp.   Give me a knife."

" A knife, sire ? "

" Yes, and a large loaf."

The valet returned carrying a large loaf, with a long knife stuck in it, on a china plate. The king made a sign to the valet to accompany him, and with a pleased air led the way to the pond.

The feeding of carp was a traditional occupation in the Bourbon family, the Grand Monarque never missing it for a single day.   Louis XV. seated himself on a mossy bank, from which the view before him was charming.

There lay the little lake, with its velvet slopes of turf; beyond it a village nestled between two hills; further off, the towers of Saint Germain, with their wooded terraces, and further still the blue declivities of Saunois and Cormeilles; whilst, above all this, the grey and rose-tinged sky hung like a magnificent cupola. The weather had been stormy, and the foliage of the trees looked dark and heavy against the pale green of the meadows; the waters of the lake, glassy and immovable as a vast surface of oil, were disturbed from time to time by some silvery flashing fish springing up to seize the unwary fly, and chequering it with wide-spreading circles of alternate black and white. At the margin might be perceived the enormous snouts of a number of fish, which, fearless of hook or net, sucked the leaves of pendent plants, and with their huge fixed eyes, which seemed incapable of sight, stared at the grey lizards and green frogs sporting among the bulrushes.

When the king, like a man profoundly skilled in the art of killing time, had looked at the landscape on all sides, when he had counted the houses in the village and the villages in the distance, he took the plate with the loaf, placed it beside him, and began to cut off large pieces of the bread.

The carp heard the sound of the knife in the crust, and accustomed to that noise, which announced their dinner hour, they immediately flocked as close as possible to the bank, to show themselves to his Majesty and solicit their daily meal. They would have done the same for any footman in his service, but the king naturally thought that all this trouble was for him alone.

He threw in one after another the pieces of bread, which first disappearing for an instant, and then returning to the surface, were contended for for some time, then, gradually crumbling away by the action of the water, were seized and seen no more. It was indeed a curious and amusing enough sight to see all these crusts pushed hither and thither by the invisible snouts, and tossed on the surface of the water, until the moment when they were swallowed.

At the end of about half an hour, his Majesty, having in that time patiently cut one hundred bits of crust, had the satisfaction of seeing that not one remained floating. He began now, however, to feel rather tired of the sport, and he remembered that Monsieur Boucher might amuse him a little; he would not certainly be as good a resource as the carp, but in the country we must take what we can get.

Louis, therefore, turned towards the summer-house. Boucher had heard that he was at Luciennes, and though he went on painting, or seeming to paint, he followed the king with his eyes, saw him turn in the direction of the summer-house, and radiant with joy, he adjusted his ruffles and mounted on his ladder; for he had been warned not to appear to know that the king was there. He heard a step on the floor of the room, and began to daub a fat Cupid stealing a rose from a shepherdess in a blue satin gown and straw hat. His hand trembled, his heart beat. The king stopped on the threshold.

"Ah, Boucher," cried he; "how you smell of turpentine!" and he walked on.

Poor Boucher, although he knew the king had no taste for the fine arts, did expect some other kind of compliment, and was nearly falling from his ladder. He came down and went away with the tears in his eyes, without scraping his pallet or washing his brushes, which, in general, he was so careful to do.

His Majesty pulled out his watch; it was seven o'clock.

Louis returned to the house, teased the monkey, made the parrot speak, pulled out all the drawers of the cabinets, one after the other, and ransacked their contents.

Evening drew on. The king was not fond of darkness, and the apartments were lighted up. But he did not like solitude either.

"My horses in a quarter of an hour!" said he. "*Ma foi!*" added he, "I shall just give her one quarter of an hour; not a minute longer."

As he said this, he stretched himself on a sofa opposite the fireplace, to watch the course of the fifteen minutes, that is, of nine hundred seconds. At the four hundredth beat of the timepiece, which represented a blue elephant carrying a pink sultana, he was asleep.

As may be supposed, the footman who came to announce his Majesty's carriage took care not to awake him. The result of this attention to his august slumber was that when he awoke of his own accord, he found himself face to face with the Countess Dubarry, who was looking at him with her eyes wide open. Zamore stood in a corner waiting for orders.

"Ah! you are here at last, countess," said the king, sitting up on the sofa.

"Yes, sire, here I am," said the countess; "and here I have been a pretty long time."

"Oh! a pretty long time?"

"An hour and a half at least. But how your Majesty does sleep!"

"Faith, countess, you were not here, and I was getting shockingly tired; and then I sleep so badly at night. Do you know, I was on the point of going away!"

"Yes, I saw your Majesty's carriage at the door."

The king looked at his watch.

"Half-past ten; then I have slept nearly three hours!"

"After that, sire, say that you cannot sleep well at Luciennes!"

"Oh, faith, very well; but what the devil do I see there?" said he, looking at Zamore.

"You see the governor of Luciennes, sire."

"Not yet, not yet," said the king, laughing. "The little wretch has put on his uniform before having been appointed; he reckons on my word, then?"

"Sire, your word is sacred, and he is right in reckoning on it. But Zamore has something more than your word, or rather something less, — he has his commission; the vice-chancellor sent it to me. The oath is now the only formality which is wanting; make him swear quickly, and then betake himself to his post."

"Approach, governor," said the king.

Zamore came forward. He was dressed in a uniform, with an embroidered collar and a captain's epaulets, with short breeches, silk stockings, and a sword like a spit. He walked with a stiff, measured step, an enormous three-cornered hat under his arm.

"Can he swear?" asked the king.

"Oh, yes, sire; try him."

"Advance," cried he, looking curiously at the black puppet.

"On your knees!" said the countess.

"Swear!" said the king.

The child placed one hand on his heart, the other in the king's hand, and said, "I swear fealty and homage to my master and mistress; I swear to defend to the death the castle in my keeping, and to eat the last pot of sweetmeats rather than surrender, should I be attacked."

The king laughed as much at the form of the oath as at the gravity with which Zamore pronounced it.

"In return for this oath," he replied, with suitable gravity, "I confer on you the sovereign rights of justice on high and low, on all inhabiting air, earth, fire, and water, in this castle."

"Thank you, master," said Zamore, rising.

"And now," said the king, "go and show off your fine clothes in the kitchens, and leave us alone; go!"

As Zamore went out at one door, Chon entered by another.

"Ah, and you there, too, my little Chon! Come, I shall hear the truth from you."

"Take care, sire, that you are not disappointed in your expectations!" said Chon; "the truth is, it would be for the first time in my life. If you wish to learn the truth, apply to my sister; she is incapable of speaking falsely."

"Is that true, countess?"

"Sire, Chon has too flattering an opinion of me. Bad example has ruined me; and from this evening forth I am determined to lie like a real countess, if the truth will not serve me."

"Oh, ho!" said the king; "I suspect Chon has something to conceal from me. I must get from the police a report of what has occurred to-day."

"From which police, sire, — Sartines' or mine?"

"Oh, from Sartines'."

"What will you pay him for it?"

"If he tell me anything worth hearing, I shall not be niggardly."

"Well, then, give my police the preference, and take my report. I shall serve you — royally."

" You will even sell your own secrets ? "

" Why not, if I am well paid ? "

" Come, then, let me hear the report, — but no fibs, remember ! "

" Sire, you insult me."

" I mean, no equivocations."

" Well, sire, get your funds ready; I am about to begin my report."

" They are ready," said the king, jingling some money in his pocket.

" In the first place, the Countess Dubarry was seen in Paris, in the Rue de Valois, about two o'clock in the afternoon."

" Well, I know that; go on ! "

" About six o'clock Zamore proceeded to join her there."

" Very possibly; but what did Madame Dubarry go to Paris for ? "

" Sire, to meet the lady who is to present her."

" Pooh !" said the king, with a grimace which he could not altogether conceal; " she is very well as she is, without being presented."

" You know the proverb, sire : ' Nothing is so dear to us as that which we have not.' "

" So she is absolutely determined to find this lady to present her ? "

" We have found her, sire."

The king started, and shrugged his shoulders.

" I like that movement, sire; it shows that your Majesty would be annoyed at the defeat of the Grammonts, the Guéménées, and all the hypocrites of the court," said the countess.

" I beg your pardon; did you speak ? "

" Yes, I am sure you are in league with those persons.'

" In league ? Countess, learn one thing, that the king only leagues with kings."

" True, but all your kings are friends of the Duke de Choiseul."

"Let us return to your chaperon, countess."

"With all my heart, sire."

"You have succeeded in manufacturing a lady, then ? "

"I found one ready made, and very well made, — a Countess de Béarn; a family who have numbered princes in their ranks. She will not dishonour the relative of the relatives of the Stuarts, I hope ! "

"The Countess de Béarn ! " exclaimed the king, with surprise. "I know only of one, who lives somewhere near Verdun."

"It is the very same; she has come to Paris on purpose to present me."

"Ha ! and when is the affair to take place ? "

"To-morrow, at eleven o'clock in the morning, I am to give her a private audience, and at the same time, if it be not too presumptuous, she will request the king to name a day; and you will name the earliest, will you not, dear France ? "

The king burst into a forced laugh.

"Certainly, certainly," said he, kissing the countess's hand. Then, all at once, "To-morrow, at eleven ? " added he.

"Yes, at breakfast."

"Impossible, my dear countess."

"Impossible ! — why ? "

"I shall not breakfast here; I must return this evening."

"What ! " said the countess, who felt an icy pang shoot through her heart at these words; "you are going to leave us, sire ? "

"I am forced to do so, dear countess; I have to meet Sartines on very important business."

"As you please, sire; but you will at least sup here, I hope ? "

"Oh, yes, I shall sup, I think; yes, I am rather hungry, — I shall sup."

"Order supper, Chon," said the countess, making at the

same time a private signal to her, which no doubt referred to some previous arrangements. Chon left the room. The king had seen the signal in a mirror, and although he could not comprehend its meaning, he suspected some snare.

"Ah!" said he, "on second thoughts I think it will be impossible to stay even for supper. I must not lose a moment; I have some papers to sign, — to-day is Saturday."

"As you please, sire; shall I order the horses?"

"Yes, fairest."

"Chon!"

Chon re-appeared.

"His Majesty's horses!" said the countess.

"Very well," said Chon with a smile, and she left the room again.

A moment afterwards her voice was heard in the ante-room, ordering the king's carriage.

CHAPTER XXXIII.

THE KING IS AMUSED.

THE king, delighted at this exercise of his authority, which punished the countess for leaving him alone so long, at the same time that it freed him from the trouble of settling the affair of her presentation, walked towards the door of the salon.

Chon entered.

" Well, are my attendants there ? "

" No, sire, there is not one of them in the ante-room."

The king advanced into the ante-room himself. " My attendants !" cried he. No one answered; there seemed not to be even an echo in the silent château.

" Who the devil would believe," said the king, returning to the salon, " that I am the grandson of the man who once said, 'I was very near having to wait ' ? " and he went to a window, opened it, and looked out.

The space in front of the château was as deserted as the ante-rooms; no horses, no attendants, no guards. Night alone displayed to the eyes and to the soul all its calmness and all its majesty. The lovely moon shone brightly on the woods of Chatou, whose lofty summits rustled gently like the waves of the sea rippled by a breeze. The Seine, on whose bosom glittered a long line of light, looked like a gigantic serpent trailing its slow length along, its windings being visible from Bougival to Maisons, that is, for four or five leagues ; and then, in the midst of this heavenly scene, a nightingale burst forth with such a sweet and varied song as she only gives in the month of May, as if she felt that nature was worthy of her music in the early days of spring alone, — days which are scarcely come ere they are gone.

All this beauty and harmony were lost on Louis XV., — a king not much of a dreamer, a poet, or an artist, but, on the contrary, a good deal of a sensualist.

"Come, countess !" said he, considerably annoyed, "give the necessary orders, I entreat; what the deuce ! — this jest must have an end."

" Sire," replied the countess, with that charming pouting air which became her so well, "I do not command here."

"Nor do I," replied the king, "for you see how I am obeyed."

" It is neither you nor I who command."

" Who is it, then ? Is it you, Chon ? "

" I ? " said the young lady, who was seated on a couch on the other side of the apartment exactly opposite the countess, who occupied a similar one on the near side; "I find the task of obeying so difficult that I have no inclination for that of commanding."

" But who is the master, then ? "

" The governor, sire, certainly."

" Monsieur Zamore ? "

" Yes."

" Ah, very true ! Well, let some one ring for him."

The countess stretched out her arm with a most graceful air of nonchalance to a silken cord ending in a tassel of beads. A footman, who had no doubt received his lesson beforehand, was ready in the ante-room and appeared.

" The governor," said the king.

" The governor," replied the valet, respectfully, "is on guard, watching over his Majesty's precious life."

" Where is he ? "

" Going his rounds, sire."

" Going his rounds ? " repeated the king.

" Yes, with four officers, sire."

The king could not help smiling.

"'That is droll enough," said he; "but it need not prevent my horses from being harnessed immediately."

"Sire, the governor ordered the stables to be closed, lest some marauder might enter them."

"And where are my grooms?"

"Gone to bed, sire."

"Gone to bed!—by whose orders?"

"The governor's, sire."

"And the gates of the castle?"

"Are locked, sire."

"Very well; then you must get the keys."

"The governor has them at his belt, sire."

"A well-guarded castle indeed! *Peste!* what order is kept!"

The footman, seeing that the king ceased to question him, retired. The countess reclining gracefully on a couch, continued to bite off the leaves of a beautiful rose, beside which her lips seemed like coral. "Come, sire," said she at length, with a fascinating smile, "I must take compassion on your Majesty; give me your arm and let us set out in search of some one to help you. Chon, light the way."

Chon went before, ready to apprise them of any dangers which they might encounter. At the very first turn in the corridor the king's nose was saluted by an odour quite sufficient to awaken the appetite of the most fastidious epicure.

"Ah, ha! what is that, countess?" said he, stopping.

"Oh, only supper, sire! I thought your Majesty intended doing me the honour of supping at Luciennes, and I made arrangements accordingly."

The king inhaled the gastronomic perfume two or three times, whilst he called to mind that his stomach had already given him certain tokens of its existence; then he thought what a fuss there must be before his grooms could be awakened; that would take half an hour at least; a quarter more to harness the horses; ten minutes to reach

Marly, and when at Marly, where he was not expected, he should only get a put-off of a supper. All these things passed through his mind as he stood at the dining-room door, inhaling the seductive steam of the viands. Two covers were placed on the table, which was splendidly lighted and sumptuously laid out.

"*Peste !* " said Louis, "you have a good cook, countess."

"Oh, sire, this is merely his first effort; the poor devil has been doing wonders to deserve your Majesty's approbation. Indeed, he is so sensitive that he might, perhaps, in his disappointment, cut his throat, as poor Vatel did."

"Really, do you think so ? "

"There was to be an omelet of pheasants' eggs, on which he especially prided himself."

"An omelet of pheasants' eggs ? I adore omelets of pheasants' eggs."

"What a pity you must go ! "

"Well, countess, we must not vex your cook," said the king, laughing; "and perhaps, whilst we are supping, Master Zamore may return from his rounds."

"Ah! sire, a capital idea," said the countess, unable to conceal her delight at having gained this first step. "Come, sire, come ! "

"But who will wait on us ? " said the king, looking round in vain for an attendant.

"Ah! sire," said Madame Dubarry, "is your coffee less grateful when presented to you by me ? "

"No, countess; and still more when you make it for me."

"Well, come then, sire."

"Two covers only ! Has Chon supped, then ? "

"Sire, I did not venture, without your Majesty's express command — "

"Come, come," said the king, taking a plate and cover from a sideboard himself, "come, my little Chon; sit there opposite us."

" Oh, sire ! " said Chon.

" Yes, yes ! play the very humble and very obedient
subject, you little hypocrite. Sit here, countess, near me
— beside me. What a beautiful profile you have ! "

" Is this the first time you have observed it, dear
France ? "

" How should I observe it, when I am so happy in looking at your full countenance ? Decidedly, countess, your
cook is first-rate. What soup ! "

" Then I was right in sending away the other ? "

" Quite right, quite right."

" Sire, follow my example ; you see it will be to your
advantage."

" I do not understand you."

" I have turned off my Choiseul ; turn off yours."

" Countess, no politics. Give me some madeira."

The king held out his glass : the countess took up a
decanter to help him, and as she raised it up, her white
fingers and rosy nails were seen to advantage.

" Pour gently and slowly," said the king.

" Not to shake the wine, sire ? "

" No, to give me more time to admire your hand."

" Assuredly, sire," said the countess, laughing ; "your
Majesty is in the vein of making discoveries ! "

" Faith, yes," said the king, now in perfect good-humour
again, " and think I am in the fair way of discovering — "

" A new world ? "

" No, I am not so ambitious ; besides, I find a kingdom
as much as I can manage. No, only an isle, — a little nook,
an enchanted mountain, a palace of which a certain fair
lady will be the Armida, and the entrance to which will
be defended by all kinds of monsters."

" Sire," said the countess, presenting the king with a
glass of iced champagne, a luxury quite new at that period,
" here is some water just drawn from the river Lethe."

" The river Lethe, countess ? Are you sure ? "

" Yes, sire ; it was poor Jean who brought it from the

shades below, from which you know he has just narrowly
escaped."

"Countess, I drink to his happy resurrection. But no
politics, I beg."

"Then I don't know what to talk about, sire. If you
would relate something, — you, who have such a happy
gift of telling a story."

"No, but I shall repeat you some verses."

"Verses ? "

"Yes, verses. Is there anything surprising in that
word ? "

"I thought your Majesty detested them."

Parbleu! out of each hundred thousand manufactured,
ninety thousand are against myself ! "

"And those which your Majesty is going to give me
belong to the ten thousand which cannot even make you
look favourably on the ninety thousand."

"No, countess ; these are addressed to you."

"To me ? By whom ? "

"By Monsieur de Voltaire."

"He charged your Majesty to deliver them ? "

"Not at all ; he sent them direct to your Highness."

"How ? — without a cover ? "

"No, enclosed in a charming letter."

"Ah, I understand ; your majesty has been at work
this morning with the postmaster. But read the verses,
sire ; read Monsieur de Voltaire's verses."

Louis XV. opened the paper and read : —

> " Goddess of pleasure, soft queen of the graces,
>   Why blend, with the fêtes which make Paphos to ring,
> Foul threat'ning suspicions and hideous disgraces —
>   The fate of a hero, oh ! why should'st thou bring ?
> Still dear our Ulysses his country shall hold,
>   The State's mighty bulwark, the monarch's delight ;
> None wiser in council, in battle more bold,
>   And Ilion can tell how resistless his might !

"Fair Venus, thy throne all the gods shall surround,
  Thy beauty celestial all tongues shall declare,
The roses of joy in thy path shall abound;
  Then calm the rough waters and smile on our prayer.
Ah! why should thy anger burn fiercely and high
  'Gainst the hero whom foemen still tremble to meet;
For how can he draw from such beauty a sigh,
  Save in breathing his vows as he kneels at her feet?"

"Decidedly, sire," said the countess, more piqued than gratified by this poetical offering, "Monsieur de Voltaire wishes to recommend himself to your favour."

"He loses his pains, then," said the king. "He is a firebrand who would burn Paris if he returned to it. Let him stay with his friend, my cousin Frederick II.; we can do very well with Monsieur Rousseau. But take the verses, countess, and study them."

She took the paper, made a match of it, and laid it beside her plate.

"Some tokay, sire," said Chon.

"From the vaults which supply his Majesty the Emperor of Austria," said the countess.

"From the emperor's vaults?" said the king. "*Pardieu!* no one is supplied from them but myself."

"Very true, sire," said the countess; "so I had it from your butler."

"Ah!" said the king, "and you have seduced —"

"No, sire, I have *ordered.*"

"Well answered, countess! I was a fool."

"Will the king take coffee?" asked Chon.

"Oh, certainly."

"And will his Majesty burn it as usual?" asked the countess.

"If the lady of the castle permit." The countess rose. "But what are you doing?"

"I am going to wait on you myself."

"Well," said the king, leaning back in his chair like a man who had made an excellent supper, and whose humours were, therefore, in a happy state of equilibrium. "Well, I see that my best plan is to let you do as you like, countess."

The countess brought a silver stand, with a little coffee-pot containing the boiling mocha; she then placed before the king a plate on which was a silver cup and a carafe of Bohemian glass, and beside the plate she laid the taper which she had just folded.

The king, with that profound attention which he always bestowed on this operation, calculated his sugar, measured his coffee, and, having gently poured on it the brandy, so that it swam on the surface, he took the little roll of paper, lighted it at a candle, and communicated the flame to the liquor. Five minutes afterward he enjoyed his coffee with all the delight of a finished epicure.

The countess looked on till he had finished the last drop; then she exclaimed, " Oh, sire, you have burned your coffee with M. de Voltaire's verses. That is a bad omen for the Choiseuls!"

"I was wrong," said he, laughing; "you are not a fairy, you are a demon."

The countess rose.

"Does your Majesty wish to know whether the governor has returned ? "

"Zamore ? Bah! for what purpose ? "

"To allow you to go to Marly, sire."

"True," said the king, making a great effort to rouse himself from that state of comfort in which he found himself. "Well, countess, let us see; let us see."

The countess made a sign to Chon, who vanished.

The king began his search for Zamore again; but, it must be confessed, with very different feelings from those which had before influenced him. Philosophers say that we behold things either dark or bright, according to the state of our stomachs, and, as kings have stomachs like other men, — in general, indeed, not so good as other men, but still communicating the sensation of comfort or discomfort to the rest of the body in the same manner, — our king appeared in the most charming humour which it was possible for a king to be in. Just inside the corridor a new perfume greeted the king's nostrils. A door leading into a delightful chamber, hung in blue satin, embroidered with natural flowers, opened, disclosing, illumined by a mysterious light, the recess toward which for the past two hours the steps of the enchantress had been pointed. "Sire," said she, "it seems that Zamore has not returned, and we are still confined, unless we leave the château through the windows."

"By the aid of the bedclothes?" asked the king.

" Sire," said the countess, with a charming smile, "let us use, not abuse."

The king, laughing, opened his arms, and the countess let fall the pretty rose, which scattered its petals on the carpet.

CHAPTER XXXIV.

VOLTAIRE AND ROUSSEAU.

At ten o'clock the next morning the king, though he had supped so well, began to think of breakfast; but going to a window, he saw his carriage and all his attendants ready for his departure. Zamore, with folded arms, was giving, or pretending to give, orders.

"What is this, countess?" said he; "are we not to breakfast? One would think you were going to send me away fasting!"

"Heaven forbid, sire! but I thought your Majesty had to meet Monsieur de Sartines at Marly."

"*Pardieu!*" said the king, "could not Sartines be told to come here? it is so near!"

"Your Majesty will do me the honour to believe that that idea occurred to me before your Majesty."

"And, besides, the morning is too fine for work; let us breakfast."

"Your Majesty must first give me a few signatures for myself."

"For the Countess de Béarn?"

"Yes; and then name the day and the hour."

"What day and hour?"

"The day and hour for my presentation."

"*Ma foi!*" said the king, "it must be so, I suppose; fix the day yourself."

"Sire, the sooner the better."

"Is all ready?"

"Yes."

" You have learned to make your three curtseys ? "

" I have practised them for more than a year."

" You have your dress ? "

" In twenty-four hours it will be ready."

" And you have your chaperon ? "

" In an hour she will be here."

" And now, countess, for a bargain! "

" What is it ? "

" That you will never again speak of that affair of the Viscount Jean with the Baron de Taverney."

" Must I sacrifice the poor viscount ? "

" Yes, faith! "

" Well, sire, I shall speak no more of it.   The day ? "

" The day after to-morrow."

" The hour ? "

" Half-past ten at night, as usual."

" It is settled ? "

" It is settled."

" On your royal word ? "

" On the word of a gentleman."

" Give me your hand on it, France! " and Madame Dubarry held out her pretty little hand, in which the king placed his own.

This morning all Luciennes felt the gaiety of its master. He had yielded on one point on which he had long before determined to yield; but then he had gained another. This was certainly a decided advantage. He would give one hundred thousand crowns to Jean on condition that he went to drink the waters of the Pyrénées, in Auvergne; that would pass for banishment in the eyes of the Choiseul party. There were louis-d'or that morning for the poor, cakes for the carp, and praises for Boucher's paintings.

Eleven o'clock struck. The countess, although attending assiduously to the king at his breakfast, could not help looking, from time to time, at the clock, which moved too slowly for her wishes. His Majesty had taken the trouble to say that when the Countess de Béarn arrived she was to be shown into the breakfast-room. The coffee was served, tasted, drunk; still, she came not. Suddenly the tramping of a horse's feet was heard. The countess ran to a window. It was a messenger from the viscount, who leaped from his horse reeking with foam. At sight of him she felt a chill run through her veins, for she knew all could not be right; but it was necessary to hide her uneasiness in order to keep the king in good-humour. She returned to his side and sat down.

A moment afterwards, Chon entered with a note in her hand. There was no means of escape; it must be read before the king.

"What is that, sweet Chon?" said the king; "a love-letter?"

"Oh, certainly, sire."

"From whom?"

"From the poor viscount."

"Are you quite certain?"

"Look at it, sire."

The king recognised the writing, and thinking the note might contain something about the Lachaussée affair, "Very well," said he, pushing it aside, "very well, — that is enough."

The countess was on thorns.

"Is the note for me?" she asked.

"Yes, countess."

"Will your Majesty permit me — "

"Oh, yes; read it, read it; and in the mean time, Chon will repeat 'Maître Corbeau' to me." So saying, he pulled her on his knee, and began to sing, — sadly out of tune, indeed, for Rousseau has recorded that Louis had the worst ear in his kingdom.

The countess retired into the recess of a window, and read the following epistle : —

Do not expect the old wretch; she pretends that she scalded her foot yesterday, and is obliged to keep her room. You may thank Chon's most opportune arrival yesterday for this. The old wretch recognised her immediately, and so put an end to our little comedy.

It was fortunate that that little wretch, Gilbert, who is the cause of this misfortune, was lost. I would have wrung his neck about! However, he may be assured it is in store for him, if ever he cross my path.

But to return to the point; come to Paris at once, or we are lost. JEAN.

"What is the matter?" inquired the king, surprised at the sudden paleness which overspread the countess's face.

"Nothing, sire; it is only a bulletin of Jean's health."

"Does not the dear viscount get better, then?"

"Oh, yes, thank you, sire, much better," said the countess. "But I hear a carriage enter the courtyard."

"Oh, our old countess, I suppose!"

"No, sire, it is Monsieur de Sartines."

"Well, what then?" exclaimed the king, seeing that Madame Dubarry was moving towards the door.

"Well, sire, I shall leave you with him and go to dress."

"And what about the Countess de Béarn?"

"When she comes, sire, I shall let your Majesty know," replied the countess, crumpling the viscount's note in the pocket of her dressing-gown.

"Then you abandon me?" said the king, with a melancholy air.

"Sire, remember this is Sunday; you have papers to sign." So saying she presented her fresh and rosy cheeks to the king, who kissed them, and she left the room.

"Devil take all signatures," said the king, "and those who bring them! Who was it that invented ministers and portfolios?"

He had scarcely finished this malediction, when the minister and the portfolio entered by a door opposite that by which the countess had departed. The king sighed again, more deeply than before.

"Ah! are you there, Sartines?" said he. "How very punctual you are."

This was said in a tone which left it very doubtful whether the words were intended as a eulogium or a reproach.

The minister opened his portfolio, and busied himself in taking out and arranging his papers. Just then the sound of the wheels of a carriage was heard, grating on the sand of the avenue.

"Wait a little, Sartines," said the king, and he ran to the window.

"What!" said he, "the countess is driving off!"

"It is she, indeed, sire," said the minister.

"But is she not going to wait for the Countess de Béarn?"

"Sire, I am inclined to think she is tired of waiting, and goes to find her."

"Yet the old lady had decided on coming this morning."

"Sire, I am almost certain that she will not come."

"Then you know something about the matter, Sartines?"

"Sire, I am obliged to know a little about everything; otherwise your Majesty would be dissatisfied with me."

"Well, what has happened? Tell me, Sartines."

"To the old countess, sire?"

"Yes."

"A very common case, sire; difficulties have arisen."

"Then the Countess de Béarn really will not come?"

"Hum! there was rather more certainty of it yesterday evening than there is this morning."

"Poor countess!" said the king, unable, in spite of himself, to conceal a gleam of satisfaction which sparkled in his eyes.

"Ah, sire, the quadruple alliance and the family compact were trifles in comparison with this presentation!"

"Poor countess!" repeated the king, shaking his head, "she will never accomplish her purpose."

"I fear it, sire, unless your Majesty concerns yourself about it."

"She was so certain that now all was in the right train."

"And what makes the matter worse for the countess," said Monsieur de Sartines, "is, that if she be not presented before the arrival of the dauphiness, it is probable she never will be presented at all."

"More than probable. Sartines, you are right. They say that my daughter-in-law is very strict, very devout, very prudish. Poor countess!"

"It will certainly annoy her very much, sire, if she be not presented; but, on the other hand, it will relieve your Majesty from many annoyances."

"Do you think so, Sartines?"

"Oh, yes, sire. The envious, the libellers, the ballad-mongers, the flatterers, the journalists, will not have so much to say. If she was presented, sire, it would cost us at least one hundred thousand francs additional for the police."

"Indeed? Poor countess! And yet she wishes so much to be presented."

"Your Majesty knows you have only to command, and her wishes will be gratified."

"What do you mean, Sartines? Do you imagine that I could meddle in such an affair? Can I, by signing an order, make people polite to Madame Dubarry? Is it you, Sartines, a man of sense, who advise such an innovation to satisfy the whims of the countess?"

"Oh, by no means, sire. I merely say, as your Majesty says, 'Poor countess!'"

"Besides," said the king, "her position is not so desperate, after all. You always look at things on the dark side, Sartines. Who can tell whether the Countess de Béarn may not change her mind? Who can be certain that the dauphiness will arrive so soon? It will take four days yet before she can reach Compiègne, and in four days much may be done. Let me see. Have you anything for me to do this morning, Sartines?"

"Oh, your Majesty, only three papers to sign;" and the minister of police drew out the first from his portfolio.

"Oh," said the king, "a *lettre-de-cachet*."

"Yes, sire."

"And against whom?"

"Your Majesty may see."

"Oh! against the Sieur Rousseau? What Rousseau is that, Sartines, and what has he done?"

"Done, sire? — written 'Le Contrat Social.'"

"Oh, then, it is Jean Jacques whom you wish to shut up in the Bastille?"

"Sire, he disturbs the public peace."

"And what the deuce did you expect he would do?"

"Besides, I don't propose to shut him up."

"Of what use is this letter, then?"

"Sire, merely to have a weapon ready."

"Not that I am at all fond of your philosophers, mark ye."

"Your Majesty has good cause not to love them."

"But people will exclaim against us. Besides, I think we authorised him to come to Paris."

"No, sire; we said we should tolerate him on condition that he did not appear in public."

"And does he appear in public?"

"He is always to be seen."

"In his Armenian dress?"

"Oh no, sire. We ordered him to lay it aside."

"And he obeyed?"

"Yes, but complaining loudly all the time of our persecution."

"And how does he dress now?"

"Oh, like other people, sire."

"Then he cannot be so much remarked?"

"What, sire! a man who has been forbidden to appear in public not remarked! And then, only guess where he goes every day?"

"To the Marshal de Luxembourg's, to Monsieur d'Alembert's, to Madame d'Epinay's?"

"To the Café de la Régence, sire! He plays chess there

every evening. He must be mad upon that point, for he
always loses; and it requires every evening a company
of soldiers to keep order among the crowds around the
house."

"Well," said the king, "the Parisians are even greater
fools than I thought them. Let them go on amusing
themselves in that way, Sartines; while they do so, they
will not shout starvation!"

"But, sire, if some fine day he should take it into his
head to make a speech, as he did in London?"

"Oh, in that case, as there would be criminality and
public infringement of the laws, you would not require a
lettre-de-cachet, Sartines."

The minister saw that the king did not wish the arrest
of Rousseau to rest on the royal responsibility, so he did
not press the matter farther.

"But, sire," said he, "there is another philosopher."

"Another!" replied the king, languidly; "shall we
never have done with them?"

"Ah, sire, it is they who have never done with us."

"And who is this one?"

"Monsieur de Voltaire."

"Has he also returned to France?"

"No, sire; it would be much better, perhaps, that he
had, for then we could watch him."

"What has he been doing?"

"It is not he who has been doing anything, it is his
partisans; they are actually going to have a statue erected
in his honour."

"Equestrian, I suppose?"

"No, sire; and yet I assure you he is a famous captor of
towns."

The king shrugged his shoulders.

"Sire, there has not been seen such a one since Polior-
cetes," continued Sartines. "He obtains information from
all quarters; his writings reach all quarters; the highest
persons in your kingdom turn smugglers for the sake of

his books. I seized, the other day, eight boxes full of them; two were addressed to the Duke de Choiseul."

"It is very amusing."

"Sire, only reflect that they are now doing for him what is only done for kings, — they are decreeing him a statue."

"Sartines, statues are not decreed by others for kings, they decree them to themselves. And who is to make this fine work of art?"

"The sculptor Pigale; he has set out for Ferney to execute the model. In the mean time, subscriptions are pouring in; and observe, sire, it is only authors who are permitted to subscribe. All come with their offerings; they make quite a procession every day. Even Rousseau brought his two louis-d'or."

"Well," said the king, "what can I do in the matter? I am not an author; it does not concern me."

"Sire, I thought of proposing to your Majesty to put an end, by royal command, to this demonstration."

"I shall take good care not to do any such thing, Sartines. Instead of decreeing him a bronze statue, they would then decree him one of gold. Let them alone. *Mon Dieu!* he will look even uglier in bronze than in flesh and blood!"

"Then your Majesty desires that the matter should take its own course?"

"Let us understand one another, Sartines. Desire is not the word. I should be very glad to put an end to these things, certainly; but how can I? — it is impossible. The time is past when royalty could say to the spirit of philosophy, as God says to the ocean, 'Thus far shalt thou go and no farther!' To blame loudly but uselessly; to aim a blow, but strike short of our aim; that would only serve to show our own weakness. Let us turn away our eyes, Sartines, and pretend not to see."

The minister sighed.

"At least, sire," said he, "if we do not punish the men,

let us suppress their works. Here is a list of books which, in my opinion, should instantly be proscribed; some attack the throne, some the altar; some teach rebellion, others sacrilege."

The king took the list, and read in a languid voice, —

" 'The Sacred Contagion; or, the Natural History of Superstition.'

" 'The System of Nature; or, Laws of the Physical and Moral world.'

" 'Instructions of the Capuchin at Ragusa, to Brother Pediculoso, on his setting out for the Holy Land.' "

He had not read one-fourth of the list, when he let it fall, whilst an expression of sadness and dejection overspread his usually unmoved countenance. He remained thoughtful, and for some minutes seemed quite overcome.

"Sartines," said he, at last, "one might as well undertake to move the world. Let others try it."

The minister looked at him with that perfect understanding of his wishes which the king loved in those who approached him, as it saved him the trouble of thinking and acting.

"A tranquil life, sire," said he, "a tranquil life,— is not that what your Majesty wishes?"

The king nodded.

"Oh, yes," said he. "I ask for nothing else from your philosophers, encyclopedists, thaumaturgi, illuminati, poets, economists, journalists,— tribes that come one knows not whence; that are always bustling, writing, croaking, calumniating, calculating, preaching, complaining. Let them be crowned; let statues be raised to them; let temples be built to them, — but let them leave me in peace."

Sartines arose, bowed, and left the apartment, muttering, as he went, "It is fortunate we have on our money, 'Domine, salvum fac regem.' "

Then the king, now left to himself, took a pen, and wrote to the dauphin the following lines: —

"You have requested me to hasten the arrival of madame the dauphiness, and I wish to gratify you.

"I have ordered that there shall be no stay made at Noyon; consequently, on Tuesday morning she will be at Compiègne.

"I shall be there myself precisely at ten o'clock, — that is to say, a quarter of an hour before her."

"Thus," said he to himself, "I shall get rid of that foolish affair of the presentation, which annoys me more than Voltaire and Rousseau, and all the philosophers, past, present, and to come. The affair will then be between the poor countess, the dauphin, and dauphiness. *Ma foi*, it is only fair that young minds, with strength for it, should contend with these vexations, hatreds, and revenges! Children should early learn to suffer; it is an excellent part of education."

Delighted at having thus got rid of the difficulty, and certain that he would not be reproached with either favouring or hindering this presentation, about which all Paris was occupied, the king entered his carriage and drove off to Marly, where the court was waiting for him.

CHAPTER XXXV.

CHAPERON AND DEBUTANTE.

THE poor countess, — let us continue to apply the epithet which the king had given her, for at this moment she truly deserved it, — the poor countess hurried like one in despair to Paris. Chon, terrified by Jean's paragraph concerning Gilbert, shut herself up in the boudoir at Luciennes to hide her grief and anxiety, lamenting the fatal whim which induced her to pick up Gilbert on the high-road.

Having reached the outskirts of Paris, the countess found a coach awaiting her. In the coach were Viscount Jean and a lawyer, with whom he seemed to be arguing in the most energetic manner. The moment he perceived the countess he leaped out, and made a sign to his sister's coachman to stop.

"Quick, countess!" said he. "Quick, get into my carriage, and drive to the Rue Saint-Germain-des-Près!"

"Is the old lady going to give us the slip?" said Madame Dubarry, changing carriages, while the lawyer, on a sign from the viscount, followed her example.

"I fear it, countess," replied Jean. "I fear she is giving us a Roland for our Oliver."

"But what has happened?"

"You shall hear. I stayed in Paris because I am always suspicious; and in this case I was not wrong, as you will see. At nine last night I went prowling about the inn of the Coq Chantant. All quiet, — no movement, no visitors; all looked well. Consequently, I thought I might go home to bed, and to bed I went. This morning I awoke

at break of day. I roused Patrice, and ordered him to go
and keep watch at the corner of the street. Well, at nine
— observe, that was an hour sooner than I had appointed
— I drove up to the hotel. Patrice had seen nothing to
cause the least anxiety, so I boldly walked upstairs. At
the door of the countess's room a maid-servant stopped me
and told me that the countess could not leave the house
to-day, and perhaps it would be eight days before she
could move from her apartment. I confess that, although
prepared for some rebuff, I was not for that. 'What,'
cried I, 'she cannot go out! What is the matter?' 'She
is ill.' 'Ill? Impossible! Yesterday she was perfectly
well.' 'Yes, monsieur, but madame likes to make her
own chocolate; and this morning, when it was boiling, she
spilled it over her foot, and she is scalded. On hearing
the countess's cries I hastened in, and I found her nearly
fainting. I carried her to her bed, and I think she is at
present asleep.' I was as white as your lace, countess,
and could not help crying out, 'It is a lie!' 'No, my dear
Viscount Dubarry,' replied a sharp voice, which seemed to
pierce the very wall, 'it is not a lie! I am in horrible
pain.' I sprang to the side whence the voice came, and
burst through a glass door which I could not open; the old
countess was really in bed. 'Ah, madame!' I exclaimed,
but it was all I could utter; I was in such a rage. I could
have strangled her with pleasure. 'Look there,' said she,
pointing to an old kettle which was lying on the floor;
'there is the coffee-pot that did all the mischief.' I flew
to the coffee-pot, and stamped on it with both feet; it will
make no more chocolate, I can answer for it. 'What a
misfortune!' cried the old lady, piteously; 'it must be
Baronne d'Alogny who will present your sister. But what
can we do? It was so written, as the Easterns say.'"

"Heavens! Jean, you drive me to despair!" exclaimed
the countess.

"Oh! I do not despair yet, if you go to her; it was for
that that I sent for you."

"But why do you not despair?"

"Why? because you are a woman, and can do what I cannot; you can have the bandage taken off; and, if you discover that it is an imposture, you can tell her that her son shall never be anything but a clown, that she shall never touch a farthing from the estate of the Saluces, — in short, you can play off the imprecations of Camilla on her, much better than I the fury of Orestes."

"Is this all a jest?" cried the countess.

"No, I assure you."

"And where does our sibyl lodge?"

"At the Coq Chantant, Rue Saint-Germain-des-Près, — a great black house, with a monstrous cock painted on an iron plate; when the iron creaks, the cock crows."

"I shall have a dreadful scene with her."

"No doubt of it; but you must take your chance. Shall I go with you?"

"No; you would spoil all."

"Just what our lawyer said; I was consulting him on that point when you drove up. For your information, I may tell you that he says to beat a person in his own house renders you liable to fine and imprisonment, while to beat him out of it —"

"Is nothing!" said the countess. "You know that better than any one else."

Jean grinned an ugly smile.

"Debts," said he, "that are long in being paid, are paid with interest; and if ever I meet my man again —"

"I would much rather, at present, speak of my woman!"

"I have nothing more to tell you; so be off!"

"But where will you wait for me?"

"In the inn itself. I shall ask for a bottle of wine, and sit there, in case you want a helping hand."

"Drive on, coachman!" cried the countess.

"Rue Saint-Germain-des-Près, at the sign of the Coq Chantant," added the viscount.

In a quarter of an hour they were in the street honoured

by possessing the Coq Chantant. At some distance from the inn Madame Dubarry left her carriage and proceeded on foot; she feared that the noise of the wheels might put the old lady on the alert, that she might suspect what visitor was coming, and might have time to hide.

Alone, then, she entered the gaping porch of the inn. No one saw her until she was at the foot of the staircase; there she encountered the hostess.

"The Countess de Béarn?" said she.

"She is very ill, madame, and cannot see any one."

"Yes, I am aware; and I came to know exactly how she is."

And, light as a bird, she was at the top of the stairs in a moment.

"Madame, madame!" cried the hostess, "a lady is going to force her way into your room!"

"Who is she?" asked the old lady, from a distant part of the room.

"I," said the favourite, appearing on the threshold with a face perfectly suited to the occasion, for she first smiled out of compliment, and then looked sad, by way of condolence.

"You here, madame?" exclaimed the old lady, turning pale.

"Yes, dear madame; I came to express my sympathy for your misfortune, of which I have just heard. Pray tell me how this accident happened."

"But, madame, I dare not ask you to sit down in such a miserable place as this."

"I know, madame, that you have a castle in Touraine, and can excuse your being obliged to receive your friends here in an inn." And she sat down so determinedly that the old lady saw she must allow her to have her way.

"You seem in great pain, madame," said the favourite.

"Oh, in dreadful pain!"

"The right leg? But, good heavens! how did you manage to scald it?"

"Nothing more simple; I held the chocolate kettle in my hand, the handle gave way, and I received the boiling water on my ankle."

"How shocking!"

The old lady sighed. "Yes, shocking, indeed," said she; "but this is always the case; misfortunes never come singly."

"You are aware that the king expected you this morning?"

"Oh, madame, that intelligence makes my sufferings infinitely greater!"

"His Majesty is far from satisfied, madame, that you did not pay your visit."

"But the pain I am in will be a sufficient apology; and I trust yet to be able to offer to his Majesty my very humble excuses."

"I do not tell you that to cause you any vexation," said the countess, seeing that the old lady was assuming a little formality, "but merely to let you know that his Majesty felt grateful for the offer you made me."

"You see, madame, that it is now impossible for me to fulfil it."

"Certainly; but may I ask you a question?"

"I shall be delighted to hear it."

"Does not your present state arise from your having experienced some sudden agitation?"

"Very possibly," said the old lady, bowing slightly; "I must acknowledge that I was deeply moved by your gracious reception of me."

"Yes; but there was another thing besides."

"Another thing? — nothing that I know of, madame."

"Oh, yes, — an unexpected meeting with a person on leaving my house."

"I did not meet any one; I was in your brother's carriage."

"Before getting into the carriage?"

The old lady seemed to be tasking her memory.

"Just as you were going down the stairs to the vestibule?"

The old lady seemed more intent in trying to recall the events of yesterday.

"Yes," said the favourite, rather impatiently; "some one entered the court as you left my house."

"I am so unfortunate, madame, as not to be able to recollect any one entering."

"A lady; now you remember."

"I am so short-sighted that at two paces from me, madame, I cannot distinguish any one."

"Oh, ho!" said the favourite to herself; "she is too cunning for me! I shall never succeed by these means. Come, to the point at once! Then, since you did not see the lady," she continued aloud, "I must tell you that she is my sister-in-law, Mademoiselle Dubarry."

"Oh, very well, madame; but as I have never had the pleasure of seeing her — "

"Yes," interrupted the other, "you have seen her; only, when you saw her it was under the name of Flageot."

"So!" cried the old lady with a bitterness which she could not dissemble, "so that pretended Mademoiselle Flageot, who caused me to undertake the journey to Paris, is your sister-in-law?"

"She is, madame."

"And who sent her to me?"

"I did."

"To mystify me?"

"No, to serve you; whilst at the same time you should serve me."

The old lady bent her thick grey eyebrows. "I do not think," said she, "her visit will turn out very profitable to me."

"Did the vice-chancellor receive you ill, then, madame?"

"Empty promises."

"But it seems to me that I offered you something more tangible than promises."

"Madame, God disposes, though man proposes."

"Come, madame, let us view the matter seriously. You have scalded your foot?"

"Scalded it very badly."

"Could you not, in spite of this accident, — painful, no doubt, but after all, nothing dangerous, — make an effort to bear the journey to Luciennes in my carriage, and stand before his Majesty for one minute?"

"It is quite impossible, madame."

"Is the injury so very serious?"

"Serious, indeed."

"And, pray, who dresses it for you, and nurses you?"

"Like all housekeepers, I have excellent receipts for burns, and I dress it myself."

"Might I take the liberty of requesting to see your specific?"

"Oh, yes; it is in that phial on the table."

"Hypocrite," thought the countess, "to carry her dissimulation to such a point! She is as cunning as a fox, but I shall match her. Madame," added she, aloud, "I also have an excellent oil for accidents of this kind; but, before applying it, it is necessary to know what kind of scald it is, — whether it is inflamed, or blistered, or the skin broken."

"Madame, the skin is broken," said the old lady.

"Oh, heavens! how you must suffer! Shall I apply my oil to it?"

"With all my heart, madame. Have you brought it?"

"No, but I shall send for it. In the mean time, I must see the state of your leg."

"Oh, madame!" exclaimed the old lady, "I could not think of permitting you to see such a spectacle! I know too well what is due to good manners."

"Delightful!" thought Madame Dubarry; "she is now fairly caught." Then she added, "Where we can serve our fellow-beings, madame, we must not stand upon etiquette," and she stretched out her hand towards the old lady's leg, which was extended on the sofa.

Madame de Béarn uttered a scream of pain.

"Very well acted," said Madame Dubarry to herself, watching her every feature distorted with anguish.

"How you frightened me, madame!" said the old lady; "it is almost death to me to touch it;" and with pale cheeks and half-closed eyes, she leaned back as if nearly fainting.

"Do you allow me to look at it?"

"If you choose, madame," said the old lady, in a weak and suffering voice.

Madame Dubarry did not lose an instant; she took out the pins in the bandages, and rapidly unrolled them. To her great surprise, she was permitted to go on.

"When it comes to the last covering," thought she, "she will scream, and try to prevent me from seeing it; but, though she kill herself calling on me to stop, I will see the leg!" and she proceeded in her task.

Madame de Béarn groaned, but offered no resistance.

At last the bandages were untied; the last covering was removed, and a real wound caused by a scald lay before Madame Dubarry's eyes. Here ended the old lady's diplomacy. Livid and inflamed, the wound spoke for itself. The Countess de Béarn might have seen and recognised Chon; but if so, her courage and determination raised her far above Portia and Mutius Scævola. Madame Dubarry gazed at her in silent admiration. The old lady, now somewhat recovered, enjoyed her victory to the utmost; her inflamed eye brooded with satisfaction on the countess kneeling at her feet. Madame Dubarry replaced the bandages with that delicate care which women exercise towards the suffering, placed the limb once more on its cushion, and took her seat beside the couch.

"Come, madame," said she, "I see of what you are capable, and I beg your pardon for not having begun this subject in the way in which I ought with such a woman as you. Make your own conditions."

The eyes of the old lady sparkled, but it was only for a

moment. "In the first place," said she, "state what your wishes are, and then I shall see if I can be of any service to you."

"Madame, I wish to be presented at Versailles by you, though it cost you another hour of the horrible suffering which you have endured this morning."

The Countess de Béarn listened unflinchingly. "Anything else, madame?" said she.

"That is all. Now for your turn."

"I must have," replied Madame de Béarn, with a decision which showed clearly that she treated with the countess as one power with another, "I must have the two hundred thousand francs of my lawsuit secured to me."

"But if you gain your cause, you will then have four hundred thousand."

"No; for I look on the disputed two hundred thousand as mine already, and the other two hundred thousand I shall reckon as merely an additional piece of good fortune to that of possessing the honour of your acquaintance."

"You shall have them, madame. Well?"

"I have a son, whom I love tenderly, madame. Our house has already been distinguished by military genius; but, born to command, we make but indifferent subalterns. My son must have a company immediately, and next year a colonel's commission."

"Who will pay all the necessary expenses, madame?"

"The king. You perceive that if I expended on my son the sum which I am to receive from you, I should be as poor to-morrow as I am to-day."

"At the lowest, I may reckon that at six hundred thousand francs."

"Four hundred thousand, supposing the commission worth two hundred thousand, which is a high estimate."

"This shall be granted you also."

"I have now to request from the king payment for a vineyard in Touraine, containing four acres, which the engineers deprived me of eleven years ago in making a canal."

"But they paid you then?"

"Yes, they paid me according to the valuator's estimate, but I value it at just double the sum."

"Well, you shall be paid a second time. Is that all?"

"Excuse me. I am out of cash, as you may suppose, madame, and I owe Master Flageot something about nine thousand francs."

"Nine thousand francs!"

"Yes; it is absolutely necessary to pay him; he is an excellent lawyer."

"I have not the least doubt of it, madame. Well, I shall pay these nine thousand francs out of my own private purse. I hope you will acknowledge that I am accommodating."

"Perfectly accommodating. But I think I have also proved that I wish to serve you."

"I have only to regret that you scalded yourself," replied the favourite, with a smile.

"I do not regret it, madame, since, in spite of the accident, my devotion to your interests will, I trust, give me strength to be useful to you."

"Let us sum up," said Madame Dubarry.

"Pardon me one moment. I had forgotten one thing. Alas, it is so long since I have been at court that I have no dress fit for it."

"I foresaw that, madame, and yesterday, after your departure, I ordered a dress for you. To-morrow, at noon, it will be ready."

"I have no diamonds."

"Bœmer and Bossange will give you to-morrow, on my order, a set of ornaments worth two hundred and ten thousand livres, which, the following day, they will take back at two hundred thousand. Thus your indemnity will be paid."

"Very well, madame; I have nothing more to wish."

"I am delighted to hear it."

"However, about my son's commission?"

"His Majesty will give it you himself."

"And for the attendant expenses?"

"The order will be given with the commission."

"Quite right. There now only remains about the vineyard, four acres —"

"How much were they worth?"

"Six thousand francs an acre; it was excellent land."

"I will now subscribe an obligation to pay you twenty-four thousand francs, which will be about the whole."

"There is the writing-desk, madame."

"I shall do myself the honour to hand the desk to you."

"To me?"

"Yes; that you may write a little letter to his Majesty which I shall dictate, — a fair return, you know."

"Very true," replied the old lady; and arranging her paper, and taking a pen, she waited. Madame Dubarry dictated: —

"SIRE, — The happiness which I feel on learning that your Majesty has accepted my offer to present my dear friend the Countess Dubarry —"

The old lady made a grimace, and her pen began to spit.

"You have a bad pen," said the favourite; "you must change it."

"It is unnecessary, madame; I shall get accustomed to it."

"Do you think so?"

"Yes."

Madame Dubarry continued: —

" — emboldens me to solicit your Majesty to look on me with a favourable eye when I shall appear at Versailles to-morrow, as you have deigned to permit me to do. I venture to hope, sire, that I merit your Majesty's favour, inasmuch as I am allied to a house every chief of which has shed his blood for the princes of your august race."

"Now sign, if you please," said the favourite.

And the countess signed: —

"ANASTASIE-EUPHÉMIE-RODOLPHE,
COMTESSE DE BÉARN."

The old lady wrote with a firm hand, in great letters, half an inch long, and sprinkled her letter with a sufficient quantity of aristocratic mistakes in orthography.

When she had signed, still holding the letter fast with one hand, she passed with the other the paper, pen, and ink to Madame Dubarry, who in a little straight, sharp hand signed the obligation to pay the sums agreed upon.

Then she wrote a letter to Bœmer and Bossange, the crown jewellers, requesting them to give the bearer the set of diamond and emerald ornaments called "Louise," because they had belonged to Madame Louise, aunt to the dauphin, who sold them to obtain funds for her charities.

That done, the ladies exchanged their papers.

"Now," said Madame Dubarry, "give me a proof of your friendship, my dear countess."

"With all my heart, madame."

"I am sure that if you come to me, Tronchin will cure you in less than three days. Come, then, and you can at the same time try my oil, which is really excellent."

"Well, but do not let me detain you, madame," said the prudent old lady; "I have some matters to settle here before I can set out."

"Then you refuse me?"

"On the contrary, madame, I accept your invitation,— but not at this moment. It is just now striking one o'clock by the abbey clock; give me until three, and at five precisely I shall be at Luciennes."

"Permit my brother, then, to return with the carriage at three."

"Certainly."

"In the mean time take care of yourself."

"Fear nothing; you have my word, and though my

death should be the consequence, I shall present you to-morrow at Versailles."

"Good-by, then, my dear madame."

"Good-by, my charming friend."

And so saying they parted, the old lady with her foot still on the cushion, and her hand on her papers; the countess in better spirits than on her arrival, but certainly rather vexed that she had not been able to make better terms with an old woman from the country,— she, who could outwit the King of France when she chose.

Passing by the door of the principal salon, she saw Jean, who, doubtless merely to prevent any one harbouring suspicions as to the cause of his long stay, was taking a second bottle of wine. Perceiving his sister, he jumped up from his chair and ran after her.

"Well?" cried he.

"Well, I may say, as Marshal Saxe once said to his Majesty in the battlefield of Fontenoy, 'Sire, learn from this spectacle how dearly a victory may be purchased.'"

"Then we have conquered?"

"Yes; only, it costs us about a million."

Jean made a frightful grimace.

"Why, I had no chance; I must either take her at that or give her up."

"But it is abominable."

"It is as I tell you; and perhaps, if you make her angry, she will make us pay double."

Pardieu! what a woman!"

"She is a Roman."

"She is a Greek."

"Never mind. Greek or Roman, be ready to bring her to Luciennes at three o'clock. I shall never be easy until I have her under lock and key."

"I shall not stir from this," said Jean.

"And I, on my side, shall hasten to prepare everything," said the countess.

She sprang into her carriage.

"To Luciennes!" said she. "To-morrow I shall say, 'To Marly'!"

Jean followed the carriage with his eyes. "We cost France a pretty little sum," said he. "No matter; it is very flattering for the Dubarrys."

CHAPTER XXXVI.

MARSHAL RICHELIEU'S FIFTH CONSPIRACY.

THE king returned to hold his court at Marly as usual. Less the slave of etiquette than Louis XIV., who sought, even in the evening parties of his courtiers, means of exhibiting his power, Louis XV. sought in them only news, of which he was inordinately fond, and, above all, a variety of faces around him, — a gratification which he preferred to all others, particularly if they were smiling ones.

In the evening of the day on which the interview just related took place, and two hours after the Countess de Béarn (who this time kept her promise faithfully) was comfortably installed in Madame Dubarry's cabinet, the king was playing cards at Marly, in the blue drawing-room.

On his left sat the Duchess d'Ayen, on his right Madame de Guéménée. His Majesty appeared very absent, losing, in consequence of inattention to his game, eight hundred louis-d'or. Rather sobered by his loss, — for, like a true descendant of Henry IV., Louis loved to win, — the king left his cards, and retired into the recess of a window to talk to Monsieur de Malesherbes, son of the ex-chancellor, whilst Monsieur de Maupeou, who was conversing with the Duke de Choiseul in an opposite window, watched the interview with an anxious eye. In the mean time, after the king left the card-table, a circle was formed near the fireplace. The Princesses Adelaide, Sophie, and Victoire, attended by their ladies of honour and their equerries, had placed themselves there on their return from a walk in the gardens.

Around the king, who must certainly have been talking of some matter of importance, as the gravity of Monsieur de Malesherbes was well known, were grouped, but at a respectful distance, generals, admirals, great dignitaries of the state, noblemen, and judges.   The little court at the fireplace, therefore, was left a good deal to itself, and seemed bent on more lively conversation, if one might judge by the skirmishing with which they began.

The principal ladies of the group, besides the three princesses, were Madame de Grammont, Madame de Guéménée, Madame de Choiseul, Madame de Mirepoix, and Madame de Polastron.

At the moment when we approach this group, Madame Adelaide had just ended an anecdote of a bishop banished from his diocese by the grand penitentiary.   It was tolerably scandalous, and it is as well unrelated here.

"Well," said Madame Victoire, "it is only a month since that bishop was sitting here among us!"

"Oh, we shall have worse than he sitting among us," said Madame de Grammont, "if his Majesty receive those who, not having been yet received, are now determined to be received."

Every one understood from the tone in which these words were uttered who was meant, and at once felt what turn the conversation was taking.

"Fortunately, wishing to be received and being received are two different things, duchess," said a little elderly man, joining in the conversation.   He was seventy-four years of age, but looked only fifty; so elegant was his shape, his voice so unbroken, his leg so well shaped, his eye so lively, his skin so fair, and his hand so beautiful.

"Ah, here is Monsieur de Richelieu," said the duchess, "advancing his scaling-ladders, and going to take our conversation by assault, as he did Mahon.   Still something of the soldier, my dear marshal!"

"Still *something* of the soldier!   Ah! duchess, you are very severe!"

"Well!   But did I not speak the truth?"

"The truth !   When?"

"Just now, when I said that a certain person wished to
force the king's doors?"

"Oh, you know, countess, I am always of your opinion,
even when you speak ill of all my friends !"

Some laughed, although it had already been whispered
that the marshal's wit was on the wane.

"If you say such things," continued the duchess, "I
shall not go on with my history, and you will lose a great
deal, I assure you."

"Heaven forbid that I should interrupt it !   I am all
attention."

The circle drew closer around the duchess.   She cast a
glance towards the window, to be certain that the king
was still there.   He was still in the same position; but
although he continued to converse with Monsieur de
Malesherbes, he kept a watchful eye on the group at the
fireplace, and just at that moment his eye met that of
Madame de Grammont.   The duchess felt somewhat intimidated by its expression, but she had made a beginning,
and would not be stopped.

"You must know," she continued, addressing herself
particularly to the three princesses, "that a certain lady
— her name is of no consequence, is it? — has lately taken
it into her head that she will see us, the privileged of the
land, sitting in our glory."

"See us?   Where?" asked the marshal.

"Oh, at Versailles, at Marly, at Fontainebleau."

"Very well, very well !"

"The poor creature knows nothing of our meetings,
except from having seen, with the rest of the mob, the
king at dinner with his guests.   How disagreeable, with
a barrier between them and the great, and an usher with
his rod driving them before him !"

The marshal took snuff noisily out of his box of Sèvres
porcelain.   "But," said he, "in order to join our circle

at Versailles, at Marly, at Fontainebleau, one must be presented."

"Precisely; the lady in question has requested to be presented."

"Then I'll wager the king has consented; he is so kind."

"Unfortunately, something more is necessary than the king's permission; there must be a chaperon to present *the lady*."

"Yes; but chaperons are rather scarce," said Marquise de Mirepoix; "witness the fair Bourbonnais, who has sought but has not found one."

"Pardon me," replied the duchess; "she has sought so well that she has found what she wants. But what a chaperon! — a frank, sincere, real country dame! She was brought away from her dovecot, petted, and caressed, and dressed — "

"It is perfectly shocking," interrupted Madame de Guéménée; "but just when the dear dame had been sufficiently petted, and caressed, and dressed, she fell downstairs from the top to the bottom and broke her leg."

"So there can be no presentation?" exclaimed Madame de Guéménée.

"Not a shadow," said the duchess.

"See how gracious Providence is!" said the marshal, raising his hands and eyes to heaven.

"Gracious!" said Madame Victoire, "not to the poor country dame; I really pity her."

"On the contrary, your Royal Highness may congratulate her" said the duchess; "of two evils she has chosen the least." She stopped short, for again her eye met the king's.

"If the ladies who have been presented," said Madame de Guéménée, "were courageous and faithful to the sentiments of honour of the ancient nobility of France, they would go in a body to return thanks to the lady from the country who showed so much sublimity of mind as to break her leg."

"Yes, faith," said the marshal, "that is a great idea! But what is the name of the excellent lady who has saved us in this great danger? We have nothing now to fear; have we, duchess?"

"Oh, nothing; she is in her bed, her leg bound up, and unable to move a step."

"But if the lady should find another chaperon?" said the princess; "she is so indefatigable."

"Oh, do not be afraid; it is not so easy to find chaperons."

At this moment the throng of courtiers separated, and the king approached; the group became silent. A moment afterwards his clear and well-known voice was heard: "Adieu, ladies. Good-night, gentlemen."

Every one rose.

The king advanced towards the door, then, turning before leaving the room, he said, "By the by, there will be a presentation to-morrow at Versailles."

These words fell like a thunderbolt on the assembly. The king glanced round the group of ladies, who looked at each other and turned pale; then he left the apartment without adding another word. Scarcely had he crossed the threshold with the long train of gentlemen attending him, when there was a general explosion among the princesses and the ladies around them.

"A presentation!" stammered Madame de Grammont, her lips quite livid. "What does his Majesty mean?"

"Eh! duchess," said the marshal, with one of those smiles which even his best friends could not pardon; "can this be the presentation you have just been speaking of?"

The princesses bit their lips with vexation.

"Oh, it is impossible!" murmured the duchess.

"Ah, duchess," said the marshal, "they do set legs so well nowadays!"

The Duke de Choiseul approached his sister, Madame de Grammont, and pressed her arm as a warning not to go too far; but she was too deeply wounded to attend to him.

"It would be an insult to us all!" she exclaimed.

"Yes, an insult indeed!" repeated Madame de Guéménée.

Monsieur de Choiseul saw he could do nothing more, and walked a short distance off.

"Oh, your Royal Highnesses," cried the duchess, addressing the king's three daughters, "there is no resource for us now but in you! You, the highest ladies in the kingdom, will you endure it? Must we be exposed, in the only asylum remaining for ladies of rank, to meet a person with whom we should not allow our chambermaids to associate?"

The princesses, instead of replying, hung down their heads.

"Oh, your Royal Highnesses, in Heaven's name," exclaimed she, "save us!"

"The king is master in this as in everything else," said the Princess Adelaide, sighing.

"That is true," said the Duke de Richelieu.

"But the entire court of France will be compromised in the affair," cried the duchess. "Gentlemen, have you, then, no regard for the honour of your families?"

"Ladies," said the Duke de Choiseul, trying to laugh, "as this seems bordering on a conspiracy, you must allow me to retire, and to take with me Monsieur de Sartines. Will you come, marshal?"

"I? — faith, I adore conspiracies! I shall certainly stay," replied Marshal Richelieu.

The two ministers departed.

There now remained around the princesses eight or ten of the ladies who had espoused most warmly the league against the presentation. Richelieu was the only gentleman. The ladies looked at him suspiciously, as if he had been a Trojan in the Grecian camp.

"I represent my daughter, the Countess d'Egmont," said he. "Go on, ladies, go on."

"Your Highnesses," Madame de Grammont began, "there

is a means by which we can show our sense of the infamous
nature of the proceedings, and for my part I shall make
use of the means."

"What is it?" all exclaimed.

"We have been told that the king is master," she
continued.

"And I reply it is just and right that he should be,"
said the marshal.

"He is master in his own palace, but we are mistresses
in our own houses. Now, what is to prevent me from
giving my coachman directions to drive to Chanteloup
to-night, instead of to Versailles?"

"Or what is to prevent others from imitating you?" said
Madame de Guéménée.

"Why should we not all imitate the duchess?" asked
Madame de Mirepoix.

"Oh, mesdames!" exclaimed the duchess, again addressing the princesses, "what a noble example it would be for
you to give the court!"

"The king would be angry with us," said Madame
Sophie.

"No, madame; I am certain he would not. On the
contrary, it would make him reflect; and he has such
exquisite sense, such perfect tact, that he will afterwards
acknowledge you to be in the right, and he will be grateful
to you."

"It is true," said Madame Victoire, encouraged by the
general spirit of rebellion; "the king said nothing when
we refused to admit the visits of the countess, but on a
public occasion like this he might not be disposed to forgive us."

"No, certainly," replied the duchess, "if you were the
only ladies who absented yourselves; but when he sees
that we have all left the court?"

"All!" exclaimed the party.

"Yes, all," repeated the old marshal.

"Then you are of the plot?" said Madame Adelaide.

"Certainly I am; and therefore I wish to speak."

"Speak, marshal, speak!" said Madame de Grammont.

"We must proceed methodically," said he. "It is not enough all to shout in chorus this or that. I have known people say, ' This is what I shall do,' but at the moment of action they have done the very contrary. Now, as I have the honour to make one in this conspiracy, I do not wish to be left by myself, as I always was when I took part in the conspiracies under the late king and under the regency."

"Upon my word, marshal, you forget yourself. Among the Amazons you take upon you the airs of a leader," said the duchess.

"Madame, I beg you to consider that I may have some right to that position. You hate Madame Dubarry,—there, I have let the name slip out, but nobody heard it; you hate her more than I, but I am more compromised than you."

"How is that?"

"I have not been at Luciennes for eight days, nor at her apartments at Versailles for four. The affair has gone so far that a footman was sent to ask if I was ill; so I am already looked on with suspicion. However, I am not ambitious; I yield the leadership to you. You have set the affair on foot; you have stirred us all; you revolutionize our consciences, — yours must be the bâton of command."

"No, I must follow their Royal Highnesses," said the duchess, respectfully.

"Oh, pray let us remain passive," said Madame Adelaide. "We are going to Saint-Denis to see our sister Louise; she will keep us there, and of course there can be nothing said."

"Nothing, nothing at all, unless by some very ill-disposed person," said the marshal.

"As for me," said the Duchess de Grammont, "I have to go to Chanteloup, because it is hay-making season."

"Bravo!" cried the duke; "an excellent reason."

"I must stay at home; one of my children is ill, and I have to nurse him," said Madame de Guéménée.

"I," said Madame de Polastron, "have felt a giddiness all this evening; I am sure I shall be dangerously ill if Tronchin do not bleed me to-morrow."

"And I," said the Marquise de Mirepoix, majestically, "I shall not go to Versailles, because I shall not; that is my reason."

"Excellent! excellent!" said the marshal; "all this is quite logical; but we must swear."

"What! we must swear?"

"Yes; conspirators always swear,—from the plot of Catiline down to that of Cellamare, in which I had the honour of participating. We always swore; it is true the thing did not succeed at all the better for it; still, let us respect old customs. Let us swear, then; you shall see how solemn it is."

He extended his hand in the midst of the group of ladies, and said with proper dignity, "I swear."

All the ladies repeated the oath, with the exception of the princesses, who slipped away.

"Now that all is over," said the marshal; "when once people have sworn in conspiracies, they never do anything more."

"Oh, what a fury she will be in," said the Duchesse de Grammont, "when she finds herself all alone in the grand salon!"

"Hum!" said the marshal; "the king will most probably banish us for a little."

"Ah!" cried Madame de Guéménée, "what kind of court would it be if we were banished? The King of Denmark is expected; who will be presented to him? The dauphiness is expected; to whom will she be presented? Besides, a whole court is never exiled; a selection is made."

"I know that very well, and I fear I run a great risk of being chosen for the distinction of banishment," said the marshal. "I have always been distinguished in that way. Four times have I been selected for it, at the lowest reckoning. This is my fifth conspiracy, ladies."

"Do not be afraid, marshal," said the Duchess de Grammont; "if any one be marked out for banishment, I shall be the person."

"Or your brother, the Duke de Choiseul; take care, duchess," replied the marshal.

"My brother is of my mind; he could submit to misfortune, not to an insult."

"It will be neither you, marshal, nor you, duchess, who will be banished," said Madame de Mirepoix; "I shall be the victim. The king will never pardon me for being less condescending to the countess than I was to the marchioness."

"That is true," said the marshal; "you were always called the favourite of the favourite. I am sorry for you now; we shall be banished together."

"Let him banish us all," said Madame de Guéménée, rising; "for I trust none of us will draw back from the resolution which we have taken."

"We cannot draw back after our oath," said the marshal.

"Besides," said the Duchess de Grammont, "I have still other resources."

"You?"

"Yes; she cannot be presented to-morrow evening without three things."

"What three?"

"A hairdresser, a dress, and a carriage."

"Certainly."

"Well, she shall not be at Versailles at ten o'clock. The king will become impatient; he will dismiss the court, and the presentation will be postponed till the Greek kalends, on account of the arrival of the dauphiness."

A burst of delight followed this new episode in the conspiracy; but while applauding even more loudly than the others, the Duke de Richelieu and Madame de Mirepoix

exchanged glances; the same idea had occurred simultan-
eously to the two old courtiers.

At eleven o'clock all the conspirators, lighted by a
lovely moon, were speeding along the roads to Versailles
and Saint Germain.

Marshal Richelieu, however, mounted his groom's horse,
and whilst his carriage, with the blinds drawn closely
down, bore him ostensibly to Versailles, he reached Paris
by a cross road.

CHAPTER XXXVII.

NO HAIRDRESSER, NO DRESS, NO CARRIAGE.

IT would have been in bad taste for the Countess Dubarry to have gone merely from her apartments in the palace of Versailles to the grand salon where the presentations took place. Besides, at Versailles there were not the necessary appliances and means for such an important day.

But a better reason than any of these was, that it was not the custom. The highly-favoured being who was to be presented always arrived with the noise and state of a foreign ambassador, whether it were from her house in the town of Versailles, or in Paris. Madame Dubarry chose to arrive from the latter place.

At eleven o'clock in the morning, therefore, she was at her house in the Rue de Valois with the Countess de Béarn, whom she kept under lock and key when she did not keep her under her smiles, and whose burn was attended to most carefully, every secret of medicine and chemistry being exhausted on it.

From the preceding evening Jean, Chon, and Dorée had been at work; and any one who could have seen them at their work would have formed an exalted idea of the power of gold, or the greatness of human intellect.

The one made sure of the hairdresser, the other harassed the sempstress. Jean took the department of the carriage to himself, but also cast an eye occasionally on the hairdresser and the dressmakers. The countess, occupied with flowers, diamonds, and lace, was buried in boxes, cases, and caskets, and gave audiences every hour to couriers from Versailles, who informed her how matters were going on. Orders had been given for lighting the queen's drawing-room, and no change had taken place in the king's intentions.

About four the viscount came in, pale, agitated, but joyful.

"Well?" asked the countess.

"Well, all will be ready."

"The hairdresser?"

"I went to him myself. Dorée was with him; but, to make sure of him, I slipped fifty louis-d'or into his hand. He will dine here at six o'clock precisely, so you may be quite easy on that score."

"My dress?"

"It will be a perfect wonder. Chon is superintending it; there are six-and-twenty workwomen at it, sewing on the pearls, the ribbons, and the trimmings. They go on breadth by breadth at the work, and it would certainly require eight days for any other persons than ourselves to have it finished. It is a prodigious undertaking."

"But do you say they are doing it breadth by breadth?"

"Yes, my dear; there are thirteen breadths of the stuff; two workwomen at each breadth; one works at the right, the other at the left, putting on the jewels and trimmings; then at the last they will all be joined together. It will take them two hours yet; at six you will have it."

"Are you quite sure, Jean?"

"Yesterday I made a calculation with an engineer about it. There are ten thousand stitches in each breadth, — that is, five thousand for each workwoman. In such thick stuff a woman can only make one stitch in five seconds, — that is, twelve in one minute, seven hundred and twenty in one hour, and seven thousand two hundred in ten hours. I leave out two thousand two hundred for needle-threading and slipped stitches, and this leaves four good hours about work."

"And what about the carriage?"

"Oh, I'll answer for it. The varnish is now getting

dry in a large store heated to fifty degrees; it is an elegant *vis-à-vis*, compared with which the carriages sent for the dauphiness are a mere trifle.   Besides the coats of arms on the four panels, there is the war-cry of the Dubarrys, '*Boutés en avant!*' on each side.   Besides that, I made them paint on one place two doves billing and cooing, and in another a heart pierced with a dart,— the whole surrounded by bows and arrows, quivers and torches.   There is such a crowd of people at Francian's to see it!   It will be here exactly at eight."

At this moment Chon and Dorée came in and confirmed all that Jean had said.

"Thank you, my brave *aides-de-camp*," said the countess.

"My sweet sister," said the viscount, "your eyes look a little dim; had you not better sleep for an hour?   It would quite revive you."

"Sleep? no!   I shall sleep to-night, and that is more than some will do."

Whilst these preparations were going on, the report of the intended presentation had spread through all Paris. Idle and careless as they appear, no people love news more than the Parisians.   None knew better all the courtiers and all the intrigues of Versailles than the Parisian cockney of the eighteenth century, though debarred from the festivities of the palace, and seeing only the hieroglyphics on the carriages and the curious liveries of the footmen.   At that period such or such a nobleman was known to the whole city.   The reason was simple; the court at that period formed the principal attraction in the theatres and in the gardens.   Marshal Richelieu in his place at the Italian opera, Madame Dubarry in a coach rivalling that of royalty itself, were constantly before the public, like some favourite comedian or admired actress of the present day.

People are much more interested in faces that are well known to them.   Every one in Paris knew Madame Dubarry's face, constantly shown where a rich and pretty

woman likes to be seen,—in the theatres, in the public
walks, in the shops. Besides, she was easily recognised
by means of portraits, caricatures, and by her negro page,
Zamore. The affair of the presentation, therefore, occupied the city nearly as much as the court. This day there
was a crowd near the Palais Royal; but, poor Philosophy!
it was not to see Rousseau playing chess at the Café de la
Régence; it was to see the favourite in her fine coach and
her handsome dress, of which they had heard so much.
There was something deep in Jean Dubarry's expression,
"We cost a pretty little sum to France!" And it was
natural that France, represented by Paris, should wish
to enjoy the sight for which they had paid so dearly.
Madame Dubarry knew her people well, for they were
much more her people than they had been Queen Maria
Leczinska's. She knew that they love to be dazzled by
magnificence; and, as she was good-natured, she laboured
to make the spectacle correspond to the expense to which
she put them.

Instead of sleeping, as her brother advised her, she took
a bath about five o'clock. Then, about six o'clock, she
began to expect her hairdresser; and while she waits we
shall explain, if we can, what hairdressing then was.

It was building a complete edifice. This was the commencement of the castles which the ladies of the court
of the young king, Louis XVI. erected with towers and
bastions on their heads. May we not, even in this
frivolity of fashion, discover something presaging that a
mine was dug beneath the feet of all who were, or all
who pretended to be, great? Or that by some mysterious
divination, the women of the aristocracy had learned they
should have a short time to enjoy their titles; that they,
therefore, made the most of them, bearing them aloft on
their heads; and as if—fatal omen!—not having long to
keep their heads, they must decorate those heads to the
utmost point which extravagance can attain, and raise
them as high as possible above the vulgar.

To plait the hair; to elevate it on a silken cushion; to roll it about a hoop of whalebone; to adorn it with diamonds, pearls, and flowers; to sprinkle it with powder, which made the eyes brilliant and the complexion fresh; to blend into harmony with the complexion pearl, ruby, opal, diamond, flowers of all hues and of all forms, — to do all this, a man must be not only a great artist, but the most patient of his race.

As a proof that such a man was esteemed great, the hairdresser was the only tradesman allowed to wear a sword.

This explanation may account for the fifty louis-d'or given by Jean Dubarry to the hairdresser of the court. It may account, also, for some fears lest the great Lubin (the court hairdresser of that day was called Lubin) might not be so punctual or so skilful on the occasion as was desirable.

The fears about his punctuality were, alas! too well founded. Six o'clock struck, and the hairdresser did not appear; then half-past six came; then a quarter to seven. One thought inspired some hope in the anxious hearts of all; it was, that a man of Monsieur Lubin's importance would naturally make people wait a little. But seven struck. The viscount feared that the dinner prepared for the hairdresser might be cold when he came, and the great artist might be dissatisfied. He sent a servant to say that dinner waited.

The servant returned in a quarter of an hour. Those only who have waited under similar circumstances can tell how many seconds there are in such a quarter of an hour.

The servant had spoken to Madame Lubin herself, who assured him that Monsieur Lubin had set out for the countess's, that if he were not then there, he must be on the way.

"Perhaps," said Jean, "he has been delayed in consequence of not getting a carriage. We will wait a little."

"Besides," said the countess, "there will be no time lost; my hair can be attended to when I am half dressed. The presentation does not take place until ten; we have still three hours, it will only take one to go to Versailles. In the mean time, to employ me, Chon, show me my dress. Where is Chon? Chon! Chon! my dress, my dress!"

"Your dress has not come yet, madame," said Dorée, "and your sister went ten minutes ago to see about it herself."

"Oh," exclaimed the viscount, "I hear a noise of wheels! It is the carriage brought home, no doubt."

The viscount was mistaken; it was Chon, who had come back full speed.

"My dress!" cried the countess, whilst Chon was still in the vestibule; "my dress!"

"Has it not come?" asked Chon, terror-stricken.

"No."

"Oh, well, it can't be long. When I got to the dressmaker's she had just set out in a fiacre with two of her women, bringing the dress to fit it on."

"It is a good way from her house to this, and as you drove very fast, no doubt you have passed her," said Jean.

"Yes, yes! certainly!" replied Chon; yet she could not suppress a vague feeling of apprehension.

"Viscount," said the countess, "you had better send about the carriage, that there may be no disappointment on that side at least."

"You are right, Jeanne," and Dubarry opened the door. "Let some of you," cried he, "take the new horses to Francian's for the carriage, so that they may be all ready harnessed when it arrives."

The coachman and the horses set off. As the sound of their trampling died away, Zamore entered with a letter.

"A letter for Mistress Barry," said he.

"Who brought it?"

"A man."

"A man ? What sort of man ? "

" A man on horseback."

"And why did he give it to you ? "

"Because Zamore was at the door."

"But read it! Read it rather than question him!" cried
Jean.

" You are right, viscount."

" Ay, provided there be nothing annoying in the letter,"
he muttered.

"Oh, no! it is some petition for his Majesty."

" It is not folded like a petition."

" Really, viscount, you are full of fears," said the countess, smiling, and she broke the seal. At the first line she
shrieked, and fell back in her chair half-dead.

"No hairdresser, no dress, no carriage!" she cried.
Chon sprang towards her. Jean seized the letter. It was
evidently the writing of a woman, and ran thus : —

MADAME,— Be not too confident. This evening you shall have no
hairdresser, no dress, no carriage. I hope this information will
reach you in time to be useful to you. As I do not desire your
gratitude, I do not give you my name. Guess who I am, and you
will have discovered

A SINCERE FRIEND.

"Oh!" shouted Dubarry, "all is over! *Sang bleu*! I
must kill somebody! By all the devils! I 'll run Lubin
through the body! It is half-past seven, and he not here!
Confound him! Damn him!"

And as Dubarry was not to be presented that evening,
he did not care about his hair, but tore it out unmercifully
in handfuls.

"But the dress! Good heavens! the dress!" cried
Chon; " a hairdresser could easily be found!"

"Oh, I defy you to find one! What sort of wretch
would he be? A murderer! A slaughterer! Oh, death
and damnation!"

The countess said nothing, but sighs burst from her

bosom, which might have softened the Choiseuls themselves could they but have heard them.

" Let us think, let us think ! " said Chon ; " a little calmness only. Let us find out another hairdresser, and send to the dressmaker to know what has become of the dress ! "

" No hairdresser ! " murmured the almost fainting countess ; " no dress ! no carriage ! "

" Yes, no carriage ! " cried Jean ; " it does not come either ! It is a plot, countess, it is a plot ! Cannot Sartines find out the authors of it ? Cannot Maupeou hang them ? Can they not with their accomplices be burned in the market-place ? I will have the hairdresser broken on the wheel ! the dressmaker torn to pieces with pincers ! the coachmaker flayed alive ! "

At length the countess recovered a little from her state of stupefaction, but it was only to feel more poignantly all the horror of her situation.

" All is lost ! " she exclaimed. Those who have bought over Lubin are rich enough to remove all the good hairdressers from Paris. None are left me but wretches who would destroy my hair ! And my dress ! — my poor dress ! And my new carriage ! I thought the sight of it would have made them burst with envy ! "

Dubarry did not answer ; but, rolling his eyes fearfully, strode up and down the room, striking himself against the angles of the apartment ; and as often as he encountered any ornament or small article of furniture, abandoning his hair, he dashed them into the smallest morsels possible, and then stamped on them with his feet.

In the midst of this scene of horror, which, spreading from the boudoir to the ante-rooms, and from the ante-rooms to the court, caused all the domestics to run hither and thither with twenty different and contradictory orders, a young man in a light green coat, a satin waistcoat, lilac breeches, and white silk stockings, got out of a cabriolet, crossed the court, stepping from stone to stone on the tips of his toes, entered the open door abandoned by all the servants, mounted the stairs, and tapped at the countess's dressing-room door.

Jean was just stamping on a tray with a set of Sèvres porcelain, which he had pulled down with the tail of his coat whilst he was dealing a blow with his fist to a great Chinese mandarin. When the noise of these feats had subsided a little, three gentle, discreet, modest taps were heard.

Then followed profound silence; all were in such a state of expectation that no one could ask who was there.

"Excuse me," said an unknown voice, "but I wish to speak to the Countess Dubarry."

"Monsieur, people do not enter here in that way!" cried a servant, who had discovered the stranger, and had run after him to prevent his farther advance.

"Never mind! never mind!" cried Jean, flinging open the door with a hand which might have driven in the gates of Gaza. "Worse cannot happen to us now. What do you want with the countess?"

The stranger avoided the shock of this sudden meeting by springing backwards, and falling into the third position.

"Monsieur," said he, "I came to offer my services to the Countess Dubarry."

"What services, monsieur?"

"My professional services, monsieur."

"What is your profession?"

"I am a hairdresser!" and the stranger bowed a second time.

"Oh," cried Jean, falling on his neck, "a hairdresser! Come in! come in!"

"Come in! Come in, my dear monsieur!" cried Chon, almost taking the astonished young man in her arms.

"A hairdresser?" cried Madame Dubarry, raising her hands to heaven.

"A hairdresser? An angel! Were you sent by Monsieur Lubin, monsieur?"

"I was not sent by any one. I read in the gazette that

the Countess Dubarry was to be presented this evening; then, said I to myself, 'Suppose that the Countess Dubarry had no hairdresser ? It is not probable, but it is possible ; so I think I shall try.'"

"What is your name, monsieur ? " asked the countess, a little cooled by this account.

"Leonard, madame.'"

"Leonard ? You are not known to any one ? "

"If you accept my services, madame, to-morrow every one will know me."

"Hum ! " said Jean, "there are two kinds of hairdressing."

"If madame distrusts my skill, I shall retire."

"We have no time to try you," said Chon.

"Why make any trial ? " cried the young man, walking round the countess in a fit of enthusiasm. "I know, madame, that all eyes must be drawn to you by the style of your hair, and already in contemplating you I have invented a head which will have a most powerful effect."

And the young man made a gesture with his hand, so full of confidence in himself that the countess's resolution was a little shaken, and hope sprang up in the hearts of Chon and Jean.

"Have you, really ? " said she, quite astonished at the young man's ease ; for he was now leaning back, hand on hip, as the great Lubin himself would have done.

"Yes ; but, madame, I must see your dress that I may make the ornaments harmonise with it."

"Oh, my dress ! my dress ! " cried the countess, recalled by his words to the terrible reality.

Jean struck his forehead fiercely. "Oh, imagine, monsieur," cried he, " imagine what a horrid trick ! They have carried off dress, dressmaker, all ! Chon, Chon, dear Chon ! " and Dubarry, tired of tearing out his hair, gave way to a downright fit of sobbing.

"Suppose you were to go back to the dressmaker's, Chon," said the countess.

"For what purpose ? You know she had set out to come hither."

"Alas! alas!" murmured the countess, falling back in her chair, "of what use is a hairdresser when I have no dress?"

At this moment the door-bell rang; all the doors had been carefully shut, and even bolted, by the porter, lest any other should slip in as the hairdresser had done."

"Some one rings," said the countess.

Chon sprang to a window.

"A bandbox!" cried she.

"A bandbox!" cried the countess.

"Coming in?" cried Jean.

"Yes — no — yes. It is given to the porter; run, Jean, run!"

He dashed down the stairs, got before all the footmen, and snatched the bandbox from the porter.

Chon looked through the window.

He pulled off the lid, plunged his hand into the depths of the bandbox, and uttered a yell of joy. It contained a beautiful dress of Chinese satin, with flowers put on, and a complete trimming of lace of immense value.

"A dress! A dress!" shouted Chon, clapping her hands.

"A dress?" repeated the countess, almost sinking under her joy, as she had before under her grief.

"Who gave it you, rogue?" asked the viscount of the porter.

"A woman, monsieur, whom I don't know."

"Where is she?"

"Monsieur, she laid it on the step of the door, cried, 'For the countess,' and disappeared."

"Well, we have got a dress; that is the main thing!"

"Come up, Jean, come up!" called Chon; "my sister is dying with impatience."

"Look!" said Jean, returning to the room, "look! admire! See what fate sends you!"

"But it will not go on; it will not fit; it was not made for me. *Mon Dieu! mon Dieu!* what a misfortune, for it is beautiful!"

Chon quickly measured it. "The same length, the same width in the waist!" she exclaimed.

"What admirable stuff!" said Jean.

"It is miraculous!" said Chon.

"It is terrible!" said the countess.

"Not at all," replied the viscount, "for it proves that, although you have great enemies, you have also devoted friends."

"It cannot be sent by a friend," said Chon; "for how should a friend know of the plot formed against us? It must be sent by a sylph."

"Let it be sent by his Satanic Majesty!" exclaimed the countess, "I care not, provided it assists me to oppose the Choiseuls! Whoever sent it, he cannot be so much of a demon as they."

"And now," said Jean, "I am sure that you may confidently submit your head to this gentleman."

"Why do you think so?"

"Because he has been sent by the same person who sent the dress."

"I?" said Leonard with the most innocent surprise.

"Come, come, my dear monsieur; acknowledge that it was all a tale about the gazette!"

"The simple truth, monsieur. Here is the paper; I kept it for curl-papers;" and he drew out the gazette in which the presentation was announced.

"Now," said Chon, "let him set to work; it is eight o'clock."

"Oh, we have time enough!" said the hairdresser, "it will only take an hour to go to Versailles."

"Yes, if we have a carriage," said the countess.

"Oh, _mordieu!_ that is true!" exclaimed Jean. "That wretch, Francian, does not come."

"You know we have been warned; no hairdresser, no dress, no carriage!" repeated the countess.

"Now, if the coachmaker should not keep his word?" said Chon.

"No ; here he is, here he is !" cried Jean.

"And the carriage, the carriage ?" exclaimed the countess.

"It is at the door, no doubt. But what is the matter with the coach-maker ?"

At that moment Francian rushed in, all in alarm.

"Oh, viscount !" cried he, "the carriage was on its way hither, when at the corner of a street it was seized by four men ; they knocked down my young man who was bringing it, seized the reins, and set off with it at a gallop."

"I told you so ! I told you so !" said Dubarry, sitting down resignedly in his chair.

"But, brother," exclaimed Chon, "exert yourself ! do something !"

"What for ?"

"To get a carriage ! the horses here are done out, and the carriages dirty. Jeanne cannot go in any of them."

"Bah ! the little birds find food when they don't expect it, and we got a hairdresser and a dress in our need. Yes, our unknown friend will not forget a carriage !"

"Hush !" cried Chon, "surely I heard carriage wheels."

"Yes, it is stopping," he replied.

Then, springing to a window which he opened, he shouted to the servants, "Run, rascals, run ! Quick, quick ! Find out our benefactor !"

A carriage lined with white satin, and drawn by two splendid bay horses, stood before the door. But neither coachman nor footman was to be seen ; a common street porter held the horses by the head. A crown had been given to him by a person unknown to him at the end of the street, with orders to lead the carriage to the countess's door.

They looked at the panels ; the arms were replaced by a simple rose.

The whole of this counterplay against the miseries with which the evening had commenced lasted about an hour.

Jean had the carriage taken into the yard, and the gates

locked on it; he carried up the key with him. On returning to the dressing-room he found the hairdresser about to give the countess the first proof of his profound knowledge of his art.

"Monsieur," cried the viscount, seizing him by the arm, "if you do not declare who is our protecting genius, that we may make known our eternal gratitude to him, I swear — "

"Allow me," said the young man, interrupting him very phlegmatically, "allow me to say, monsieur, that you are doing me the honour of squeezing my arm so tight that I fear my hand will be quite stiff when I shall have to dress the countess's hair, and it is now eight o'clock."

"Leave him alone, Jean, leave him alone!" cried the countess.

Jean sank down in his chair.

"A miracle!" exclaimed Chon; "it is a perfect fit, — only an inch too long in front; but ten minutes will alter that!"

"And what is the carriage like?" asked the countess.

"It is in the best style," replied Jean; "I got into it: it is lined with white satin, and perfumed with essence of roses."

"All is right, all is right!" cried the countess, clapping her little hands with delight. "Now, Monsieur Leonard, if you succeed on this occasion, your fortune is made!"

Leonard took possession of her head, and the very first touch of the comb revealed a skilful hand. Rapidity, taste, marvellous precision, a complete knowledge of the relation between the moral and the physical, — all these he displayed in the accomplishment of his important duty.

When he had, at the end of three-quarters of an hour, given the finishing touch to the splendid edifice which he had reared on the countess's head, he would have modestly retired, after having washed his hands in a basin

which Chon presented to him as if he had been a king.
The countess appeared more beautiful than Aphrodite, less
nude and not less fair.

"Now, monsieur," said Dubarry, "you must know that
I am as ardent in my loves as in my hatreds.   As you
have gained my esteem, pray tell me who you are."

"You know already, monsieur, who I am.   My name
is Leonard; I am only a beginner."

"A beginner ? —*Sang bleu!* you are a thorough master
of your profession ! "

"You shall be my hairdresser, Monsieur Leonard," said
the countess, looking at herself in a little glass which she
had in her hand; "and I shall pay you on each occasion
like this fifty louis-d'or.   Chon, count out one hundred
for this time; he shall have fifty of earnest money."

"I told you, madame, that you would make my
reputation."

"But you must dress no one's hair but mine."

"Keep your hundred louis-d'or, then, madame.   I prefer my liberty; to it I owe the honour of having this
evening dressed your hair.   Liberty is the first of human
blessings."

"A philosophical hairdresser! " exclaimed Dubarry, raising his hands to heaven; "to what shall we come at last ?
Well, my dear Monsieur Leonard, I shall not quarrel
with you; take your hundred louis-d'or, and keep your
secret and your liberty.   Now, countess, to your carriage ! "

The last words were addressed to the Countess de Béarn.
who entered stiff and stately, and dressed like an image
in a shrine.   She was brought out of her room just when
she was to be made use of.

"Now," cried Jean to the servants, "let four of you
take her, and carry her downstairs; and if you hurt her,
so as to make her heave one sigh, I'll flay you alive ! "

Whilst he was superintending this delicate and important
operation, assisted by Chon, the countess turned to seek
for Monsieur Leonard; he had disappeared.

"But how did he go?" murmured Madame Dubarry, who had not yet quite recovered from the influence of the many surprises of the evening.

"How did he go? Why, through the floor, or up through the ceiling, of course, as all genii do. Take care, countess, that your head-dress does not turn into a heap of mud, your dress into a spider's web, and your coach into a pumpkin, drawn by two rats!"

Having given utterance to this last fear, Jean took his place beside the Countess de Béarn, and her fortunate god-daughter.

CHAPTER XXXVIII.

THE PRESENTATION.

VERSAILLES, like everything really great, is and will long be a fair and lovely scene. Though moss should cover its mouldering walls, though its gods of marble, bronze, and lead should lie shattered around their broken fountains, though its broad alleys of clipped trees should remain in all the wild luxuriance of nature, though it should become but a heap of ruins, — it will always present to the thinker and the poet a great and touching spectacle. Let such look from its circle of ephemeral splendour to the eternal horizon beyond, and it will be long ere thought and fancy sink to rest again !

But it was, above all, in its days of pomp and splendour that Versailles was fairest to look upon, — when its gay and thoughtless population, restrained by a crowd of soldiers still more gay than themselves, thronged its gilded gates ; when carriages lined with velvet and satin, blazoned with armorial bearings, thundered over its pavements at the full speed of their prancing steeds ; when every window, blazing with light like those of an enchanted palace, exposed to view the moving throng, radiant with diamonds, rubies, sapphires, and bending to the gesture of one man, as bends before the wind a field of golden corn, with its bright flowers of crimson, white, and blue ; yes, Versailles was brilliant indeed when its gates sent forth couriers to all the powers of the earth, when kings, princes, nobles, generals, learned men, from all parts of the civilized world, trod its rich carpets and its inlaid floors !

But when, for some great ceremony, all its sumptuous furniture was displayed, and its sumptuousness doubled by the magic of a thousand lights, even the coldest imagination must have glowed on beholding what human invention and human power could do. Such was the ceremony observed on the reception of an ambassador, or the presentation of the nobles attending the court.

Louis XIV., the creator of etiquette, a system which shut up each individual within bounds beyond which he could not pass, desired that the favoured few initiated into the magnificence of his regal life should be struck with such veneration that ever afterwards they could only regard the palace as a temple, and the king as its presiding deity, to whose presence some had the right of approaching nearer than others.

Versailles, then, still magnificent although already showing symptoms of degeneration, had opened all its doors, lighted all its chandeliers, and exhibited all its splendour for the presentation of Madame Dubarry. The people, inquisitive though hungry and wretched, forgetting, strange anomaly, both their hunger and wretchedness, that they might gaze on so much grandeur, filled the Place d'Armes and the avenues leading to the palace. Every window of the château poured out floods of light, and the lustres from a distance looked like stars gleaming in an atmosphere of golden dust.

The king left his private apartments exactly at ten. He was dressed rather more richly than usual, — that is, his lace was finer, and the buckles alone of his garters and his shoes were worth a million.

The Count de Sartines had informed him of the conspiracy entered into by the ladies the evening before, so that there was a shade of anxiety on his brow, and he trembled lest he should see only gentlemen in the grand salon. But he was soon reassured when, on entering the salon set apart for presentations, he saw, amid a cloud of lace and powder mingled with the blaze of diamonds, first, his three daughters, then the Marquise de Mirepoix, who had talked so loudly among the plotters, — in short, all the turbulent spirits who had sworn not to come were there.

Marshal Richelieu, like a general on the eve of an engagement, hurried from one to another, saying to this one, "Ah, I have caught you, perfidious one!" whispering to another, "I was certain you would not keep your oath!" and to a third, "Remember what I told you about conspiracies!"

"But, marshal," replied the ladies, "you are here yourself!"

"Oh, I represent my daughter! I represent Madame d'Egmont. Look around, you will not find Septimanie! She alone has kept faith with Madame de Grammont and Madame de Guéménée; so I am pretty certain what my fate will be. To-morrow I shall enter on my fifth banishment, or my fourth trip to the Bastile. Most certainly I shall never again conspire."

The king entered. There was a profound silence, during which ten o'clock struck,— the hour fixed for the ceremony. His Majesty was surrounded by a numerous court, and was attended by about fifty gentlemen, who, not having sworn to come to the presentation, were probably for that reason present.

The king observed, at the first glance, that Madame de Grammont, Madame de Guéménée, and Madame d'Egmont were wanting in this splendid assembly.

He approached the Duke de Choiseul, who affected great calmness, but in spite of all his efforts was somewhat disturbed.

"I do not see the Duchess de Grammont here," said the king.

"Sire, my sister is ill," replied the Duke de Choiseul, "and desired me to present her very humble respects to your Majesty."

"So much the worse!" said the king; and he turned his

back on the duke. In doing so, he found himself face to face with the Prince de Guéménée.

"And Madame de Guéménée," said he, "where is she? have you not brought her, prince?"

"It was impossible, sire; when I called at her hotel in order to accompany her here, I found her in bed."

"Oh! so much the worse! so much the worse! Ah, here is the marshal! Good-evening, marshal."

The old courtier bowed with all the suppleness of a youth.

"*You* are not ill, at least!" said the king, loud enough for De Choiseul and De Guéménée to hear him.

"Whenever, sire, I have in prospect the happiness of seeing your Majesty, I am perfectly well," replied Richelieu.

"But," said the king, looking round, "I do not see your daughter, Madame d'Egmont; how comes it that she is not here?"

The duke's features assumed an expression of deep regret.

"Alas! sire, my poor daughter is really not able to lay her humble homage at your Majesty's feet, this evening, above all others; ill, sire, ill!"

"So much the worse!" said the king. "Ill! — the Countess d'Egmont, who enjoys the finest health in France! So much the worse! so much the worse!" And the king left the marshal as he had left Monsieur de Choiseul and Monsieur de Guéménée.

Then he completed the circuit of the salon, and particularly complimented Madame de Mirepoix, who did not feel altogether at her ease.

"You see what the price of treachery is," whispered the marshal in her ear. "To-morrow you will be loaded with honours, whilst we — I shudder to think of it!" and he sighed.

"But I think you have rather betrayed the Choiseuls yourself, since you are here; and yet you swore — "

"For my daughter, for my poor Septimanie, marquise; she will be disgraced for being too faithful."

"To her father," replied the marquise.

The marshal pretended not to hear this remark, which might have passed for an epigram.

"Do you not think," said he, " that the king is uneasy?"

"I think he has reason to be so; it is a quarter past ten."

"True; and the countess not here! Shall I tell you what I think?"

"Yes."

"I have some fears."

"Fears about what?"

"Fears that something disagreeable may have happened to that poor countess. You know whether I am right or not, marquise."

"I! how should I know?"

"Yes; you were up to the neck in the conspiracy."

"Well, I may tell you in confidence, marshal, that I cannot help sharing your fears."

"Oh! our friend the duchess is a fierce antagonist; she has fled, and like the Parthians she wounds in fleeing. See how restless the Duke de Choiseul is, although he wishes to appear calm; he cannot stay a moment in one position, and he keeps his eye always on the king. Come, confess that there is some plot in the wind!"

"I know nothing of it, duke; but, like you, I have suspicions."

"But what can they gain by their plot?"

"Time, my dear marshal; and you know the proverb, ' He who gains time, gains all.' To-morrow something may occur to put off the presentation *sine die*. The dauphiness may reach Compiègne to-morrow instead of four days hence; perhaps they only wished to gain to-morrow."

"Do you know, marquise, this little tale of yours has all the appearance of truth. There is no sign of her coming."

"And see, the king is becoming impatient!"

"That is the third time he has approached the window; he is really annoyed."

"Things will be much worse presently."

"How so?"

"It is twenty minutes past ten, is it not?"

"Yes."

"Then I may now tell you—"

"What?"

The marquise looked around, then whispered, "She will not come."

"Oh, heavens! but, marquise, it will be a scandalous affair."

"It will perhaps cause a lawsuit,—a criminal suit. I know from good authority that there will be in the case robbery, abduction, treason. The Choiseuls have played a bold game."

"Very imprudent in them."

"Passion rendered them blind."

"You see what an advantage we have over them, in not being governed by our passions; we are cool, and can look at things calmly."

"Observe, the king is going again to the window."

Gloomy, anxious, and irritated, Louis had drawn near a window, leaned his head on a carved frame, and pressed his forehead to the cool glass.

During this time the conversation of the courtiers sounded like the rustling of the leaves of a forest before a tempest. All eyes wandered from the king to the timepiece, and from the timepiece to the king. The half-hour struck; the clear, vibrating sound died away in the vast salon.

Monsieur de Maupeou approached the king.

"Delightful weather, sire," said he, timidly.

"Very fine, very fine! Do you understand anything of this matter, Monsieur de Maupeou?"

"Of what, sire?"

"About this delay, the poor countess."

"She must be ill, sire," replied the chancellor.

"I can comprehend that Madame de Grammont may be ill, that Madame de Guéménée may be ill, that Madame d'Egmont may be ill, but not that she should be ill."

"Sire, very great emotion often causes illness, and the countess's joy was so great."

"Ah! there is no longer any hope," said Louis, shaking his head; "she will not come now."

Although the king had uttered these words in a low voice, there was so profound a silence in the salon that every one heard them. No one, however, had time to reply, even in thought, for just then the noise of a carriage was heard in the court of the palace. All heads moved; eyes interrogated eyes.

The king came forward to the middle of the salon, that through the open doors he might see the whole length of the gallery.

"I am afraid," whispered the marchioness to the marshal, with a meaning smile, "that some bad news is coming."

But suddenly the king's face brightened, and his eyes flashed with pleasure.

"The Countess Dubarry! the Countess de Béarn!" cried the usher to the grand master of the ceremonies.

These two names made all hearts beat, many with very opposite emotions. A crowd of courtiers, impelled by ungovernable curiosity, drew near the king.

The Marquise de Mirepoix was nearest him; clasping her hands, she exclaimed, as if ready to fall down and worship, "Oh, how beautiful she is! how beautiful she is!"

The king turned a gracious smile on her.

"She is not a woman," said Richelieu; "she is a fairy."

The king sent the remainder of the smile in the direction of the old courtier.

In fact, the countess never had appeared more lovely; never had such a perfect representation of gentle agitation and modesty, never had a more charming figure or more noble carriage graced the queen's salon at Versailles, which, nevertheless, as we have said, was the salon of presentations.

Lovely in the extreme, dressed with the most perfect taste, and above all, her hair dressed exquisitely, the countess advanced, conducted by Madame de Béarn, who, notwithstanding her suffering, did not betray it by the slightest gesture; yet every movement caused each fibre of her frame to quiver, whilst from her dry and fevered cheeks the rouge dropped off atom by atom.

Every eye was fixed upon the pair who presented such a strange contrast. The old lady, her neck uncovered as in the time of her youth, her head-dress standing up a foot above her head, and her large eyes glittering in their deep sockets, like those of an osprey, seemed, in her splendid dress and with her skeleton appearance, the type of the past leading forward the present.

So striking was the contrast that it seemed to the king as if his favourite had never looked so beautiful as now, when he received her from the hand of the old Countess de Béarn.

Just as the countess, according to the etiquette, sank on her knee to kiss the king's hand, Louis seized her arm, raised her up, and in a few words rewarded her for all she had suffered during the last fortnight.

"You at my feet, countess!" said he. "It is I who should be, and who always wish to be, at yours."

Then he extended his arms to her, following the usual ceremonial, but on this occasion the embrace was not a pretended, but a real one.

"You have a lovely god-daughter, madame," said the king to the Countess de Béarn; "but she has as noble a chaperon, and one whom I rejoice to see again in my court."

The old lady bowed.

"Go and pay your respects to my daughters," whispered the king to Madame Dubarry, "and show them that you know how to make a curtsey. I hope you will have cause to be satisfied with their reception of you."

The two ladies advanced in the space which was formed around them, whilst the eager looks of all followed every movement which they made.

The king's three daughters, seeing them approach, rose as if moved by springs, and remained standing. Their father fixed a look on them which commanded them to be polite.

The princesses, a little agitated, returned Madame Dubarry's curtsey, which she made much lower than etiquette demanded, and this they thought such good taste that they embraced her as the king had done, and delighted him by their cordiality.

From that moment the countess's success became a triumph, and the slower and less adroit courtiers had to wait an hour before they could get their bow made to the queen of the night.

She, free from coldness or any feelings of recrimination, received all advances favourably, and seemed to forget all the treachery used against her. Nor was this mere pretence; for her heart was too full of joy to be anything but magnanimous, or to have room for a single unamiable feeling.

Marshal Richelieu showed a knowledge of tactics worthy of the victor of Mahon. Whilst vulgar courtiers waited in their places the result of the presentation, in order to decide whether they should offer incense to the idol or turn their backs on her, he took up a position behind the countess's chair, like a fugleman who serves as a guide by which to deploy a troop of cavalry on a given point. The result was that at last he found himself close to Madame Dubarry, without being troubled by the crowd. The Marquise de Mirepoix knew that her old friend had been successful in war; she therefore imitated his tactics, and gradually drew her seat near that of the favourite.

Conversation now commenced among the different groups;

the countess was criticised from head to foot. She, supported by the love of the king, by the gracious reception of the princesses, and by the high rank of the lady who had presented her, looked round less timidly on the men, and sought out her enemies among the women.

An opaque body obscured her view.

"Ah! Marshal Richelieu," said she, "I was obliged to come here in order to meet you."

"How so, madame?"

"Is it not eight days since I have seen you, either at Versailles, or in Paris, or at Luciennes?"

"I wished to render the pleasure greater of seeing you here this evening," replied the old courtier.

"You guessed that I should be here?"

"I was certain of it."

"Oh, marshal, you knew it, and you did not tell your poor friend, who knew nothing about it."

"What! madame, you did not know that you were to be here?"

"No; I was like Æsop when a magistrate arrested him in the street. 'Where are you going?' said he. 'I don't know,' replied the fabulist. 'Then you shall go to prison,' the other replied. 'You see plainly,' said Æsop, 'that I did not know where I was going.' In like manner, duke, I had some idea that I should go to Versailles, but I was not sure. That is why you would have done me a great service, had you come and told me that I should be here. But you will come to see me now; will you not?"

"Madame," replied Richelieu, without being moved by her raillery, "I really do not understand how it was that you were not sure of being here."

"I shall tell you; it was because snares were laid on all sides for me;" and she looked steadily at him, but he bore her look without wincing.

"Snares! Good heavens! How could that be?"

"First, they stole my hairdresser."

"Stole your hairdresser!"

"Yes."

"But why did you not inform me? I could have sent you — but let us speak low, if you please — I could have sent you a treasure; my daughter, Madame d'Egmont, found him out. He is quite a superior artist to all others, even the royal hairdressers, — my little Leonard."

"Leonard?" cried Madame Dubarry.

"Yes; a young man whom she hides from every one. But you have no reason to complain, countess; your hair is charmingly dressed; and, singularly enough, the design is exactly like the sketch which the Countess d'Egmont ordered from Boucher for her own head-dress, and which she intended to have used this evening had she not been ill. Poor Septimanie!"

The countess started, and again fixed a searching look upon the marshal; but he continued, smiling and impenetrable.

"But pardon me, countess, for interrupting you," said he; "you were speaking of snares."

"Yes; after having carried off my hairdresser, they stole my dress, — a most beautiful dress."

"How shocking! However, it was not of much consequence, as you had another dress so wonderfully beautiful as that you wear. It is Chinese silk, with flowers embroidered on it. Well, if you had applied to me in your trouble, as you must always do for the future, I could have sent you a dress which my daughter had ordered, so like that that I could swear it was the same."

Madame Dubarry seized both the duke's hands, for she now began to suspect who was the enchanter who had befriended her in her difficulties.

"Do you know in whose carriage I came, marshal?" said she.

"In your own, no doubt."

"No; they stole my carriage as well as my hairdresser."

"Why, it was a regular ambuscade! In whose carriage, then, did you come?"

"Will you tell me first what the Countess d'Egmont's carriage is like?"

"I think that for this evening she had ordered one lined with white satin; but there was not time to paint the coat of arms."

"Yes," exclaimed the countess, "and they substituted a rose instead! Marshal, marshal, you are an adorable man!" and she held out to him both her hands, which he covered with kisses. All at once he felt her start.

"What is the matter, countess?" inquired he, looking round.

"Marshal," said the countess, with an alarmed air, "who is that man near the Prince de Guéménée?"

"In a Prussian uniform?"

"Yes; the dark man with black eyes, and such an expressive countenance."

"He is some officer of rank, countess, whom his Prussian Majesty has sent, no doubt, to do honour to your presentation."

"Do not jest, marshal; I know that man. He was in France three or four years ago; I have sought him everywhere, but could never discover him."

"I think you must be mistaken, countess. He is the Count de Fenix, a foreigner, and only arrived in France yesterday or the day before."

"Observe how he looks at me."

"Every one looks at you, you are so beautiful."

"He bows to me! he bows to me! Do you see him?"

"Every one bows to you,—at least, all who have not already done so."

But the countess, who seemed greatly agitated, paid no attention to the duke's gallant speeches, but kept her eyes riveted on the stranger who had attracted her attention. Then rising, as if involuntarily, she advanced a few steps towards the unknown.

The king, who kept his eye fixed on her, observed this movement, and thought that she desired to be near him; and as etiquette had been sufficiently attended to in keep-

ing so long from her side, he approached to congratulate
her on her success. Her thoughts were, however, too
much engaged to be turned from their object.

"Sire," said she, "who is that Prussian officer with his
back to the Prince de Guéménée?"

"And who is looking at us at this moment?" asked the
king.

"Yes."

"That strongly marked face, that square head, framed
as it were in the gold collar?"

"Yes, yes; the same."

"He is an accredited agent of my cousin of Prussia, —
some philosopher like himself, I think. I desired him to
be here this evening, as I wished Prussian philosophy to
enhance, by its ambassador, the triumph of Cotillon III."

"But what is his name, sire?"

"Let me think. Ah! yes, the Count de Fenix."

"It is the same," murmured she to herself; "yes, I am
sure it is he."

The king waited a few moments, in order to give
Madame Dubarry time to ask further questions if she
wished to do so; but finding that she did not speak, he
said in a loud voice, "Ladies, her Royal Highness, the
dauphiness, will arrive to-morrow at Compiègne; we shall
meet her precisely at noon. All the ladies who have been
presented will go, except, however, those who are ill, for
the journey might be fatiguing, and her Royal Highness
would be sorry to aggravate their indisposition."

As the king pronounced these words, he looked sternly
at the Duke de Choiseul, the Prince de Guéménée, and the
Marshal de Richelieu.

There was a profound silence; every one understood the
meaning of the royal words; they carried disgrace in their
front.

"Sire," said Madame Dubarry, who had remained near
the king, "may I request your gracious pardon for the
Countess d'Egmont?"

"Why so, may I ask?"

"Because she is the daughter of Marshal Richelieu, who is my most faithful friend."

"Richelieu?"

"I am certain he is, sire."

"I shall do what you wish, countess," said the king.

The king then approached the marshal, who had watched every movement of the countess's lips, and, if he had not heard her words, had at least guessed their meaning.

"I hope, my dear marshal," said he, that the Countess d'Egmont will be better to-morrow."

"Certainly, sire; if your Majesty desire it, she will even come out this evening."

And Richelieu made a bow which expressed at once respect and gratitude.

The king then whispered a word in the countess's ear.

"Sire," replied she, with a curtsey accompanied by a charming smile, "I am your Majesty's obedient servant."

The king, by a wave of his hand, saluted all the assembly and retired. Scarcely had he crossed the threshold when the countess's eyes turned again on the singular man who had before attracted her so strongly.

This man bowed like the rest as the king passed along; but even as he bowed there was something haughty, almost threatening, in the expression of his countenance. When Louis XV. had disappeared, he made way for himself through the different groups, and stopped within two paces of Madame Dubarry. The countess, attracted by an inexpressible curiosity, made one step forward, so that, as the unknown bowed to her, he could say in a low voice, and so as not to be overheard, "Do you know me again, madame?"

"Yes, monsieur; you are the prophet whom I met in the Place Louis XV."

The stranger fixed his clear and penetrating glance on her.

"Well, did I speak falsely, madame, when I predicted you should be queen of France?"

"No, monsieur; your prediction is accomplished, or at least nearly so, and I am ready to fulfil my part of the engagement. Speak, monsieur; what do you desire?"

"This place is ill chosen for such a purpose; besides, the moment for me to make my request is not yet come."

"Whenever it does come, you will find me ready to grant it."

"May I, at any time, in any place, at any hour, have liberty to be admitted to your presence?"

"I promise it."

"Thanks."

"But under what name shall I expect you? Under that of the Count de Fenix?"

"No; under that of Joseph Balsamo."

"Joseph Balsamo," repeated the countess to herself, whilst the mysterious stranger disappeared among the groups of courtiers, — "Joseph Balsamo. I shall not forget it."

CHAPTER XXXIX.

COMPIÈGNE.

THE following morning Compiègne awoke transported, intoxicated with joy; or rather, to be more exact, Compiègne never went to rest.

The evening before, the first detachment of the king's guards had entered the town, and whilst the officers took up their position, the magistrates, assisted by the lord high steward and other functionaries, prepared the town for the distinguished honour which was to be conferred on it. Triumphal arches composed of evergreens, roses, and lilacs; inscriptions in Latin, French, and German; compositions in verse and prose,— occupied all the sub-magistracy of Picardy from night till morn.

Young girls dressed in white, according to immemorial usage; municipal officers clad in black; monks attired in grey; the clergy in their richest vestures; officers and soldiers in their new uniforms, — all were at their posts, ready to advance on the first signal of the arrival of the dauphiness.

The dauphin had arrived incognito with his two brothers about eleven o'clock the night before. Very early in the morning he mounted his horse, as if he had been a private gentleman, and, followed by his brothers, the Count de Provence and the Count d'Artois, the one fifteen and the other thirteen years of age, he galloped off in the direction of Ribecourt, the road by which the princess was to approach. It was not to the young prince, we must confess, that this gallant idea had first occurred; it was suggested by his tutor, Monsieur de Lavanguyon, who had been desired by the king to instruct his august pupil in all the duties which the next twenty-four hours would impose upon him. The tutor, therefore, had thought it right, in order to maintain the honour of the monarchy, to cause him to follow the traditional example of the kings of his race, — Henry IV., Louis XIII., Louis XIV., and Louis XV., — who desired to see their future wives without any of the illusions of dress and ornament, and therefore met them when not expected, on the road.

Mounted on swift horses, the three brothers accomplished three or four leagues in half an hour; the eldest had set out serious, the two others laughing. At half-past eight they returned, — the dauphin still serious, the Count de Provence almost ill-tempered, the Count d'Artois more gay than before. The dauphin was uneasy, the Count de Provence envious, and the Count d'Artois enchanted, about one and the same thing, — the beauty of the dauphiness. The grave, jealous, and careless character of each prince respectively was written on his face.

At ten o'clock the look-out employed to watch for the expected train announced that a white flag was displayed on the steeple of the church of Claives, which was to be the signal that the dauphiness was approaching. The bells of the church commenced to ring, and were answered by the firing of cannon.

At that instant, as if he had only waited for this signal, the king entered Compiègne in a carriage drawn by eight horses, between a double file of his body-guards, and followed by the immense train of the carriages of the court. The guards and dragoons, at a gallop, opened a passage through the crowd, which was divided between two feelings, — desire to see the king, and curiosity with regard to the dauphiness. One hundred carriages drawn by four horses, extending nearly a league in length, contained four hundred ladies, and as many lords of the noblest families of France. These hundred carriages were escorted by outriders, heyducks, footmen, and pages. The gentlemen of the king's household were on horseback, and formed a brilliant army, glittering like a sea of velvet and gold, waving plumes and silk, in the midst of the dust raised by the horses' feet.

They halted an instant at Compiègne, then slowly proceeded to the spot agreed on for the meeting, and marked by a cross, near the village of Magny. All the young nobility thronged around the dauphin, and all the old around the king.

On the other side the dauphiness was also slowly approaching the appointed place.

At length the two parties met. On both sides the courtiers left their carriages; two only remained occupied, —that of the king and that of the dauphiness. The door of the dauphiness's carriage was open, and the young archduchess sprang lightly to the ground, and advanced to the royal carriage. The king, on perceiving his daughter-in-law, ordered the door to be opened, and hurriedly got out.

The dauphiness had calculated her time so well that just as the king put his foot to the ground she was close to him, and she sank on her knee. He raised the young princess, and embraced her tenderly, yet casting a look upon her which made her blush.

"Monseigneur the Dauphin," said the king, introducing his grandson, who had kept behind the dauphiness without being perceived by her, at least ostensibly.

The dauphiness made him a graceful curtsey; he bowed, blushing in his turn.

Then, after the dauphin, came his two brothers, then the three princesses; the dauphiness had something gracious to say to each.

Whilst these introductions were going on, Madame Dubarry stood anxiously behind the princesses. Would she be thought of? Would she be forgotten?

After the introduction of Madame Sophie, the last of the king's daughters, there was a pause; every breath was suspended. The king seemed to hesitate; the dauphiness

seemed to expect some incident concerning which she had been previously informed.

The king looked round, and seeing the countess within reach, took her hand; all near him stepped back, and he found himself in the midst of a circle with the dauphiness.

"The Countess Dubarry," said he, "my very dear friend."

The dauphiness turned pale, yet a gracious smile appeared on her white lips. "Your Majesty is happy," said she, "in possessing so charming a friend; and I am not surprised at the attachment which she inspires."

Every one heard these words with astonishment amounting to stupefaction. It was evident that the dauphiness followed the instructions of the court of Austria; perhaps the very words she repeated were dictated by Maria Theresa.

The Duke de Choiseul then thought that his presence was necessary. He advanced to be presented in his turn; but the king made a sign with his head, the trumpets sounded, the drums beat, the cannon were fired. His Majesty took the young princess's hand to conduct her to her carriage. She passed close to the Duke de Choiseul. Did she see him or did she not? It was impossible to say; but it is certain that she made no sign of recognition. At the moment when she entered her carriage, the bells of the town pealed out, and their clear tones were heard above all the other festive sounds.

The countess returned to her carriage, all radiant with delight and pride.

There was a halt for about ten minutes whilst the king was re-entering his carriage and giving his orders to return to Compiègne. During this time conversation, which had been suspended from respect, or by the interest of the scene, again became general. Dubarry drew near his sister's carriage; she received him with smiles, expecting his congratulations.

"Jeanne," said he, pointing to a gentleman on horseback, who was talking at the door of a carriage in the train of the dauphiness, "do you know that young man?"

"No," replied the countess; "but do you know what the dauphiness said when the king presented me to her?"

"I am not thinking of that. That young man is the Chevalier Philip de Taverney."

"He who wounded you?"

"Yes; and do you know who that beautiful creature is with whom he is talking?"

"The young girl so pale and so majestic?"

"Yes; she at whom the king is looking at this moment. I think he is asking the dauphiness her name."

"Well, what then?"

"That young girl is Taverney's sister."

"Ah!" exclaimed the countess.

"Jeanne, I don't know why, but I think you have as much reason to fear the sister as I the brother."

"You are a fool!"

"No, I am tolerably wise; and I shall, at all events, look after the youth."

"Well, then, I shall keep an eye on the girl."

"Hush! here is your friend, Marshal Richelieu!"

The marshal drew near, shaking his head.

"What is the matter, my dear marshal?" inquired the countess, with her most fascinating smile; "you seem dissatisfied with something."

"Don't you think, countess," said the duke, "that we all seem very grave, not to say sorrowful, for such a joyous occasion? Formerly, I know, we were much more gay when we went to meet a princess as amiable and as beautiful as this, the mother of his Royal Highness the dauphin. Was it because we were younger then?"

No," answered a voice behind the marshal; "no, my dear marshal, but because the monarchy was not so old."

"Heaven and earth!" exclaimed the marshal, "it is the Baron de Taverney! Countess, one of my oldest friends, for whom I solicit your kindness,— the Baron de Taverney-Maison-Rouge."

"The father," whispered Jean and the countess to each other, as they stooped to salute the baron.

"To your carriages, gentlemen, to your carriages!" cried the major of the guards commanding the escort.

The two old gentlemen bowed to the countess and to the viscount, and both entered the same carriage, delighted to meet once more after so long a separation.

"And now," said the viscount, "shall I tell you another thing, my dear? I have as little love for the father as for the children."

"What a pity," replied the countess, "that that little wretch, Gilbert, ran away! He was brought up in their house, and could have told us so much about them."

"Pshaw! I shall find him again, now that I have nothing else to think about."

Their conversation was interrupted by the carriages being again put in motion.

After having passed the night in Compiègne, the two courts — the one the sunset, the other the dawn, of an age — set out on the following day for Paris, — that yawning gulf which was to entomb them both.

CHAPTER XL.

THE PATRONESS AND THE PATRONISED.

IT is now time that we should return to Gilbert, of whose flight the reader has been made aware by an imprudent exclamation of his protectress, Mademoiselle Chon, but of whom we have since heard nothing.

Our philosopher had cooled very much in his admiration, of his patroness from the moment that he had, during the preliminaries of the duel between Philip de Taverney and Viscount Jean, become aware that her name was Dubarry.

Often at Taverney, when, hidden by some hedge, he had followed Andrée and her father in their walks, he had heard the baron explain, at great length, all about the Dubarry family. The hatred of the old baron to Madame Dubarry — a feeling which in him, however, sprang from no dislike to what was in itself vicious — found a ready echo in Gilbert's heart, arising principally from her conduct being regarded by Andrée with contempt and reprobation, sentiments which may be taken as expressing the general opinion of the nation towards her whole family.

During the journey Chon was too much occupied with matters of a more serious import to pay any attention to the change of feeling which the knowledge of who were his travelling companions had produced in Gilbert. She reached Versailles, therefore, only thinking of how the viscount's wound, since it would not redound to his honour, might be turned to his greatest profit.

As to Gilbert, scarcely had he entered the capital — if not of France, at least of the French monarchy — when he forgot every unpleasant thought, and gave free scope to

his undisguised admiration. Versailles, so majestic and stately, with its lofty trees already beginning to show symptoms of decay, touched his heart with that religious sadness which poetic minds always experience in contemplating the mighty works of nature, or those erected by the perseverance of man.

From this impression — a very novel one to Gilbert, and one against which his innate pride struggled in vain — he became silent and submissive, overcome by wonder and admiration.

The feeling of his inferiority crushed him to the earth. When the great lords in their stars and ribbons passed by him, how deeply did he feel the wretchedness of his attire! How inferior did he feel, even to the porters and footmen! How did he tremble when, in his hob-nailed shoes, he had to walk over the shining marble or polished inlaid floors!

At such times he felt that the protection of his patroness was indispensable to him, unless he wished to sink into absolute nothingness. He drew near her, that it might be seen he belonged to her; yet it was for the very reason that he needed her that he disliked her.

We are already aware that Madame Dubarry occupied at Versailles the magnificent suite of rooms formerly inhabited by the Princess Adelaide. The gold, the marble, the perfumes, the carpets, the hangings, at first intoxicated Gilbert; and it was only after these had become somewhat familiar to him that his understanding — dazzled by the reflected light which so many marvels cast on it — roused itself in the end to a clear perception of surrounding objects, and he found that he was in a little attic room, hung with serge; that there had been placed before him a basin of soup, some cold mutton, and a custard. The servant who brought these eatables had said, with the tone of a master, "Remain here!" and then left him.

But Gilbert soon found that the picture had its sunny side. From the window of his garret he could see the park of Versailles, studded with marble statues, and ornamented with fountains. Beyond were the dense and lofty summits of the trees, rolling like a sea of verdure; and farther still, the chequered plains, and the blue horizon of the neighbouring mountains. The only subject which occupied Gilbert's mind whilst eating his dinner was that, like the greatest lords of France, without being either a courtier or a lackey, without having been introduced there either by birth or baseness, he was living in Versailles, in the palace of the king.

His dinner, too, was an excellent one, when compared with those to which he had been accustomed. When it was over, he returned to his contemplation at the window. Meantime Chon had, as the reader may remember, joined her sister, had whispered that her business with Madame de Béarn was happily executed, and then related aloud the accident which their brother met with at Lachaussée. This accident, although it made a great noise at first, was lost, as the reader has seen, in that great gulf which swallowed up so many things much more important, — the king's indifference.

Gilbert had fallen into one of those reveries to which he often gave way while meditating on what was beyond his comprehension, or on what was impracticable for him to accomplish, when he was told that his patroness requested his presence. He took his hat, brushed it, compared by a glance his old worn coat with the new one of the footman, and saying to himself that that of the latter was a livery coat, he followed him. Yet, notwithstanding this philosophic reflection, he could not help blushing with shame to observe how little he resembled the men who elbowed him, and how much out of keeping he was with everything around him.

Chon was descending to the court at the same time as himself, with this difference, that she took the grand staircase, he a little back one more resembling a ladder. A carriage was waiting for them. It was a kind of low phaeton, containing seats for four persons, and resembled that historical vehicle in which the great king used to drive out with Madame de Montespan, Madame de Fontanges, and frequently with them the queen.

Chon got in and took the front seat, with a large box and a little dog beside her; the other seat was for Gilbert and a kind of steward called Monsieur Grange. Gilbert hastened to take the place behind Chon, in order to keep up his dignity; the steward, without thinking there was any degradation in the matter, placed himself behind the box and the dog.

As Mademoiselle Chon, like all who inhabited Versailles, felt joyous on leaving the great palace to inhale the air of the woods and the meadows, she became communicative, and was scarcely out of the town, when she turned half round and said, "Well, what do you think of Versailles, Monsieur Philosopher?"

"It is very beautiful, madame; but are we quitting it already?"

"Yes; now we are going to our own home."

"That is to say, to *your* home, madame," said Gilbert, with the tone of a half-tamed bear.

"That is what I meant. I shall introduce you to my sister; try to please her. All the greatest noblemen in France are only too happy if they can succeed in doing so. By the by, Grange, you must order a complete suit for this boy."

Gilbert blushed up to the eyes.

"What kind of suit, madame?" asked the steward. "The usual livery?"

Gilbert half started from his seat.

"Livery?" cried he, with a fierce look at the steward.

Chon burst into a laugh.

"No," said she; "you will order — but no matter, I will tell you another time. I have an idea, on which I wish for my sister's opinion. But take care to have the suit ready at the same time as Zamore's."

"Very well, madame."

"Do you know Zamore?" asked Chon, turning to Gilbert, who began to be very much alarmed by the conversation.

"No, madame, I have not that honour," replied he.

"He will be a young companion of yours; he is going to be governor of the château of Luciennes. Endeavour to gain his friendship; for Zamore is a good creature, in spite of his colour."

Gilbert was about to ask of what colour he was; but recollecting the reproof he had already received on the subject of curiosity, he refrained, for fear of another reprimand.

"I shall try," he answered, with a dignified smile.

They reached Luciennes. The philosopher saw everything, — the road, lately planted; the shady slopes; the great aqueduct, which resembled a work of the Romans; the dense wood of chestnut-trees; the varied and magnificent prospect of plains and woods stretching away on both sides of the Seine to Maisons.

"This, then," said he to himself, "is the country-seat which cost France so much, and of which I have heard the baron often speak."

Bounding dogs and eager domestics ran out to welcome Chon, and interrupted Gilbert in the midst of his aristo-cratico-philosophical reflections.

"Has my sister arrived?" asked Chon.

"No, madame, but there are visitors waiting for her."

"Who are they?"

"The chancellor, the minister of police, and the Duke d'Aiguillon."

"Well, run quickly and open my sister's private cabinet, and tell her when she arrives that I am there; do you understand? Oh, Sylvia," added she, addressing a *femme-de-chambre* who had taken from her the box and the little dog, "give the box and Misapouf to Grange, and take my little philosopher to Zamore."

Sylvia looked all round, doubtless to find out what sort of animal Chon was speaking of; but her eyes and those

of her mistress happening to rest on Gilbert at the same
moment, Chon made a sign that the young man was the
person in question.

"Come!" said Sylvia.

Gilbert, still more and more surprised at all that he saw,
followed the *femme-de-chambre*, whilst Chon, light as a
bird, disappeared by a side door of the pavilion.

Had it not been for the commanding tone in which Chon
addressed her, Gilbert would have taken Mademoiselle
Sylvia to be a great lady rather than a *femme-de-chambre*,
as her dress resembled Andrée's much more than Nicole's.
The young and handsome waiting-woman took him by the
hand with a gracious smile; for her mistress's words
showed that, if not an object of affection, he was chosen
at least through some new whim.

"What is your name, monsieur?" said she.

"Gilbert, mademoiselle," replied the young man, in a
gentle voice.

"Well, monsieur, I am going to introduce you to my
lord Zamore."

"To the governor of the château of Luciennes?"

"Yes, to the governor."

Gilbert pulled down his sleeves, dusted his coat a little,
and wiped his hands with his handkerchief. He was in
reality rather intimidated at the idea of appearing before
so important a personage; but he recalled Chon's remark,
"Zamore is a good creature," and recovered his courage.
He was already the friend of a countess and a viscount;
he was going to be the friend of a governor. "Well,"
thought he, "surely people calumniate the court; it is
certainly easy enough to find friends in it; at least, as far
as my experience goes; I have found every one kind and
hospitable."

Sylvia threw open the door of an ante-room, which from
its splendour, might rather have been supposed a boudoir.
The panels of the walls were of tortoise-shell, inlaid with
copper gilt; and one might have imagined himself in the

atrium of Lucullus, but that that ancient Roman used pure gold to decorate his walls.

There, in an immense arm-chair, half-buried in cushions, sitting cross-legged and gnawing chocolate cakes, reposed my lord Zamore, whom we already know, but whom Gilbert till now had never seen. The effect, therefore, which the governor of Luciennes produced on the mind of the philosopher was rather curiously depicted in his face. He stared with all his might at the strange being, for it was the first time he had ever seen a negro.

"Oh, oh!" cried he, "what is that?"

As for Zamore, he never raised his head, but continued to munch his cakes, rolling his eyes and showing the whites of them in the excess of his enjoyment.

"That," said Sylvia, "is my lord Zamore."

"That person?" said Gilbert, almost dumb with amazement.

"Yes, to be sure," answered Sylvia, laughing in spite of herself at the turn the scene was taking.

"He, the governor?" continued Gilbert. "That ape the governor of the château of Luciennes? Oh, mademoiselle, you are certainly jesting with me."

At these words Zamore raised his head, and showed his white teeth.

"Me governor," said he; "me not ape."

Gilbert looked from Zamore to Sylvia, and his glance, at first uneasy, became wrathful, when the young woman, in spite of all her efforts, burst into a fit of laughter. As for Zamore, grave and solemn as an Indian fetish, he plunged his black claw in a satin bag, and took out a handful of his cakes.

At this moment the door opened, and the steward entered, followed by a tailor.

"Here," said he, pointing to Gilbert, "is the person for whom you are to make the suit; take the measure according to the directions I gave you."

Gilbert mechanically submitted his arms and shoulders

to be measured, whilst Sylvia and Grange were talking in another part of the room, and at every word of the steward the chambermaid laughed louder and louder.

"Oh, it will be delightful!" she said; "and will he wear a pointed cap, like Sganarelle?"

Gilbert heard no more; he rudely pushed the tailor aside, and absolutely refused to submit to the rest of the ceremony. He knew nothing about Sganarelle; but the name, and particularly Sylvia's mirth, plainly declared that he was some pre-eminently ridiculous personage.

"It is of no consequence," said the steward to the tailor; "don't hurt him! I suppose you can do very well with the measure you have taken."

"Certainly," replied the tailor, "for width does no harm in such suits. I shall make it very wide."

Whereupon Sylvia, the steward, and the tailor, walked off, leaving Gilbert with the little negro, who continued to gnaw his cakes and roll his great eyes. What an enigma was all this to the poor country lad! What fears, what anguish, did the philosopher experience, in seeing his dignity as a man evidently more compromised at Luciennes than ever it had been at Taverney!

However, he tried to talk to Zamore. It occurred to him that he might be some Indian prince, such as he had read of in the romances of Monsieur Crebillon the younger. But the Indian prince, instead of replying, made the circuit of the apartment from mirror to mirror, admiring his splendid clothes like a bride in her wedding-dress. After that he got astride on a chair with wheels, and impelling it with his feet, he whirled round the ante-chamber some dozen times with a velocity which showed that he had made a profound study of that ingenious exercise.

Suddenly a bell rang. Zamore jumped up from his chair, and hurried through one of the doors in the direction of the sound. This promptness in obeying the silvery tinkling convinced Gilbert that Zamore was not a prince.

For a moment he entertained the idea of following him;

but on reaching the end of the passage which led into a salon, he saw so many blue ribbons and red ribbons, guarded by lackeys so bold, impudent, and noisy, that he felt a chill run through his veins, and, with the cold perspiration on his forehead, he returned to his ante-room.

An hour passed. Zamore did not return; Sylvia was seen no more. Any human face would have seemed then to Gilbert better than none, were it even that of the dreaded tailor who was to complete the mystification with which he was threatened.

Just at that moment the door by which he had entered the room opened, and a footman appeared and said, "Come!"

CHAPTER XLI.

THE PHYSICIAN AGAINST HIS WILL.

GILBERT felt it rather disagreeable to be obliged to obey a footman; nevertheless, he lost no time in following him, for he thought that now there was some prospect of a change in his condition, and it seemed to him that any change must be for the better.

Chon, now completely her own mistress, after having initiated her sister into the whole affair of the Countess de Béarn, was breakfasting very much at her ease in a charming morning-dress, beside a window shaded with acacias and chestnut-trees.

She was eating with an excellent appetite, and Gilbert remarked that a pheasant and truffles justified the relish with which she enjoyed her breakfast.

The philosopher, having entered the apartment, looked around to discover his place at the table, but there was no plate for him, and he was not even asked to sit down.

Chon merely cast a glance on him; then, after swallowing a little glass of wine, as clear and yellow as a topaz —

" Well, my dear doctor," said she, " how have you got on with Zamore ? "

" How have I got on with him ? "

" Yes; I hope you have become acquainted with him ? "

" How could one make acquaintance with an animal like that, who never speaks, and who, when one speaks to him, only rolls his eyes ? "

" Really, you frighten me ! " said Chon, without stopping one moment in her repast, and without her countenance showing any expression at all corresponding to her words. " Your friendship is difficult to gain, then ? "

"Friendship presupposes equality, madame."

"A noble maxim," said Chon. "Then you don't think yourself the equal of Zamore?"

"That is to say, I do not think him my equal," replied Gilbert.

"In truth," said Chon, as if talking to herself, "he is charming!"

Then turning to Gilbert, she remarked his stately air.

"So, my dear doctor," said she, "you do not easily bestow your affections?"

"No, madame, not easily."

"Then I was mistaken when I thought you held me as your friend, and as a good friend too?"

"Madame," said Gilbert, very stiffly, "I feel for you naturally a liking, but —"

"Oh! a thousand thanks for your condescension! you really overwhelm me! And how long do you think, my scornful young gentleman, it would require to gain your affection?"

"A long time, madame; and there are even persons who, whatever they did, could never obtain it."

"Oh! then that explains the reason why, after having been eighteen years in the Baron de Taverney's house, you left it all at once. The Taverneys were not so fortunate as to obtain your affections, — that was it, was it not?"

Gilbert blushed.

"Well? you don't answer," continued Chon.

"I have nothing to reply, madame, but that friendship and confidence must be merited."

"Oh! it appears, then, that your friends at Taverney did not merit your friendship and confidence?"

"Not all of them, madame."

"Ah! and what had those done who were so unfortunate as not to please you?"

"I do not complain of them, madame," answered he, proudly.

"Well, well, I perceive, Monsieur Gilbert, that I am also

one of the unfortunates excluded from your confidence;
yet, believe me, it is not from want of a desire to obtain it,
but from my not knowing the right means of doing so!"

Gilbert bit his lip.

"But to shorten the matter," added she, with an inquisi-
tiveness which he felt must be for some object, "the
Taverneys did not behave quite satisfactorily to you. Tell
me, if you please, what was your occupation in their
establishment?"

This was rather an embarrassing question, as Gilbert
certainly could not say that he held any particular office at
Taverney.

"Madame," said he, "I was their confidential adviser."

At these words, which he pronounced most phlegmatically
and philosophically, Chon was seized with such a fit of
laughter that she threw herself back in her chair.

"Do you doubt my words?" asked Gilbert, frowning.

"Heaven preserve me from such a rash act, my dear
friend! Really, you are so fierce that one can scarcely
venture to speak to you. I merely asked what sort of
people the Taverneys were. Believe me, it was with no
other intention than that of serving you, by assisting you
to be revenged on them."

"If I am revenged, madame, it must be by myself."

"All very well; but we have a cause of complaint
against the Taverneys ourselves; and, as you have one,
or perhaps indeed several, we are naturally allies in our
wish for revenge."

"You are quite mistaken, madame. Should I think of
vengeance, mine could have no connexion with yours. You
speak of all the Taverneys, while I have different shades
of feeling towards different members of the family."

"The Chevalier Philip de Taverney, for instance, — is
he in the number of your friends or enemies?"

"I have nothing to say against the chevalier. He never
did me either good or ill. I neither love him nor hate him:
I am quite indifferent to him."

"Then you would not give evidence before the king, or before the Duke de Choiseul, against Monsieur Philip de Taverney?"

"Give evidence about what?"

"About the duel with my brother."

"I should say all that I know about it, if I were called upon to give evidence."

"And what do you know about it?"

"The truth."

"But what do you call truth! That is a word whose meaning is very vague."

"No, not to the man who can distinguish between good and evil — between justice and injustice."

"I understand you; justice is on the side of the Chevalier de Taverney, injustice on that of Viscount Dubarry?"

"Yes, madame, so I think, if I must speak conscientiously."

"So this is the creature I picked up on the highway!" said Chon, sharply; "I am rewarded in this way by one who owes it to me that he is living!"

"That is to say, madame, who does not owe you his death."

"It is all the same."

"On the contrary, madame, it is very different."

"How different?"

"I do not owe my life to you; you merely prevented your horses from depriving me of it; besides it was not you, but the postilion."

Chon fixed a penetrating look on the young logician, who showed so little scruple in the choice of his terms.

"I should have expected," said she, in a milder tone, and allowing a smile to steal over her features, "a little more gallantry from you who travelled with your head upon my arm and my foot on your knee. Come, come! you will give evidence against the chevalier, will you not?"

"No, madame, never!"

"And why not, you foolish fellow?"

"Because the viscount was in the wrong."

"And, pray, how was he in the wrong?"

"By insulting the dauphiness; whilst, on the contrary, the chevalier — "

"Well, what ? "

"Was right in defending her."

"Oh, ho ! then it appears you belong to the dauphiness's party ? "

"No, I am only for justice."

"Hold your tongue, Gilbert; you are a fool ! Do not let one hear you talk in that way here."

"Then permit me to remain silent when I am questioned."

"In that case, let us change the subject."

Gilbert bowed, in token of assent.

"And, now, my little friend," said the young lady, in rather a harsh tone of voice, "what do you intend to do here, if you refuse to make yourself agreeable ? "

"Must I perjure myself in order to make myself agreeable ? "

"Perjure ! where did you learn all those grand words ? "

"In the knowledge that I have a conscience to which I must be faithful."

"Pshaw ! " said Chon; "when we serve a master, the master takes all the responsibility from our conscience."

"But I have no master," growled Gilbert.

"You will never have a mistress, you fool, if you act this way," said Chon rising. "Well, answer my question. What do you mean to do here ? "

"1 did not think that I required to study to be agreeable when I could be useful."

"You are mistaken, we can get useful people anywhere ; we are tired of them."

"Then I shall go away."

"You will go away ? "

"Yes, of course. I did not ask to come here; I am therefore free."

"Free ? " exclaimed Chon, who began to get angry at this resistance to her will, a thing to which she was by no means accustomed. "Free ? indeed you are not ! "

Gilbert's brow contracted.

"Come, come!" said she, seeing by his frown that he would not easily renounce his freedom, "let us be friends. You are a handsome lad, and very virtuous, which makes you very amusing, were it only for the contrast which you will present to everybody else about us. Only, keep a guard upon that love of truth of yours."

"I shall take care to keep it," said Gilbert.

"Yes, but we understand the word in two different senses; I mean to keep it to yourself. You need not exhibit it in the lobbies and ante-rooms of Luciennes or Versailles."

"Hum!" said Gilbert.

"There is no occasion for 'Hum!' You are not so learned, Monsieur Philosopher, but that you may learn something from a woman; and let this be your first maxim: 'To hold your tongue is not to lie.' Remember that!"

"But if any one questions me?"

"Who would question you? Are you mad, my friend? Who in the world would ever think about you but myself? You have not yet founded a school, Monsieur Philosopher, I presume. It will require some little searching and trouble before you happen upon a body of followers. You shall live with me; and before four times four-and-twenty hours, I shall transform you into a perfect courtier."

"I doubt that," replied Gilbert, majestically.

Chon shrugged her shoulders.

Gilbert smiled.

"Now," said Chon, "to settle the matter at once, you have only to endeavour to please three persons."

"What three?"

"The king, my sister, and myself."

"What must I do to please?"

"Have you not seen Zamore?" asked the young lady, avoiding a direct reply.

"The negro?" said Gilbert, with the utmost contempt.

"Yes, the negro."

" What similarity is there between him and me ? "

" Try to make a similarity of fortune, my good friend.
That negro has already two thousand livres per annum
from the king's privy purse. He is to be appointed governor of Luciennes ; and even those that laugh at his thick
lips and his black face call him 'monsieur,' and even
' monseigneur.' "

" I shall not be one of those," said Gilbert.

" Oh ! I thought that the first principle of you philosophers was that all men are equal."

" That is the very reason that I shall not call Zamore
' monseigneur.' "

Chon was beaten with her own weapons. It was her
turn to bite her lips.

" So you are not ambitious ? " said she.

" Oh, yes, I am ! " replied Gilbert, with sparkling eyes.

" And if I remember rightly, your ambition was to be a
physician."

" I look upon the mission of soothing the pain and suffering of our fellow-creatures as the noblest in the world."

" Well, your dream shall be realised."

" How so ? "

" You shall be a physician, — and the king's physician to
boot."

" I ? " cried Gilbert, " I, who know not even the first
principles of medical science ? You jest, madame."

" Well, and what does Zamore know about portcullises,
and drawbridges, and counterscarps ? He does not trouble
his head about such things, yet that does not prevent him
from being governor of Luciennes, with all a governor's
privileges."

" Ah, yes, yes, I understand ! " said Gilbert, bitterly.
" You have only one buffoon, and that is not sufficient.
The king is getting tired and wishes for another."

" There," said Chon, " you are putting on your long face
again. You make yourself so ugly, my little man, it is
really quite delightful to see you. Keep all those ridicu-

lous faces till the wig is on your head and the sugar-loaf
hat over the wig; then, instead of being ugly, they will be
comical."

Gilbert frowned more darkly still.

"I should think you might be glad of the post of the
king's physician, when the Duc de Tresmes solicits that of
my sister's monkey."

Gilbert made no answer.   Chon thought of the proverb,
"Silence gives consent."

"As a proof that you are in favour," said she, "you shall
not eat with servants."

"Ah! thank you, madame," replied Gilbert.

"I have already given orders to that effect."

"And where shall I eat?"

"Along with Zamore."

"I!"

"Yes, the king's governor and his physician may surely
eat together; go now to your dinner."

"I am not hungry," answered Gilbert, rudely.

"Very well," said Chon, quietly; "you are not hungry
now, but you will be in the evening."

Gilbert shook his head.

"To-morrow, then, or the day after to-morrow you may
be. Oh, we know how to tame rebels here; and if you
continue obstinate we have, besides, the corrector of our
pages to do our will!"

Gilbert shuddered and turned pale.

"Go to my lord Zamore now," she added sharply; "you
will be very well treated with him; his table is excellent.
But no ingratitude, remember, or we shall teach you to be
grateful."

Gilbert let his head fall on his breast, an invariable
symptom that instead of going to reply, he was going to
act.

The footman who had showed him to Chon's apartment
waited at the door, and on his dismissal conducted him to a
little dining-room adjoining the ante-room.

Zamore was at table. Gilbert took his place at the table, but he could not be made to eat.

Three o'clock struck. Madame Dubarry set off for Paris. Chon, who was to join her there a short time after, left instructions for the taming of her bear. Plenty of sweetmeats were to be his reward if he became docile; plenty of threats, and at last the dungeon, if he continued rebellious.

At four o'clock a complete suit, such as that worn by the 'médecin malgré lui,' was brought into Gilbert's apartment. There was the pointed cap, the wig, the black jacket, and the long black robe; in addition to these, they sent him a collar, a wand, and a large book. The footman who carried them in exhibited the various articles one by one. Gilbert no longer manifested any disposition to rebel.

Grange entered after the footman, and instructed him how all the different parts of the dress should be worn. Gilbert listened most patiently.

"I thought," said he at length, "that doctors formerly carried a little writing-case and a roll of paper?"

"Yes, faith, he is right," replied the steward; "go and bring him a long writing-case, which he can hang at his girdle."

"With pen and paper," added Gilbert; "I must have every part of my costume complete."

The footman hastened to execute the order, and at the same time to tell Chon how obliging Gilbert had become. Chon was so much delighted that she gave the messenger a little purse with eight crowns in it, to hang with the writing-case at the girdle of this model of a physician.

"Thank you," said Gilbert to the person who brought it; "now may I be left alone to dress?"

"Well, make haste," replied Grange, "so that mademoiselle may see you before she goes to Paris."

"Half an hour," said Gilbert; "I only ask half an hour!"

"You may take three-quarters, if you like, my dear doctor," said the steward, shutting the door carefully, as if it had been that of his money-box.

Gilbert stole on tiptoe to the door, to be certain that the footsteps were dying away in the distance ; then he glided to the window and looked down.   There was a terrace about eighteen feet below him, covered with fine gravel, and bordered by lofty trees, which shaded the balconies of the windows.

Gilbert tore his long robe into three pieces, which he tied lengthwise together, placed the hat on the table, and near it the purse and the following note : —

MADAME, — Liberty is the first of blessings.   Man's most sacred duty is to preserve it.   You endeavoured to enslave me ; I set myself free.   GILBERT.

This letter he folded and addressed to Mademoiselle Chon, then he tied his twelve feet of serge to the bars of the window, slipped between them with the suppleness of an eel, and when at the end of his cord, dropped down to the terrace at the risk of breaking his neck.   Though a little stunned by the fall, he lost not a moment in gaining the trees, among which he glided stealthily, and running as fast as his limbs would carry him, he disappeared in the direction of Ville d'Avray.

When, at the end of half an hour, they came to seek for him, he was already far beyond their reach.

CHAPTER XLII.

THE OLD MAN.

GILBERT had avoided the highway through fear of pursuit; he glided from one plantation to another, until he reached a sort of forest, and there he stopped. He had travelled a league and a half in about three-quarters of an hour.

The fugitive looked around him, and finding himself quite alone, he felt so much courage that he thought he might venture nearer the high-road. He therefore turned in the direction which, according to his calculation of his position, he supposed would lead to Paris.

But some horses which he saw near the village of Roquencourt, led by grooms in orange liveries, frightened him so much that he was cured of all desire to be on the public road, and he returned to the woods.

"Let me keep in the shade of the trees," said he to himself; "if I am pursued, it will certainly be on the high-road. In the evening, from tree to tree, from one opening to another, I shall steal on to Paris. They say Paris is very large, and as I am little, I can easily hide there."

This idea was rendered still more agreeable to him by the fineness of the weather, the shade of the forest, and the softness of the mossy sward. The sun was now disappearing behind the hills of Marly, and the vegetation, dried by the scorching heat of the day, exhaled the sweet perfume of the spring, — a mingled odour of the plant and of the flower.

Evening came on. It was the hour when, beneath the darkening skies, silence falls more softly and more deeply on all things; when the closing flower-cup shuts in the insect sleeping on its bosom; the gilded flies return with

ceaseless hum to the hollow oak which serves them as an
asylum; the birds hurry silently to their nests, their wings
rustling through the foliage; and the only song which is
heard is the clear whistle of the blackbird, and the timid
warble of the redbreast.

Gilbert was familiar with the woods; he was well acquainted both with their sounds and with their silence.
Without giving way therefore to reflection, or to idle fear,
he threw himself at full length on the heath, on which there
yet remained here and there a red leaf of the preceding
winter.

Far from feeling anxious or disturbed, he experienced
rather a vague and boundless sense of joy. He inhaled
with rapture the pure and free air, feeling, with the pride
of a stoic, that he had once more triumphed over the snares
laid for human weakness. What though he had neither
bread, nor money, nor shelter, — had he not his beloved
liberty ? Was he not the free and uncontrolled master of
his destiny ?

He stretched himself, therefore, at the foot of a gigantic
chestnut-tree, where between two of its moss-covered roots
he found a luxurious couch; then, gazing up at the calm
and smiling heavens, he gradually sank to sleep.

The warbling of the birds awoke him; it was scarcely
day. Raising himself on his elbow, stiff and painful from
contact with the hard wood, he saw, in the dawning light,
an opening from which three paths branched off through
the wood. Here and there a rabbit scudded past him with
its ears drooping, and brushing away the dew in its course,
or a stag bounded past, with its sharp, quick leaps, stopped
to gaze at the unknown object under the tree, and then,
alarmed, darted off with a more rapid flight.

Gilbert jumped to his feet, but no sooner had he done so
than he felt he was hungry. The reader may remember
that he had refused to dine with Zamore, so that since his
breakfast in the attic at Versailles he had eaten nothing.
On finding himself once more under the leafy arches of a

forest, he who had so boldly traversed the great woods of
Lorraine and Champagne, he almost thought himself beneath
the trees of Taverney or among the brakes of Pierrefitte,
surprised by the morning beams after a nocturnal expedi-
tion to procure game for his fair mistress.

But at Taverney he had always found by his side a partridge or a pheasant which he had shot, while here he
found only his hat, rather the worse for his journey, and
now nearly unfit to wear after the damps of the night.

It was not, then, all a dream, as he had on first awaken-
ing supposed. Versailles and Luciennes were realities,
from his triumphal entry into the first till his forcible
escape from the last.

But what more than all else served to recall him to his
real position was his hunger, now becoming sharper and
sharper every moment.

Then he mechanically sought around for some of those
delicious mulberries, those wild cherries, or pungent roots,
which, though acrid like the radish, the woodman loves to
find as he plods in the morning to his labour with his tools
on his shoulder. But this was not the season for such
things; and besides, he saw around him only the ash, the
beech, and other trees which bear no fruit.

"Well," said he to himself, "I will go direct to Paris.
I cannot be more than three or four leagues from it, — five
at the most; I can be there in two hours. What matter
is it to suffer for a couple of hours, when I am sure after
that of not having to suffer any longer? In Paris every
one has bread, and the first artisan whom I meet will not
refuse me bread for my work, when he knows that I am
honest and industrious. In Paris I shall be able in one
day to procure food for the next. What do I want more?
Nothing, except that every succeeding day may see me increase in strength, in elevation of character, in greatness
of mind, and approach nearer and nearer the object of my
wishes."

Gilbert redoubled his speed; he now wished to find the

high-road, but he had lost all means of directing his course. At Taverney, and in the woods around it, he knew the east and the west; every ray of light was to him an index of the hour. At night every star, although unknown to him by its name of Venus, Lucifer, or Saturn, served him as a guide. But here he was in a new world; he knew neither places nor objects, and was forced to seek his way, groping by chance.

"Fortunately," said he, "I saw finger-posts, on which the roads were pointed out."

He proceeded towards an opening where one of these directing-posts was placed. It pointed to three roads; one road led to Marais-Jaune, another to Champ-de-l'Alouette, a third to Trou-Salé. Gilbert was not much assisted by this; he ran for three hours from one place to another, very often finding himself in the same spot from which he set out, and as far from the high-road as ever.

The perspiration poured down his face. A dozen times he threw off his coat and vest to climb some colossal chestnut-tree; but when he had reached its summit, he saw nothing but Versailles, — Versailles, now on his right, now on his left, — Versailles, towards which, by some fatality, he seemed constantly impelled. He was half frantic with rage; but at last his efforts were so far successful that he first passed Viroflay, then Chaville, then Sèvres."

Half-past five sounded from the clock-tower of Meudon when he reached the Capuchin Convent between Sèvres and Bellevue; there, climbing on a cross at the risk of breaking it, and of being himself broken on the wheel by order of the parliament, as Sirven had been, he saw from that height the Seine, the village, and the smoke of the nearest houses. Beyond this he saw a great mass of buildings on the horizon, dimly distinguished in the morning vapours. That must be Paris, he thought; so feeling no longer either fatigue or hunger, he directed his course thither, and only stopped when out of breath from his excessive speed.

He was now in the woods of Meudon, between Fleury and Plessis-Piquet.

"Come," said he, looking around, "no false shame! I shall no doubt soon meet some early workman going to his day's labour with a loaf under his arm. I shall say to him, 'All men are brethren, and ought to help one another. You have more bread there than you will want this day, whilst I am dying of hunger,' and then he will give me the half of his loaf."

Hunger rendering Gilbert more and more philosophical, he continued his reflections.

"In truth," said he, "should not everything be in common among men on this earth? Has the Eternal Source of all things given to this man or to that the air which fertilizes the soil, or the soil which produces the fruits? No. Some, it is true, have usurped a power over these things; but in the eyes of their Maker, in the eyes of the philosopher, no one possesses them. He who holds them is only the man to whom the Creator has lent them."

Gilbert, in all this, was but condensing by a natural instinct the vague and indefinite ideas of the period which men felt, as it were, floating in the air and hovering above their heads, like clouds impelled in one direction, and forming a threatening mass, from which at length the tempest would burst.

"Some," continued he, "retain by force what should belong to all. Well, then, from such we should tear by force what by right they should share with us. If my brother who has too much bread refuse me a portion of that bread, why, then, I shall take it from him by force; I shall follow the law of nature, the source of all sound sense and of all justice, since it arises from our natural wants. But I must yield if my brother say to me, 'The portion you ask for is that of my wife and of my children,' or if he should say, 'I am stronger than you, and I shall keep what I have, in spite of you.'"

He was in this temper of mind, which bore a striking resemblance to that of a hungry wolf, when he reached an open space among the trees; in its centre was a pond of muddy water, margined with reeds and water-lilies, on the surface of which sported myriads of flies, dotting its glassy bosom with innumerable circles. The grassy slope which descended to the water's edge was closely studded with bunches of myosotis, and resembled a bed of turquoises and emeralds. The background of the picture, that is, the circle around the pool and the bank, was formed of a hedge of tall aspens, the interstices between whose golden trunks was filled up with the thick and leafy branches of the alder. Six paths led down to this spot; two of which, radiant with golden light, might have seemed to the imagination avenues to the palace of the glorious luminary of day; the four others, diverging like rays of a star, were lost in the blue depths of the forest.

This verdant salon seemed fresher and more flowery than any other part of the wood. Gilbert entered it by one of the dark alleys.

The first object which he perceived, when, after having at a glance taken in its extent and circumference, his eye rested on nearer objects, was a man seated on the fallen trunk of a tree, near a deep ditch. The expression of his face was mild, yet refined and penetrating, and he was dressed in a coat of coarse brown cloth, breeches of the same, and a waistcoat of grey jean. His well-made, sinewy legs were encased in grey cotton stockings, and his shoes with buckles were dusty here and there, yet showed on the soles and points traces of the morning dew.

Near him on the grass was placed a box, painted green, wide open, and filled with plants recently gathered. He had between his legs a stout stick, with a smooth round handle, and terminated at the opposite end by a little spade about two inches broad and three long.

Gilbert embraced in one rapid glance all these details which we have given; but what first drew his attention was a piece of bread, from which the old man from time to time broke off small pieces to eat, sharing them benevolently with the linnets and the wrens, who fixed from

afar a longing eye on the food, swooped on it the moment
it was thrown to them, and then, flew with joyful twitter-
ing to their thick foliage above.

The old man watched them with an eye at once gentle
and animated, then, extending his hand to a checked
handkerchief beside him, he drew from it a cherry from
time to time, as a relish with his mouthful of bread.

"Ha! this is the man for me!" said Gilbert, brushing
aside the branches of the trees and making four steps
towards the solitary man, who looked up as he approached;
but he had not advanced a third of the distance which
separated them, when, perceiving the calmness and gentleness of the old man's countenance, he stopped and took
off his hat.

The old man, finding himself no longer alone, cast a
hurried glance on his box and then on his coat. He shut
the former and buttoned up the latter.

CHAPTER XLIII.

THE BOTANIST.

GILBERT took courage and walked close up; but he opened his mouth and shut it again before he could utter a word. His philosophy wavered, and it seemed to him that he was about to entreat alms, and not to demand a right.

The old man observed this timidity, and it seemed to banish on his side all feelings of apprehension.

"Do you wish to speak to me, my friend?" said he, smiling, and laying down his bread on the trunk of the tree on which he sat.

"Yes, monsieur," replied Gilbert.

"What do you wish to say?"

"Monsieur, I see you throw your bread to the birds as if we were not told that God feeds them."

"Doubtless he does feed them, young man; but the hand of man is one of the means which he employs for that purpose. If you mean your words as a reproach, you are wrong; for neither in the silent wood nor in the crowded street is the bread ever lost which we cast from our hand. In the one place the birds pick it up; in the other, the poor.

"Well, monsieur," said Gilbert, singularly moved by the soft, penetrating voice of the old man, "although we are in the woods, I know a man who would dispute your bread with the birds."

"Can it be you, my friend?" cried the old man; "are you, then, hungry?"

"Very, very hungry, monsieur; and if you will permit me —"

The old man seized his bread at once with eager compassion. Then reflecting for a moment, he looked at Gilbert with a keen and searching glance.

In fact, Gilbert so little resembled a starving man that some consideration might be permitted. His coat was clean, except where it was in some places stained by its contact with the ground; his shirt was white, for at Versailles the evening before he had taken a clean one from his bundle, yet it was rendered damp by the dews; it was quite evident that he had passed the night in the wood.

Besides all this, his hands were white and slender, like those of a man of thought rather than of labour.

Gilbert did not want tact; he read the stranger's distrust and hesitation in his countenance, and hastened to anticipate further conjectures which he readily saw would not be favourable to him.

"We are always hungry, monsieur," he said, "when we have not eaten for twelve hours, and it is now twenty-four since I have had any food."

The emotion expressed on the young man's face, his tremulous voice, and his extreme paleness, all declared that his words were true. The old man hesitated, or rather feared, no longer; he held out to Gilbert his bread and the handkerchief containing his cherries.

"Thank you, monsieur, thank you," said Gilbert, gently pushing aside the handkerchief containing the cherries; "nothing but the bread, it is quite sufficient."

And he broke it in two, keeping one-half for himself and returning the other to the old man; then he sat down on the grass a couple of paces from his companion, who looked at him with increasing wonder.

The repast did not last very long. There was but little bread, and Gilbert was very hungry. The old man did not disturb his occupation by a word; he continued to observe him furtively but silently, bestowing apparently great attention on the plants and flowers in his box, which, when he opened it again, raised their odoriferous heads to the level of the edge, as if to inhale the air. But seeing Gilbert approach the pond, he cried hastily, " Do not drink that water, young man; it is rendered unwholesome by the remains of last year's plants, and by the spawn of frogs now on its surface. Take instead a few of these cherries; they will refresh you as much as the water. Take them, I beg of you, for you are not a forward guest, I see."

" It is true, monsieur; forwardness is the reverse of my nature, and I fear nothing so much as being intrusive. I have just experienced that at Versailles."

" Oh, you come from Versailles ? " said the stranger, eyeing Gilbert with a strong expression of curiosity.

" Yes, monsieur."

" It is a rich town ; one must be either very poor or very proud to be starving there."

" I am both, monsieur."

" You have had a quarrel with your master, perhaps ? " said the stranger, while he apparently arranged the plants in his box, yet giving Gilbert a rapid interrogating glance.

" I have no master, monsieur."

" My friend," replied the old man, putting on his hat, " that is too ambitious a reply."

" It is the truth, however."

" No, young man. Every one has his master here below; we do not place our pride on a proper object when we say that we have no master."

" How ? "

" Yes. Whether old or young, it is so ordered that we must submit to some ruling power. Some are ruled by men, others by principles ; and the severest masters are not always those who order with the voice or strike with the hand."

" Be it so," said Gilbert. " Then I am governed by principles, I confess. Principles are the only masters which a reflecting mind can recognise without shame."

" And what are your principles ? Let me hear them ?

You seem to be very young, my friend, to have any decided principles."

"Monsieur, I know that all men are brethren, and that every man from his birth is bound to fulfil certain duties towards his fellow-men. I know that God has bestowed on me a certain amount of value in society; and as I acknowledge the worth of other men, I have a right to exact from them that they should acknowledge mine, if I do not exaggerate its importance. So long as I do nothing unjust and dishonourable, I merit some regard, even were it only as a human being."

"Oh, oh!" said the stranger, "you have studied, I perceive."

"Alas! monsieur, I have not; but I have read the "Discours sur l'Inégalité des Conditions," and "Le Contrat Social." From those two books I have learned all that I know, and even all that I have dreamed."

At these words the eyes of the stranger flashed, and by an involuntary movement he was nearly destroying a beautiful xeranthemum, which he was trying to place securely in his box.

"And such are the principles which you profess?" said he.

"They may not be yours, monsieur," replied the young man; "but they are those of Jean-Jacques Rousseau."

"But," said the stranger, with a distrust so apparent that it was rather humbling to Gilbert's vanity; "but are you sure you have rightly understood those principles?"

"I understand French, I think, monsieur, particularly when it is pure and poetical."

"You see that you do not," said the old man, smiling; "for what I ask you, if not poetical, is at least quite plain. I mean, have your philosophical studies enabled you to understand the groundwork of the system of — "

He stopped, almost blushing.

"Of Rousseau, monsieur?" continued Gilbert. "Oh, monsieur! I have not studied my philosophy in a college;

but there is an instinct within me which revealed the excellence and utility of "Le Contrat Social," above all other books that I had read."

"A dry book for a young man, monsieur; a barren subject for reverie at twenty years of age; a bitter and unfragrant flower for fancy in its springtime!" said the old man with gentle sadness.

"Misfortune ripens man before his time, monsieur," answered Gilbert; "and as to reverie, if we give it a free and unrestrained course, it very often leads to ill."

The stranger opened his eyes, which he usually kept half closed in his moments of calmness and reflection, a peculiarity which gave an indefinable charm to his countenance.

"To whom do you allude?" asked he, reddening.

"Not to any one, monsieur," said Gilbert.

"Oh, yes, you do."

"No, I assure you I do not."

"You appear to have studied the philosopher of Geneva. Did you not allude to his life?"

"I know nothing of his life," replied Gilbert, frankly.

"Do you not?" and the stranger sighed. "Young man, he is a wretched creature."

"Impossible! Jean-Jacques Rousseau wretched? Then there is no justice on earth. Wretched? The man who has devoted his life to the happiness of mankind?"

"Well, well! I see that you know nothing about him. Let us speak of yourself, my friend, if you please."

"I should prefer going on with our present subject. What can I tell you of myself worth hearing, monsieur, — I, who am a mere nobody?"

"And besides, you do not know me, and are afraid of trusting a stranger."

"Oh, monsieur, what have I to fear from any one? Who can make me more wretched than I am? Recollect in what guise I came before you, — alone, poor, hungry."

"Where were you going?"

"I was going to Paris. Are you a Parisian, monsieur?"

"Yes, — that is to say, no."

"Which of the two am I to believe?" asked Gilbert, smiling.

"I abhor falsehood, and every moment I perceive how necessary it is to reflect before speaking. I am a Parisian, if by that is meant a man who has lived in Paris for a long time, and has mixed in its society; but I was not born in that city. But why do you ask?"

"It was from an association of ideas, arising out of our conversation. I thought if you lived in Paris you might have seen Rousseau, of whom we were speaking just now."

"I have indeed seen him sometimes."

"People look at him as he passes by, do they not? He is admired, and pointed out as the benefactor of the human race?"

"No; children, incited by their parents, follow him, and throw stones at him!"

"Good Heavens!" exclaimed Gilbert, with the most painful astonishment; "but at least he is rich?"

"He has sometimes to ask himself, as you asked yourself this morning, 'Where shall I procure a breakfast?'"

"But poor as he is, he is esteemed, has influence, is respected?"

"He knows not at night, when he lies down, whether he may not in the morning awake in the Bastille."

"Oh, how he must hate mankind!"

"He neither loves them nor hates them; he is disgusted with them, that is all."

"How can we avoid hating people who treat us ill?" cried Gilbert; "I cannot comprehend that."

"Rousseau has always been free, monsieur; Rousseau has always been strong enough to rely on himself alone. It is strength and freedom which make men mild and kind, — slavery and weakness alone make them malevolent."

"Those are my reasons for wishing to be free," said Gilbert, proudly. "I have long thought what you have just so well explained to me."

"But one may be free even in prison, my friend," replied the stranger. "Suppose Rousseau were in the Bastille to-morrow, — and he certainly will be in it one day or other; he would think and write as freely as among the mountains of Switzerland. I have always thought, for my part, that man's freedom consists in his being able to do whatever he wills, but that he should not, by any human power, be forced to do what is against his will."

"Has Rousseau written what you have just said, monsieur?"

"I think he has."

"It is not in "The Social Contract.""

"No, it is in a new work of his, called 'The Reveries of a Solitary Walker.'"

"Monsieur," said Gilbert, warmly, "I think we shall agree on one point."

"What is that?"

"That we both love and admire Rousseau."

"Speak for yourself, young man; you are still in the age of illusions."

"We may be deceived about things, but not about men."

"Alas! you will learn at a later period that it is in the characters of men more than in aught else that we are deceived. Rousseau may be a little more just than other men, but believe me, he has faults, and very great ones."

Gilbert shook his head in a way which showed that he was far from being convinced; but notwithstanding this rather uncivil demonstration, the stranger continued to treat him with the same kindness.

"Let us return to the point at which we set out," said the stranger. "I was saying that you had quitted your master at Versailles."

"And I," replied Gilbert, but more mildly than before, "I answered that I had no master: I should have added that it depended entirely on myself to have one, and a very illustrious one too, and that I had refused a situation which many would have sought eagerly."

"A situation ? "

"Yes; one in which I should only have had to talk for
the amusement of great lords in want of such an occupation; but I thought that being young and able to study
and push my way in life, I ought not to lose my most
precious years, and compromise in my person the dignity
of man."

"And you decided well. But have you any fixed plan of
pursuing your career ? "

"Monsieur, I should wish to be a physician."

"A noble profession. In it you may choose between
real science, ever modest and self-sacrificing, and quackery,
ever noisy and empty. If you would become a physician,
young man, study ; if a quack, nothing but impudence and
effrontery are necessary."

"But it requires a great deal of money to study, does it
not, sir ? "

"It certainly requires some money; I should not say a
great deal."

"In fact, I believe that Jean-Jacques Rousseau, who
knows everything, studied at no expense."

"At no expense ? Oh, young man ! " said the stranger,
with a sad smile, "do you call it no expense when we
expend the most precious of God's gifts, — innocence, health,
sleep ? These are what it has cost the philosopher of
Geneva to acquire the little that he knows."

"The little ? " repeated Gilbert, almost angrily.

"Yes; ask any one about him, and you will hear him
spoken of as I speak of him."

"In the first place, he is a great musician."

"Oh, because King Louis XV. sang a song out of an
opera of Rousseau's composing, that does not make it a
good opera."

"But he is a great botanist. I have only seen a few odd
sheets of his letters on botany, but you, who gather plants
in the woods, have read them, I dare to say."

"Oh, sometimes a person thinks himself a botanist, and
is only — "

" Only what ? "

" Only an herborist and even — "

" And which are you, herborist or botanist ? "

" A very humble herborist, and a very ignorant one,
when I contemplate those marvels of God's creation, plants
and flowers ! "

" He is a Latin scholar."

" A very bad one."

" But I read in a newspaper that he translated an
ancient author called Tacitus."

" Because, in his pride, — alas ! every man has his moment
of pride, — because, in his pride, he thought he could undertake anything. In the preface, however, to the first book,
the only one which he translated, he says he does not
understand Latin well ; and Tacitus, who is a rude antagonist, soon wearied him. No, no, my good young man, in
spite of your admiration, there is no such thing as a
man of universal knowledge ; and believe me, almost all
men lose in depth what they gain in superficies. A little
river, when swollen by the rains, may overflow its banks
till it looks like a lake, but try to sail on it, and your boat
will soon touch the ground."

" Then you think Rousseau a superficial man ? "

" Yes ; perhaps he presents a greater superficies than
other men, but that is all."

" There are some, I think, who would be very glad to be
superficial in his fashion."

" Do you intend that for me ? " asked the stranger, with
a good-natured frankness which quite disarmed Gilbert.

" Oh no, monsieur ! I am too much delighted to converse
with you to say anything disagreeable to you."

" In what way does my conversation delight you? Let
me hear, for I do not think you would flatter me for
a morsel of bread and a few cherries."

" You do me justice ; I would not flatter to obtain the
empire of the world. You shall hear why I am pleased :
you are the first person who has ever spoken to me without

haughtiness, who has reasoned with me in a tone of kindness, — as if speaking to a young man, and not to a child. Although we did not agree about Rousseau, there has been in all that you have said something so calm and elevated that it attracted me. I seem, when talking to you, to be in a richly-furnished salon, the window-shutters of which are closed, but of which, notwithstanding the darkness, I can guess the richness and magnificence. I know that you could, if you wished, permit a ray of light to penetrate into your conversation which would dazzle me."

" But you yourself speak with a certain degree of refinement, which might lead me to think that you had received a better education than you have confessed."

"It is the first time, monsieur, that I have spoken so, and I am surprised myself at the terms which I have employed; there are even some of them of which I do not quite understand the signification, and which I have only heard once. I have met with them in books, but I did not comprehend them."

" Have you read much ? "

" Too much ; but I shall re-read."

The old man looked at Gilbert in astonishment.

" Yes, I read all that fell in my way, whether good or bad; I devoured all. Ah, if I had only had some one to direct me what I ought to forget and what I ought to remember ! But excuse me, monsieur, I was forgetting that although your conversation is delightful to me, it does not therefore follow that mine must be so to you. You are herborising, and I perhaps interfere with your occupation."

Gilbert made a movement as if to withdraw, but at the same time with the greatest desire to be detained. The little grey eyes of the stranger were fixed on him, and they seemed to read his heart.

" No," said he, " my box is almost full; I only want a few mosses ; I have been told there are some very beautiful hair-mosses in this quarter."

" Stay, stay," said Gilbert, " I think I have seen what you want on a rock just now."

" Far from this ? "

" No, not more than fifty paces."

" But how do you know that description of moss ? "

" I have lived almost all my life in the woods, monsieur; and then the daughter of the gentleman at whose house I was brought up was fond of botany ; she had an herbal, and under each plant the name was written in her own hand. I have often looked at the plants and the writing, and then I knew them when I saw them again in the woods."

" Then you felt a taste for botany ? "

" Oh, monsieur, whenever I heard Nicole say, — Nicole was the waiting-maid of Mademoiselle Andrée, — when I heard Nicole say that her mistress had been trying in vain to find some particular plant, I asked her to get me the form of that plant. Then, without knowing that I had asked for it, Mademoiselle Andrée would frequently sketch it in a moment, and Nicole would bring the drawing to me. I would then scour the fields, meadows, and woods until I had found the plant in question. When found, I dug it up and planted it in the lawn, where Mademoiselle Andrée could see it; and full of joy, she would exclaim on discovering it, ' How strange ! Here is the very plant which I have been searching for everywhere. ' "

The old man looked at Gilbert with even more attention than he had yet bestowed on him; and if Gilbert, on reflecting on the purport of what he had said, had not cast down his eyes and blushed, he would have seen that this attention was mingled with an expression of tender interest.

" Well, young man," said he, " continue to study botany ; it will lead by a short route to a knowledge of medicine. God has made nothing in vain, and one day or other the utility of each plant will be distinctly marked in the book of science. Learn first to know simples, afterwards you can study their properties."

" Are there not schools in Paris ? "

"Yes, and even some gratuitous ones. The school of surgery, for instance, is one of the benefits which we owe to the present reign."

"I shall follow the course prescribed in it."

"Nothing can be more easy, for your parents, seeing your inclinations, will no doubt provide you an adequate maintenance."

"I have no parents; but I am not afraid; I can provide for myself by my labour."

"Certainly, and as you have read Rousseau's works, you know that he says that every man, even a prince, ought to be taught some manual trade."

"I have not read 'Émile.' I think it is in 'Émile' he has given that recommendation?"

"It is."

"I have heard the Baron de Taverney turn that advice into ridicule, and regret that he had not made his son a carpenter."

"And what did he make him?"

"An officer."

The old man smiled.

"Yes, our nobles are all so. Instead of teaching their children any trade by which life might be preserved, they teach them the trade of killing. When a revolution comes, and exile after revolution, they will be forced to beg their bread from foreigners, or to sell them their swords, which is still worse. You, however, are not the son of a noble; you know a trade, I presume?"

"Monsieur, I have already told you I know nothing. Besides, I must confess that I have always had an invincible repugnance for all labours requiring strong rough movements of the body."

"Ah," said the old man, "you are lazy."

"Oh no; I am not lazy. Instead of putting me to the labour of a mechanic, place me in a room half dark, and give me books, and you shall see whether I will not work day and night at the labour of my own choosing."

The stranger looked at the young man's white and slender hands.

"It is a sort of predisposition or instinct," said he. "Sometimes this repugnance for manual labour leads to a good result; but it must be well directed. "Well," continued he, "if you have not been at college, you have at least been at school?"

Gilbert shook his head.

"You can read and write?"

"My mother had just time before she died to teach me to read. My poor mother, seeing that I was not strong, always said, 'He will never make a good workman; he must be a priest or a learned man.' When I showed any distaste for my lessons, she would say, 'Learn to read, Gilbert, and you will not have to cut wood, drive a team, or break stones.' So I commenced to learn, but unfortunately I could scarcely read when she died."

"And who taught you to write?"

"I taught myself."

"You taught yourself?"

"Yes, with a stick which I pointed, and with some sand which I made fine by putting it through a sieve. For two years I wrote the letters which are used in printing, copying them from a book. I did not know that there were any others than these, and I could soon imitate them very well. But one day about three years ago, when Mademoiselle Andrée had gone to a convent, the steward handed me a letter from her for her father, and then I saw that there existed other characters. Monsieur de Taverney, having broken the seal, threw the cover away; I picked it up very carefully, and when the postman came again, I made him read me what was on it. It was, 'To the Baron de Taverney-Maison-Rouge, at his château, near Pierrefitte.' Under each of these letters I put its corresponding printed letter, and found that I had nearly all the alphabet. Then I imitated the writing; and in a week had copied the address ten thousand times perhaps, and had taught myself to write.

You see, monsieur, that I am not extravagant in my expectations. Since I can read and write, have read all that I could, have reflected on all that I read, why may I not perhaps find a man who requires my pen, a blind man who wants eyes, or a dumb man who wants a tongue?"

"But you forget that then you will have a master, and that is what you do not want. A secretary or a reader is only a sort of upper servant, after all."

"That is true," replied Gilbert, a little downcast; "but no matter, I must accomplish my object. I shall stir the paving-stones of Paris; I shall turn water-carrier if necessary, but I will attain my object, or I shall die in attempting it, — and that will also be accomplishing an object."

"Well," replied the stranger, "you seem indeed full of ardour and courage, — excellent qualities."

"But have you not a profession yourself, monsieur? You are dressed like a man employed in the finances."

The old man smiled sadly.

"I have a profession," said he. "Every man ought to have one, but mine is a complete stranger to everything connected with finance. A financier would not come out herborising."

"Are you an herborist by profession, then?"

"Almost."

"Then you are poor?"

"Yes."

"It is the poor who are charitable, for poverty makes them wise, and good advice is better than a louis-d'or. Give me your advice then."

"I shall do more than that."

Gilbert smiled. "I suspected that," said he.

"On how much do you think you could live?"

"Oh, very little!"

"But perhaps you do not know how expensive living is in Paris."

"Yesterday I saw Paris for the first time from the hills near Luciennes."

"Then you are not aware that living in great towns is dear?"

"How much does it cost? Give me an idea."

"Willingly. For instance, what costs a sou in the country, costs three sous in Paris."

"Well, said Gilbert, "if I got any kind of shelter to rest in after my work, I should only need for my food six sous a day."

"Ah!" cried the stranger, "that is what I like, young man! Come with me to Paris, and I shall find you an independent profession by which you may live."

"Oh, monsieur!" cried Gilbert, with rapture. Then, after a moment's reflection, "But it must really be an occupation; I must not live on alms."

"Do not be afraid of that, my child. I am not rich enough to bestow much in charity, and not foolish enough to do it without knowing the object better."

This little sally of misanthropy pleased Gilbert instead of giving him offence. "That is right!" said he; "I like such language. I accept your offer and thank you for it."

"So you decide upon coming to Paris with me?"

"Yes, monsieur, if you have no objection."

"Of course I have no objection, since I make you the offer."

"What shall I have to do with you?"

"Nothing, but to work. But you shall regulate the quantity of your work yourself. You are young, you ought to be happy and free, — even idle if you like, after you have gained the privileges of leisure," said the stranger, smiling in spite of himself. Then, raising his eyes to heaven, he exclaimed with a deep sigh, "O youth! O vigour! O freedom!" Then he rose with the assistance of his stick.

As he said these words, an expression of deep and poetic melancholy overspread his fine features.

"And now," he continued, in a more cheerful voice, "now that you have got an employment, will you object to help me to fill another box with plants? I have some sheets of paper here in which we can class the others according to their orders. But, by the by, are you hungry ? I have still some bread."

"Keep it for the afternoon, if you please, monsieur."

"Well, but at least eat the cherries; they will be troublesome to carry with us."

"On that account I shall eat them. But allow me to carry your box; you will then be more at your ease, and I think, thanks to habit, my legs will tire yours."

"Ah, see! you bring me good fortune. There is the *vicris hieracioïdes,* which I sought in vain until now, and just under your foot — take care ! — the *cerastium aquaticum.* Stop, stop! Do not gather them! Oh! you are not an herborist yet. The one is too moist to be gathered now, the other not advanced enough. We can get the *vicris hieracioïdes* in the afternoon when we pass this way, and the *cerastium* a week hence. Besides, I wish to show it growing to a friend whose patronage I mean to solicit for you. And now, show me the place where you saw the beautiful mosses."

Gilbert walked on, the old man followed him, and both disappeared in the shades of the forest.

CHAPTER XLIV.

MONSIEUR JACQUES.

GILBERT, delighted at his good fortune, which had hitherto befriended him in his utmost need, walked on, turning from time to time towards the stranger who had by a few words made him at once so submissive and docile. In this manner he led him to the spot where the mosses grew; they were really splendid specimens, and when the old man had made a collection of them, they went in search of other plants.

Gilbert was a much better botanist than he thought himself. Accustomed to the woods from his infancy, he was familiar with all the plants that grew in them; but he knew them only by their vulgar names. When he named them in that manner, his companion told him the corresponding scientific term, which Gilbert, on finding another plant of the same family, would endeavour to repeat. If he miscalled the Greek or Latin term, the stranger repeated it in syllables, and gave him its derivation. Then he explained how it was adapted to the nature of the plant; and thus Gilbert learned not only its botanical name, but the Greek or Latin one by which Pliny, Linnæus, or Jussieu had distinguished it.

From time to time he said, "What a pity, monsieur, that I cannot gain my six sous by botanising every day with you! Oh, I should never rest a moment, and indeed I should not want even the six sous; a piece of bread such as you gave me this morning would be sufficient for the whole day. I have just drunk from a spring of excellent water, as good as that at Taverney; and last night I slept under a tree here, and I am sure I slept better than I should have done under the roof of a château."

"My friend," replied the stranger, with a smile, "winter will come; the plants will be withered and the spring frozen; the north wind will whistle through the naked trees instead of this gentle breeze which agitates their leaves. You will then require a shelter, clothes, and fire, and you must be economical with your six sous that you may obtain them."

Gilbert sighed, gathered more plants, and asked more questions.

They spent thus the greater part of the day in the woods of Alnay, Plessis-Piquet, and Clamart-sous-Meudon.

Gilbert, according to his usual custom, soon became familiar with his companion, who questioned him with admirable address ; but there was in the young man something distrustful and circumspect, and he revealed as little as possible of his past life.

At Châtillon the stranger bought some bread and milk, but it was with difficulty he prevailed upon Gilbert to take the half of his purchase. Then, refreshed, they set out for Paris, that Gilbert might enter it whilst it was yet daylight.

The young man's heart beat high at the mere thought of being in Paris, and he could not conceal his emotion when, from the hill of Vanvres, he perceived St. Geneviève, the Invalides, Notre-Dame, and that vast sea of houses whose rolling billows seemed to lave the declivities of Montmartres, Belleville, and Menil Montant.

"Oh, Paris ! Paris !" murmured he.

"Yes, Paris, a mass of houses, an abyss of ills !" said the old man. "If the griefs and crimes which those houses inclose were to appear on their exteriors, from every stone would ooze a tear or a drop of blood !"

Gilbert heard, and repressed his enthusiasm, and thus checked, it soon died away of itself.

The suburb by which they entered the city was filthy and squalid ; sick persons on litters were carried past him to the hospitals ; children, half-naked, were playing in the dirt, among dogs, cows, and pigs. His brow grew dark.

" You think all this hideous," said the stranger ; "well, in a short time you will not even see these things ! People are rich who have a pig or a cow; they will soon have neither one nor other. Their children give them pleasure ; soon they will bring them only sorrow. As to filth, you will always find that everywhere."

Gilbert had been inclined to look on Paris with a gloomy eye ; the picture of it which his companion drew did not, therefore, displease him. The old man, at first prolix in his declamation, gradually sank into abstraction and silence as they approached the centre of the city. He seemed so full of anxious thoughts that Gilbert had not courage to ask him the name of a large garden which he saw through a railing, nor of a bridge by which the Seine was crossed. The garden was the Luxembourg ; the bridge the Pont Neuf. At last, however, as they still proceeded onwards, and as the stranger's meditation appeared to have changed into uneasiness, he ventured to say, " Do you live far from this, monsieur ? "

" Not very far," answered the stranger, whom this question evidently made more morose.

They proceeded along the Rue du Four, passing the magnificent Hôtel de Soissons, the windows and the principal entrance of which look on the street, but whose splendid gardens extend to the streets of Grenelle and Deux-Écus.

They passed by a church which Gilbert thought very beautiful; he stopped a moment to gaze at it.

" That is a beautiful building," said he.

" It is Saint-Eustache," replied the old man. Then, looking up, " Éight o'clock ! Good heavens ! make haste, young man, make haste ! "

The stranger strode on faster ; Gilbert followed him.

"By the by," said he, after some minutes of a silence so ungenial that Gilbert began to feel uneasy, " I forgot to tell you that I am married."

" Oh ! " said Gilbert.

"Yes; and my wife, like a true Parisian housekeeper, will scold us, I dare say, for coming in so late. Besides, I must tell you, she is very suspicious of strangers."

"Do you wish me to leave you, monsieur?" said Gilbert, whose heart was chilled by these words.

"Not at all, not at all! I invited you to come home with me, and you shall come."

"I follow you, then," answered the young man.

"Now, here we are! — down this street, to the right!"

Gilbert raised his eyes, and by the last gleams of expiring day, he read at the corner of the street, above a grocer's shop, the words "Rue Plastrière."

The old man continued to hurry on faster, and as he approached nearer his house his feverish agitation seemed to increase. Gilbert feared to lose sight of him, and in his haste, knocked against the passers-by, the burdens of the porters, and the poles of carriages and litters. His companion seemed to have completely forgotten him in his hurried progress, absorbed as he was by one disagreeable thought.

At last he stopped before a door, in the upper part of which was a grating. A little string hung out through a hole; the stranger pulled it, and the door opened. He then turned, and seeing Gilbert standing undecided whether to enter or not, he said, "Come on!" Gilbert obeyed, and the old man shut the door.

After a few steps forward in the dark, Gilbert's foot struck against a narrow, steep staircase; but the old man, accustomed to the place, had already mounted half the flight. Gilbert overtook him, ascended with him, and stopped when he stopped. This was on an old half worn-out mat, in a lobby with two doors in it.

The stranger pulled a cord near one of these doors, and a sharp tinkling bell rang; then, from the interior of one of the rooms was heard the shuffling of slip-shod feet dragging along the floor. The door opened, and a woman from fifty to fifty-five years of age appeared.

Two voices immediately arose together, — one that of the stranger; the other, that of the woman who opened the door.

"Am I too late, dear Thérèse?" he murmured, timidly.

"A pretty hour, Jacques, to sup at!" she replied, rudely.

"Come, come, we shall soon make all that right!" replied the stranger, affectionately, shutting the door, and then turning to receive the tin box from Gilbert's hands.

"Oh, a porter to carry your box!" cried the old woman; "it only wanted that! So you could not carry all that nasty stuff of grass and herbs yourself! Indeed! a porter for Monsieur Jacques! I beg pardon, he is becoming quite a great gentleman!"

"Well, well, be calm, Thérèse," quietly replied he whom she addressed so insolently by the name of Jacques, arranging his plants on the mantel-piece.

"Pay him, then, and send him away; we don't want a spy here."

Gilbert turned as pale as death, and sprang to the door. Jacques stopped him.

"This gentleman," said he, with less timidity than he had shown at first, "is not a porter, still less a spy. He is a guest whom I have brought."

The old woman's arms fell powerless by her side.

"A guest?" said she. "Certainly, we are in great need of guests."

"Come, Thérèse," said the stranger, in a tone still affectionate, but in which a shade of decision might be detected, "light a candle; I am heated, and we are thirsty."

The old woman still grumbled, loudly at first, but gradually subsiding. Then she proceeded to strike a light.

Whilst the dialogue lasted, and the murmurs succeeding it, Gilbert remained silent and immovable, nailed to the floor within a step or two of the door, which he deeply regretted having entered.

Jacques perceived what the young man was suffering.

"Come forward, Monsieur Gilbert," said he; "come forward, I beg of you."

The old woman turned to see the person to whom her husband spoke with such politeness, and Gilbert had thus an opportunity of seeing her yellow, morose face, by the first light of the miserable candle which she had placed in a copper candlestick.

That face awoke in him, at the first glance, a violent antipathy. It was wrinkled, pimpled, and filled, as it were, with gall; the eyes were sharp but meaningless; there was also a pretended softness spread over those vulgar features at that moment, which the old woman's voice and manner so completely contradicted that Gilbert's dislike was if possible increased.

The old woman, on her side, found the thin, pale face, circumspect silence, and stiff demeanour of the young man little to her taste.

"I see, gentlemen," said she, "that you are hot, and I am sure you must be thirsty. Indeed, passing a day in the shade of the woods is so fatiguing, and stooping from time to time to gather a plant so laborious an occupation! For this gentleman is a botanist also, no doubt; that is the trade of people who have no trade!"

"The gentleman," replied Jacques, in a voice becoming every moment firmer, "is a kind, good young man, who did me the honour to bear me company all the day, and whom my Thérèse will, I am sure, receive like a friend."

"There is enough of supper for two, but not for three," grumbled she.

"He is easily satisfied, and so am I."

"Oh, yes; all very fine, — I know what that means. I tell you plainly, there is not bread enough for your double moderation, and I am not going down three flights of stairs to get any more, I assure you. Besides, at this hour the baker's would be shut."

"Then I shall go down myself," replied Jacques, frowning. "Open the door, Thérèse."

"Oh, but —"

"I will go down, I tell you!"

"Well, well," said the old woman, in a discontented voice, but at the same time yielding to the absolute tone which her opposition had called forth from Jacques ; "am I not always ready to satisfy your whims ? I think we can do with what we have. Come to supper."

"Sit by me," said Jacques, leading Gilbert into the next room, where a little table was prepared for the master and mistress of the house. On it were laid two plates, beside one of which a napkin folded and tied with a red ribbon, and beside the other, one tied with white, pointed out where each took his seat.

The walls of the room, which was small and of a square shape, were covered with a pale blue paper, with a white pattern, and its only ornaments were two large maps. The rest of the furniture consisted of six straw-seated chairs, the aforesaid table, and a kind of cabinet filled with stockings to be mended.

Gilbert sat down. The old woman placed a plate before him, then she brought a spoon, worn thin by use, a knife and fork, and a brightly polished pewter goblet.

"Are you not going down ? " asked Jacques.

"It is not necessary," she replied, in a sharp tone, showing the spite which filled her heart at his having gained a victory over her. "It is not necessary. I found half a loaf in the pantry. That makes a pound and a half of bread for us all ; we must make it do."

So saying, she put the soup on the table.

Jacques was helped first, then Gilbert, and the old woman ate out of the tureen. All three were very hungry. Gilbert, intimidated by the discussion on domestic economy to which he had given rise, kept his appetite as much within bounds as possible ; but, notwithstanding, he had finished his soup first. The old woman cast a wrathful look on his plate so prematurely empty.

"Who called to-day ? " inquired Jacques, in order to change the current of her thoughts.

"Oh, everybody, as usual ! " replied she. "You pro-

mised Madame de Boufflers her four pieces, Madame
d'Escars two airs, Madame de Penthièvre a quartette with
an accompaniment; some persons came themselves, others
sent for what they wanted. But what of that? Monsieur
was botanising; and as people cannot amuse themselves
and do their work at the same time, the ladies had to go
without their music!"

Jacques did not say a word, to the great astonishment
of Gilbert, who expected to see him get angry; but as it
only concerned himself, it did not disturb him.

To the soup succeeded a morsel of boiled beef, served on
a common earthenware dish, scraped and cracked by the
edge of the knife. Jacques helped Gilbert, moderately
enough, for Thérèse had her eye upon him; then he took a
piece about the same size for himself, and handed the dish
to her.

The old woman seized on the loaf and cut a slice for
Gilbert, — so small a slice that Jacques blushed. He
waited until she had helped him and herself; then he took
the loaf into his own hands.

"You shall cut your own bread, my young friend," said
he; "and cut it according to your appetite, I beg of you.
Bread ought to be doled out only to those who waste it."

A moment afterwards appeared a dish of kidney-beans
stewed in butter.

"Look how green they are!" said Jacques. "They are
of our own keeping; we have an excellent method for
that." And he passed the dish to Gilbert.

"Thank you, monsieur," said the latter, "but I have
eaten quite enough; I am not hungry."

"The young gentleman is not of your opinion about my
kidney beans," said Thérèse, angrily. "He prefers, no
doubt, fresh-gathered ones; but they are early vegetables,
and rather above our means."

"No, madame. On the contrary, I think these appear
very nice indeed, and I am sure I should like them; but I
never eat of more than one dish."

"And you drink water?" said Jacques, handing him the jug."

"Always, monsieur."

Jacques poured out a small glass of wine for himself.

"And now, wife," said he, "you will begin and get this young man's bed ready; he must be tired, I am sure."

Thérèse let her knife and fork fall from her hands, and fixed her angry eyes on her husband.

"Bed? Are you mad? If you bring any one to sleep here, he must sleep in your own bed, I can tell you. You are really becoming deranged! Or perhaps you are going to take up a boarding-house? If you are, you may get a cook and waiting-maid; it is quite enough for me to be your servant, without being servant to other people."

"Thérèse," replied Jacques, resuming his serious and firm tone, "Thérèse, pray listen to me; it is only for one night. This young man has never set foot in Paris before; he came under my protection, and I will not permit him to sleep in an inn; I will not, though I should, as you say, have to resign to him my own bed."

After this second exhibition of firmness and resolution, the old man awaited the result.

Thérèse, who had watched him whilst he spoke, appearing to study every muscle of his face, seemed now to understand that she must give up the contest, and she suddenly changed her tactics. She was certain of being beaten if she continued Gilbert's enemy; she therefore began to fight for him, but certainly like an ally who intended treachery.

"Well, well," said she, "since the young gentleman has come home with you, he must be a friend of yours; and it is better, as you say, that he should remain under our roof. I shall make him a bed as well as I can in your study, near the bundles of papers."

"No, no," said Jacques, quickly. "A study is not a fit place to sleep in; he might set fire to the papers."

"A great misfortune, truly," muttered Thérèse to herself. Then she added aloud: "In that case, I can put him in front of the cupboard in the ante-room."

"No, no!"

"Well, you see, however much I wish it, I can't manage it, unless he take your bed or mine."

"I do not think, Thérèse, you are looking in the right quarter."

"What do you mean?"

"Why, we have the garret, you know."

"The garret? The loft, you mean."

"No, it is not a loft; it is a room, a little garret-like, I confess, but wholesome, and with a splendid view of the neighbouring gardens, — a thing very unusual in Paris."

"Oh, what matters it, monsieur," exclaimed Gilbert, "whether it be a loft or not? Even if it were, I should be but too glad of it, I assure you."

"But stay, that cannot be," cried Thérèse; "it is there that I dry our linen."

"The young man will not disturb it, Thérèse. You will take care, will you not, my young friend, that no accident happens to my good housekeeper's linen? We are poor, and any loss is serious to us."

"Oh, do not be afraid, monsieur."

Jacques rose and approached Thérèse. "I do not wish, my dear Thérèse," said he, "that this young man should be ruined. Paris is a dangerous place for a stranger; while here we can watch over his conduct."

"Then you have taken him to educate? He will pay for his board, this pupil of yours?"

"No, but I answer for it he shall cost you nothing. From to-morrow he will provide for himself. As for lodging, since the garret is almost useless to us, let us do him this slight service."

"How well idle people understand each other!" muttered Thérèse, shrugging her shoulders.

"Monsieur," said Gilbert, more wearied even than his host of this struggle for a hospitality which was so humbling to him, and which was only gained by fighting for every inch of ground, "monsieur, I have never yet given trouble to any one, and I shall certainly not begin with you, who have been so good to me. Permit me, therefore, to leave you, if you please. I saw, near the bridge which we crossed, some trees with benches under them. I shall sleep very well, I assure you, on one of those benches."

"Yes," said Jacques, "to be taken up by the watch as a vagabond."

"Which he is," muttered Thérèse to herself, as she removed the supper things.

"Come, come, young man," Jacques added, "there is, as well as I can remember, a very good straw mattress upstairs, and that is surely better than a bench?"

"Oh, monsieur, I have never slept on anything but a straw mattress," said Gilbert; then correcting this truth by a slight fib, "a soft mattress always overheated me," added he.

Jacques smiled. "Straw is certainly cool and refreshing," said he. "Take that bit of candle which is on the table, and follow me."

Thérèse did not even look at them. She sighed; she was defeated.

Gilbert rose gravely and followed his protector. Passing through the ante-room he saw a cistern of water. "Monsieur," asked he, "is water dear in Paris?"

"No, my friend; but were it dear, water and bread are two things which no man has a right to refuse his fellowman who begs for them."

"Oh, the reason I asked is, that at Taverney water cost nothing, and cleanliness is the luxury of the poor."

"Take some, my friend," said Jacques, pointing to a large earthenware pitcher; and he preceded the young man to his sleeping apartment, surprised to find united in a youth of his age all the strength of mind of the lower classes with all the refined tastes of the higher.

END OF VOL. I.

www.ingramcontent.com/pod-product-compliance
Lightning Source LLC
Chambersburg PA
CBHW020500020726
47493CB00001B/108